AN ILL-FITTING MAN

PETER TWOHIG

ALSO BY PETER TWOHIG

The Cartographer
The Torch
The Mazemaster

AN ILL-FITTING MAN

PETER TWOHIG

NED KELLY
AWARD WINNING AUTHOR

Warburton Press

Warburton Press

An Ill-fitting Man
First published in Australia in 2022

Warburton Press
PO Box 9305
Wyoming NSW 2250 Australia

ISBN 978 1 922470 12 6 (paperback)
ISBN 978 1 922470 13 3 (ebook)

A catalogue record for this book is available from the National Library of Australia

Literary Agent
Lyn Tranter, Australian Literary Management
2A Booth St, BALMAIN NSW 2041 Australia

Cover design & illustration: Kate Twohig
Visit PeterTwohig.com

To my sons with love,
Jason, Marcus and Andrew

Peter Twohig was born in Melbourne in 1948 and grew up in Richmond and Dandenong. He endured a Catholic education and worked in the Australian Public Service until 1992, mainly in the area of systems analysis and design. He then moved to Sydney to undergo training as a naturopath and homoeopath. He has degrees in English, philosophy and complementary medicine.

Peter's first novel, *The Cartographer*, received the Ned Kelly Award for Best First Fiction in 2012 and was long-listed for the Commonwealth Book Prize in 2013. His second novel *The Torch*, and third, *The Mazemaster*, completed a trilogy.

petertwohig.com

There is no road. The road is made by walking.
Anthony Machado

A creative person has little control over his own life. He is not free.
C.G.Jung

Contents

Part 1 A Name for Myself

1 A Little Smack

The only thing that ever made me feel smooth was hitting some other bloke; that and making up poetry. I was lousy at just about everything else, especially school stuff – everything except English: I was the best in the class at that. Jesus, I got into strife so often I reckon I'm lucky to be alive. Bloody nuns, I hated them. And the brothers were worse. As for my old man, he only ever told me one thing that paid off. There was a kid at our school, Mick Donahue, a bully, who decided to bash me up for being an awkward kind of kid and a bit of a runt. I went home covered in dirt and with a loose tooth. Dad went round the bend, and told me it was time I learnt how to box. I hated the idea of fighting – you wouldn't think it now, would you? It was the idea of actually hitting someone, of reaching out in that sudden way, and then bunging one on him. So I thought: *Here we go, he's going to spend the next two hours bashing me up, and call it a bloody boxing lesson.* But no, that's not what happened. See, he only wanted to tell me one thing, and there wasn't even any demo. He only wanted to tell me this: blokes hate getting punched in the nose.

'Yeah, Dad, that hurts like hell,' I said.

'I'm not talking about pain, son. I'm talking about self-respect. Gettin' punched in the nose wrecks it; it leaves him and passes to *you* instead. See?'

'Nuh.'

'Jesus. Let's see: he'll feel worse about himself, but better about you – something like that.'

'He'll like me.'

'I wouldn't go *that* far, but he won't hate you.'

'Alright, I'll try it.'

'And don't forget, whatever you do, don't break his nose, or he *will* hate you.'

That was my first boxing lesson, and my best one – I wouldn't get another one until I left school. But when I punched Mick Donahue in the nose my life as a little bastard with a funny voice and an odd way of walking ended, and my life as a little bastard with a funny voice and an odd way of walking, and a reputation for busting kids noses began.

I discovered that day that reaching out to people, touching them, wasn't nearly as smooth as reaching for the *inside* of their bodies, and the inside their heads, with my knuckles, past the place where their skin was, and straight in to the place where their bones were, where the blood was, and feeling the stuff inside give way, and letting my fist have its way. There was mateship in the conversation between the insides of the other bloke and my fist. And I just stood and watched as the echoes of that conversation rang up my arm and into my brain, like the fuzzy messages that pass up a string stretched between two jam tins, and bounce around inside my head. I think I hit Mick too hard on the day, however he took it well. I think he was glad to stop being the bully.

Naturally, it turned out that Mick Donahue had a big brother who was keen on killing me. He sent me a note, through Mick. Mick gave it to me right at the start of school, at the beginning of the Christian Doctrine class. I think it was a Friday. I remember what the note said, because it scared me cold. It said:

Cum over to my plas after school and fas up to me like a man
for what yu did to Mick. Or are yu gutless.

Well, he had me worked out, of course: I was as gutless as
they come. I only had one trick, and that was punching kids in
the nose, and I'd only done that once. I read the note and looked
up. All the kids were staring at me. They'd all seen the note, of
course: I was the last to see it. Normally, if a kid my age got a
note like that from Bazza Donahue, he'd be as sick as a spaniel
and would probably run away from home.

So I looked at the kids, and at Mick, who was no longer my
enemy, in spite of having plaster all over his face. To tell the
truth, I was paralysed with fear, and my whole body had sort of
seized up like a drunk just before he falls over, except I was still
standing. In the end, I spent the whole day like that, not
speaking, hardly moving. Not eating. Nothing. So by the end of
the day, the kids thought I had gone mad, and that I was going to
kill Mick's brother - that or get murdered. Every few hours after
that I had to go to the toilet. I reckon that by the end of the day
I'd lost so much weight that if I'd been a boxer I would have
dropped a whole weight division, probably down to a
strawweight.

But I managed to keep my fear from the other kids. And
after school I went with Mick back to his place. Half the bloody
school came with us, so that we looked like a St Patrick's Day
parade as we walked down his street, leaving no room for horses
and carts at all. As I dragged myself along I wondered what would
happen to my immortal soul after Bazza Donahue killed me.
Sister Adrian had informed me only a few days before that I
would be going to Hell when I died, but that had been for

making faces at her behind her back, but really, I thought, would probably not get me more than a few days in Purgatory. As for the other sins I still had to confess, I was sure they would not get me more than a short sentence in Purgatory, as long as you didn't count pinching a box of coloured chalk from the store room, and I didn't. On the whole I couldn't see God getting too upset with me, though I freely admit that my opinion was based on the Archbishop's well-known view that God always smiled on the Irish.

When we got to Donahue's place, there was an even bigger crowd of kids waiting, and most of the neighbours as well. It was one of those days. When the two crowds merged, they engulfed us, so that we found ourselves in a kind of clearing. Despite being a Donahue, Mick leaned over to me and said to me quietly: 'Don't let him shake hands with you. If he does he won't let go – that's what he does. Then he'll kill you.'

Then he left my side and took up his place with his family. I walked out to the middle of the clearing and waited for death to come and take me away from all this, as I thought it must. Bazza came over to me and leaned over to me so that his long, greasy hair fell on my forehead. He was a few years older than me and built like a brick dunny. His breath smelled of grog. I inhaled it, because I suddenly hungered for one more sensual experience before I was killed. He looked into my eyes, and I could feel his breathing. He was excited, red in the face, and his eyes were shining.

'Now listen to me, Taggerty. You're a game little bugger for showing up, but if we fight, I'll prob'ly kill you, and then I'll go to jail, and me mum'll have no one to look after her 'cept Mick, who's just a kid – oh, and Dad, I s'pose. So I want you to let me punch you once, then you fall down, and when I ask you if you've had enough, you say yes, and that'll be that, and we'll shake hands. Alright?'

I couldn't speak. In fact I hadn't said a word all day, and my jaws were locked together so hard they were aching. I wanted to nod - anything. But my head wouldn't work either. He took a few steps back and looked at me; then he licked his lips. That lick told me something. It was like a little gift, only not so little.

He held out his hand to me, just as Mick said he would. I took a step toward him and looked up at him. Then I punched him in the nose, just the same way I had punched Mick, only not, I thought, as hard. Nevertheless, he didn't duck at all. He didn't even move. I don't think he saw it coming. For the first time that day, I felt my body free up as if all of it wanted to be a part of the punch, and none of me wanted to miss out. In a split second I went from being rusted up to being clean and oiled. I felt the thrill of the punch even before it was a punch, when it was still on the way to his face, when, if it had missed, it would have been just another stupid attempt by Archie Taggerty to be likes ... someone.

A whole lot of things seemed to go on inside Bazza's head when I threw that punch, which was, just for the books, a straight right. I discovered - everyone did, I think - that Bazza had what I later heard called a glass nose, in other words, a nose that couldn't take a punch. *Must run in the family*, I remember thinking. Anyway, down he went in a heap, blood everywhere. I looked at Mick, and he looked at me, and his face said: *I'd piss off quick, if I were you, mate.* But before I could move a muscle, out steps a big skinny bloke with a nose like a chook, and a really shitty look on his dial, and says to me pretty unsteadily, because he was half stung:

'You rotten little bastard, hittin' a bloke when he's trying to shake your hand. I oughta tan your fuckin' hide. In fact, I *will* tan your fuckin' hide.'

'You lay a hand on me, Mr Donahue, and I'll do the same thing to you. And then when I'm finished with you, so will my old man. And he takes a dim view of blokes who bash up kids.'

Now this was all horseshit, of course, as my old man couldn't have cared less whether I got my bashings from him or from some other bastard, and would have said that it was about time someone wiped the smile off my face. I put up my fists as if I meant it and took a step towards him, ignoring Bazza, who was hanging on to his face with one hand, and crawling out of the ring on his bum with the other. I was pretty sure at that point that I could feel my own piddle running down my leg, and hoped to God I was wrong, because if the Donahues saw it, I reckoned I was dead.

'Fuck off, yer little bastard, back to your drunkard of a father, if he is your bloody father, and your useless bloody cow of a mother, whose had every bloke in Richmond, and a few from even worse places, so I hear.'

At that point Mrs Donahue stepped up behind him and landed him a mighty smack across the back of the head.

'You save that filthy talk for your tram driver mates, Doolan Donahue.'

'Jesus, woman, you'll kill a man. I didn't mean *me*.'

The contest was over. Final score: visitors: two busted bugles and one back-down; home: bugger all.

But the feeling of it!

I slowly backed all the way down to the corner – because it was a safe bet that someone in the Donahue family would have a knife – then I ran like hell. When I got home, I went straight to the bathroom, and looked at myself in the mirror. I was trembling, and breathless. I was still holding my hand in a fist, and now I held it up and looked at it in the mirror. Dad had been right, but I had discovered something about myself that I know I couldn't have discovered any other way. I had discovered that punching blokes is the sweetest feeling in the world. Two weren't enough; I wanted more. But I still felt the same way about fights. They were for mugs.

The dual realisation made my mind change, from a normal *What's next?* sort of mind, to a kind of messy, confused mind, but one that seemed to be on the point of thinking something important. I was embarrassed for myself, of letting my mind push me around, as if I was a girl. Blokes didn't think like that. Blokes always knew what was what. Only girls didn't. As I looked at my eyes in the mirror, I had an urge to stop seeing myself as I always had, and to see myself in a new way, perhaps for the first time. I wanted to - *Christ*, I wanted to. But I was afraid. I took a step closer to the mirror and stared at the eyes I saw. There was change, and less fear. Closer. I felt as if I were falling, and grabbed the edge of the mirror, not so much for support as to remind me that I was still there. Then, in the space between the image and me came a suggestion - I don't know if it was in my mind or in the mind of the other. It was the suggestion of a word, two words, a phrase, a new expression, a couple more. Then strings of them, silly but meaningful. It was my celebration. I said the expressions out loud, because that was what they wanted me to do.

Like Christ's Passion, bent and hurt, the noses of Dunbar Street
Blood's a Passion, too, but straight
In the heart.

Bluestone gutters, square and hard, the boxer boy's home
Bluestone gutters, cold and hot
In the blood.

Last to move, first to fall, the Big Nipper
Next to move, the boxer boy
Like mad.

It was unsatisfactory, but satisfying, like excretion. I knew what it was, of course – I didn't come down in the last shower – it was a kind of poetry. I hoped that, being a kind of regurgitation of events, it would have no special meaning, just as a cough and a sneeze can't be taken for the flu. But really, I had got the family disease.

My old man had it, though it touched him only lightly, and only when he was drunk, which was often enough, but fair, as he was Irish. Always, he would shout it out, and occasionally, write scraps of it down, though only while still drunk. However, his writing was so poor that I took no notice of it; I don't know what he did with those scraps. On the odd occasion when I said my evening prayers, I hoped to God that he would stop embarrassing himself. It wasn't the drunkenness: it was the poetry. Later, my cousin Seamus would have it even worse.

However my prayers went bung. And now I saw that I was going to end up like my old man: a laughing stock. Worse, I was not even a drunk: I was not going to sober up. I wished the poetry thoughts away, and away they went, leaving a kind of peace, though I knew it wouldn't last. It was like the peace in the house between Mum and Dad's stoushes. It was only the peace that kept them from being continuous, the way words get in the way of commas.

They did, but I didn't like the space they left behind, like a fizzy hole in a pitch dark room, which you know is full of something, despite there being nothing to be seen, a *know*-hole. So reluctantly, I wrote the words down – that fixed them. I looked down at them lying on the paper, not breathing, and even I could see that they were, at the very least, out cold. I was tempted to read them out loud one more time, but I resisted. That poetry is as strong as the demon drink, I reckoned, even though I hadn't yet fallen under its spell, as I knew from school many men had, including a few who weren't even Irish.

I had always blamed the grog. We had a brewery down the street and a pub on the corner. All day we were tickled under the chin by their warm, friendly smells, tickled like trouts, we were, without a hope of escape. It had charmed the O'Deas, the O'Riordans, the O'Reillys, the O'Shaunessys the O'Donnells, and the O'Neills. And a lot of other O's. And a few Fitzes, and Macs. And the Ryans, of course, who bred like rabbits, and had a family connection in every second bloody home between Bridge Road and the river. Though mum said the Ryans weren't true Irishmen but something the English had got at, way back. However, while they were drinkers, they weren't poets.

But this poetry stuff just about knocked the stuffing out of me. I knew right then what I'd only suspected: that I was no friend of myself. I felt that it was a bomb inside me, waiting to go off. And if it did, or even if it ever escaped, so that others could hear it, I'd be thought of as no better than a sissy; it wouldn't matter how many noses I broke. The words were written down, and while that felt right and natural, it was going no further. I folded up that paper and stashed it in a safe place, in a place where no one would ever dream of looking: under the loose floorboard under the mat in my bedroom. That'd do the trick.

The reason I mention this event, this punching and poeting thing, is that it was the starting point of the whole bloody mess that I call my life. I now saw that until that day I had been merely mooching. And after that it seemed to me that I was always going somewhere and getting into this trouble or that. Always.

See, this is how it worked. I'd get into a stoush with some cove or other, and give him a smack or two – not counting Danny O'Neill, who smacked *me* around a bit – I was fighting way out of my weight that day – valuable lesson there. As I said, I'd smack him around a bit, then, next thing you know, my head would feel like it was full of words. At first I thought that's *all* they were. Words can't do you any harm. *Sticks and stones may break my bones, but names'll never hurt me.* Something like that. That's what I'd always thought. So of course I'd ignore the bastards. Then the next thing you know they'd be giving me a hard time, like the wowsers that stand on boxes down at the Yarra Bank. They call you 'brother' but they don't know anything about you. But they're good at giving you a bloody ear-bashing. Always on about the bloody government and the demon drink, and kids smoking, and so on. Fuck 'em.

My words wanted to be read out loud, preferably from a sheet of paper – see, they knew what they wanted, like the wowsers. Like bloody women, come to think of it. But they weren't right, the poems. They wanted to make me do what *they* wanted. A man who lets words take over his soul is a man in trouble, like those kids the nuns told us about who do what the Devil says. Pretty soon, the Devil is giving them a hard time, pulling their leg about all kinds of things, telling them porkies about how lovely they look or what a handsome figure they cut about town. Can you imagine me falling for that one? People would fall about laughing. They'd pass out from the bloody effort. Me, handsome.

But I'd believe it if the Devil got his hands on me. And then after a lifetime of this folly, I'd get run over by a cable tram, and go straight to Hell, and who'd be waiting for me there but the fucking Donahues, the whole bloody family, including the ones from Carlton, who are all dead-set fucking lunatics. Those words'd be the bloody death of me, if anyone ever got wind of them. I hated the bastards.

But they gave me such a bloody headache and such an itch. Jack Duncan, who's years older than me, and goes to the High School, told me one that whenever anything's bothering him he gives the old feller a bit of a tug, and pretty soon all his troubles are little ones. I went home and tried it, wondering if it would cure me of poetry, but all it did was hurt like mad. That's the last time I take the advice of one of those High School bastards, I thought.

So I continued to write the poems down. At night, when I was by myself in my room, I'd take them out and read them. It made me feel like a dog sniffing his own turds: you know, you can tell they're as embarrassed as hell, but they can't help themselves. Terrific, now I was turning into a bloody mongrel, a mongrel bloody poet.

2 Queenie

A couple of years after I began dongin' kids' noses, my old man got murdered down at the docks. He was always getting up to things with his crooked mates, and one night someone decided to cut his throat, then set fire to him. At least that's what it said in the paper. But I heard from a little bird at the footy that, while trying to avoid an unpleasant conversation he fell overboard from one of the coastal traders that was in port that night – he would have been picking up some medicine for a sick mate – and drowned. Then one of the gang fished him out and did those other things to the body to throw a scare into the locals. Apparently, it was all a misunderstanding: my old man misunderstood, the papers had misunderstood, and I then I had gone and misunderstood. Well, it all came as a bit of a blow to everyone: to my mother, who now had no bread-winner about the house; to me, as I was going to have to fill in for him in that department; and to the Richmond Police, because half of their coppers would now have to be laid off.

So there I was, one minute sitting in a classroom staring at Brother Anselm, a very nasty piece of work with a sad, droopy face, and the next sitting in a tiny office down at the Jam Factory, staring at a cove whose face was so similar I could have sworn he and Brother Anselm were out of the same stable. But they weren't, as Brother Anselm was Irish, as Irish as you can get – I don't think he could even pronounce half the words in the

English language, which he called the *Australian* language, though he made up for it by knowing a lot of them anyway. But this new bloke, this Mr. Levinson, was Jewish, I reckoned, and only knew a small collection of words, though he made up for it by using them over and over till I was bored stiff.

The gist of what he had to say was that pilfering was actually a very serious crime (said slowly), and punishable by immediate dismissal with loss of any pay owed (which I doubted), and prosecution by the police, which I already knew was bull, otherwise half of Richmond would be out of work, in jail, and broke, and that didn't seem to be the case. He also said he had heard of me, and that he wouldn't tolerate any violence. If I so much as raised my voice to another employee, I would get the bum's rush.

You can imagine how happy I was to hear that he had already knew of me. That was all I needed to make my blooming day. Shows that all those years of punching blokes inside out hadn't been for nothing. People were getting the message, even people who worked in dark offices in jam factories alongside jam machines.

It must have been all this talk of misbehaviour and threat that did it. Amid the tension of this conversation a singsong poem flowed by. I caught it's phrases as they bobbed up in the stream, and adopted its theme and silly scenes.

...the boss's room, I'll tell you all this much:
...sweetish dreams of fruitly scenes...of cakes and such
It lies behind a jam machine that has a lovely heart.
Its song gets to me better side, and make me heartstrings start.

...the place to bring back luscious times:

16

*Of Christmas puds, and birthday foods, of nuts and stinging
limes.*
*I remember chocs, and jubes red and sugared purple plums
... not safe from hungry tongues.*

By what right does this office box enjoy these friendly thrills?
The answer lies amid these piles of papers, slips and bills.
*This Levinson's a bloke who knows which side the butter's
on:*
The side that has the jam machine, that flamin' side, my son.

I said: *Yes sir* every now and then to show that I was paying
attention, but all the while I was wondering what all the wonderful
sweet smells were. No sooner would I get one of those smells on
the ropes when it would skip away out of smelling distance and
taunt me to have another go.

In the end, Levinson finished by telling me that I was going
to start on Monday, and sat back and peered over his glasses at
me.

'Do you have any questions?'

I sniffed.

'Is that marmalade?'

'No, it's lemon quince. If you see Mr Scudds in the outer
office when you leave, he will fetch a tin for you to take home.
You see, Mr Taggerty, here we have made pilfering completely
unnecessary. You will be charged half price against your first
week's wages. Good day.'

Work in the jam factory was hard, as all the really rotten jobs
were given to the apprentices. I was an apprentice tinsmith, which
meant that if anything heavy needed lifting, I was the silly bugger
who got to lift it, drag it, pour it out or whatever had to be done.

Sometimes the lifting was beyond one kid, and it would take a couple of us to get the job done. I reckon I made more tins than there were things to put in them, but still we kept making them. And of course, the Germans would have to pick a fight with the Poms, and we would have to get involved, though Christ knows why. And so all of a sudden the Mother Country – not mine: England – seemed to have a sudden need for tins full of all kinds of things I'd never seen put into a tin – didn't know you *could* put into a tin.

But there it was. I couldn't have cared less if those Poms had asked us to put dog turds into tins, as long as I got paid. But it wasn't as simple as that. It turned out that Australia couldn't wait to send all the young coves it could find – and, to be fair, a few older coves as well – to Europe to fight anyone who thought their old fellas were bigger than the Pommies' old fellas. It was basically the biggest dick measuring competition ever held. I wasn't worried. I knew that I'd never get sent off to war as long as I had a dick that looked like a whitebait out of water. Besides, I was an awkward little bugger who couldn't even stand up straight. The Germans'd laugh themselves silly. I was safe as eggs as long as I stayed in the jam factory. Besides, they needed the tins.

So you can see that I had it all worked out, and was prepared to mind my own business and stay put in the sticky world of jam and the acrid world of solder and acid, in exchange for the sticky world of blood, and the acrid world of guncotton and cordite. The papers went on about it constantly. Blokes were marching down to the docks and getting on ships with names like pretty places, like *Palermo*, and *Persia*, and *Wiltshire*. They had feathers in their hats and waved and cheered, and carried on like it was bloody Cup Day. Then the wounded started to come home. The same ships would come back and dock at Station

Pier, and a much smaller group of blokes would get off. And this time they'd have to bust a gut to raise a smile, but at least their injuries seemed to be little ones, you know, a bandage here, a patch there. To tell the truth, I'd seen worse injuries at the factory.

Well, I went down to the wharf one Sunday with Tiger Kelly to welcome his cousin home. There was a brass band playing on the wharf, and all the ladies had their long dresses on, and their sun hats. In fact, everyone and his dog would go along to one of these arrivals, to cheer the brave lads safely home from the war. In Tiger's case, he'd had a letter from his brother saying that he'd been injured somewhere or other and lost a foot, and now they were sending him home on the *Thermostocles*.

'He lost a foot?' I said to Tiger. 'Mate, how do you lose a whole bloody foot?'

He shrugged. 'Why don't yer ask 'im?'

We waited until the ship had docked and all the blokes had been hurried down the gang plank, but there was no sign of Tiger's brother.

'I don't get it. Come on,' he said, and we went up the gang plank and went for a walk around.

'What're you blokes after?' said a seaman.

'Looking for me brother. He didn't get off.'

'He'll be getting off at the next stop then.'

'Where's that?'

'Coode Island, up the river.'

'So he's still on the ship, then?'

'Couldn't say, but we're shoving off in a few minutes. If you go down to the stern and look scarce, you can get a lift. You didn't talk to me, okay?'

'Okay.'

Well, we took the *Thermostocles* up the Yarra to Coode Island, and watched as a horrible sight met our eyes from the stern of the ship, where we had made ourselves scarce behind a stack of tenting. It turned out that most of the ship's passengers had not been the walking wounded, as they were called, but stretcher cases. And it was these men that were now taken off the ship with a lot of clattering and groaning, and surrounded by a foul stink that issued from belowdecks when the hatches were opened. We looked over the side, as the men and their ambulance people passed below us, but could make out none of the faces, and ended up following the miserable procession into the Coode Island military hospital, a place we'd never heard of.

This hospital, this so-called hospital, I say, covered the whole Island, and was full of thousands of blokes, most of them men in various stages of death and wishing for death. I reckoned that between each three blokes there would have been enough bits to make up one man. This was the real homecoming. And after going around the new arrivals with Tiger for an hour or so, and asking every one we met, we gave up when we found out that the ship we had been on had in fact been the *SS Clan MacCorquodale*, and that it was common practice to disguise the names of ships, to confuse enemy agents.

We left stinking, crying Coode Island, and walked up the main thoroughfare, which took us through the Leprosy Hospital – the only way out – and made our way across the bridge to South Kensington, where we hailed a tram. We didn't say much. We were travelling with a small crowd of people who'd fallen for the same trick, and gone to visit a man in one piece, only to find themselves knee deep in other people's pain and pus. It was one of those events that just confirms that everything you hear is bullshit, from the newspapers to the politicians, to the bosses, to the unions, to the pub talk, to your own bloody parents. Once you've been to Coode Island on a Sunday afternoon, you've been bullshitted for the last time, and you can consider yourself an honest man, because you know what real lies look – and smell – like.

After that I was never got into arguments about politics, because they were all about the war, really, and put the war out of my mind. It had nothing to do with me. I was an apprentice tinsmith from Richmond with a funny sound in my voice which I recognised in the tin as it bent in my hands at work. It let out a little cry as it gave, and it was one of the other wise-crackers, Ben Newman, the manager's nephew, who pointed it out to me. The mystery that had bothered me my whole life was solved. I had a tin voice. From that moment on Ben called me Tinny, and the name spread around the factory. Of course, everyone thought it was a reference either to my trade, or to my remarkable luck. And yet I was not, in fact, particularly lucky at all. But such is the nature of nicknames, especially, I would say, those bestowed mischievously, that they tend to stick like tattoos.

The factory was to me the sweetest smelling place on earth, and there was no shortage of fruit and sugar to take home to mum, so that she gave my ear a rest most nights. I was therefore able to slip out and meet the blokes at the local sly grog, the wowsers having made it bloody near impossible for an apprentice with a dry throat to get a drink in a pub.

Naturally, the talk was of women, and though I'd seen a few, some of them close up, I'd had nothing to do with them. In fact, the general opinion was that my chances of getting a girlfriend were pretty slim, in view of my reputation as a bloke who bashed people up just for looking sideways at him. No girl in her right mind would be interested in the likes of me, they said.

And that was before she got close enough to me to see that I wasn't going to win any prizes in the looks department either. When I finally got sick of the listening to other blokes talking about girls, I went looking for a girl for myself, down at the Temperance Hall dance on a Saturday night.

It was a tough crowd, and I'm just talking about the girls, all of whom were lined up on one side of the hall, waiting to be asked for a dance. The fellers stood on the other side, looking like stunned mullets. There were two other types in the room: the band, which was a group of old-age pensioners trying to keep up with each other while they played some kind of whinging waltz, and at the other end of the room the temperance coves, who asked me as I walked through the door if I'd taken the pledge yet. I just gave them my polite smile, a big hello, and my promise to take the pledge just as soon as my parish priest, Father Fitzgerald, took it. That wiped the smiles off their faces, not that they were smiling a lot to begin with. God save me from bloody wowsers.

As for the girls, they were as it turned out all older than me. And the blokes, well, they all looked taller, straighter and less bad-looking than me. I could tell that a few of them were just biding their time and would have no trouble pouncing once they got up the nerve. As for the rest, there were no pouncers. I was with my old man one time, up near the brewery, when a tram rolled a brewery truck over. There were crates of beer all over the place. Quick as a flash, my old man ran out on to the road, grabbed a crate of beer, and hefted it onto his shoulder. 'The Lord helps those that help themselves,' he said. That was how I felt just then. I picked the best looking girl in the place and got going. She had a pretty face, and large breasts, and for me, that was a double bonus. She was not shorter than me, which was what society demanded in those days, but she was not so tall that I would look even more ridiculous dancing with her. It was hard for a girl to refuse a dance: you'd have to have rabies or something to get a knock-back. So when I popped the question I knew I was home and hosed. See, all it took was front, and I'd punched so many blokes out by then that I had about half a mile of that, and I could feel it expanding by the second.

Her name was Queenie, and it turned out she was as bold as brass, so that I felt like all my Christmases had come at once. When we danced, even though I held her at respectable distance, her breasts touched me just enough so that I couldn't think of anything else, that and her smile, which was mocking and open. And I knew why, of course; it was because she was older than me and a lot more experienced. Hell, she was experienced and I wasn't – I don't mind saying it. When it came to girls I was no genius. All I had going was the front I told you about, and I was using it for all it was worth.

The other thing I thought I had going for me was my anonymity. I reckoned that as long as none of these girls knew that I was the bloke who probably bashed their brother, or cousin, or best friend's boyfriend last week, I was going to pass as a bloke who never gets into strife or causes trouble. I'd already heard that I had a bad reputation around South Richmond, and I didn't want it to spread to the Temperance Hall about that time of the night. Fat chance.

'Hello,' she said. 'My name's Queenie, what's yours?'

'Ar...Ar.' Shit, I couldn't think of a new name on the spur of the moment.

'It's Archie, isn't it?'

'Hell, if you already knew, why'd yer ask?'

'I was just teasing. Everyone knows who you are. D'ya see that girl over there with the blue dress? Well, that's Mary Jackson. She reckons you broke her cousin's nose. And d'ya see that girl over there, with the yellow dress, well she reckons that you bashed up her friend's brother. And –'

'Yeah, I get it. There's no need to go on. I might have got into a few dust-ups. It gets a bit rough down near the river.'

'Yes, but they all live up the hill.'

She was still smiling at me, and I reckoned she was having a ball.

'Well,' I said, smiling back, 'I like to spread myself around.'

'You also knocked out one of Ruby Scott's teeth.'

'I don't know any Ruby Scott,' I said, but I knew exactly who she was talking about, and I reckoned my night was probably over. 'Yeah, well I might have given her a little tap, but it was only because she pulled a knife on me mate.'

This was all perfectly true. Anyone who knew me knew I'd never hit a girl without a bloody good reason, as most of them had brothers and cousins, and what have you. But this Scott girl was a nut case, and should have been locked up; and the only reason she wasn't was because her old man was a copper. So there you are. The world's a strange place, and no mistake.

'Anyway,' says Queenie, pulling me a little closer, so that I can feel both of her breasts pushing my chest and I can feel a lot more besides, 'I like you.' She came a little bit closer, until I felt as if I was going to pass out from the sudden heat, or from a heart attack or something, and them she whispered in my ear, something that I couldn't catch, owing to a sudden blast from the saxophonist, who seemed to have worked out what the tune was at last. But my ear was wet from the closeness of her mouth, and my brain was whistling the way it does when you stick your head out of the train window to enjoy the fresh air. When I turned my head to face her, she was open-mouthed in front of me, and had a questioning look on her face.

'What?'

But I never heard what she'd asked, because at that moment a burly bloke in a suit grabbed me by the shoulder and pulled me away from Queenie.

'Get out,' he said to me, giving me a shake and a push towards the door. 'We don't want people like you in here. And neither do these young ladies. Now piss off before we call the police.'

I made a mental note to come back one night when the Temperance Union was having one of its meetings, and heave a brick through the front window, then left. Queenie was left standing in the middle of the dance floor, as embarrassed as hell. But I couldn't do much about it. When I got outside the door, I stood there for a long time trying to work out what to do next, then the next thing I knew, Queenie was standing beside me.

'You didn't have to leave,' I said. 'You should have stayed with your friends.'

'They're not my friends any more. They were not very nice about what happened. You know what I think? I think they were jealous.'

'What, because of me?'

'Yeah, because the best looking bloke came up to me.'

'Go on.'

Then she kissed me. And everything I had touched everything she had. It was one hell of a serious kiss. And when we were finished, she smiled at me as if she had never been so happy in her life, and kissed me again. That night I couldn't do anything wrong. I walked Queenie home, sat with her on the sofa on her front porch for ages, while she let me feel her body all over, and then felt mine. I'd never seen Queenie before, and I reckoned I'd never see her again. But I was very wrong about that, wronger than I'd been about anything.

3. The Richmond Terrier

I'm skipping bits, because, well, because I can. No, that's not true. I'm skipping bits because I'm excited, and I want to get to the point, as usual. I've been told that before. Anyway, after that, I was okay about girls, at least the ones who were older than me. The younger ones I couldn't abide. They were, well, different. I knew that no matter how keen they were, they could never hold a candle to Queenie. As for the older ones, well, they gave me a run for my money, and they knew things, like how to protect themselves from getting up the duff. And they didn't seem to care what I looked like, how I sounded, or how I walked. At least, I was never able to work out whether they cared or not, though they all said they liked me just the way I was. The married ones liked me best of all, as young as I was. And I had a few. In those days, there were a lot of women around whose husbands were in the Police Force, as there was a general breakdown of law and order in Richmond, which, it seemed to me, had spread like the itch from the rest of Melbourne. I blamed the proddies, myself, as did we all.

The point is, the police were as busy as a snake with hives, and the little lady often got neglected in the rush to catch the miscreants that made Richmond one of the nastier parts of Melbourne. So in steps A.T., bold as you please, to do the local constabulary a favour by servicing its cows. I'd heard that a policeman's lot is not a happy one, but I knew that it bloody well would be if he stayed home and did the housework a bit more, because some of those ladies had what it took, and I soon figured out what it took as well. And imagine my surprise when I discovered one of them – it was Florrie Hardy, I think – yes it was – worked in a cat-house over Wing's laundry just off Swan Street. No wonder she was good. But I dropped her after that – in the interest of not catching a dose of plague and having the mighty member, such as it was, drop off while I was in the act of running away from some minor fracas I was involved in. *You will observe, ladies and gentlemen of the jury that the prick the police found in Ginty's Lane on the night of the crime matches the defendant's vacant lot.* No thanks. It was a pity too, because Florrie ran a close second to Queenie, for whom I had many a vision on a lonely night.

Well, of course, there was a war on, and women were in abundance, while rivals were not, so a bloke the likes of me could do well with the ladies; and it wasn't long before I bumped into Queenie again, but this time she was working a few yards off Dynon Lane for some bastard called, of all things, Randy Ryan. Well, it made my blood boil to see her in such a state, she being such a beauty, a natural beauty, as my mother used to say of Queen Mary, though I couldn't see that at all. But this Ryan was a big bastard, and six weights above me, so I reckoned I had two chances of putting one over on him. All I could do was go around to Queenie's place one night and put it to her straight.

'Listen, love,' I said, 'that Ryan's only gunna hurt you like mad, like he does to all the girls. And you're the best of the best, especially to me. Why don't you give this bloke a miss, and chuck your lot in with me. I'll see you right.' Or something like that. I was feeling awkward, not my normal self. I was saying something to a girl I'd never let myself think, let alone say, and was yet to be convinced that it was one of my best ideas. But Queenie was no ordinary girl, and I knew that she thought something like that about me as well, regardless of the facts, and when in a sober state, because she has let me know as much.

'Archie,' she'd say. 'I don't know what it is about you, but you're different.'

'I wish I had a quid for every time I've heard that,' I'd say. 'I'd have a flamin' mansion on Toorak Bloody Road.'

'You know what I mean, Arch, you know who you are, and you act it, not like those other bastards, always trying to big-note themselves, trying to show a girl how big and tough they are, what a great catch, and so on.'

'Jeez, Queenie, you're not exactly making me feel terrific over here.'

'No, love, I didn't mean that. Everyone knows you're as tough as a fox terrier, but you don't go around telling everyone who'll listen. You just quietly bash some big bastard up every now and then, and go on your way. A girl admires that in a man. And you are a good catch, or at least you will be, when you're ready. But you're not, are you. I mean, you're still an apprentice, and we all know what apprentices make, don't we? Sweet Fanny Adams. The only way you can get by is finding a little something to do on the side, to make a quid or two to tack onto your income. Isn't it?'

'Well –'

'Yes, well, a girl's no different. I make bugger all down at the shop, less than you do. And the only reason the boss took me is because I've got these –' and she lifts her tits up in front of me, so they just about jump out of her clothes. 'Without 'em I'd be dead. They're my bread and butter.'

'I don't like that boss of yours. He's a pig. I've seen the way he looks at the girls. He looks like he could be a bad bastard.'

'Let me tell you something, Arch. It's only the possibility of a naughty with any one of us that keeps us on the books. He's not gunna get it, of course, but he lives in hope. And his wife watches him like a bloody hawk. So I wouldn't be too worried. And what about you, Arch? I hear all kinds of stories about you. *Archie knocked off something or other, Archie'll look after you, Archie this, Archie that.* Whatever you're up to, every man and his bloody dog knows about it, so you can be sure the local coppers do too. You just be careful, love. And don't you worry about Randy, he won't hurt me. He knows about you and me being friends, and he heard that you've cut a few blokes bad, so he'll watch himself.'

'Jesus, Queenie, you know I hate knives. Where'd he get an idea like that?'

'P'raps from me. See? I'm looking after you. Now, you leave Randy alone, and he'll leave you alone, and I'll do what I have to do. Course, if you was to get a fair dinkum job, one with some real money in it, I might reconsider. What d'yer reckon?'

'Strewth, Queenie, a bloke needs an apprenticeship. Hell.'

'And I need a real man, Arch. I know you haven't asked me, but I'm saying yes. But you have to have something better than tin goin' for you. I mean, even when you finish that bloody apprenticeship, where are you gunna work? I'll tell you: at the flamin' Jam Factory. Who else makes bloody tins? Think about it, love. It's the tins, or me.'

She opens her blouse and lets me slide my hands inside and kisses me.

'Nobody gets these kisses, Arch. They're all for you. It can all be just for you. Think about it.'

Well I thought about it until my brain just about fell out, and in the end, I took myself down to Ryrie's Boxing Gym and introduced myself.

'G'day, Mr Ryrie, I'm Archie Taggert, the next Australian bantamweight champion.'

'Piss off.'

'You wouldn't say that if you lived in Richmond.'

'I do live in Richmond. Now piss off.'

'Well, I know how to handle meself, or so I've been told. And besides, I could use a few quid.'

'You couldn't fight yer way out of a wet paper bag.'

'See, that's where you come in, Mr Ryrie. Come on.'

'Piss off, or I'll sick me dog onto you.'

I looked around.

'You haven't got a dog.'

'Then I'll sick me old lady onto you. Then you'll wish I *did* have a dog.'

'You don't allow women in the gym. The sign says so.'

'So you can read, can you? Smart arse.'

'I can punch, too. Get me a bantamweight, and I'll show you.'

'Get some gloves and get into the ring.'

I got some gloves and got into the ring. Or so they told me. I don't remember. But when I was able to talk again, I fronted up to Ryrie, and said to him: 'You don't frighten me, Mr Ryrie. They told me you put me in with some kind of bloody giant. Well, that's the last time you treat me like a fool. I'm coming back, and I'm going to get a trainer, and I'm going to fight. And I will be the next champ. And when I am, I'll come back and buy your bloody gym, and you with it.'

He didn't say a word, just smiled at me. But he had that look in his eyes, I'd seen it a hundred times. He'd gone too far, and he knew it. He'd let me come back, and he'd help me find a trainer, and it would all work out just the way I said.

After that you could always find me at the gym. And work? I worked like a fucking navvy. The first thing I discovered about myself was that I had no stamina at all. I was basically a cart without a bloody horse. I was born with a dodgy hip, which was in perpetual pain, especially in the wet weather, which Melbourne seemed to specialise in. My mum told me when I was a kid that when she was expecting she was bitten by a three-legged wombat. It was only when I mentioned this in the classroom one day that I discovered a wombat is not a monster that hangs upside down from trees and preys on helpless pregnant women. I trace my loss of trust in the world to that moment.

My hip hurt; I was never out of pain. So I favoured the other, and tended to limp a little, and wandered to the right a touch. Only swimming in seawater eased the pain, so I spent many long hours down at Port Melbourne soaking in the water, weightless, praying that one day I would get out of the water, put pressure on my leg, and feel no pain. That was how I learned that God was a funny bugger.

So the only way I could stay on my feet in the ring was by learning the tricks of the trade. And I mean *all* the buggers. The name of the game was early knockout, and I had the punch to do it. My best punch was still my straight right, and everyone I fought was very careful to keep an eye out for it, because it came of nowhere, disguised as a jab, and fooled a lot of people.

So to keep a long story short, I kept my promise to Dave Ryrie and got a manager, Les Parker, and managed to stay off the canvas. Queenie came to watch all my fights, and was always pretty excited, treating the whole thing like a flamin' footy match, screaming out that someone ought to kill the flaming umpire. After I explained to her that he was called a ref, she switched to: 'Will someone please kill the flamin' ref for me, bugger it?' until we told her to just stick to barracking for me, and tell the other bloke to drop dead, that being my intention anyway.

Well, despite the good run of luck I had hitting blokes, and the support I got from Queenie, support which I knew young Randy Ryan did not approve of, I was still not making any real money. After you've paid every one off, including a few people who collected a cut for looking the other way about various official matters, like the coppers who turned up and turned a blind eye to the sale of grog, and the bookmaking. After everyone and his dog had had a go at the take, you were lucky if you had enough left to get you a tram home. Boxing was a mug's game, they said, and I was beginning to think they were right. So I branched out a bit, doing a bit of door-keeping for Wing the Chinaman down at his casino, near East Richmond Station.

Charlie Wing had a finger in every pie in Richmond. Basically, nothing went on down our way without him getting involved, usually at approval level. And he was a bad bastard, too. But he had a soft spot for fighters, and for me in particular, even though I was as straight as a die, and never took a dive. I think he had a soft spot for me because I looked after his girls at the fuck-shop over the laundry whenever I was available, and I never took advantage, never tickled Peter, as we say, and never spoiled the merchandise. The fact is, I let it be known by everyone that I had a girlfriend, and that I was keen on keeping it that way. So things were pretty smooth in the minding department.

But that place was murder to work in, if you can call what I did work. For a start it was right above a laundry, so it got as hot as hell, especially in summer, and it was widely known that a punter could lose a couple of pounds just getting caught up in the heat of the moment, so to speak. A client would therefore do well to pace himself, lest he pass out, or have a heart attack, or both. Many's the time I'd answer some young lady's distress call, half expecting to find that one of the clients had gone too far and needed a smack, dragging down the stairs, and throwing out into the street, stark naked, only to find some cove who'd succumbed to the heat, and just sort of melted all over his hostess, like cheese on cauliflower. In those cases there was nothing to be done but try to revive him with a bit of water. A few never did come round, and we'd have to have to drag them out into the lane, and call the mortuary, who probably would have gone out of business but for Wing. Mind you, that sort of thing happened even in our competitors' places, where the temperature was relatively cool and they had fans in summer.

But who'd have thought that a cat-house above a Chinese laundry would be successful? It was all in the location, explained Charlie to me, one night. The place abutted the upper storey of a hotel, the Lord Cardigan, and there was even an adjoining door, so in the event of any unpleasantness downstairs, involving, say, the client's wife, then the said client could make a dash for the pub through the upstairs door, and make an exit. Naturally, this door got more use than the main turnstile at the Royal Agricultural Show, and had to be oiled every five minutes to keep it from bursting into flames. But it was one of the attractions of Wing's place.

Another was the fact that clients were able to have their clothes laundered downstairs for free, if they were staying for the long haul, and many a city official or policeman did just that. The members and employees of the Richmond local government were in consequence a smart and sweet smelling lot, despite not really deserving it. Wing's also had stairs out the back that lead down into the lane, and those who were in a particular hurry, or who needed to avoid the pub, and there were a lot of these types, too, would use this particular facility. The result of these arrangements was that the front door of Wing's place was often no more than an entrance, spitting out only bachelors, men who owed no one money, and wowsers, who'd come into to complain about the noise, hoping to catch a glimpse of a half-naked tart.

So there I was, having a pretty lazy time of it, except on pay nights, when I'd be busier than a one-legged waiter, when who should decide to come in to the establishment and stir up a bit of trouble but Randy Ryan, who did not approve of me at all, not that the feeling wasn't mutual. He'd come up to give a hard time to one of the new girls, who'd left the street and decided to throw in her lot with Wing and Co, the Co being Rita Rouse, a woman of manly proportions, who frightened everyone who'd ever met her, bar me. And to this day, I don't know why that is. Little Archie, she'd call me – she had my number.

So one Thursday night in walks this Ryan bastard, and starts giving this hostess a hard time, and I go in to give him a helping hand out to the street, though I'm not looking forward to it, because he's a big bastard and mean. But I'm stopped at the door by a bloke with a nose like a ferret and wearing a suit, as though he was going out on the town, which he might have been as, for a lot of desperate characters, that's just what a visit to Wing's was. This bloke was bigger than me, as were most of the locals over the age of fourteen, but he had the look of a bloke who drinks too much and doesn't look after himself, so I decided that he wouldn't be too hard to deal with. I was thinking that to save time, I might just bust his bugle, do my trick, if you see what I mean.

'Scuse, me, brother,' I say, polite as a priest's housekeeper.

'And who the hell would you be, shorty?'

Well, it might have been the shorty comment, it might have been the stinking weather, it might have been the Chinese stew I had downstairs at the back of the laundry before starting work, but I was not happy with his tone and I told him so.

'I'm sorry to hear that little feller, but I don't give a stuff. If you want to go in there, you'll have to wait till my friend's finished.'

And he pulls up his right coat sleeve to reveal a cut-throat razor that's doubled back and running up his wrist. I know that if he's fast, he can get my face with that before I can blink, so I decide not to give him a chance, and give him a fast right to the stomach, that should have just about knocked him flat. But he's wearing some kind of armour under his clothes, and my fist slams into a sheet of tin. Then it dawns on me who this bloke is. He's a feller they call Ned Kelly, because he goes out wearing all this tin sheeting, and causes mayhem wherever he goes. He's a slasher, as well. Altogether, a very nasty bastard.

Anyway in the split second it takes me to realise all this, he takes a swipe at my face, aiming to miss with his fist, and connect with his forearm, to that he can open me up with the razor. Well, he might have had more success if he'd tried a punch, of course, because he was well within range, and I was in agony from punching what I was pretty sure was a bit of tin from someone's back gate. So I pulled my head back an inch and let the punch miss. Then, because I didn't know how much of that junk he was wearing under his fancy suit, I let him have one in the face. But he must have been a bit of a fighter himself, because quick as a flash he whipped his right hand up to defend his face, just as he might have if we were in the ring. My fist connected with the bottom of his wrist, and drove the razor tip into his eye, skewering his eyeball like a pickled onion, and he let out a mighty scream, and squirted blood all over me. I didn't want to touch him, because he still had the razor, but just then the door opened, and Ryan appeared in the doorway, and sized up the situation.

'Cut me mate, will ya, ya fuckin' loony. I'll fuckin' kill yer.'

He lunged at me, and as I dodged I kicked him in the shins as hard as I could, and he sort of took off like one of those swans down as Albert Park Lake, and went flying through the air, cleared the top of the stairs, and landed half way down to the ground floor. When he landed there was as loud snap that told me he'd busted something he probably had a use for. I felt good about that, but on the whole, not good about the other bloke, as I never set out when I went to work to seriously hurt anyone, and now I had.

Charlie was good about it.

'Archie, better you take a trip.' He kept talking while he dipped into his pocket and produce a wallet full of pound notes. 'New Zealand is my advice. Never been there meself, but I hear the pussy is first class; though not the beer – black stuff.' He stuffed some money into my hand. 'Not tomorrow: tonight, now. Get down to the wharf. Keep in touch, and I'll let you know how things turned out.'

'Charlie, that's not my style, running away. You know that. I'll stay and look after Queenie and your girls. It was him who had the knife, anyway.'

'No, Archie, he'll say it was you. Archie, that Ned Kelly bastard, you don't know him, do you?'

'Not really, mate. Why?'

He lowered his voice, almost to a whisper.

'Not supposed to know this, but he's a police detective – undercover – he's in with the Razor Gang, down here from Sydney looking for some bloke whose been cutting women all over the place. At least he was. Now he's just plain fucked, and so are you. So get going.'

'You'll stand up for me, Charlie.'

'Yes, I will, but not if they put you on trial.'

'Why not?'

'Because they'd have me closed down – a judge wouldn't hesitate, too close to home...sorry, mate.'

'Ah, Jesus. Well, I still won't go to New Zealand.'

'Look, why don't you go over and ask Queenie to go with you. She must have a few quid put away for a rainy day, and believe me, this is a rainy day. And my offer still stands. But you'll have to do it tonight.'

'Look, you said he was a Sydney cop. And he had a razor. I think I'll be okay. We know a few people too, don't we?'

'There's no *we*, Arch. There's just you.'

So I left that place and went over to look for Queenie, to tell her what happened, and ask her what she thought of living in New Zealand.

'Why New Zealand?' she said.

'It was Charlie's idea.'

'What would a Chinaman know about New Zealand?'

'Not a lot, by the sound of it. But he reckons it's easy to get to. We just get down to Port Melbourne and look up a few ships, and Bob's your uncle.'

'Well, I'm doing quite well here,' she says. 'I reckon if I go anywhere I'll lose me corner, and it's paying like a drunken sailor. You go, love, and write me a letter. When things blow over, I'll let you know and you can come back.'

'Trouble is, Queenie love, I also busted up Randy pretty bad too, I reckon.'

'What, Randy! I'd've thought he'd be a bit big for you, Arch. Aren't you a surprise package?'

'Lucky punch, I think. Anyway, he broke something important, and they lugged him off to hospital. He'll live, but he won't be good company for a while. So what d'yer say?'

'I'd love to, Arch, but it's just this flamin' corner of mine. It's makin' me stinkin' rich. I tell you I'm sittin' on a bloody fortune.'

She laughed that wide open laugh that made me fall in love with her two years before, at the time when the poetry began, and my mind was made up.

'That settles it, love. I'm staying. We'll sort things out, somehow. I'm starting to make money in the ring now. Soon, I'll be able to get some serious matches. And if worse comes to worse, I'll probably only get a month or two in the city lock-up, and you can come and visit me and tell me all the news.'

I got five years, bugger it.

4 Pentridge

His Majesty's Pentridge Gaol was where they sent me. It was a
difficult place to get ahead if you were a bloke with shortcomings
which, as I've told you, I was. But my point is that in Pentridge,
there's not much a bloke can do to get by. Fighting is one way, of
course, because all the new blokes have to get bashed on arrival,
and a lot of blokes reckon you're better off being one of the
bashers. So it wasn't long before I had scores to settle, and that
meant that I was soon punching well out of my weight, but as
fighting came natural to me that wasn't a problem. And one lot
that gave me no trouble at all were the other boxers in the place.
And you would be surprised, no doubt, to hear who they were.
While I was there, I either met, or heard of the following, whom
I have made into a kind of boxing programme for you, as they do
at the Stadium.

There was, in order of their preferred fighting weight:

Marmaduke "Duke" Hobson, Heavyweight
Manny O'Brien, Heavyweight
Jack "Jackhammer" Baskett, Heavyweight
Terry "General" Denahy, Light Heavyweight
Rex "Chaff-cutter" Corrie, Light Heavyweight
Albert "Froggy" Froggatt, Middleweight
Colm Byrne, Welterweight
Danny "Nigger" Jackson, former Australian Welterweight
Champion

Mick "Sugar" Sweetman, Lightweight
Paddy O'Donovan, Lightweight
"Flash" Harry Williams, Lightweight (not looking too flash
when I saw him, though)
Fergus Toohey, Lightweight (and mad as a snake)
John Withers, Featherweight
Sam Burns, Featherweight
Ray Sidebottom, Flyweight (and looked it)

Of course, most of these blokes were so far out of shape they looked either like great overgrown potatoes or wilted sticks of celery, depending on which end of the weight scale you were looking at. And when push came to shove, the weights went out the window, and someone just plain clobbered someone else, and that was an end to the matter. So it paid to be careful how you went. But naturally, the boxers had too much respect for each other to do this very often, and more often than not the blokes these ex-fighters fought were just ordinary cons trying to make a name for themselves – a dangerous game. Naturally, all the youngsters wanted to go a round with yours truly, and I even got to bust a few noses, which didn't really surprise any of the fighters and caused most to leave me alone.

The poetry gave me hell, more that it usually did, to the point where it would run through my head whenever I let my guard down, which was too often. Sometimes, it would strike in the form of a stanza I'd sort of got stuck on, that kept on running round and round in my head, and sometimes it would be a line, or sometimes a funny little poem with not much of a body, a bit like me, that would visit me every now and then to say hello, or so it seemed. Occasionally I would give in to it completely and sit down in a corner and just let it happen, because that's what it seemed to want. On those days, I'd feel dreamy and odd, as if I was dreaming while I was awake.

We had a bloke in our division who was a bit of a painter. He was a curious cove. If he had been a boxer I'd describe him as a lightweight with a long reach, because he had very long arms for his size. But he told me that it was a big advantage for him because he was an artist. His job was to illustrate magazines, while in his spare time he painted pictures and sold them through art galleries. I'd heard of these painter coves, of course, but this was the first one I'd actually met. This Daryl bloke was in for doing his block and donging another bloke with a chair, and doing him quite a bit of harm. Now, while this was the kind of place where very little judgement went on as to the whys and wherefores of how a cove got into it, I couldn't help telling Daryl that I would have smacked the bloke in the bugle, and that would have been that. But apparently painters are not like that, and prefer to involve the furniture in the discussion.

So one day I says to Daryl: 'So Daryl, do you mean to tell me that you busted a perfectly good chair over a bloke's head, when you could have just given him a fistful of fivers? I don't get it.'

'Well, I don't like fighting: it's not in my nature. I just got so upset I picked up the nearest thing, and it was his chair – he loved that chair.'

'Hang on minute, didn't you just tell me that it was your chair.'

'Well, it was, but as I said, he just adored it.'

This Daryl was clearly finding the conversation a bit awkward – you know how it is when you touch on a subject without meaning to, that sort of makes everyone start fiddling with the buttons on their shirts, and so on – one of those moments.

'So what was the fight about, a woman?' I said, hopefully.

He tossed his head a bit, and looked over my head – people tended to do that with me – sort of into the distance.

'No, it wasn't a woman.'

I reckoned that if the argument wasn't over a woman then it might have been over money, and that's something that a bloke doesn't want everyone to know about, so I decided not to push it.

'I think I understand,' I said, to put an end to the conversation.

'Actually, Archie,' he says to me, inclining his head as if he's hearing my bloody confession of something, 'I'm glad you don't. But let's say it *was* about a woman, and leave it there. Now, tell me all about your poetry.'

I nearly fell over when Daryl said this, as I'd never told a soul, and never would, but somehow he'd managed to read my flamin' mind.

'For Christ's sake, Dazza, what makes you think I know anything about poetry?'

'*Daryl*, please.'

'What? Oh, okay. Daryl.'

'Because I heard you reciting it in the kitchen, when you thought you were alone:

Mmm...To my shame, I doubted the convicts' scrawls
Aah...
Til I placed my fingers in the wounded walls
And felt the chiselled rows myself –

I memorised it.'

'Christ Almighty, Dazza, what're yer doin'?'

'Sorry.'

'Jesus, Dazza ... Daryl ... if anyone finds out, I'm fucked.'

'Don't be silly, Archie. I know a lot of men who write poetry.'

'Don't come the raw prawn with me, mate. We both know what kind of blokes you're talkin' about. I'm talking about real men. Look, I'm a fighter, not a bloody poet. A man's got a flamin' reputation, hasn't he - outside?'

'Oh, Archie, *real* men. Don't give me that 'real men' rubbish. I could tell you stories about some of these real men.' He waved an arm around him.

'I know the stories. It's a bloody prison, for Christ's sake. It's like a shovel for all the crap in town, no offence to you, Dazza ... Daryl, as you seem to be a nice enough bloke when you're not trying to murder your mates with the furniture.'

'No, I mean, some of your so-called tough blokes. Take Bob Wright, for instance –

'The welterweight? Don't make me laugh. That bloke eats nails for brekky.'

'I heard he eats more than nails –'

'Now, listen, cobber –'

'Alright, don't get into a tizz. Look, I was only trying to make you laugh, Archie. I just think you should wake up, that's all. You secret's safe with me. If you ever want to let me hear any of you poetry, I'd love to.'

'Now listen, Dazza. I'm no bloody wowser. I was the upstairsman in a cathouse when I got landed in this place, and a few of them cats were more like tommycats, if you catch my meanin', so I didn't come down in the last shower. But if you keep talking like that, some bad bastards gunna hear you and you're gunna wake up one day in the bloody infirmary, minus your block and tackle. So be careful. And no more of this 'Daryl' bullshit. From now on you call yourself Dazza, and you call the cook a cunt.'

'Why, for heaven's sake?'

''Cos he is.'

In Pentridge, every day was as slow as a wet weekend, and a bloke had do whatever he could to while away the time, though they had us cutting and shaping bluestone, which was at least good for the arm muscles, and did get you out in the fresh air, though that was usually full of fresh rain. At that time there were a lot of blokes in my division doing overly long sentences for comparatively minor crimes, so many, in fact that the old hands were soon complaining about the quality of the new prisoners, many of whom were guilty of no more than shoplifting, or receiving something of no particular value at all. This strange phenomenon – that's what it was – became the centre of conversation among the prisoners, and one morning at breakfast, I struck up a conversation with the cove sitting next to me, a new chum who had seaman written all over him.

'What's yer name, young feller,' says I, judging him to be about five years older than me.

'Jack Delaney,' says he, quick as a flash.

'Well, I'm Archie Taggerty, and I'm no seaman, but I know one when I see one.'

'Able seaman, *SS Morocco*. At least I was. Got three months for going on strike. Half the bloody crew did.'

'You can't get locked up for going on strike,' I said. 'Even I know that, and I'm a bloody fighter.'

'You can when there's a war on. The *Morocco's* a troop transport. See all these new blokes?' He waved his spoon around the dining room. 'Half of them are seamen, and that surly crowd, down the end? They're off the *Morocco*, the lot of 'em.'

'But, surely, you wouldn't have gone on strike would you, I mean, knowing what would happen?'

'They declared it a troop transport after the strike had started, and forgot to tell the crew. Then they pinched half of us.'

'Why didn't they just tell you to end the strike?'

'Because that's how they get blokes into Pentridge – haven't you heard?'

'Nuh. What're yer talkin' about?'

'They're finding any excuse to bang blokes up; the union brief told us. Any little offence, no matter how minor, maximum penalty, but only if it's a prison offence. You can get three months for looking the wrong way out there.'

'Jesus, this place'll be full in nothing flat.'

'It's full already, that's what the barrister says. He says in D Division, they've got blokes sleeping on the floor, there's so many of 'em.'

'But what's the point?'

When I asked him this, he laughed so loud a guard came over and punched him in the kidneys extra hard, so that he spewed up his breakfast on the spot, and most of it ended up back in his bowl. It looked exactly the same – funny, that.

Well, I discovered the point straight after breakfast – we all did. The whole division was paraded in the yard in three long ranks, and as our numbers were called we were marched one at a time into the masonry overseer's office. None came out. When it was my turn, I was marched in, and found myself facing a table with an army officer sitting at it. He was surrounded by some very nasty looking prison officers.

'Name.'

I began to recite my number, and a guard behind me hit me so hard with his truncheon I thought he'd broken my shoulder blade.

'The officer said *name!*' he said.

'Archbold Patrick Taggerty, sir,' I said, not wanting to cop another one.

The officer looked at his list and checked my name with his pen.

'*Grievous bodily harm*, I see. Well, you'll be doing plenty of that where you're going, my lad. Sign here.'

I signed.

'Your sentence has been commuted in exchange for volunteering to join His Majesty's Australian Imperial Force. Should you wish to change your mind you will be shot. Next.'

The rear door of the office was opened by a guard who motioned with his head for me to walk through. On the other side, I walked down a passage that came out into the chapel, then through the chapel into another yard. Next thing I knew I was inside a Black Maria that was crammed full of prisoners. The barred door on the back was closed, and the outer door shut, and we were off.

An hour later, the doors were opened and I discovered that we had arrived inside a large warehouse of some kind, full of trucks coming and going, and blokes from Pentridge, and soldiers. Under guard, we were issued with uniforms, which we changed into on the spot, and a mysterious kit bag, then were formed up in ranks by a little bloke with a giant moustache and a loud voice. He then saluted another bloke, who addressed us as follows.

'Welcome to the 25th Reinforcements. I am Captain Wren. In a few minutes we will be boarding *HMAT Boorara*, and proceeding to Egypt. There you will complete the training began on the ship, and join your regiment. Any questions?'

'You –', someone began, but was cut short by the bossy bloke with the moustache, who nearly had a fit.

'Stand to attention when you address an officer, or I'll have you!' he shouted, red in the face.

The bloke stood to attention. He was used to this kind of treatment.

'I have a –'

'You will address the officer as *Sir*!'

'Sir, you said reinforcements – reinforcements for who?'

'The 4th Light Horse Regiment.'

'But sir, I can't ride a horse.'

Everyone had their first laugh for the day.

'Shuddup!' yelled the little bloke.

'Neither can I, Trooper. Carry on Sar' Major.'

'Sir!'

The moustache and the captain saluted each other and the captain walked off. The moustache then made a little speech of his own, telling us how horrible we were, and how by the time we arrived in Egypt we'd be soldiers, not the scum that we had been up to this point. We then marched out through a back door onto a wharf, and up a gangplank onto our new home.

Ah, the smell of the sea! It hit me with the force of a happy memory. But I couldn't see how I could avoid writing some lines about it, as the poetry demon had crept aboard inside me, and was niggling at me already.

> Boorara, *is this all a joke? And will you bring me home*
> *Hidden in your stinking bowels, like a thing of shame?*
> *Is that where you were yesterday, up at the Island of Tears?*
> *Is this your secret plan, and is* Boorara *your real name?*
>
> *I hope we go our separate ways,* Boorara, *you and me*

I've seen your kind before, my son, I've seen you spewing boys

And I would pray that when I get back to Station Pier

There'll be a band, and grog to hand, and lots of bloody noise.

The *Boorara*, a smallish and unattractive ship, shoved off straight away, and pretty soon we were going flat out which, for the *Boorara,* was about as fast, I thought, as Duke Hobson could probably run. I wondered if he and the others had made it. Another troop transport shoved off just before ours, the *Suevic,* a big bastard. We raced her to the open sea, both sides barracking like hell as we caught up to her, but in the end she beat the crap out of us. I shouldn't have cared, I know, but it gave me a bad feeling.

5 Beersheba

Cairo was a bloody oven. And the 4th Light Horse Training Regiment didn't help. For one thing they made me ride a horse, which was a stupid bloody idea. I fell off more times that I've had hot feeds, and pretty soon word got around that the horses were making book on which of them I would fall off next. So I wasn't too good as a starter in the Light Horse, and the riding instructor, a burly sergeant with no neck, called Brooks, told me that he was considering scratching me from the Spring Carnival altogether.

'Taggerty,' he said, looking down at me sitting in the dust, still holding the horse's reins, and looking into its pitying eyes. 'Taggerty, you're a bloody disgrace to the Unit, and to the country you come from. Are you sure you're an Australian?'

'Yes, Sergeant, last time I looked.'

'Look, even the bloody horse is embarrassed. You're enough to make a grown man cry, you are. But I'll tell you a little secret.' He got down on his haunches, so that his hat brim was touching mine. 'If you don't pull your socks up and learn how to ride this bloody horse, I'm going to tie you to it and put you out in front of the first battle we go on. How d'yer like that? That's what we do to shirkers.'

I jumped to my feet.

'Who said I'm a bloody shirker? I'll have the bastard. I don't think there's a man in the place who's climbed on a horse as often as me.'

This was true.

'Well if you're not a shirker, you stay on that horse and prove it, Trooper.'

So I did. The last horse I fell off turned out to be the most forgiving horse in the Regiment. Her name was Dasher, like Santa's reindeer, and she'd started out not as a brumby, as many of the horses had, but as a stock horse, so she was used to being ridden by flaming idiots and made to go into impossible places. I worked this out when I accidentally let her run into a wadi, and she seemed to think it was in all in a day's work and calmly waited for me to choose which way to go. A brumby would have been a lot more worried, and nervous. But either way, the Walers were terrific horses, to the extent that a horse can be terrific, just because they seemed to be able to do anything you asked them to do, provided it was some other bugger who was doing the asking.

But though I only just passed muster as a rider, which was not good enough to be a trooper in the Regiment, the Walers loved me, as long as I didn't try to ride them – I reckoned they sensed my nervousness – and when I was around they usually became as gentle as lambs, and would let me do anything with them. For that reason, at the end of my training, and because the army discovered that I couldn't shoot straight to save myself (which, as it happened, was the very reason they needed us to shoot straight) they ended up posting me to the 4th Light Horse Regiment Supply Section. My job was to look after the horses' supplies, fetch up new horses, and so on. It was hard yakka, but it got me off the horses' backs, and around to the front of them, where I could quietly recite poetry to them when no one was around. The horses loved it, and I swear they would come close to me just to hear a poem. Reciting poetry to horses, that's all I was good for.

When eventually the CO reckoned we'd learned enough about shooting and riding, and were beginning to look like we could frighten the Turks, we were sent to the Regiment, which had by then become part of the 4th Light Horse Brigade, and was over the other side of the Sinai. I was considered to be too much of a risk to my own mates to be trusted with a rifle, so I was posted to the 4th Light Horse Brigade Supply Train with the rank of Corporal. As my main job involved taking care of horses, I found that if I recited a little scrap of poetry to a horse, no matter how irritable he pretended to be, he'd let me mount and ride him till the cows came home. This trick came in pretty handy whenever I had to ride a replacement horse out to the lines to hand over to his new rider, or ride out to collect a horse for the vet, which was often, as we liked to keep an eye on all the horses, no matter how tough they pretended to be, because it's in the nature of a Waler to bullshit about being crook.

Every now and then, when I was sure no one was paying attention, I'd try my luck with a horse by asking him to canter for me, and once or twice I got a quiet horse to gallop, knowing that he'd done with far heavier weights than me on board. It was these little achievements that gave me a little bit of confidence on horseback, though I preferred, as I think did the horses, to have me around the front feeding them treats and giving them the drum.

Things were a bit touchy in the Brigade, as there had been two unsuccessful attempts to get the Turks out of Gaza, and a lot of Aussies and Kiwis had already been killed and wounded, not to mention embarrassed. So they reckoned that when we turned up, their worries would be over. But first they decided to send us to Beersheba, which was held by the Turks with artillery. I couldn't see the problem myself, as I was just a supply bloke, you know, feeding the odd horse, and so on. I would have said *watering* the odd horse but water was a bit hard to get your hands on at that time, and the gee-gees were going around with their tongues hanging out. I know for a fact that a lot of blokes were sharing their water with their horses. One look at a horse and I could tell.

As for the Turks, we heard that their supply train was cactus, and that they were out on their feet inside the fortress, though they had water to burn. We sent them notes every five minutes telling them that we had bonza tucker, and we knew that they were receiving them because we had more Turkish deserters than you could shake a stick at, and nowhere to put them, and no spare munga to feed them. It didn't seem to bother these blokes that we'd been pulling their legs, as they were happier working for us than the Germans.

But they were keen on holding onto Beersheba, because of the wells, I reckon. They knew that without water we could never take Gaza. My crowd was at Karm station before the attack, waiting for food and water to arrive on the train, and when it did, we all took a load the twelve miles or so to the position of the Desert Mounted Corps. We found them, and fed and watered the horses, and they took up their positions. I could see Beersheba in the distance, and the brigade getting ready for the attack. It was an impressive sight, and one that I knew must have been worrying the Turks.

While I sat on a wagon and watched, a scrap of poetry came to me, and filled my ears and my sight, so that I could imagine that it was being played on the desert stage in front of me.

I've seen them on their way to the casualty clearing station

- it sounds almost polite;
Wagonloads of busted bodies, still alive, and crying out for
Mum;
I've watched them pass, and felt screwed up at feeling nothing
- but: I'm alright*;*
I've turned away, and discovered that I had work to be do.

They want to pass a bloke who'll shed a tear and curse,
and take them water to sip,
A man standing straight in the shadow feeling their darkest
fear;
They want a friend to see their pain and follow and hold their
hand;
It's no good standing idly by and gawking like a fool;
They gets a peek from me, that's all.

This was the kind of thing that worried me a lot, as I had come to recognise it as a kind of bad omen, the sort of thing that happens before trouble turns up. And in I was in a lousy place to start getting premonitions of trouble.

'Is that you, young Taggerty,' says a horribly familiar voice.

I looked over to my right, and there was Captain Wren, who I hadn't seen for a couple of months, he having been assigned to the Light Horse.

'G'day, sir,' says I, standing up and saluting.

'Can you ride, Corporal?'

This was no time for bullshit. Wren knew me, and I knew him.

'Yes, sir.'

He points at a Waler, all saddled up and ready to go, beside his own.

'My galloper's horse is up for grabs. I reckon she's yours, if you want to get back at the Turks for killing your mates.'

Put like that, it was bloody hard to refuse, though I had a polite go at drawing out the conversation.

'Well where's your galloper, sir? Won't he want her?'

'He was just commandeered by a Kiwi major. Rotten luck. So I'm stuck with two horses.'

This was one of those moments when a refusal might not only have offended but got me shot, or at least branded a coward. I opted for the smile the Richmond Terrier is famous for - in Richmond, anyway.

'Then this is my lucky bloody day, sir. God help those Turks now.'

'That's the spirit. Better check your ammo and water supply. Dawkins is a good galloper, but I don't know how prepared he was for battle.'

Well, as luck would have it, Dawkins had been armed to the teeth, and everything was in spit-polish order. I walked around and looked his horse, a lovely black mare, in the face and whispered to her while I gave her a potato from my pocket. She seemed to be calm enough, which was good, because I could see that a few of the horses in the line were a bit nervous. Horses can smell trouble, and, being sensible animals, prefer to stay away from it. The only thing that'll make a horse head for trouble is a friend, and in the little time left, I wanted this horse to be my friend.

'Has she got a name, sir.'

'Daisy, I believe.'

'Daisy, Daisy.' I whispered the word to the horse and held her head in my hands. She was a shade under fifteen hands, and seemed a little small for a soldier's mount.

'She's not exactly a draft horse, is she, sir?'

'Yes, well, Dawkins isn't much taller than you, and he picked her himself. She should suit you down to the ground. Seen any action yet?'

'No sir.'

'Then it *is* your lucky day. If you like, when we get to Beersheba, I'll send a message to your CO asking you to release you to us. You don't want to be a supply driver for the rest of the war, do you?'

I wanted to point out to him that the casualty rate among my fellow supply blokes was exactly zero, but he was enjoying himself so much, I didn't have the heart to spoil his day, and I went back to my horse, and sang *Daisy Bell* to her about half a dozen times, though I couldn't keep the shake out of my voice.

Well, the attack was due to start early, but didn't, of course. And by the time all the farting around had been done, it was almost dark and the Turks had had time to bring all their most bloodthirsty blokes out and dig them in. And to make matters worse, the little water we'd been given hadn't made the slightest bit of difference, and the horses were out on their feet.

So off we went, with Daisy happy to walk to within a mile of Beersheba with the hundreds of others, in three ranks. At the beginning we'd been walking so as to touch each other, as that was the style of the Light Horse, and they did that so that, when they were within firing distance, they'd jump off and go to ground, and one of each group of three or four would grab the reins, and lead the horses back out of the firing until it was time to go back and pick up the riders. And for some reason that now escapes me – I suppose it had something to do with being terrified – I had assumed that I was going to be a horse holder.

We were still walking, there was the sudden scream of shot just over our heads, as the Turks fired long in their haste to find our range. Next came the order to open ranks and canter, which I would have been only too happy to do, had we been facing in some other direction. We fanned out, and the Turks started to find our range, though it was hard to do any damage to us, we were so far apart.

I was in the rearmost of three squadrons, and just as the bombs started to fall the order was changed and we were told to unfix bayonets and holster our rifles. We were going to charge with our bayonets in our hands, as if we were cavalry, or lancers, which we were not, or bloody lunatics, which we were. At the charge we broke into a gallop and after only a few hundred yards were onto their forward defensive trenches, which were quite shallow, and screaming our heads off. The two squadrons ahead of us were copping machine gun fire and rifle fire, and blokes were falling down here and there, though not as many as I expected, and mainly because the Turks were shooting at the horses and not at the men. The forward squadrons jumped clean over the trenches, then the blokes wheeled around and jumped to the ground to face the Turks, who took one look at the bayonets, and put their hands up like a bunch of old women, despite being heavily armed. Well, we were right on top of this lot and jumped the trenches full of surrendering blokes and kept on going, straight for the defensive wadi.

I had never jumped anything at all on a horse without coming off, so I was quite amazed when Daisy cleared the six foot hole full of waving hands without even breaking her stride, and even more amazed when I didn't fall off, which I later put down to being so terrified that my knees and hands were gripping the horse like grim death. A couple of Turks with a machine gun were kneeling right in my path, and frozen stiff, with their mouths open. Daisy was in a hurry, and ran the buggers down. Down the wadi we went and up the other side, and there in front of us was the town. We passed through the many gates, which had been left open so that the men in the trenches might retreat, and rode through the town screaming like maniacs, with Turks down on their knees with their hands in the air all over the place, thousands of the buggers. I cornered about fifty Turkish soldiers in a little square and pulled out my rife and waved it at them, and down they got on their knees, without a murmur.

Not one of the Turks inside the town fired a shot. I didn't know whether to laugh or cry, unlike the Turks, who were on the side of having a good cry and getting it out of their systems. After we had collected all the weapons and found their water supply, we settled down to rounding up all the Turks and putting them in the one place. All this took most of the night. The Turks pitched in and helped wherever they could, and they didn't bear us any grudge at all for making them look like a bunch of sissies. Turns out they were starving, and buggered, and thoroughly pissed off with the way their officers had been running their lives lately. I knew that feeling. It also turned out that half the garrison had run like hell up the Hebron road when they first saw us massing earlier in the day, and were by now well away, and probably digging in somewhere else. I didn't give them another thought - they were gone, and good riddance. But it turned out they hadn't gone very far.

'Let's go and get the rest of them bloody Turks, boys,' says the sergeant major, one morning. And we all give a big cheer and wave our hats, and start moving, to find the rest of the Turkish army and make it surrender. How bloody naive can you get, eh?

And here's me, suddenly thinking that I was a bit of a horse soldier, and asking Wren to let me stay in the Regiment.

'Corporal Taggerty,' he says, 'I heard how you charged those machine gunners yesterday, and I'm proud of you, and I'd be damned happy to ride beside you.'

I now know that the correct reply my request to stay with the regiment would have been: *'Sorry, young Taggerty, but the Army needs you shovelling chaff and humping water cans, there's a good chap.'* Though, to be fair to Wren, I shouldn't have asked.

We had had a few days' rest, during which time a film company turned up, and made us pretend to attack Beersheba all over again, for the newsreel. I was sure I'd come unstuck if I tried that charge again, so I didn't volunteer to ride Daisy. Next, we had to catch the retreating Turks before they got established somewhere else. But they beat us to it, and so we were told to cut them off by marching north then west, to the coast.

At Huj, two squadrons stopped to get stuck into the Turks, while the rest of us went to the coast and were picked up by boats, horses and all, and taken down to Gaza. The idea was to attack Gaza from the sea, which had been tried before, of course, though not with the added burden of frightened horses. Naturally, we were told that the Turks would get the surprise of their lives when we turned up, and naturally, because there can be no secrets in a country where the Gyppos are everywhere and all looking the same, and talk about you nonstop, our arrival was about as surprising to the Turks as the rising of the bloody sun. So we turned up at the coast in small ships, chugging along and towing the horses in great long barges that were, I think, originally designed to carry cotton. The engineers had built the sides up, so that the horses wouldn't get a big surprise at being at sea, though a lot of the horses got instantly sea sick and stayed that way, and were consequently useless at the landing next morning, as were a lot of other things.

It took all day to get ashore, and get stuck into the enemy, who amused themselves by lobbing mortar bombs onto us, and managing to splatter some good horse flesh all over yours truly, who was looking after the horses on one of the barges. Just as the boat towing my barge was about to land, it was blown to bits, and I was forced to grab an axe and sever the towing rope, to stop the horses all going down, because they were all tethered together. It was a bloody mess. Riding one of the horse, I went paddling around in the middle of all the bombs and blood and crashing wood, and rounded up as many horse as I could, cutting their tethers from the barge's on-board tether, and dragged them to shore with me.

On the shore, no bastard would come and drag us from the surf, and I had to get the horses out the water alone, while half a dozen of them were shot and drowned on the spot. When the squadron had gotten the horses ready, they hopped on and charged the Gaza position. It was only five hundred yards, but it was uphill, and the Turks seemed to have an easy time of it. We ended up having to dismount and walk, then crawl, then stop. We'd been joined by a bunch of Kiwis, and they were having a hard time of it, too. At the lowest point of my confidence, I found myself hiding in a shallow bomb crater.

It had been the end of the day, a stupid bloody time to mount an attack. We were supposed to be the bloody Light Horse. Now we were so light on for horses, it wasn't funny. There was a dead one pretty close by, a nice bay that looked familiar. Legs blown off. I wondered how a horse could get it's legs blown off by an artillery piece. I'm still flaming wondering. I could hear a horse crying somewhere, too, not that I was sticking my bloody head up to get a clearer picture. Blokes moaning everywhere. Moaning for water. I was one of 'em. My left leg was numb. It was still there, thank Christ; it was just numb. So standing up and getting shot by a Turk sharp-shooter was out of the question.

Lying with me in the crater was another bloke, who was staring up into the darkening sky. Oh well, waste not, want not, my dear sainted bitch of a mother always said. I slipped the bloke's canteen and gave it a shake.

'Ere, what the hell d'yer think you're doing?' he whispered.

'Jesus, cobber, you scared the bloody life out of me. I thought you were dead.'

'I was just admirin' the Gaza fucking sky. Course I'm not flamin' dead. But you will be if you don't give me that bloody water.'

'How's about we split it? A bloke's dying o' thirst. An' I think me leg's busted.'

'Yer sound like a fucken sheila. Go on then.'

'Ta. Archie Taggerty.'

'I don't want to know yer fuckin' life story. Just give me the bloody water.'

I took a slurp and gave it to him, but it only made him vomit about half his blood all over me. If he wasn't dead before, now he was definitely past the half-way point. He looked at me and a parachute flare went off over our heads, turning his face and body white like ash, and his blood a black shadow that we shared. His upturned eyes glistened as they reflected the flare above us, and when they turned to me they told me that he was going to die there, with me.

'What did you say your name was?' he said.

'Arch – you?'

'They call me Polly. There's two of us: I'm Polly Corbett; the other bloke's Polly Passmore, a lieutenant.'

That rang a bell. 'I knew a Polly,' I started to say. 'In –'

There was a long silence, during which he coughed a horrible bubbly cough that turned into a new way of breathing.

'You were going to say 'in Pentridge' – thought I recognised that voice.'

'Yeah, I was there. I would have done anything to get out. I thought this would be a push-over. You?'

'Yeah. Arch?'

'Yeah.'

'I'm going. I can feel it.'

'Might be joinin' you soon, I reckon. I think the bastards got the better of us this time. The horses didn't scare 'em.'

'Yeah. Shit, them horses were fun. Me mates at home would have laughed themselves silly to see me. Arch, do me a favour, will you: don't leave me till I'm dead, mate.'

'I won't. I'll even tell you a poem to pass the time.'

The flare started to sputter as I wriggled close to him.'

'That'd be nice, Arch. I'd like that. I've never heard a poem.'

Speckles of the moon drip on the soldier in his hide
As he contemplates what might have been, today and in
former days
And gathers up his soul just as he would his kit
And makes to pass from harshest sun to coolest moon, away.

It's sweetness and it's gentleness; this fragrant path of old
Is waiting there rolled out for him, like the carpet at his nan's.
He'll meet old mates – their neddies, too – his family in time
As pain rolls off his soldier's brow, his angel takes his hand.

'Thanks mate. Arch, I can hear the surf.'
'Me too.'

6 Polly Beer

I had a rough journey to the coast by camel, and was only aware of pain, nothing else, and occasional rest stops, when the driver would give me water. Truth to tell, I would have settled for a rest in the shade, a cold beer, and being allowed to die. I had an interesting visit from my Troop Commander, Mr Beaumont, before I left. I didn't feel much like talking, and neither did he, as he had a lot of blokes to have a word with before they went off to hospital.

'You were lucky to be found, my boy,' he says.

'I was born lucky, sir,' I say.

'That's the spirit. You know, the only reason you're alive is that you were buried by dirt from a mortar round, and a couple of quick-thinking men crawled over and dug you out before you could suffocate.'

'Strewth, sir. Please thank those blokes for me. Did they get Polly as well?'

'Was there another man? God, I'm sorry, Taggerty. I don't think they knew.'

'It's alright, sir. He died in the night.'

'Ah. There's something I thought you might like to know, Taggerty. I heard about you charging those machine gunners at Beersheba. And I was on the beach when you rescued those horses. I've recommended you for a decoration. Well done. Well, you have a good rest in Cairo, and try to stay out of mischief.'

He shook my left hand, as my other one wasn't working, and I was off for the worst ride of my life.

Port Said was a hole. They were whipping off arms and legs right, left and centre at the hospital there. I was spared the hacksaw, but they had to set every bone in my body and they put so many splints on me I looked like a two pound cocky in a one pound cockies cage. But I was alive, though by the time I arrived at the hospital, which was at the Heliopolis Oasis, I had influenza, and was half dead. The whole time I was at the hospital I never saw the faces of the nurses, because I was put in the Flu Ward, despite having broken half the bones in my body and a few other bits that weren't actually bones at all, and the nurses were all wearing veils.

'Sir,' I said to the doctor, as soon as I was back in the land of the living, 'will I be able to box, I mean, after the war?'

'You mean fight? Well, that's pretty unlikely, my boy. You're not really built to be a boxer. But you were reciting some very nice poetry when you were feverish. Didn't recognise it, though. Perhaps you could be a teacher.'

'No sir, what I meant was, will I be able to box *again*. See, I was a boxer before the war, leastways, I was training to be one. I was the Richmond Terrier.'

'Richmond Terrier, eh? Well, I think those days are over. You've fractured your leg pretty badly. The bad news is you'll never ride again. Sorry, old chap, I know how you fellows love to ride. And you'll need a walking stick to get around. The good news is that you'll be going home as soon as you're up and about.'

'And when will that be, sir?'

'Not for a while yet, I'm afraid.'

He wasn't wrong about that, but I paid a couple of Gyppos to lug me around in a sedan chair, so I got to see the sights, though I'd been to Helio' before. And the poetry was there all the time, because it came with the pain, and not just mine, either. In the hospital, which was really just a series of bloody great warehouses of some kind, I was surrounded by blokes in terrific pain, so much so that the only way I could think straight was to let the poetry come to me sort of soothe me by being let out to play, like a kid, when it stops raining and the sun comes out.

But it wasn't enough for the poetry to just waft through me and out the other side like a daydream. No, it had to be written down. That's the kind of poetry it was, you see, like a pushy woman. It was always telling me to write it down. So I had done just that, making sure that no one ever saw me doing this and always keeping it in a special diary I got in a lovely-smelling shop in Cairo.

But eventually a day came when the poetry wasn't content to just be written down, and it insisted on being sent to someone who might be in a position to publish it, not that I wanted that – I didn't – but the poetry did, and it wouldn't give me any peace until I'd written some of it down, and made a few enquiries and ended up sending it to the editor of *The Argus* back in Melbourne. It was a pretty reminiscence of Richmond itself, the place I came from. I'd never heard of anyone writing about a Melbourne suburb before, so I reckoned the poem wouldn't stand a chance against all those poems about rivers and flowers, and so on. But blow down me if a few months later I didn't get a letter from the editor thanking me for the poem, and enclosing a copy of the issue in which it appeared. Also, the editor had published the poem under the name I the name I gave him, me not wishing to thought of as some girlie type who couldn't punch his way out a wet paper bag. The name was Polly Beer, after the bloke who died with me at Beersheba; I never knew his last name. I was happy with Polly Beer.

I don't want to rave on about the bloody poem, but I do want to mention that the editor wanted to know if I had any more of the stuff.

Part 2 Taggerty versus Beer

7 Starting From Scratch

The first thing I did when I got back to Melbourne was visit the Editor of *The Argus*, Jack Galloway, and tell him that he was never to reveal the real name of Polly Beer, or Polly's secret career as a boxer would probably turn into a joke. Mr Galloway was surprised to receive a visit from a small, banged up soldier using a walking stick.

'You've been in the wars haven't you,' he said, laughing his head off. 'Do you take a drink?'

'I'm sorry, Mr Galloway, but I don't, normally. Me neither,' says he. Let's have an abnormal one, then.' And he grabs his coat, and off we go down to the local rubbity, where he buys me the best beer I've tasted all year.

'I can see I'll have to take up the grog again, Mr Galloway,' I says, after a sip or two.

'Jack, please. That's good poetry, that stuff of yours, and I should know. And there's other rags that'll publish it, too. I'll give you a list.

So I was a published poet, without wanting anything more than the bloody poetry would get out of my system and go and plague some other poor bastard.

First thing I did after leaving *The Argus* was to take the tram up to Swanston Street, and visit Ryrie's Boxing Gym.

The last time these blokes heard my name was when they found out I'd been put away for what I did to Randy and that copper at Wing's. I don't think they would have had a clue that I'd been in the Army.

I walked into the gym with my uniform on, and a feather in my hat, being careful to leave my walking stick outside the door.

'Well, look what the cat's dragged in,' said some wag.

'Hey Arch, how'd you get out of jail? And where'd you nick that uniform?'

'G'day, fellers. They let me out provided I joined the Army, then they sent me to Egypt.'

'Go on! Never!'

'S'true. Sent me off to have a go at killing Abdul, which I did.'

'Looks like Abdul got his own back,' said Ryrie, who had an eye for a fighter who's got a problem.

'Nothing a bit of training won't fix.'

'Training won't fix that list to starboard, mate. Jesus, Arch, you can hardly walk. What happened to yer?'

'Got blown up, that's what. Bloody Turks!'

Just then one of the trainers comes in waving my bloody walking stick.

'Hello, mate. You left your stick outside. Thought you might need it.'

'Jesus, what a mate you are,' I says. 'I oughta bloody hit you with the bugger.'

'Arch, we'll talk about fighting when you're back in one piece, okay?'

'I'm almost ready for a fight. Been keeping in shape. Gyppo food keeps you regular as hell. I just gotta get this leg working properly. I might come down and do a bit of training if I get the chance. They're gunna give me my walking papers, they reckon. Dunno why. Nothing to do with me leg. I think they just want to get rid of me.'

'I see you got a few medals, Arch.'

'Pinched 'em.'

'Yeah. Well good on yer, kid. We'll have to wait and see how you go, won't we?'

'Reckon.'

I could see that look in their eyes. That was the look they gave dead-enders, fighters who were finished, who'd hit the end of the road, and who'd never get into the ring again. They didn't know the Richmond Terrier too well. They didn't know me at all.

The Army didn't want me. I was an embarrassment to them. I'd been lifted out of prison to be cannon fodder. That was how it worked. I wasn't supposed to live, let alone get a bloody medal. I was supposed to die a rude death in the sand, at the hands of some lucky Turk. I was supposed to be executed. I wasn't supposed to be a soldier's bootlace. And they let me know it, too.

Eventually, I was discharged on medical grounds by a bloke who wasn't even a bloody doctor, but some kind of bloody pen pusher, and a rude one at that. And when I walked out onto St Kilda Road, I had the look of a man who'd just come home from war, and was as brown as a berry from the Gyppo sun, and scarred here and there from the Turkish shrapnel, and the surgeon's patch-up jobs, and I swear my hip creaked out loud when I walked. And while any one can tell you I never did have a particularly graceful gait, now I had a lurch that made me look as if I was on the verge of falling over with every step, and depended on a walking stick. *You'll have to correct that*, says I to myself as I looked at my reflection in a shop window, and struck a boxing pose. But as soon as I put the stick down I nearly fell over with the lameness in my hip. But I'd be damned if I'd give up fighting.

It was the one thing that I could do well that I loved to do, they only thing I had ever done that gave me a chance at fitting in, or at least of kidding myself that I did, and I wasn't going to give that up for anything or anybody.

So I went back to Ryrie's day after day, though I was lucky if I could even climb onto the tram without help, which I hated. Everyone and his dog could see where I'd been and how and I got banged up, and besides, word gets around. Eventually, I got my hands on a lovely brown suit and a smart hat to match, and wore them everywhere. And I found out years later, that when coves saw that titfer lurching all over the place, they'd give each other a knowing wink, because they'd know who was under it, sweating in pain, and cursing the bloke who invented lace-up shoes, because mine were always coming undone, and I couldn't bend down to do the buggers up. People would stop and offer to do them up for me, and I'd always accept their help.

On the day Ryrie let me get into the ring for the first time after my return, I was walking down the steps to the gym when I nearly broke my neck on my own shoe laces, and a kindly lady says to me:

'You'll have to watch out, you nearly tripped over. Will you let me do those shoe laces up for you?'

And I, being weary of refusing such requests, and feeling sorry for myself as it was, and appreciating the young lady's way of addressing me, you know, straight and to the point, say to her:

'That'd be bonza, sister. I have such trouble reaching those little buggers.'

'What you need is some of those elastic-sided boots,' she says. 'I've seen some very well-dressed gentlemen wearing them lately.'

'Thanks, sister, I'll make enquiries.'

74

Well, having exhausted the subject of footwear, and she having retied my shoes laces with neat double bows, I bid her good-day.

'Ruth,' she says, shoving out a long, pale hand.

'Pleased to meet you. Archie.'

'Archie Taggerty. I know. The Richmond Terrier.'

'Now how would you know that? I mean, were not even in blood – I mean bloomin' Richmond. And I've been...travelling for the last few years.'

'I know.'

She did know, I could tell. But she seemed determined, as I was, to put the past behind us.

'My brother told me he saw you at Ryrie's.'

'Your brother's a fighter?'

'He's Billy Magee. He calls himself the Burnley Bruiser. He says he got the idea off you. I'm off to Ryrie's right now, if you're going that way.'

'Well I am, Ruth, but I'm afraid I can't walk very fast, if you can call this walking.'

'Here, let me put my arm through yours, and steady you.'

I didn't argue, because I was in a hell of a lot of pain about then, and I think she could tell by looking at me, though I prided myself on keeping a straight face.

'So you're off to Ryrie's are you? I suppose you know that Ryrie don't allow females into the place?'

'He will when he sees that I'm giving you a hand. What's he going to do, throw me into the river?'

She laughed like a bell, and the sound stunned me for a moment. She stopped laughing and walking, and looked at me with concern, something I hadn't seen in a woman's eyes since the 1st Australian General, in Heliopolis.

'What's wrong?'

I smiled, and felt the warmth of her hand around my upper arm.

'Nothing at all. It was just the sound of your laugh. I haven't heard that sound for a long while.'

I regretted saying that straight away, but Ruth showed no embarrassment at all, and looked at me straight and true, the way soldiers look at each other, the way fighters look. It was the look of a person who was used to both hard times and good times, and wasn't afraid to say so.

'So tell me about your brother, Billy. I don't know him.'

'Well, he's a Bantamweight, like you.'

'My God, you know your weights, don't you. I *am* a bantamweight, and that's a fact.'

'Oh, our family's been producing boxers since Adam was a pup. I'm probably one of the few women in the family who's not in favour of our young men getting their blocks knocked off every second Saturday.'

'You don't approve of boxing?'

'I don't approve of men hurting each other. There's enough pain to go around, the way I see it. I'd be just as proud of Billy if he got an ordinary job.'

'Well, then, you won't approve of what I'm going to do as soon as I get to Ryrie's.'

'What's that?'

'Have a go, that's what.'

'She gave another of those ringing laughs that warmed me to hear. She seemed to enjoy laughing a lot, and I didn't take offence.

'I'm sorry Archie. I didn't mean to take the mick. I was just thinking that now I know why they called you the Richmond Terrier.'

'Well, I may not be able to dance around like your gentlemen pugilists, but then, I never could really. I've always had a funny way of boxing. No, I just want to get the feel of it again, that's all. I need to be in the ring again.'

'Well, a part of me would like to see that, and another part wouldn't. I mean, you've seen enough fighting, I think.'

'I have seen a lot, that's true, but it was mad, blokes killing each other for no reason at all. I met a lot of Turks, you know, and they were just ordinary blokes, same age as us, except with different uniforms. Some of them had pictures of their sweethearts and families. They all had these big moustaches, which made them look quite dashing. Some of them, the lancers, were the most amazing horsemen I've ever seen, except that their horses were a bit temperamental, not like the Walers at all.

'What's a Waler?'

'A Waler's a horse, an Aussie, horse. Lovely animals, too. A horse'd be your mate. Funny thing is, the Walers come from the Arab world in the first place. But life in the bush toughened them up, gave them character. Least, that's what we were told.'

This brought us to the top of the steps going down to the River Walk, where Ryrie's was, and it took me a fair while to get down, as I wouldn't let Ruth take my arm, for if her brother was down there, I didn't want any trouble. I didn't know Ruth at all, though I felt as though I did, but I knew all I needed to know about Billy Magee: he was the Burnley Bruiser.

Inside the gym I was greeted with the big hello from all the blokes I knew, which was most of them. But Ryrie was not too happy with the appearance of Ruth, though she looked pretty enough to fit into any place, I thought.

'Now, you know the rules, Arch – I'm sorry, Miss, but Arch should have told you.'

'You must be Mr Ryrie,' she says, as sweet as marmalade, but with a little bit of a left jab in the voice. 'I'm Billy Magee's sister, and I can speak for myself, thank you. And as for your rules, we Magees don't care too much for them, as you've probably noticed. As a matter of fact, Billy said I could look in for a minute, as long as I didn't get in the way.'

She spotted Billy and gave him a wave which he returned. He was a pleasant enough looking cove about my weight, but when he spotted me he frowned like a short-changed Chinaman.

'Miss, these rules are there to protect the likes of you – young ladies, that is – from hearing the general kind of rough language that goes on in a place like this, this being language that will definitely offend you, I'd bet my life on it.'

'That would be an expensive bet for you, Mr Ryrie, for I come from an Irish household, where you call the dog a bastard, and a spade a bloody shovel.'

And all the while she was speaking, she had her eyes fixed on her brother and a sweet smile on her face, as if she and Ryrie were discussing the price of curtain material, or whatever it is women talk about – I'm pretty certain it's curtain material.

'You'd better stay near the door, then, so that you'll have less distance to cover if you have to leave suddenly.'

He turns to me next, and if he was in a good mood before we arrived, he isn't now.

'And what the hell d'*you* want?'

'Well, *Mister* Ryrie,' I says, all the air having been drained out of my balloon by the sight of this conversation, and in an

78

effort to pump some back in, 'if you'll recall, you said it was high time I got in the ring and had a bit of a run around, show the lads I'm back, and a force to be reckoned with, as we say in the Light Horse. So here I am.'

I had prepared this little speech a few minutes earlier while trying to get myself down the steps outside, and I thought it had the right mixture of determination and cockiness for which I was, and I mean was, well known.

'I recall nothing of the kind, you little twerp, but if you want to get into the ring and have bit of a run around, be my guest. Everybody knows you can't walk without a stick, so don't blame me if you get your bloody head knocked off. So I walk up to the ring, and say to Billy Magee: 'Will you have a little spar with me, just so I can get the feel of the ring again?'

'What, and have everyone know that I flattened a bloke who'd just come back from the War with one leg missing? Not bloody likely.'

'Listen,' I say, getting all wound up to tell one of my best porkies, but kind of looking forward to it at the same time. 'We had a flyweight in the Light Horse, a Moonee Ponds bloke called Ray Sidebottom – Jesus was he thin. He was so thin, it rained one day, and he had to run around just to get wet. I don't know how he stayed on a bloody horse, really. Anyway, when we charged the Turkish trenches at Beersheba, he jumped off his horse and took ten prisoners with only a bayonet for a weapon. Those Turks were scared shitless, not because he was waving a big knife at them – hell, they all had guns, for Christ's sake – but because his other hand had been blown off. And in my unit, that bloke was generally considered to be a bit of a mummy's boy. After that, the Turks always referred him as *Effendi*, in other words, *My Lord*, or some such, which was very polite of them, under the circ's. Just wanted you to remember that there's more to us funny looking blokes than meets the eye. Now give us a go, so I won't look silly in front of me old mates.'

So we climb into the ring, and I made it look as hard as hell, but on purpose, you understand, not wanting the young Magee to think I was as fit as a fiddle. And then I hang onto the rope for a few seconds pretending something was wrong. Then I put up my gloves and sort of hobble out to the centre and plant my feet as well as could. Well, Billy and me kind of reach out and trade a few polite taps at each other and I let fly a flurry of straights to his face, so that his vision is a little blocked by all the leather, then I give him a straight that knocks him off his feet, as he was not really ready for anything serious, and was well off balance. He lands on his bum on the canvas, and I go in the other direction and land on my bum a couple of yards away. The pain nearly made me pass out, and I sat there looking at his surprised face, knowing that I couldn't move for the sheer pain that was in my hip. Finally, Billy climbs to his feet and comes over and hauls me to my feet, and looks at me, really for the first time.

'If you were anyone else, I'd say that was a lucky punch, but I know it wasn't. Serves me bloody right for being a smart-arse.' And he give his sister a wink, to show that he's alright.

'You bloody fool,' says Ryrie, taking the gloves off me. 'He could have killed you.'

'It was him that was the bloody fool, Mr Ryrie. He fell for the oldest trick in the book, and he forgot to protect himself at all times. You told him to take it easy on me didn't you – I saw you give him the office. They told me I'd never fight again, you know, but you just watch me. I never was one for dancin' and prancin' – you know that – and now I'm even less of a dancer. But I'll make up for me, by being the sneakiest bloody fighter you ever saw, you just watch. Hey, what happened to Billy's sister?'

'Reckon she's seen enough. Still think puttin' Billy on his arse was a good idea?'

'Oh hell, I dunno anything these days.'

8 Woman Trouble

I went to Ryrie's every chance I got after that, and worked on the few weights he had there, until I found out that there was a fair dinkum weight training gym in Punt Road, and after that I tried to spend as much time as I could at each of the two places, trying to teach myself a new boxing style at one, and trying to build up my week leg at the other. I couldn't disguise the fact that I was carrying an injury of some kind, and so I decided to trade on it by making myself as strong as possible, so that when my opponent was drawn in and started to lean to one side in sympathy, which is what boxers tend to do, I'd surprise him with a left hook that'd catch him off balance. I developed a whole bag of tricks like that one, and managed to find my old trainer, Les Parker, who'd gone to New South Wales to train the mighty Ronny Judge, who was lost to the war, and come back again, pretty down about life in general.

I thought I'd cheer Les up when I saw him, so I said: 'Les this is your lucky day, for I need a manager, and you need a new champ.'

'I'll bite,' he says. 'Who's the champ?'

'That's right,' I says, 'put the boot in when a bloke's down; that'd be you.'

'Nah, never. I've heard all about your plans for a comeback. Let me see your hands.'

I gave him my hands, and he kneaded them and twisted them in every direction he could.

'Well now, Arch, you're in luck, for those hands are in pretty good nick. But the rest of you – Jesus, son, look at you.'

'See, that's where you come in, Les. I reckon I've got to be sneaky as hell if I'm going to face anyone bigger than a circus midget. I need to know all the lurks. I need to keep my feet planted and get into their heads, then surprise 'em, because if have to dance, I'll be fuckin' ratshit.'

'I think you might end up ratshit no matter what you do, but you do have a lovely pair of hands, and you are as sneaky as a shithouse rat, so let's see what you've got left.'

After that it was all just me getting exhausted and irritable and Les just getting irritable. And that went on for months.

In the meantime, I did the rounds, trying to get in as much walking as possible, and caught up with old friends and acquaintances. My family were happy enough to see me out of jail, but I can't say the same for my mother, who could be a hard bugger. Charlie Wing didn't want to know me, of course, and more than a couple of coves told me that the whole of Randy Ryan's mob had heard I was back, and were looking for a piece of me. That was one thing I wasn't really worried about, however, as I knew that he and his whole family were a bunch of cowards, and hardly worth the time of day.

When I next saw Queenie, she had been given the flick by Randy and was working for another useless bugger called Dago Dargie, though it was a well-known fact that he wasn't a dago at all, but an Irishman, just like the rest of us, and should have had more self-respect. Of course, they called him Dago partly because of his dark skin, he being one of those swarthy Irishmen – my old man was another – who would have passed for an Arab

84

camel driver if you wrapped a sheet around him, and especially as he had one of those great hooked noses you occasionally see on the more sensitive races. And the other reason was his surname. It was also a well-known fact that while he answered tolerably well to Dago, he couldn't abide his other nick-name, Darky, which drove him round the bend.

'Well, well, well,' I say, when I first spied him and Queenie sitting side by side in the back garden of the Commercial in Swan Street. 'If it isn't Darky Dargie, sittin' with the prettiest girl in Richmond. Your luck must've changed, cobber, else why would a lady like this been seen dead with a hopeless bastard like you, eh?'

Dargie kept his mouth shut, no doubt because he'd heard that I was looking all over Richmond for Queenie, and he probably remembered, like everyone else in the Southern Bloody Hemisphere, that I was a dangerous bastard, and had for the last twelve months been gutting' Turks for a crust, a story that I swear I did my level best to discourage.

But Queenie knew me better than anyone, and she piped up like a magpie with a toothache.

'So you survived, did you Archie? Lookin' a bit the worse for wear, too, I see. I hope you won't be giving our Paddy a hard time, as he's a respectable businessman, and treats me as good as he can, I reckon.'

At hearing this fine speech, which was good enough for the Yarra Bank, and which I know must have been rehearsed about a hundred times in front of the flamin' mirror, Dago looks at me all philosophical like and nods, puffing at his pipe like a saint with a chimney in his fizzog. He come so close to getting that look wiped off his face and that briar shove up his arse (which I once seen done, in Pentridge) it wasn't funny. And I reckon

Queenie knew it, too, as she shoots a hand out and grabs me by the wrist, with a nervous smile.

'Pull up a chair, Arch, and have a beer with us. It's ages before I have to start work, anyway. Paddy, how about getting us all another round, eh?'

'Lemonade for me,' I says. 'I'm in trainin'.

Dargie slopes off without a word, as he knows which side his bread's buttered on, and there's a general silence until he's out of earshot. Then Queenie turns to me quickly, and gives me a hug. She tries to kiss me, but I'm still pissed off at finding her working for Dargie.

'Come on, Arch, you know the score. A girl has to get by, you above all people know that. I wrote to you didn't I? I wrote to you every month. I never wrote so many bloody words in my whole life.'

'That's true enough, Queenie, love. And between you and me and Reilly's dog, I think I might have died without those letters, as Pentridge is such a hole of a place, not fit for a river rat.'

'And not one bloody word back not until you went to Egypt.'

'Now that's not true at all. I replied to every letter, and they let you do that, too, so I know them letters were sent. Bloody Dago,' I says, and Queenie looked at me in a very sad way, so that in that moment she knew she'd been denied something precious.

'Don't hurt him, Arch – they'll put you away again. I don't know if I could –'

'What?'

I looked at her, but she wasn't going to finish, for it wouldn't have been the way for a girl in her position to talk that way. But it was too late, anyway. I'd seen what was in her heart, and I reckoned this life of hers would have to come to an end.

'Don't you worry, love,' I says, I won't hurt him, though God knows he deserves a spanking. And where is the bugger, anyway?'

I went into the bar to see if I could see him, and the barman, who was an old cobber, gives me a little nod in the direction of the main door. I said to him: 'Tell Queenie I'll see her at her place.' And I took off like hell for Dargie's place.

Well, Dargie is off home, of course, but he's not in a big hurry, and, being a stupid bastard, he's on foot. Meanwhile, I'm on the first tram that comes along and off up Swan Street. I get to his place before he's got a clue, pouring with sweat from pain, and place myself in the shadow of the front porch of his house, so that when he walks up to the door, I reach out and grab him by the neck first with one hand, then with both. I can tell by the feel of his body that he knows it's me, and I take advantage of the knowledge by slamming his head against a plywood door panel so hard, it goes right through.

'Best we go in, I reckon, Darky. Don't want the neighbours to see you beating the crap out of a war veteran, do we?'

And he opens the door, which isn't even locked, and we go in. Once inside, I smell the familiar odour of opium, which I guess Dargie likes, and which can be got at half the easy houses in Richmond, and all those in Arab lands, too, come to think of it. It makes me feel a little bit easier about knocking his block off, as I know he will have a little something for the pain. Inside, the house it apparently dark, the sun outside being so bright, and the house is tranquil, like an oasis at night.

'The letters, give 'em to me.'

'What bloody letters?'

I give him a hard short right just below the ribs, and down he goes, with a sound like a frightened mongrel. He makes no attempt to get up, even after gets his breath back a little.

'I'm going to be here for hours,' I say, and when I'm finished, you'll either be dead, or you'll have no unbroken bones left, includin' yer teeth. Unless you hand over the letters, of course.'

He lies there, all bunched up, and I can tell he's looking for a way out. He quickly crawls to the wall, and pulls a shiv from his boot and waves it at me with a wild look on his face, like he thinks he's got the upper hand. I walk around him until I'm near one of his feet, then I stomp on his foot as hard as I can with my good leg. It hurts him like mad, but I fold up like a bloody ironing board, and end up right beside him on the floor. He lashed out blindly, just to keep me away, as he's in so much pain, he can't fight. The shiv slices through my shirt and into my chest, but I can tell by the sting, that he's barely touched me. I punch him once in the forehead, and he loses interest in the proceedings. I take the shiv off him and help him to his feet with a few punches to the skull, just to let him know that he'd be better off standing up, which he does.

'The letters.'

He doesn't talk, but staggers into one of rooms, with me hanging onto is collar, and giving him helpful little taps in the back of the head, you know, by way of motivation. I follow him around like this being extra careful, unless he pulls another knife, or even a gun, as a few of the pimps in those days were starting to carry. And eventually, he gives me a packet of letters, which I see is all of them.

'Ta. No hard feelings, I hope, Darky.'

I put my hand out for him to shake, politeness being a bit of thing with me, but he spits at me.

'Fuck you.'

That was the last thing Dargie said for a few days, as it took him that long to find a dentist who could restore his fetching smile. But I honestly had no hard feelings, as it always feels good to smash a bloke's face in, and I do believe it took that to properly put me in the mood to box again. Queenie didn't have to be told what I'd been up to. I put the letters in her hand, and she looked at the packet, and started crying all over the place. I pulled her to me and told her it was all right, but she let out a shriek, and jumped back with blood all over her.

'Dargie pulled a shiv.'

'Arch, darling. Don't ever say that bastard's name again. Now take me home, and read me some of these.'

'Queenie, I don't want you on the game. I want you for myself.'

'The game pays the rent.'

'Not anymore.'

I next saw Ruth under circumstances that I thought at the time were pretty coincidental. It was at the new cinema in Church Street, the New Mayfair, the old Mayfair having burnt down. The New Mayfair was up near the cop shop, so a lot of the younger players gave it a wide berth, but the film was Leonard Doogood in *Algie's Romance*, so naturally, all the women wanted to see that. Personally, though, I couldn't see myself going to see a film that had anything to do with a bloke called Doogood, even though I suspected the name might have started out its unfortunate life as an Irish one. However, on this particular Saturday , the New Mayfair had decided to show a special film that they had made of the fighting in Palestine, including the charge on Beersheba, so I had gone along to see if I recognised anyone, or anything. The film turned out to be a hotchpotch of short bits of films of various battles, more or less in the right order, though some of them looked pretty fake to me.

I have mentioned the film company that turned up after the battle. They decided to make a film of the attack, which they had missed. So they rounded up all the blokes who were interested and not dead or wounded, bunged them on horses, and made them attack the walls all over again, only this time from just across the sand near the wadi, which was quite close to the town. They also got all the Turks who were interested, which turned out to be bloody nearly all of them, and shoved them down on the sand. A lot of them were actually firing their rifles, though well over the heads of the riders, as these were the Melbourne boys they'd put down there, who pretended to be Turks.

As I'd had enough of horses to last me a lifetime, I went down to the slit trenches with a couple of dozen Light Horse blokes and about two hundred other coves called Abdullah, and we all made as much noise as we could and screamed: *Amina kodu mun pii!* which is an impolite way of telling someone to fuck off. The only thing that was missing really was the artillery defence, which is what had killed so many of the blokes and chopped up so many horses. The guns were already on their way to the north of the city, in case the Turks remembered that they'd left something important behind, and decided to come back for it. We all ended up having a great time, though a lot of the Turks thought we were being pretty disrespectful to ride over the blood of our mates, and would have no part of it. But I don't think those blokes had ever been to the flicks.

It was at the end of the film that I saw Ruth. I was with Queenie, and she was having a good look around to see if she knew anyone, that being what women do at the flicks, or

90

anywhere else, for that matter, while I was just wondering if they put the Men's in the same place in the old Mayfair, that being what coves do after the flicks. And I see Ruth with her brother Billy, who has already spotted me and gives me a wink that has a touch of mischief in it. He gives his sister's arm a little shake, and nods in my direction, so that she will see me with Queenie, and she nods at me politely, and gives a little smile, though I couldn't for the life of me work that smile out, though I took it home with me and turned it around every which-way, like a jam tin with no label, to work out what was inside. That Billy Magee was obviously having a ball with me, but I couldn't have cared less, and Ruth didn't seem to care either. So neither of us could have cared less.

Queenie was still looking around when I resumed my search for the Men's, and I saw that she was frowning a little, and staring at something. I followed her eyes, and saw that it was Ruth, who was now having a conversation with a slightly older and shorter man who was wearing a suit, which a lot of coves wore to the picture theatre, as though they were filling in time until Mass started.

'Isn't that Billy Magee, the bloke you floored at Ryrie's place?'

'So it is. I hope I didn't hurt him.'

'Hurt him. You little twerp, I hear that you're lucky to be alive. Don't tell me you didn't see him over there, with him looking like his hair's on fire.'

'I was busy looking for the Mens. You haven't seen it, have you?'

'So that's it, is it - it's that girl he's with. I might have known. Why couldn't you have been born ugly, like all the other little blokes? Well, you can forget that one. I'd say she was a bit out of your class, 'specially if he's got anything to say about it.'

She waited until Ruth glanced at us again and then tightened her grip on my upper arm.

'Jeez, girl, you're squashing me punching arm.'

'I'll squash more than that when I get you home.'

As usual, I didn't have a clue what she was on about, as Queenie was one of those women who had the gift of the riddle, and spoke like that all the time. Her odd way of talking to me, which she used most of the time, was half threat and half joke, as if she was daydreaming out loud, and the words had got stuck halfway out of her mind. Just hearing that funny remark made a poem drift by, like a cloud, and I was able to rope it and haul it in, as if it was a loose horse in a corral.

The riddle poem was how I thought of it, and still do, and whenever I hear someone come out with one of those riddles, or puzzles, I say that poem to myself, and if the riddle isn't exactly solved, well at least I feel that I have it by the scruff of the neck, which is at least better than the other way around.

So we passed out into the street, and that was the last I saw of Ruth Magee for a long time, which I think suited Queenie down to the ground. When we got home, which was Queenie's place, she roughed me up in play, and then rolled around with me on the bed for a mo, then stopped and looked at me dreamily.

'Arch, before we left the flicks, you had a funny look on your face, like you were a thousand miles away. Were you back in Egypt, or wherever you went, remembering the fightin', or were you remembering some Egyptian women you rode like one of your horses?'

'Neither, love. I was –'

I was on the point of telling her about the poetry, when I realised that she didn't know, and I also realised, with embarrassment, that I didn't want to know. We were as close as ever, and yet something told me to take it easy and not get carried away. After all, she was a working girl. What if she and I were to call it a day, and go our separate ways, and what if she was to get a bee in her bonnet something or other, the way females often do, and tell one or two of her professional acquaintances? Or worse, what if she got up in the middle of Mass and make an announcement about it, to save them putting it on the wireless.

'Scuse me, Father, but I just want to announce to those people down the back and out in Church Street that Archie Taggert is a sissy, and probably has a St Bridget's uniform tucked away under his bed.' I could see it.

'You was what?'

'I was just remembering the first time we met.'

'Oh yeah? Well, when was it, then?'

I had her. There was nothing sweeter to a girl's ears that the 'where we met' thing. I'd heard that from Fatty Ferguson when I was at Coburg. Fatty was lousy at burglary, but he was a bit of a dab hand at knocking over ladies, despite being shaped like a medicine ball.

'It was at the old Mayfair, wasn't it?'

'You drongo, it was –'

'Ah, I know, it was down at the Temperance Hall. I've never been so frightened in my life.'

'But you still danced with me, Arch.'

'No, I mean when I saw the band. I was terrified that the old bloke playin' the sax was going to keel over in the middle of something.'

'Dancin' with you was a piece of cake.'

'You were packin' death, go on, say it.'

'Oh all right.'

'Go on, say it.'

'I was packin' death.'

'And just for being good, you can have a handful of these, which is more than you'd get from your skinny girl.'

It was on the tip of my tongue to correct Queenie about Ruth's skinniness, but the way she put it, I didn't have the heart.

9 The War is Over

It wasn't until the war ended that I realise that I had been undergoing change, not as the result of any particular experience, like a lot of blokes, but in the course of becoming a man. It took growing up in Richmond, going to prison, being sent to Palestine to die killing Turks (who'd probably been dragged out some bloody prison in Turkey), busted up like the bottommost cornflake, and being sent home to be laughed at and to fail at the one thing I loved before I even realised it. I had been changing, but for the life of me, I couldn't see that I'd been growing in any way at all.

One day, I looked in the mirror, and I was a man, that was all, without having done anything to myself, without having noticed, without having had any fun. I was crooked, my body was crazy. Just then, I didn't know what made me think I could be a fighter. I didn't seem to belong in the same society as polite people, and they put me away for that, I think, not for fighting a bad bastard in a brothel, which was all legal and above board, if you see what I mean, being, well, at least a legitimate job. Then they had sent me to the war that blokes were busting a gut to get into, because they had nothing and never would have and they sensed the madness of it, like the possibility of another mask to hide their anguish. I couldn't have become aware of this in myself, as I was just so relieved to get out of Pentridge, which was the worst place on earth as far as I was concerned and not as much a place to punish bad people as to crush the Irish heart of Australia.

It was well known, for example, by everyone associated with the place that the population of women prisoners was way out of proportion to that of the male prisoners, there being not so many bad women in Melbourne, and I'm talking bad enough to warrant being sent to Hell. Prostitution was only a crime if some local police inspector decided to big-note himself, and clean up his slice of the town, in which case you could bet that he'd leave his own girlfriend, and those of his mates, alone, and just scoop up the women who'd laughed at him for one reason or another, usually one reason.

It therefore paid to have friends in high places. Queenie had these, and was virtually guaranteed a peaceful existence as long as she kept her nose clean, which she did. The trouble with working the upper end of the street, however, was that the high life tended to go to a working girl's head, especially if she came from the bottom end, and they all did. And Queenie was no different. She was a girl with a head, I'll give her that, and though she was careful not to let coves know it, probably would have made a fine go of it in some profession that required a person who could think.

But it was the high life that turned her head, and in particular the drink, which Queenie enjoyed altogether too much for my liking. I had never myself been much of a drinking man, and the most grog I think I had ever drunk in any one period of my life was the enormous quantity of Gyppo beer I knocked over when I was away scaring the poor bloody Turk, who couldn't drink, for religious reasons. A lot of blokes reckoned that anyone who will let God tell him when he can and can't drink has lost control of his God, it being a man's job to tell God what's what, and bugger the consequences.

It was a well-known fact that the Catholics had a firm grip on God, and even kept Him locked him up in a box in the church, so that they could do their drinking in peace. The Turks, though, let Him run around loose, and He was able to make a man feel bad any time he felt like it, just by whispering bullshit in his ear, stuff like: 'Hey, Abdul, d'yer see those lazy bloody Australian bastards over there? I'll bet you could beat the crap out of them if you wanted to.' The Irishman who hears that voice doesn't really give a bugger. He'll fight when he's good and ready, which is usually when he's had a skinful. Your Turk, on the other hand, gives his camel a shove, and says to his mates: 'Well, fellers, I don't know about you, but I just feel like getting myself killed for no particular reason, so I will now be toddling off to the Aussie lines, to stir for a while.'

What I'm trying to say is that, while I drank a ton of beer when I was away, mainly when I was training and then recuperating in Cairo, the Gyppo grog was as weak as widdle, whereas the Melbourne drop was a bit strong for my liking, and I hardly touched it. Also, a bloke like me, who tends to get into trouble even when he's not looking for it, needs to keep a clear head at all times.

Look at that Randy, for instance, a nasty piece of work, and that Dargie bloke, both bad bastards. But Queenie, as I was saying, had been hitting the bottle a bit lately, and while I will say that the grog didn't have the effect that it had on most people in those days of making them angry and bitter about life in general, it did have the effect of making her even more amorous, which is a bad sign in a working girl, who must be able to turn it off and on like a tap, otherwise she will find herself giving it away to all and sundry, and maybe even having annual sales, like Dimmeys. And where would we be then? And the reason I ask is that Queenie represented the top shelf of the street. She might not have been one of those lah-di-dah Toorak pros, but she had looks that could kill or, at the very least, stun a man long enough for him to get the odd funny feeling, first in his old feller, then in his wallet.

She was a front runner. And it does no good for a champion in any field of endeavour to take to drink, unless that person is a drinking champion, of course, in which case it does no good for them to take the pledge, may God forgive me for even bringing the subject up.

I had a word about it with Queenie one night. I'd just about had it with her drinking, and of course I knew the reason, for it's damned hard to be doing something you're bloody at good one minute and the next, sitting in the Hibiscus Tea Shop pretending your one of the hoity-toity crowd. I was making a bit of money looking after the upstairs in Wing's new posh place on Waverley Street, and Wing had changed the rules so that it was a club for members only. I therefore knew everyone who turned up, and was allowed to bounce anyone else, regardless of country, class or creed, as they say, though they were all of the same country and class.

Occasionally, one of the members would turn up with one of his mates, of course, and then I would be nice to them both. But woe betide any man who was a complete stranger to me. I had Wing's permission to teach them a lesson they'd never forget, but I always trod very warily, in view of the danger of donging some bloke who might turn out to be a County Court Judge, or the like. I always let the downstairs man, a big bloke with copper hair whom everyone except Mr Wing called Big Red, because he boxed like a kangaroo, all straight backed and very businesslike, know that I was keen to avoid trouble, and he should feel free to dong any bloke who he thought was likely to come up the stairs in a bad mood, for my job was to protect the hostesses. Mr Wing paid well, at least well enough that Queenie didn't have to work, which was the point, but the boredom, not to mention the drink were getting to her.

'So, Queenie, my girl,' I says one night while we were taking the air in Swan Street, 'I've been doing a bit of thinking. I've been thinking that you and me could do with a change of scenery.'

'A change of scenery, you mean like catch a tram into the city.'

'You know what I'm talking about,' I says. 'I'm talking about taking a trip. Richmond's a rotten place for a girl who's lost her trade – I know how I'd feel.'

'What d'yer mean, 'how you'd feel'. You did lose yer trade, and you didn't give a tinker's.'

'Well, tinsmithin' wasn't really a big hit with me, as it turned out.'

'The only thing that was ever a big hit with you was getting stuck into someone. And you're strugglin' to do that nowadays.'

'I never lost me punch, and Les says I'll soon be fit to fight again.'

'*Les says*. He doesn't care if you get yerself killed. But I do.'

'That's nice to hear, Queenie love, but it's you I wanted to talk about. I reckon you might be less restless if we took a trip, say, to New Zealand, for a while. What d'yer reckon? Sound good?'

'Have you gone mad? Leave Melbourne? What would we do? We don't even speak the language, for God's sake.'

'They speak the King's English,' I say, spitting on the footpath, automatically.

'Oh, they speak bloody English. That's all right then, isn't it?'

'Come on, Queenie, I know what's eatin' you, and I'm just tryin' to help.'

'Yeah, well you can just stop tryin' to bloody help. I can do whatever I like. And what I like is to have a good time, which I'm not flamin' havin'.'

'But we can do whatever we like –'

'You mean you can, and all you like is hanging around at Ryrie's and with Wing's stuck-up bitches.'

'Now come, on, that's not fair. That's what I do, and Wing pays well. He likes to have a name on the door.'

'Yeah, and those bitches like to have a name on the bed.'

'I don't touch those girls –'

'So it's 'girls', is it. *Girls.* Well, excuse me, Mr Taggerty, and what does that make me? Some fuckin' old tart that can't have her own corner, because she's past it?'

'Now, Queenie, you know you're worth any two of those girls –'

'Two –'

'Three...at least.'

'Jesus Christ, Archie. I'm a businesswoman. I need to be in business.'

'I don't want –'

'*I don't want.* You don't bloody-well want. Well I've had it. I need a drink.'

We were outside the Royal, at the time, so she grabs me and pulls me in, before I could think of a smart reply. The barman stops talking and gives us a look that you could chop meat with, and I drag Queenie, through a side door, and into the ladies lounge. I'm reluctant to give Queenie a drink, because she's in such a rotten mood, but she insists on brandy, so I get it for her.

'Listen, love –'

'No, more listening, Arch. Just drink up. I've made up me mind, and that's that.' I do as I'm told, while Queenie mutters loud enough to be heard all over the lounge. 'I'm a flamin' businesswoman, I am.'

'Stone the crows, love, keep it down.'

'Yer don't like that, do yer, Arch? Well stiff. From now on, I do as I bloody please. And you can either help out, or let me get someone who will.'

'I won't pimp for you.'

'You will, and you'll like it.'

'I got my self-respect to think of.'

'Self-respect, don't make me laugh. You work in a fuck-shop.'

The few other patrons who were in the lounge, a couple of couples, looking as smart as they could, got up and left, huffing and puffing like a pair of bloody steam engines.

The barman, who was still not impressed at all, appeared at the bar and, catching our attention, tilted his head and eyes towards the door, telling us to piss off.

'Come on,' I said. 'And thanks very much for getting me thrown out of a pub in me own town.'

'It's a lousy pub,' she said, loud enough to be heard across the road. 'Yer hear me?'

'They heard you – the whole bloody town heard you.'

I poured Queenie out into the street, and she looked up and down for a moment, then made her mind up.

'The Balaclava,' she says. 'That'll do.'

'Let's call it a day, Queenie. I'm buggered if I want to get banned from every pub in Richmond. I've got a reputation –'

'Well, fuck your reputation, then,' she says, and does her disappearing act.

The next time I saw Queenie was four months later. I'd looked for her, of course, looked everywhere, even in the pubs and sly grogs, but she really had disappeared. People told me that she'd left town, and I have to admit that that worried me a bit, because the furthest she'd ever been from Richmond was when she accidentally got on the Dandenong train one night and fell asleep – I remember because she told me the next day (when the train came back) that she'd seen a horse with horns – so I couldn't for the life of me imagine a place Queenie might want to go outside of Melbourne, and I went to all her haunts asking around.

Turned out she'd shot through with a young bloke of her acquaintance called Arty Curran. I knew him, a bit of a smart-arse with an eye for a woman of natural gifts, but an eye for other things, of which it was better not to speak. I had no argument with Curran's taste, of course. In fact I had no argument with Curran at all, except that I knew him to be a bit of a Flash Harry, which wasn't my style. I knew that Queenie's heart couldn't have been with Arty, even though he was part of the mob we'd hung around with all our lives. And I knew just as well that Arty didn't need a reason to go with Queenie, she being a well-endowed beauty, and named right. But I was curious and kept pushing for news. Finally, in desperation – you have to be desperate to think you can get a straight answer from an Irishman – I went over to Arty's home, to talk to his family.

'G'day, Mrs Curran,' I says, doffing my hat very politely. 'I'm a friend of Arty's, and I was wondering what's become of him lately, as he seems to have disappeared off the face of the earth, and all his friends are enquiring after him.'

'I know who you are. You're that boxer who used to be in jail. He talks about you all the time. Taggerty this, Taggerty that. So, what's it to you where he is?'

'Nothing at all, Mrs Curran. I was just passing, and thought I'd drop in and introduce meself, and make enquiries.'

'I wasn't born yesterday, Mr Taggerty. I know why you're here, and I think that young lady is better off without the likes of you. At least Arthur has a steady job in an office, and can keep out of trouble. As to where he is, well, I don't think he'd like a ruffian to be chasing him all over the place, giving him a hard time, do you?'

'I didn't –'

'No, he wouldn't. So on our bike. I'm sure if Arthur is as worried about you as you say you are about him, he'll send you a postcard. Good day to you, Mr Taggerty.'

I thought that went rather well, really. She didn't actually threaten or assault me, which is what most women in her place might have done. And while she didn't tell me where the happy couple were, I knew it was probably one of those places that had postcards. Next, I went round to the back of the Post Office at ten o'clock, when I knew the Post Office workers were having their smoke-oh, and found, among the throng of unhappy blokes of which Arthur had been one, his mate Shady Lane, emerging into the yard with a rollie between his lips.

'G'day, Arch. You'd be looking for Arty, that's right, isn't it?'

'G'day, Shade. Actually, I don't give a stuff about Arty, as you well know. I'm just looking for Queenie, and I heard him and her took a trip together.'

'Yeah, he upped and quit the Post Office, and shot through to New Zealand. Said he was going to buy a sheep station. He knows all about the place, y'know. Sorry about Queenie. Who knows? She mightn't like having a sheep station. I know I wouldn't.' He sucked on his weed. 'Don't even know what a sheep station is. D'you?'

'Bloody New Zealand! Bloody women!'

'Language, Arch. No swearing on Post Office premises - it's a rule.'

'Hell, Shade, I asked her only the other day to go with me to New Bloody Zealand, and she turned me down flat.'

'Must have been the way you asked her.'

'I'll give you *must have been the way I asked her.*'

'Anyway, it won't last.'

'How d'yer know?'

'Because I know Arty, and with him nothin' ever lasts - nothing. He'll get tired of trainin' sheep, and come back, and he'll get tired of worrying about you creeping up on him and cutting his throat, and he'll stop seeing Queenie, too, because' - he gave a little chuckle - 'he likes to be boss, and Queenie's not the kind of girl who likes to be pushed around. That's true, isn't it?'

'Yeah, though I s'pose I never thought of it that way. So how come you're such a bloody expert on Queenie all of a sudden?'

'Arch, I'll speak plain to you because we've known each other for years -'

'Only since we were born.'

'Well, that's years, isn't it? Look, there isn't a bloke in Richmond who hasn't asked himself at some time: *What the hell does that Queenie see in that bloody Taggerty bloke? What has he got that I haven't got for Christ's sake?'*

'Language -'

'Yeah. Well, nobody knows, of course, cos if they did, they'd get some of it for themselves. So don't you worry about us other

104

blokes. You just concentrate on the boxing. I probl'y shouldn't be telling you, as Arty's me mate, but it's the boxing she likes, you know. You get back into the ring, and your worries'll be over, mark my words. Oops, smoke-oh's over. Cheerio.'

As you can imagine, I went straight back over to Ryrie's, and started working on my boxing technique. Lane was right, and I could see that with a mind like that, he'd probably end up being the Postmaster-Bloody-General one day. Ryrie thought he'd seen the last of me, but he had to admit he was wrong. Les came in and started training me again, and I paid him what I could afford.

'Don't quit your night job just yet,' he says to me, after picking me up off the training mat for the hundredth time.

'Just shut up and train me,' I says back. 'I'm not leaving this place 'till you've taught me a new trick.'

By that I meant a *dirty* trick, because we both knew that the only way I was ever going to make a comeback was by fighting dirty. Of course, I knew all the tricks already, but just not how to perform them with my gammy. It's a well-known fact in the fight game that a boxer who can't move is a dead man. I had two things going for me: my stature, being short, even for a bantamweight, and my unusual stance, which made me look a bit lop-sided (which I was), and just the way a boxer looks when he drops one shoulder, and therefore, one hand.

Both of these features tend to draw the other bloke in. The taller boxer comes close to the smaller man to give him a hard time – lean on him and so on, especially if the little bloke likes to tie him up in the clinches. The straighter fighter is drawn to the dropped shoulder, because he thinks his man is hurt, and instinctively get in close to punch, then leaving himself open to all the dirty punches, because you have to be close to get away with them, unless you can afford to bribe the ref, and I couldn't, at least not yet.

So Les says to me: 'You know, Arch, when you weave to the right, your right glove always drops to the level of his left hip.'

'You want to punch him in the hip? He'll dodge it.'

'Not if you do this,' he says, and shows me how to hold the other bloke.

'Arch, it's your hip that bothers you, isn't it?'

'Bloody oath.'

'Well, let's make the other bloke feel the same way. That should even things up a bit.'

So a week later, I'm in the gym, doing my level best to scare the crap out of the bloke in the mirror, when in walks Les.

'Got a bout.'

'Les, I'm not –'

'Yes, you are.'

'Bloke's a warrior, like you. Had a few bouts in France, and a few up the bush. But he likes to fight below his weight. He's never had a real match. Paddy Smith.'

'Never heard of him.'

'Polite Patrick Smith.'

'Tall bloke.'

'That's him. Like Jack and the Beanstalk.'

'But why do they call him 'Polite'?'

'Because he's forever apologising to his man. He lost his last fight by picking his man up off the canvas – copped an uppercut.'

'He doesn't sound too bright.'

'Then that should even things up, shouldn't it?'

The fight was put off for a month, as Les sent a message to the other camp telling them that I had malaria, which I got fighting the Turks, and mightn't pull through. In the meantime, me and Les shot through to Wonthaggi to do a bit of secret training at his brother's place. I learnt a few tricks he thought might work on a tall bloke, and also a way of favouring my right leg, so that Paddy would be confused and go the for other leg.

'I've been thinking,' said Les.

'Jeez, don't hurt yerself, son.'

'No, I mean, Paddy's trainer is bound to tell him you've got a crook hip, and he's bound to go for it.'

'If he catches me on this hip, it's all over, Les'.

'Yeah but what if gets the hips mixed up, and goes for the other?'

'You said he was wasn't too bright, you didn't say he was a complete bloody moron.'

'Just do this.'

He starts to imitate the way I stand, only like a mirror image. I slowly shift my weight onto my right leg, until it begins to hurt.

'More.'

'He'll see the pain on me face.'

'He won't know where it's coming from – more.'

I lean a little to the right.

'Straighten that leg.'

'It won't straighten, fuck yer.'

'Then switch to southpaw.'

I switch to southpaw and lead with me bad leg, and we spar for a while.

'You'll fight Smith southpaw.'

'I'm no southpaw.'

'It puts all the weight on the back leg. You can use that to drive forward. Also, he won't know if he's Arthur or Martha.'

'Yeah, well I know which one of us is gunna look like Martha.'

10 The Digger and the Galloper

The fight was held in the Liberty Theatre in Fitzroy, so the gate percentage was always going to be low. But the betting had been stirred up with all kinds of rumours, including the advertising of the fight as the Galloper versus the Digger. They said that we were both half dead from malaria, and that we had been fortified with strychnine so that we could take one another apart. They also said that I had a false leg, and that Paddy was permanent shell-shocked, and that at the sound of the bell, he would go berserk and probably murder me. Finally, they said that we were fighting for the honour of Britain, which made me see red.

'What would the British know of honour, Les?'

'It's true, they don't know the meaning of the word. And I hear Paddy is none too pleased, either.'

Paddy was in the room next door, getting gloved up for the fight and I got up from the chair.

'Best I go in and say hello.'

'You'll do no such thing. I don't want him to get a look at that leg. You let him come in here. Tell you what –'

He disappeared for a minute, then reappeared, and resumed bandaging my hands.

'I told him you were busy throwing up, but that you said you would like it if he could drop in to shake hands.'

Just then in walks Paddy, looking like a lamp post wearing boxing boots.

'I'm sorry you've been a bit crook. Best of luck, mate.'

We touched fists, and he was off.

'There, wasn't that polite?'

'Was he on the up and up?'

'That's how he talks, but he has a punch, so stay in close. And remember, you're a southpaw.'

The Liberty was full that night, because a couple of up and coming names were appearing, to see who would get a bout at the Stadium, so that meant that the winner of our bout would get a few extra quid, despite us being only the curtain raiser. It was because blokes like us tended to string their fights out to give the crowd what they paid for that the fights were usually pretty short, and ours was five rounds.

The crowd was happy to see a couple of ex-soldiers fight it out, and Bob Purcell, the promoter, had found me a Light Horse hat with an emu feather to wear into the ring, and Paddy some kind of bloody great army coat to wear, which he did, despite it being a stinking hot night. They all let out big cheers when we enter the ring and a lot of young blokes stand up and salute, and I can tell by their bearing that they are old soldiers. I can even see one of them wearing the Light Horse hat, which chuffs me like hell.

Well, of course, when we go to centre ring for the Ref's directions, I am careful to drag me left leg a touch, as I rehearsed with Les, and when we stand together I can see that this bloke's got about a hand and a half on me, and I wonder what the hell does Les think he's doing. I can't help noticing as we're standing there eyeing each other off that the Ref is directing all his comments about clean fighting to me, as he seems to have heard the rumours. But then I remember that he refereed a few of my bouts when we were kids, and probably remembers what a lovely style I have, especially when I think he can't see me. But Paddy seems like a nice enough bloke, and as we touch gloves, I give him a wink, to show that I've got his number, though really, I'm not so sure I have.

The punters are sweating on the first round bell, because they've heard that when Paddy hears it he will go troppo, and think he is back in France again, killing Germans. And in fact, when the bell goes, he does let out a roar and raise his hands like one of those circus weight-lifters, and the crowd appreciate that very much. But I remember my directions: get in close, fight dirty, and get an early knockout. And on no account box him. So I walk straight up to him, with my good leg a little stiff, put my right foot forward, and adopt a southpaw stance, which makes Paddy step back and glance at his corner in confusion. His trainer yells: 'Just box him', and he starts to concentrate on me again. Meanwhile, I walk up to him again, and poke my right hand into his face as hard as possible, and catch him right on the nose. It is definitely the luckiest punch I am going to get on the night, and we both know it. He is a little shaken, and steps back again. And again I am forced to walk up to him, knowing that if he keeps back-pedalling, I'm going to be in trouble, because my instructions were not to travel. So I let him get me into the centre ring, and plant my feet, and wait for him to come to me. But he knows about my big punch, and is confused by my southpaw stance, so he decides to box me. But I make him work without giving much in return, and he is gives me a pounding from a distance.

In the second round, he can see that I'm breathing extra hard, and I am, because of the pain in my hip, which is giving me hell, so finally he does just what Les said he would do. He lets me get in close and trade a few body punches, them he leans on my left shoulder real hard, to hurt me. You could hear me groan outside in the street, but the Ref was on the left side, so I hung on to his arm, and buried my head as low as I could in his chest, and let go my best right hook into the point of his left hip. To half the punters it looked like a foul blow, and they howled blue murder, when the young digger let go of me and buckled a bit on one side. Well, it was a foul technically, but no one was dead, so the Ref let it go. But after that the fight was a lot more even, with Paddy not able to dance and having to fight flat-footed.

By round five I was definitely behind, and I told Les I was rooted. But he wasn't worried, because young Paddy had adjusted his stance to protect himself from my right, which was for him the danger punch, so as I walk up to Paddy for the last time, I drop the pretence and adopt my orthodox stance, and take the weight on my crook hip for the first time. And this had been the plan all along. Then while Paddy's trying to work out what's happening I let fly a flurry of lefts into the face and step forward inside his reach and give him a right to the throat that hurts him so much he can hardly breath.

For this I am given a warning, but I am already so far behind on points that I don't give a stuff. Before the Ref can finish talking I brush him aside and walk straight up to Paddy, who is busy coughing his head off as if air is hard to get, and knock him over with a big left hook. The only reason he falls over is because he's coughing as the punch connects, and his body has momentarily lost its resistance. He takes a standing count of eight, and comes back at me, this time looking more dangerous than he has at any time in the fight, and this time he's trying to box again. Again he lets me walk up close, though it costs me a couple of hard bangs against the side of the head, and when I get close enough to put my hands around his ribs, he throws his arms over my shoulders and I can feel him begin to lean on me again, this time on both shoulders at once, as he's not sure now which side is my crook side.

Well, the Ref can't see a thing in close, so I let rip an uppercut and pull it toward my own face just before it reaches his chin, and shove my elbow as hard as I can into the bottom of his breast-bone. He lets out a cry, and relaxes for a split second, and I put my left hand on his chest to steady him, and give him my Sunday punch, which sends him to the canvas, perhaps wondering where the moral is in all this. I could have told him.

After the fight I go over to Paddy's corner to tell him he fought well, and his corner men tell me to fuck off, and Paddy's too busy coughing and groaning to take part in the conversation so I leave them to it, and go back to the centre of the ring, where I have a victory walk, and even to a bit of boxing to show that I've still got some petrol in the tank. The punters love a dodgy fight, and a lot of them are throwing coins into the ring, which is a very good sign for the curtain raisers, so I turn to Reg Paterson, my cornerman, and tell him to give it to Paddy, and he looks at me like I'm mad, then shrugs. Well, of course, the crowd sees this and throw even more money. Punters are a funny lot. I look at Les, and he shrugs, and smiles, and nods his head in the direction of the crowd to the left. I follow the direction of his eyes, and who should I see in the third row but Queenie, and she's smiling and waving as if she's been trying to catch my eye for the last half an hour. Thank God she didn't.

It turned out that with Queenie in my corner, I couldn't put a foot wrong. She carried on as if she'd never gone away, and there was never a word about Arty Curran, so, of course, I didn't ask, me being a polite sort of cove when it came to a lady's feelings.

But I knew that she'd tell me when she was good and ready. I also noticed that she'd cut down on the drink, and seemed to be willing to go along with whatever I said, though I wasn't really saying anything new. In particular, she'd stopped all that talk about being Number One on Church St Hill. She was changed. And after I'd had a few more fights, and had become more or less notorious, she told me what had happened.

The papers were a touch unkind to me over the fight with Smith and called me a cheat, which was alright with me, because I won. And in boxing, there's no such thing as fair and square, just as there's no such thing as fair and square in life itself. Life gives to you when you reach out with what you've got. I've got fists, and that's about it.

As the boxing progressed, of course, I had to pay the penalty, the little joke penalty that life had decided to lump me with, the poetry. The more I trained and the harder and the more violent I became – and that was a necessity in my line of work – the more the poetry appeared in my mind, to the extent that sometimes it interrupted me at the worst possible times. The only time it didn't bother me was when I was when I was fighting and even then I felt that it was still there, but had simply changed form, so that instead of words, it was now boxing – punches, steps, ducks, weaves, dodges – and so on.

I hated the thought that the boxing might be turning into poetry, and I thought about this for a long time. But I hated even more a new thought that came to me one day, that boxing might already be a form of poetry. That thought frightened me, and as always, the fear was about something in the poetry I was ignoring or trying to shove into the background. But one thing I knew, that my deliberate attempts to ignore the poetry were not going to succeed. It was going to keep appearing, grow stronger and remain connected to my boxing.

After the Smith fight, despite the reactions of just about everyone except my own team, I felt good about the result and gave into an irresistible impulse to write. I felt that the poem was not a bad one so I mailed it to Jack Galloway, and sure enough there it was in the following Saturday's paper, looking like it had only it's simple story to tell, the story of the words you were reading, but in fact, telling a much different story, you might say the real story.

It told a story of conflict that sucks in, and spits out of prejudice, and the discovery of the person authentic. I had discovered the authentic person in myself, I had seen him – it. I had observed that he was not me but himself, that he had a way of being, and that he knew all about me and why I did the things I did and thought the thoughts I thought. He knew my weaknesses and tended to adopt them carelessly, you might say bravely, or in spite of them, for he was not prejudiced against me for my shortcomings, my ill-fittingness.

He was a real person, and offered me that real person as a gift. I saw all this not through the poetry and not through the boxing, but through their meeting place, in the place where they, heading in different directions as they were, cut across each other's paths, like the blades of a pair of scissors when you work them. The scissor blades, beginning at rest and pointed in different direction, and having nothing in common except their mechanical nature, suddenly, on their purpose coming into view and being brought into play, are activated so that the paths tend to align, and a great conflict builds between them, a great potential relationship, a powerful cutting and severing and chopping motion that is going to render the thing that's being cut separated and the thing that's doing the cutting one.

I – we – the separate paths, were coming together, the poetry told me, and the something we held in our grasp was going to be sacrificed. The question the poetry seemed to be asking me was: *Is this alright with you, Arch? Is it okay for God to do what He has to do? Or have you got a problem with that?* In a trance, the day I read the poem in the *The Argus* I contemplated these questions and realised that I had always had a problem with that, and with everything else in life. Of course I disapproved with the way God was running the world. Of course I disapproved of His choice of bodies for me, even His choice of my name. I disapproved of God interfering in a life that He wasn't living with His own poetry, that told me nothing useful, but only pointed to what I didn't need to know, that it was a part of a coming together that was going to cause destruction. As long as the destruction was about others, that was the main thing. As long as there was something in life for me. That was the main thing.

I was aware, of course, being a Catholic, that this kind of thinking was a sin of some kind, though not the kind that you needed to confess to a priest, but I was not sure just how this worked. I only knew that if you got any satisfaction out of anything at all, then that thinking was a sin, and was enough to get you barred from Heaven. Well, I'd made up mind up a long time ago, of course, that Heaven was out of my reach, and this had been confirmed for me the Prison Chaplain, Father Mulcahy, at Pentridge. He told me that the best I could hope for was an easy Purgatory, so I did.

The Smith fight got me the Galway fight. Stephen Galway was a bantamweight who was the same shape as me, and could fight

116

southpaw, so I was not going to be able to pull any of those switching stunts on this bloke. Also, unlike Paddy Smith, he had a brain of some kind, and it hadn't been scrambled by fighting or by being shell-shocked or by being just plain dumb, which I think might have been Paddy's problem. Stephen Galway was a ring-in, and came from Adelaide. I got a seven rounder against him at the Brunswick Town Hall, and had to really practise my bag of tricks. I had a look at him sparring one day, before he was moved to the suburbs to train, and he looked impressive, defended himself well, didn't waste much energy dancing, and tended to favour head shots. I was impressed, and went home thinking about how I might go up against him. He was an unknown quantity, so I asked Les.

'Oh, I asked around, but he trains out at Camberwell, and nobody's seen him. But I do know he's won a few amateur fights and was a contender for the South Australia flyweight championship until the war. Don't know what he's being doing since then. Putting himself back together, I s'pose.'

'Les, I need to know. I can't beat him unless I know his weakness. All I got was a quick look before I was thrown out.'

'I'll see,' was all he said.

I kept the training up, and found that I could switch sides from orthodox to southpaw pretty easily, and wondered why I'd never done it before. I also found that I could fight unorthodox, which is switching arm positions, without switching feet positions. I was happy with that, but that was not a trick, and many boxers for forced to adopt these sorts of tactics during a fight when they'd been injured.

About a week after our conversation Reg Paterson turned up and gives me a wink, which is a good sign, coming from Reg, whose whole way of conversing is with nods, winks and facial expressions. For a cornerman, he can be so quiet it's bloody eerie.

'I've been over to Camberwell,' he says, in a quiet voice, without any expression at all.

'And?'

'They've got a lovely railway station. Flowers all over the place. Won a prize, so they tell me.'

'Sounds wonderful.'

'The Station Master over there –'

'Bugger the Station Master.'

'I was going to say, the Station Master's a keen boxing follower.'

'You say they have a lovely garden, Reg.'

'His sister married a bloke from Adelaide and her husband beat her. He hates anyone from Adelaide. We got to talking, and he ended up getting me a long look at young Galway. A long look. I even got an invitation to his home, met his family – they're all there, in Camberwell. I'm practically one of them. Turns out he has got a few weaknesses, though I wouldn't call them that. More like little quirks.

'Idiosyncrasies.'

'What?'

'Quirks.'

'That's what I said. Do you wanna know or what?'

'Go on, then.'

'I've lost me thread.'

'You were havin' dinner with the family.'

'Paterson is blind in one eye.'

'You're pullin' me leg.'

'Lost it at Gallipoli.'

'Jesus Christ, not another bloody war hero. Don't tell me he got the VC or something. The punters'll kill me.'

'He deserves to be beaten for turnin' up.'

'So is that it? He's half blind?'

'Isn't that enough?'

'So what's the bad news?'

'He's a sweet boxer, very straight backed, long reach, and moves quickly.'

'What do the punters say?'

'Better you don't ask. It's bad luck.'

'Jesus.'

'A lot of people want you to get done, after what you done to Paddy Smith.'

'It was him or me.'

'They don't see it that way.'

'What if it had been me who'd beaten me?'

'Then they would've said you got what you deserved. That was one fight you were only ever going to win in the ring.'

'Maybe I should take a dive, improve me popularity.'

'I hope that was meant to be funny.'

'How the hell would you know what funny is?'

'Now, now.'

'Oh well, which is his blind side, then?'

'His left.'

'Then he'll be expecting a left.'

'D'yer reckon?'

'Oh yeah. Does Les know?'

'Not yet. I thought he'd be here.'

'You find him, and I'll do a bit of sparring with one of the lads. Reg?'

'Yeah?'

'Get me an eye patch, will you?'

11 Blind Man's Bluff

Stephen Galway turned to be a very angry man, and the reason for his anger was standing in my corner looking at him. It was Reg. One of his blokes comes over to Reg after we climb into the ring, and stands so close to Reg and Les and me, I can smell what he had for dinner the previous Thursday.

'You'd be a bit of a bastard, wouldn't yer? The kid tells me you went to his home and spied on his family.'

'Come on, cobber, look at him. He looked like he was going to give my boy a hiding. Everyone said so. We needed to know what we were up against, that's all.'

'I oughta kill yer.'

'I wouldn't even think accusations like that in front of my boy. I s'pose you haven't heard that he got five years for carving out a bloke's eye with a cut-throat razor, have yer? Why don't you tell your boy that? I bet that'd bring back a few unpleasant memories.'

'You lousy cunt. We'll wipe the floor with your boy, then I'll do the same thing with *you*.'

'Tell you what,' says Reg, 'if your boy can still walk, why don't you bring him with you, and we'll make it an even fight.'

Suddenly a new voice pipes up, kind of gravelly and slow.

'I've had enough of this bullshit. You get back to your corner,' says Vic Norton, the ref, and that seems to be that.

'This'll all work in our favour,' says Les. 'The kid'll be ropable. He'll make mistakes. He'll use energy early. He may need a little bit of boxing.

'I think I'll spend a bit of time on the canvas,' I says. 'That'll slow down things a bit.'

'Good idea,' says Les. 'Just don't hurt that hip on the way down. And don't forget our fight strategy.'

So I take a couple of dives early the match, just to please young Galway, who turns out to be the Galway Kid, even though he's ten years older than me, always being careful to fall on my left side. The crowd hates me, of course, as they're not blind, and the referee gives me one of those looks that tells me he's losing patience with me, as he too wants to get home in one piece. So I say I him: 'So, Vic, how're the wife and kids?' and give him wink, and he says to me: 'Are you here to fight, or do I have to disqualify you?'

'So it's fightin' you want, is it Vic? Well, why didn't you say so.'

And I quickly walk around the back of the ref to the Kid's blind side, and give him a hard cuff across the left ear with the lacing of my glove, which stings him like hell, and make him rub hard. The ref does nothing, as to the punters lacing is a pretty standard way of intimidating a new opponent, and seems fair considering I've been on the canvas twice.

So off we go, with the Kid fighting a pretty fight indeed, speed being his one big trick, but accuracy being absent. In the end, only half of his punches make the distance, and most of *them* miss badly, and I catch so many punches on the forearms, they're bruised all over, while he's able to dodge most of mine altogether. I beckon him to come close constantly, but his trainers have told him that I'm dirty in close, so he's content to throw them from out in the foyer. The fight would have progressed this way, with neither of us wanting to come to grief, except that at the end of round four, Queenie suddenly appears behind me outside the ring, and gives me a hey.

'Not now, Queenie,' says Les, who hates women like the flu.

'I just wanted to tell you I know something that might help.'

'Oh yeah, what?'

'He can't take a low punch.'

'Is that it?'

'I heard he's got some kind of problem, that's all I know.'

That Queenie had a real nasty streak in her, and no mistake.

Anyway I got a chance to test her suggestion in one of the clinches, when I dropped my right hand down as low as could and gave him a sharp tap in the family jewels with the back of my flat hand. I was standing so close to him that it looked like I was defending my own nuts, but I could tell by his eyes and by the way he sucked in air that he was hurt when a fit bloke wouldn't have been. His corner went crazy, but the ref hadn't seen anything unusual, and let it go.

But after that, the Kid was walking wounded, and near the end of that round, I gave him the left hook he wasn't expecting, twice, and the ref decided it was time for the next fight.

They had to take the Kid to hospital straight after that fight, and I heard he gave up fighting straight away. A lot of blokes, good fighters, some of them, came back carrying injuries like that one. A lucky punch, or a well-calculated one, could retire them from the game for good. It would be a few years before all those blokes had been taken out of the running by clever or ruthless bastards like me. I reckoned my time would come as well.

Queenie was pleased as punch about being right about the Kid's trouble, and I asked about it when we were out celebrating.

'Oh, it's just girl stuff,' she said. 'You don't want to know.'

'Yes I bloody well do.'

'Well he's one of Dora's fellers, or at least he was, and she wanted to make a few extra quid, so she asked me to put a few quid on you. Guess he won't need her anymore.'

'Christ, Queenie, I'm glad you're on my side.'

'I'll be on your side for ever, Arch.'

Her eyes glistened as she said this and I felt a powerful mixture of feelings take hold of me, poetry included.

The next bout was another seven rounder, this time with Michael "Lance" Boyle, who also went by the name of Basher Boyle. Boyle had never been in the Army, having worked in one of those jobs that protected him from the war: he was a wharfie, and as a result had probably gotten into a lot of scraps in his time. I happened to know that he was a doorman in one of the rowdier casinos on the dock, one of those ones that moved from ship to ship, and paid the house – or in this case, ship – a nice little earner by way of rent. It wouldn't have surprised me to hear that he'd helped more than a few dissatisfied customers into the chilly waters of Port Phillip Bay late at night. He was a featherweight who'd made a special effort to lose weight just so that he could knock my block off, though to this day I don't know the reason why, as the wharves are one place I try to avoid, mainly because of blokes like him.

I was one of those blokes coves either like or hate – usually it's hate. I don't know why. God knows I've asked the poetry, and a lot of stuff has come out. It's got to the stage where I just have to feel it coming, like vomit that's still in your stomach, for it to make an appearance in my mind. It'd make me feel like a fool but it gives me directions, it always did that. I suppose I just never paid a lot of attention to them. Anyway, that's how it is with me. And I'd give up the poetry tomorrow, if it'd let me. And I'd give up the boxing too, if I could get that sweet feeling some other way, some way that made it unnecessary for coves to choose between hating and liking me. I mean, it's too easy not to like me, it's just too easy. Not that liking me is a breeze, I'm not saying that. But Queenie likes me, and so do a lot of the other girls, and so do their mums, as a matter of fact. And that is a very strange thing, of course, given my body's disinclination to fit into any mould.

So I was not particularly worried about this Basher character, because I knew how those blokes fight, and usually it's hell for leather, and big impressive punches all over the place, and lots of misses. And to make matters better, he hates me, which is always an advantage for the bloke that's copping the hatred, and the other bloke tends to lose his focus, and that's one thing I'm shit-hot at keeping. It's a crying shame, I often think, that God made me so keen to be a fighter, and give me the natural focus and the natural gifts to fight dirty, and then give me a body that doesn't fit the game at all. I reckon if God had made me a woman I'd be on the street and ugly to boot, and would probably starve to death.

On the night, Basher turned up with a big audience of his mates, and finally we got a bout at the West Melbourne Stadium, which was a bit of feather in everyone's caps, but I was in no doubt that it was me who had got the Stadium, and for once it was some other bloke who was riding on my good fortune. We knew nothing new about Basher, and we had no idea why he was so upset about me, so I says to him while the referee's going over the rules:

'Lance, what's this I hear about you being upset at me? I didn't even know you knew me. Have we met or something?'

'Yeah, we've met alright, in the old days at College. You denied me a fight by begging the screws to put you on the boat to Egypt – I heard all about it. You chickened out.'

'I don't think I'd ever heard of you. Someone's been pulling your leg. But what's all this Egypt stuff? Didn't we all go to Egypt?'

'Don't pull that crap on me. I rotted in that fucking hole for two more years.'

'Jesus, you must have pissed someone off pretty good, mate. Anyway, forgive and forget, eh?'

'Go and fuck yourself, Taggerty.'

'What, and end up looking like your mum?'

'You're dead.'

'What was that all about?' asked Les.

'He's an old mate from the College. We were just swapping yarns.'

'Fair enough.'

When the bell went, Boyle made no attempt to box, and walked out with his hands in the grappling position. I tried to fend him off, but he just walked in and grabbed me and head butted me in the ear so hard that I went immediately deaf on that side. In return, I grabbed him by the lower elbow and turned him around a little and punched him as hard as I could in the kidney.

The ref could see it was tit for tat. 'So it's love at first sight, is it?' says he, holding us both by the neck and drawing us to him. 'Well the next bloke who fouls again is going to get DQ-ed. This is the Stadium, not the Collingwood Town Hall. Now, touch gloves.'

We touch gloves and get stuck into each other again, but even though Boyle is keen to kill me, he is now less than keen to get into a wrestling match, and we throw punches at each other until we're both breathing hard. I cop a lot of leather from Boyle, but in the process I discover that he's no boxer, and lacks speed, and holds his right out from his body like he's waiting to throw the big punch. So I give him a chance to throw the right, to see how he does it, and he throws it so far out to the right that it takes a fortnight to reach me, and I pull back a little to let it sail past. As it goes by, I step a little closer to him, and let my left go as hard as I can into his triceps, which hurts him, and makes him walk back and shake his arm like mad, to get the feeling back into it. He's still shaking his arm when the bell goes, and his corner complains to the ref about my dirty tactics. I don't know what the ref says, but it's apparent that he's one of those refs who think corners should keep their mouths shut, and that he is quite capable of making up his own mind what is and what is not a foul. Boyle glares at me like mad, and I give him the finger, which is a bit hard when you're wearing a boxing glove, but to his credit he does get the message.

Round two was a replay of round one, with me succeeding in tying Boyle up on the ropes a couple of times, and forcing him to put his hands up high, which gives me a chance to uppercut his crook upper arm a couple of time. As this is the kind of punch that might be seen as legitimately trying to get through the defence of a bloke who's not trying to box you, which is a bit of a mortal sin, I get away with it, though the crowd are less forgiving.

But the result of all this close work was that Boyle could hardly move his right arm, let alone get one of his haymakers in, and he could only use if for blocking, which exposes it to more punishment. But the price I paid was being close to him most of the time, and copping a bit of a hiding, mainly from his left, which seemed to be in good form. At the end of the round my hip was giving me hell, from pushing against it and resisting his grappling, and I was pretty tired. I wasn't going to make it to seven. I didn't even feel like a boxer. I went back to my corner, feeling bushed, and hearing the poetry demon whispering to me.

'Go away, you bastard,' I said out loud, as a stool was put down for me.

Les slapped my face a few times.

'Pay attention.'

He was interrupted by the ref, who stuck his head in, and said: 'One more arm foul, and he's out,' he said. 'He can box, or he can go home.'

'Bastard,' I said, quietly.

'Listen,' says Les. 'He's a slugger. You can out-box him. It's time to move around.'

'I'm knackered.'

'Rubbish, what about him? He's only got one good arm. You're doing fine. If you don't like, it put him down, and we can all go home early.'

Well, round three, normally a round used for picking up the pace, was bound to be hard, because we'd been fighting flat out since the opening bell, and the crowd were very pleased, especially at the dirty tricks yours truly was using. Nothing buggers up a night out at the boxing faster than a clean fight. Well, we walk out in the middle, and the bell goes, and the ref sees out of the corner of his eye that the stool from my corner still hasn't been removed from the ring, so he puts his hand out to the both of us, to indicate that we should wait, and says to Reg: 'Get that bloody stool out of the ring,' or something. And I can see in a flash what's going on, and I take a step back up against Boyle and pretend to bump into him, while hitting him hard below the water-line. He falls to his knees and I quickly step forward again, and all this in the second that the ref's head is turned. He can do nothing but tell us to box, because his only alternative is to ask the crowd's opinion – and believe me, they're not backward in coming forward – and there hasn't been a ref in history who's done that.

So as soon as Boyle regains his feet, and while he is trying to regain his composure, which is bloody hard yakka when everything down there is giving you hell, I plant my feet and give him a right cross that stuns him so hard he staggers around the ring backward with his hands spread out at waste level as if he's singing the last line of Danny Boy. Before he can fall to the floor and have a bit of a free lie down I run up to him and give a big thump on the ear that send him smack into the cross buckle, which he throws his arms backwards over. At this point he is pretty much off with the fairies, but the second rule of boxing is to fight on until you can't fight any more, so I walk up to him and prepare to let fly one of my 'two year' punches. I call it my two year because that's what you'd get if you tried it outside the ring. But the ref grabs me by the glove, and walks in between us, and gives the 'all over' wave, to stop me murdering young Lance. Well, the crowd is very pleased at the clever way I take advantage of every opportunity, but not happy at being robbed of the better part of a fight, and only throw a couple of bob in the ring. As usual, I let my opponent have it. After all, I cheated.

12 The Tourist Season

'You're not welcome in Melbourne, anymore.'

It was Les, telling me the what day it was.

'What're yer talkin' about, *not welcome*. Who says?'

'The owners of the game.'

'Nobody owns boxing.'

'Come on, mate, everyone knows the Sportsmen's Syndicate owns all of the boxing venues in Australia, bar a few that can't pull a crowd. And the Syndicate has banned you. The promoters are at one on this. Archie Taggerty is too dirty to touch, they're sayin'. They're goin' all respectable –'

'Don't make me laugh.'

'It's true.'

'But I was going to have a shot for the title. State Bantamweight. I'm one fight off...I'll fight clean.'

'Yeah, and pigs'll fly.'

'I could learn,' I say. 'How hard can it be?'

'This is no joke: they mean it.'

'But we're just startin' to make money.'

'There is a way you can keep making money, and box, and build your reputation.'

He shows me a sheet of paper.

'*World's Greatest Boxers.* Hey, most of this is in a foreign bloody language.'

'World boxing. You travel – India, Great Britain, the United States, and so on – thumping blokes left, right and centre; we make a packet, we move on. We're talking big money. And the beauty of it is, you can be as dirty as you like. I was planning on taking an Aussie stable, you know, Bantamweight, Lightweight, Welterweight – a good range of weights. They say travel broadens the mind, yer know.'

'I'm already broadminded.'

'I'm serious. Blokes are coming home rich and buying mansions in Toorak. What d'yer say?'

'I'll have to talk to Queenie.'

'She's already packed.'

'Nice of you to remember to ask me – all right, then. No sense in wasting me vast knowledge of foreign lands, I s'pose.'

We went to New Zealand first, and met a bloke who'd been putting together a few fighters from there. They reckoned they were going to call us the Anzac Diggers, but I refused point blank to be called a digger, so they decided to call us the Anzac Fighters, which suited me fine, as I'd known many a Kiwi, and they seemed to be almost as keen on hitting people as the Aussies did.

Queenie took to travel like a brumby, and wanted to see everything, fuck everybody, and drink everything she saw. It was all I could do just keeping her from sloping off to make a few quid on the side. But she reminded me that she'd been here before and the place was a very friendly place for an Aussie girl to be. But the biggest problem with Queenie was the drink, a problem that she took with her, and made no attempt to hide, as if it was some peccadillo she's decided she could get away with. Not to put too fine a point on it, Queenie drank everything that wasn't nailed down. Trouble was, in the few moments of the day when she was not actually drinking, but merely contemplating it, she seemed to be sober and loving. Indeed, it was as easy for me to love Queenie, at those times as it was for me to hate her at other times.

Boxers tend to be a rough lot, you'll no doubt be surprised to hear, so Queenie's behaviour wasn't a whole lot different from the other women in our travelling boxing show, and she seemed to fit in, regardless of her shenanigans. We had a few bouts in Auckland that were definitely not exhibitions, and I managed to lose on points to a Maori fighter called Jack Tui, who we later took with us, although at that time, we didn't know him from a bar of soap. I liked Jack. Apart from being one of the few coves who got a decision over me, he'd been in the Camel Corps in Palestine, and had been one of those Anzacs who'd beaten Laurence to Damascus, which made the Brits as mad as hell. He still had his funny Kiwi slouch hat, which had some kind of bird's feather in it – a chook's, I think – and used to wear it all the time. Naturally, nobody ever told him to take it off, and he told me in private, that he intended to die with it on, as he'd expected to many times in Palestine. Can't argue with that.

We did a little tour of New Zealand looking for boxers, and ended up with only the blokes we found in Auckland, they being capable of outclassing in three rounds the best the locals could rake up, I suppose because they had access to professional training. It wasn't until we got to India that we found any serious competition, and we soon discovered that we could fill an arena with thousands of people, though they didn't pay a lot for the privilege. The size of India was astonishing, as it seemed that wherever we went, there was never a shortage of people who wanted to see a good boxing match, and never a shortage of well-trained fighters, either. So, doing as we had done in New Zealand, we double the size of our stable, and left India with some very handy fighters.

Our next stop was Cairo, where we had a bit of a rest, and I took in the sights. Heliopolis had changed, as the new Egyptian government had gone crazy. We staged some fights while I was there, as it is well known that your Gyppo loves nothing better than a stoush, though they like to do a lot of talking at the same time, you know, name calling and what have you. Really, though, unless you mind your mum being likened to a camel, it's pretty hard to take offence. Truth is, those Gyppos are hopeless bloody barrackers, so God help them if they ever decide to take up footy.

Our circus ended in Great Britain, where we found lots of interest, and some great fighters, but very little money, thanks to the bloody war, so we stayed there only long enough to pick a few fighters, and then go over to the United States, where they not only had money up to here, but prohibition of alcohol, which ensured that there would be a lot of watering holes, and a lot of people with more money than sense. It was in the US that things started to happen for us.

We were offered a fight by every second bloke we met, many of whom were boxers. In New York, where we went first, Queenie became very popular with the locals, which I was used to, and managed to get us introductions, where just plain knocking on doors achieved bugger all. In the end we were fighting all over the place, and I had hopes, which were never realised, of getting a shot at the bantamweight title. I did see Jack Dempsey KO Luis Firpo in two rounds, and that alone was worth the trip. But it was just before that bout that a very strange thing happened, something that shook me like a chin punch.

We had all decided to go up to Saratoga Springs to watch Dempsey prepare for his defence – we knew the place would be filled with boxers, all hoping for a chance to spar with the champ. One young man about my age was dead keen on fighting the big man, not to make a name for himself, like all the other mugs, but because he wanted the experience pitting himself against a dangerous man, one on one. We had met this man, a writer called Paul Gallico, on the train, and he had spoken of the many great poets who were also fighters, and told us his theory that they had fought as a way of coming to grips with their daimons, or creative spirits, though he did not tell us what he was about to do. It is history now that Jack knocked him cold. But what is not generally known is that Gallico got a big kick out of it.

Later, when were alone together, he smiled at me and said: 'Now I feel free to write. Before this, something was holding me back. Then, when I punched Dempsey in the face, I felt a freeing-up. I was free, I'd finally stopped resisting my daimon.' My face must have revealed something, because he begin to explain. 'Most men are left alone by their one daimon, but some of us – the writers, or at least the poets, have one that gives them hell. Now my writer knows he can – *I* can – take the punches and dish 'em out and my boxer can be happy just to have a front-row seat. Oh, but I just remembered: you're a fighter yourself, so you probably know what I mean.'

I knew, all right, but I hadn't *known* that I knew. All these years I'd been dishing out the punches while this daimon had been giving me hell, not to punish me but to get my attention. But I pushed it away. It wasn't part of my plan; it didn't fit in with it, nor I with it.

We travelled to the West Coast in the end, not because we weren't making money in the Eastern States – because we were making the stuff hand over fist – but because the really big money was in movies, and we figured it was worth a shot.

Our manager, Shorty Long, a funny bugger, formed a stunt man company called Stage Fight Inc, and we all went into the movies, even Queenie, who never actually performed on camera, though her performances off camera probably saved our bacon a few times at the beginning.

Stage Fight was a big success, and soon our blokes, myself included became so good at our jobs, we were being asked to do non-fight stunts, so a couple of us formed a new company with Shorty Long, called Hard Knocks Inc, and this we plugged all over town, performing stunts everywhere we went, usually in the streets, to attract publicity. We learned the tricks of the trade from the few local stuntmen we dug up, some of them too banged up to continue, but only too happy to pass on all they had learned for a few dollars.

When the producers found out I could ride, they had me doing all kind of horse-riding stunts I didn't even know I could do, and I pitched in and gave then plenty of advice about their horses, which had gotten into a pretty sorry state. They were pretty horses, too, not Walers, of course, but retired quarter horses, and great for cowboy scenes. The one thing I shied away from, however was falling off a horse, as my hip couldn't have stood it. And I passed up some good money as a result. But there were always plenty of cowboys willing to break their necks for a buck, so I made it my job to tell them how to do it. After all, I'd fallen off a horse more times than all of them put together.

After a year of this, we were in the chips up to our elbows, and Hard Knocks was being asked to supply charioteers, bloodthirsty revolutionaries, soldiers, and the like. And we weren't above doing the odd non-violent scene, either. No job too large or too small. And we picked up a few bouts, as well. When finally I discovered that Queenie had developed a fondness for one of the bigger producers, I left Hollywood and came home. I had made a packet, and I missed Melbourne. I'd kept in shape and I still wanted to box, and Les was never keen on the stunt business in the first place. The plan was to get a few top boxing matches, and clean up.

Our eyes had been opened in New York. The yanks were efficient when it came to boxing, and had everything organised for months ahead. Of course, the boxing in Australia was controlled by the Syndicate, so there were limitations everywhere you turned, but the possibility of making money and having a good time were still there. And there was something else, too. The poetry had ceased as soon as I had left for the States. It was mysterious, but there it was, and good riddance. I'd be hopping into blokes, giving then a hard time in the ring, and though there'd be that sweet feeling I liked so much when I was fighting – and winning – I didn't have to put up with any strange stuff appearing in my head and forcing me to write it down.

The feeling that everything was alright seemed pretty strong as our ship docked at Sydney, and Les and I went over to Festival Hall to see a fight, it being Saturday night. We missed the first fight, in which a bantamweight, Billy Magee, punched the living daylights out of a state contender, Ronny Futaba, an odd sort of name, but not one that we were likely to see again, in any case.

'Billy Magee,' I says to Les. 'That's that bloke I sparred with at Ryrie's.'

'You? And Billy Magee? When was that?'

'Oh, that would have been before my comeback.'

'You're lucky to be alive. They reckon he made mincemeat out of that Futaba kid.'

'Wonder what he's doing up here?'

'He's fightin', that's what. And that's what you should be doing. I'll be glad to get back to Melbourne,' he says, looking around the place. 'These Sydney buggers couldn't organise a piss-up in a brewery.'

So we end up back at the ship, and the next morning, it's off to Melbourne. Well, that afternoon, I'm up on the promenade deck, watching the coast go by, when who should I see but the kid himself, Billy Magee.

'Hello, Billy. Hear you had a win. Good on yer. Mind you, anyone with a name like a vegetable deserves to be flattened.'

'Futaba's Japanese. Good fighter, too. Just not on the night.'

'So what the hell are you doin' here? I hear you won a shot at the title?'

'I did, but they wanted me to go up a division, and I told them to get whatsanamed. That wasn't the deal. I've had it with these people. So what's your story? Haven't seen you for ages, not since you tricked that wharfie bloke. Good stoush, that.'

'Been in the USA, in Hollywood. A few of us formed a stunt company. Made a packet, too. But I'm a boxer.'

'Yeah.'

We stared for a while at a distant town half buried in factory smoke.

'So how's your sister? Married yet?'

'What d'you know about my sister?'

'Me and Ruthie are old friends – didn't she tell you?'

'What d'yer mean *Ruthie*?' No one calls her Ruthie.'

'Well, I do.'

'When I was down in Melbourne you had a girlfriend; as I remember you and her were as thick as thieves.'

'That was years ago,' I say, looking down into the sloshing sea. 'History.'

'Well, if you know Ruth so well, I suppose you've heard all the news, been writing letters and such, haven't you?'

'I can't write,' I say, without thinking. It's a gift.

'Well, Ruth isn't keen on fighters. She even hates *me* doing it. And she won't like you doing it, either. So you can just keep it up for good, as far as I'm concerned.'

'We'll see, won't we?'

He catches me staring all around the place, and starts looking around too, to see what I'm looking at.

'What's wrong?'

'It's funny, but this ship, the *Orsova*, I've been on it for days, and I didn't realise it was the same ship I came back from Egypt on, in nineteen-eighteen. It's completely different.'

'How can you not recognise a whole bloody ship?'

'It was a hospital ship, it was painted white and besides, it was full of crook people. We weren't taking any notice. But it's the same ship, alright. Big bastard. I remember that when it arrived in Port Said, it was already chockers with blokes from France. These decks were covered in blokes. Christ.'

Billy was quiet, and watched me look around.

'Must've been rotten.'

'It smelt bloody awful.'

'No, I mean the war.'

'It was for those other poor bastards, the ones in France. It was different in Palestine.' I laughed. 'And I had poetry to keep me company.'

'Poetry?'

I'd said too much, but it was easy to talk to this bloke, as I liked him right off the bat.

'Never mind. The Gyppos like poetry, that's all.'

'Poetry,' he says, with a dreamy look on his face. 'Nope, dunno it.'

'Me neither,' I says, trying to change the conversation.

'S'pose yer wondering why I didn't enlist.'

'Not really. I couldn't give a continental, as a matter of fact. War's a mug's game, anyway.'

'Essential job. I tried to, but they knocked me back.'

'What were yer, the Prime Bloody Minister, or something?'

'Nah, I was a printer's mate. We were printing all this stuff for the war, you know, telling people things.'

'Newspaper'.'

'No, pamphlets, posters, and the like. We were at it day and night.'

'Well, you were lucky. They prob'ly would've sent you to France. Ah, fuck it. I wonder if they sell beer on this thing. You game?'

'Yeah.'

So that's how me and Billy Magee became mates. It was a natural thing. I told myself I was just having a beer with a bloke I met on a ship. But there was more to it than that. I was up to my old tricks, a little voice told me. He knew Ruth, who had come back into my mind, all of a sudden. It was being back here that did it. There were times when the ship was so close to the coast that I could smell the Eucalyptus pouring down off the steep hills and out to sea like invisible water. And when that happened it was as if I'd never been away, and I was a boxer again, looking for a fight, and Queenie had shot through with some new feller, and I was feeling okay, and so, of course, I'd think of that tall, quietish girl I'd met near Ryrie's place that day.

Why I thought of her I didn't know. Why I couldn't stop, I didn't know. Billy Magee was the reason. They shared the same parents. That made me stop and think. It stood to reason that they'd have a lot in common. But that thought was as phoney as bootleg beer. Magee was okay, that was all. I'd take my chances with Ruth, if I ever saw her again, when I got back to Melbourne. I'd take my chances, just as I always had.

When we left Sydney the sun was shining, and it was a perfect day, though I heard someone say Sydney always looked like that – I doubt it. But my point is, as we got further south the weather got rottener and rottener, and when we finally reached Port Phillip Bay, it was positively foul. We drove our way through freezing cold bloody rain in a straight line from The Rip to Station Pier, and stopped there, with the *Orsova* just sitting and feeling sorry for itself, and nobody game to move towards the gangway for rain, which was pissing down.

Good old Melbourne, I thought. I would have been disappointed if we'd had nice weather. I would have gone up to the Captain, and said: 'Scuse me, sir, but I believe I've hopped on the wrong bloody boat, and ended up in New Bloody Zealand by mistake.' So, while some brave souls started ashore, the rest of us, especially those from Melbourne, who knew a bit about her temperament, just stood on the decks, and watched and waited, and many simply waited in the saloon, even though it was closed for business. Well, after a while, the Captain can put up with us no more, and apologises for the weather and asks us to begin disembarking, so we do. But all I can think of is the poetry in my head, which has come back and is giving me hell.

I went for a walk and tried to find someone I knew, but I couldn't even find Les or Shorty, or Billy, and I guessed they'd already shot through. Thus, when I finally set foot in Melbourne again I was alone, drenched, and had a head full of unwanted poetry, which was demanding to be written down with considerable urgency, so that I couldn't have ignored it if I'd tried. I walked down the gangway, thinking that if I could just make it to the shelter that ran the length of the pier, I'd be okay, as I could then catch a train from Port Melbourne station, down at the far end. So I hurry down the gangway and wade across to the shelter, and out of the downpour.

'Hello, Mr Taggerty.'

Well, now, at the sound of that voice, I nearly fell over.

'Ruthie...Ruth Magee.' I must have looked bewildered as I removed my hat, because she laughed that bell-like laugh that I remembered from our first – in fact, our only – meeting.

'You should see yourself. I came down to meet Billy. He should have got off ages ago. I wasn't expecting to see you.'

I let the sentence resonate in my head for a second, to see if she'd meant anything by it, but it seemed friendly enough.

'I've been overseas – America – just got back. I met Billy in Sydney. He didn't say he was expecting you to be here to meet him. In fact, I'd bet he didn't know.'

'And how would you know about that?'

'Well, me and Billy had a few conversations, mainly boxing stuff.'

'I see, and are you still a boxer, Mr Taggerty?'

'Please call me Archie, everyone does, even me mother.'

'Well what else would she call you?'

'If she wanted to stick it into me, she could call me Archbold.'

142

'Archibald?'

'No, though that's what everyone thinks. It's even what the army called me. But it's Archbold. It's a family name, or something.'

'Well, you may not like it, but I think it's very dignified, though I shall call you Archie – but only one condition.'

'Oh yes?' I hate conditions.

'Yes, you must give up boxing. Otherwise I shall follow you around calling you Archbold out loud. I don't think that would do much to help the reputation of the Richmond Terrier. Or do you now call yourself the Yankee Doodle?'

She blushed suddenly, as she realised she had made a faux pas, and I suddenly realised that it was the most beautiful thing I'd ever seen, or ever would. It was one of those moments that you realise, as the years go by, that you were born to experience; it gives your life on earth meaning, because most of it is, let's face it, bloody meaningless. In that moment, I prayed to God, who I was sure had probably forgotten me, I prayed, embarrassed that I'd neglected to keep in touch with Him, except when I cursed him occasionally for what He did in the war, and what I prayed for was that I would never forget that look as long as I lived.

13 Missionary Ruth

I nearly panicked when I saw that blush on Ruth's face, in case I never saw it again, but I needn't have worried, because I saw it again, a couple of times, as we waited for the train, and again, as we sat on the rickety train, on the way to Flinders Street. Ruth was like no other woman I had ever met. She wasn't backward in coming forward, as I've said, but she had that in common with the Richmond girls, and I would've been disappointed if it had been otherwise. But there was a lot more to her. She had some kind of personal idea about what works in a person's life that had nothing to do with the tub-thumpers and bible-bashers. She didn't approve of drunkenness, though she was, I discovered, a drinker herself. She didn't approve of boxing, though it was only because she said she didn't like to see so many fine young Irishmen being hoodwinked by the English landlord, meaning those with money. She didn't approve of the war because we were, she said, fighting for a cause we knew nothing about. It was all true, of course, every word.

'You're right, Ruthie,' I says, the next time I saw her, which was a week later, as arranged, at the tram shelter in Swan Street.

'About what?' she says, and I notice she has no problem with the name I call her.

'About everything.'

'Don't be silly. I don't want to be right. That's not why I say what I say. I say those things because I must, because someone must, and it seems like no one is game enough to put his best foot forward. It's always left to the women to speak up when the men make a blooming mess of things.'

I loved it when she got all hot under the collar like this, and I could look at her face all day, especially when her eyes got that red look about them, like he was about to cry, or dong someone, or maybe both. But she never did cry or dong someone, though I made a note to myself not to ever take her down to the Yarra Bank, as she was bound to get into trouble and clock some copper – I wouldn't put it past her.

'Where are we going?' she says to me, even though we'd talked about it the week before, when she'd accidentally met me at Station Pier. I chuckled, because she was so hot under the collar, she'd forgotten.

'What's so funny?'

'You are. I thought we decided to go to Luna Park.'

'Yes, we did, didn't we? It should be good. I haven't been over there for ages.'

'And you're not worried about being seen with Archie Taggerty, the Richmond Terrier?'

'I don't see any terrier,' she says. 'I wouldn't be seen dead with you if I thought that rubbish I read about you in the papers was true.'

'Oh, and what did they say?' For I never took any notice of the papers. In the old days, the papers wrote me off week after week. They'd had me die a thousand deaths. Don't talk to me about the bloody papers.'

'They say you're a low hitter.'

'Well, I'm not a tall man, as you can see, and if I happen to be fightin' someone who's shaped more like a telegraph pole, well, of course, he'll cop a few where he doesn't want – that's how a short boxer gets by. The tall boxer hits you on the top of your noggin in return. That's how it works. But I wouldn't say I was a low puncher. What else do they say?'

'They say that you're dirtier than ...'

'Yeah, than what?'

'Than a sewer rat.'

'Oh, is that all?'

'Hell, Arch.'

'Yes, you're right, Ruthie, it's horrible, the things they say about a man.'

'I know it's partly true, Arch – I've been around boxers for years – but what I don't like is that this is the kind of world decent men get into when they get into the fight game. I hate it, Arch.'

'I can see that, yes, I can. But what can I do? There's something about it, it gets into a bloke. It can feel good, y'know – I know that's not you want me to say, but it's true.'

'Other things can feel good, too, Arch, if you'll let them.'

'Like what?'

But she never answered, she just looked out the window of the tram at the passing parade of shops and pubs, as if there was something outside worth seeing.

'Ruthie?' I says, getting a bit worried about this turn of the conversation. 'Ruthie?'

I was talking to Ruth for only the third time, and already I felt as though we were joined in some way, that I was somehow responsible, for ... something I couldn't put my finger on – something. She slowly turned away from the window, as you tend to on a Richmond tram, and her eyes were lowered. I realised that I wanted to see her eyes, that not being able to see them was a terrible thing. The tension in my head, in my whole body, started to speak to me, poetically, and wanted, I knew to be spoken or written, or both. It was the only thing in my life I couldn't control. If I had have been free to, I would have let the words fall out on my lap, so she could see them, because they would have been for her, like flowers.

But I was terrified. I didn't trust my own mouth. I wasn't game, in fact, to move a muscle. Ruth knew something I didn't know – about us. Hell, I knew she knew a lot more than that. But what was I to do? I was fighting a battle in my head, and all my bones and muscles were involved.

When she raised her eyes they were soft and pink, a little swollen. That's what you get from staring at Richmond on a Saturday, I could have told her.

'You're squirming. Am I that hard to be with?' she says, landing a fair blow, I suppose.

'You're not hard to be with at all. I've never met anyone ... easier to be with.'

'Yes, I feel the same way.'

'Well, good. So you wouldn't be seen dead with me if you thought I was a dirty fighter. As I was trying' to tell you, we have to do things, to get by, to win. In the end, that's all the punters care about: who won.'

'I'm not a punter, Arch. Haven't you noticed?'

'Oh, I've noticed alright. I've noticed everything about you. I haven't missed a single detail.'

I looked in the reflection a glass covered advertisement, and saw Ruth and I side by side. She had her eyes on me, and it seemed to me that she was looking at me in a new way. The poem was cutting its way out. I was now afraid of it. I was a grown man, well, not much of a one, and this poem, and its brothers, were trying to make an even bigger fool of me, trying to show me up.

It was Ruth's closeness that was doing it. I could feel her warm thigh touching my painful one, and it was more soothing than the touch of the nurses' hands when I was dying of the flu in Cairo. She talked as if she liked me, but in a way that was causing me to feel a pain in every part of my body. Queenie had never tortured me like this. She told me I was the best, and that was that. I told her she was the best too; and that was that. She didn't reach inside me and rummage around for any old poetry, or feelings that were there for the taking, if someone only knew how.

Only one other person before had managed to get me to spill my guts about the poetry, and that was the dying trooper at Beersheba. And I knew he was dying. I could be responsible for his passing – that's what had happened, I had been responsible. Hadn't we been told that it was okay to share our water with our fellow soldiers? Well, I had no water for his particular kind of thirst. What he wanted was to have some beauty in his life as he let go of it. He wanted what I was having right then, just by being with Ruth.

Just then I saw Ruth looking at me in the reflection, and our eyes met. She was looking at me so softly, I thought it was just something about the reflection, but when I looked to my side, she turned and looked into my eyes, and took my hand, gently, as if she had been asked to hold the Holy Host itself. I don't think she'd ever held a bloke's hand before. As for me, I didn't deserve it.

Neither of us spoke until the tram got to the city, then we got off, still holding hands, and headed for the tram stop for St Kilda. We held hands all afternoon, not speaking of it, as if we had been doing it for years. I had a lot of questions for her, mostly about her choice of bloke to hold hands with, and I asked none of them. I had none for myself, because I wouldn't have known how to answer.

At Luna Park, I saw and smelled everything for the first time. We pointed things out to each other as if we were showing the place to a country visitor, but we didn't care. We said funny things, and all the while she laughed her bell-like laugh, and I laughed my silly idiot's laugh, which she seemed to like a hell of a lot. I hadn't heard that laugh for so long, I'd forgotten how bloody foolish it sounded, just like the rest of me, I reckoned.

'You were overseas doing what, boxing?'

'Well, in the beginning I was. Me and Les, and Reg, and Shorty Long ...'

'Shorty Long!'

'Yeah. We went over to America to get a few bouts, and ended up in Hollywood, in the film business.'

'Shorty Long!'

'Do you want to hear or not?'

'Don't tell me you're a film star!'

'Not a film star, but I was in a lot of films, mostly as a charioteer or a cowboy, or some such. It was because I knew so much about horses.'

'Horses!' That tickled her funny bone.

'Yeah. It's a long story, but when I was in the Army I was taught how to ride, and ended up in the Light Horse Regiment. I fell off just about every horse they found for me, but finally it all worked out in the end. I'll tell you the long version one day.'

'And just what makes you think I'll let you stick around long enough for you to tell it to me.'

'I dunno - I see what you mean.'

'You silly duffer, I'm not going anywhere. Are you?'

'A man'd be a fool to, wouldn't he?'

'Well, it's not a very elegant answer, but I suppose it'll have to do.'

'What d'yer mean?'

'Archbold Taggerty, what am I going to do with you?'

I kept my trap shut.

Ruth was keen for me to quit fighting, but I was contracted for three more fights, each of them more important than the one before. There was a possibility that I'd end up fighting for the Australian championship. The truth was I didn't need the money, but I just had to box again. Les was enthusiastic, of course, but I should have seen that he was bound to be, once the decision was made.

I didn't have to be told what was bothering him; it was the fact that since the war, I had only been able to win by pulling a fast one on my opponent, and in the few years since we'd been away, the fight game had been cleaned up a little. He was worried that I wouldn't be able to last the distance. I had reservations too, of course, but I was a good enough boxer to realise that all it took was training, and the odd shot of pain killer to get through a bout.

This time, the first bout was to be over twelve rounds against Ambrose Farley, who was making a comeback, like me. Ruth wanted no part of it, and wouldn't turn up at the gym I was training at, except to bring me some lunch. She didn't turn up to the fight, when it took place, which was a bit of a relief. And she was not particularly happy at the news that I got the decision, though she was very happy that I was not injured, apart from looking like I'd just gone twelve rounds with Ambrose Farley. It was a nerve-racking fight, because Farley was a bit of a dirty trickster himself, but the crowd didn't seem to mind at all, though they went troppo every time I gave him a little tap that looked in any way sus. That's the story of my life, I reckon.

The second bout was another twelve-rounder against Brian "The Bushman" O'Brien, whose nickname was apparently Oby. When we met in the middle of the ring, I said to him: 'G'day, Oby, I hope you put some plaster in that glove, because you're a fool if you didn't'. And the ref says to me: 'Now Arch, was that nice?'

'Sorry, Ref. Me and Oby are old mates, aren't we Oby?'

O'Brien spat in my face for a reply, and I took that to mean that he was a man of few words, so I gave him my trademark wink, and touched gloves. That fight went my way, but only, I think, because I was lucky to cop young Brian in the eye with my thumb, oddly, not because I had gouged him – I'd never gouged anyone in my life – but because he zigged when he should have zagged. After that, he had the devil of a time trying to see what was going on, and I found it necessary to give him a running commentary, like at the races, which I did. He was so riled by all my quiet talking that he tried to shut me up, which is a sure way to lose your focus.

This time, I got the best of a split decision, and that twelfth round was so hard on me that I could barely walk, and had to be lifted to my feet to accept the decision. For the first time in my life, I didn't want to box again. I felt sorry for myself, and I could see that Ruth had a point. The problem was that I felt sorry for O'Brien, for getting himself hurt, and I'd never had that feeling before, and I was so ashamed that I couldn't tell Les, because I think he would have had a fit.

And the poetry from both fights was killing me. I had written it down as soon as I was by myself, of course, because it was that or bust. But the verses were like ropes that tied me and had to be untied. I thought about what Gallico had said, but reckoned he must have been mistaken about the daimon, at least in my case. It hung around no matter what I did, fight or write.

Strangely, I wasn't looking forward to the third fight – I could see only trouble. I knew what was coming up if I beat Farley and O'Brien: a shot at the Australian title. And that had recently passed to the last man I wanted to fight, Billy Magee. I'd been seeing Ruth, of course, and wondered what she thought of the whole thing, but wasn't game to raise the subject, as being with her was the most peaceful I had ever been, and I didn't want to spoil that.

I don't see how Ruth couldn't have known about Billy being the new Australian Bantamweight Champion, as every man, woman and child and their dogs in Richmond would have known about it, and she was his sister. The promoters had expected me to get creamed by either Farley or O'Brien, of course and the punters has lost a packet, and it did no one any good to have two Richmond boys fighting each other for a bit of the purse, as it looked too much like a put-up job.

But there it was. We were lined up to fight, just by the turning of the world, and not by any intentional doings of any persons.

Well, Billy was the better fighter of the two of us on the face of it. He wasn't carrying any injuries that we knew of, and he was fit. He'd beaten everyone who counted on the way up, and the only reason he wasn't getting a return bout for his first fight as champion was because his last opponent, Herbert "Lord" Nelson, had been so badly beaten he had decided to retire, he being a bit long in the tooth for the fight game.

The bookies had me down and out in an assortment of rounds, and the only thing they couldn't agree on was which round would be my last, it being generally agreed that I wouldn't last the distance. I had the feeling, for once, that they were on the money, and felt like putting a few bob on Billy myself. As for me, everyone in Melbourne, and probably a few neighbouring countries, knew that I was carrying an old injury, and that I couldn't take any kind of injury to my right side.

The only money on me was from people who thought I'd fight dirty to protect myself or avoid going the distance. A few people in the paper reckoned that I was a tough little bugger and might just go the distance to spite them. So that will give you an idea of the general atmosphere in which the fight lead-up was conducted. As for me, I trained as hard as I could, and urged Reg to do a bit of spying to see what he could discover about the kid.

'What d'yer mean, spy? You're knocking around with his bloody sister.'

'And if I even look as though I'm going to talk boxing, she jumps down me throat.'

'Surely, she must talk about Billy, you know: "Oh, by the way, Archie dear, Billy's not at all well lately – been off his steak and veg something terrible."'

'No, mate. The only time she talks about him is to tell me about the things they used to get up to when they were kids, stuff like that.'

'Well, I'll have a sniff around, of course, but I've seen him train and fight before, and I can tell you that he does nothing special, eats nothing special, and goes nowhere special. He's as fit as a fiddle, and that's all he cares about, being fit. He runs a lot.'

'Where?'

'All over the place. The Boulevard, for instance. He likes to run. You'll never tire him out by making him dance. He is very long-winded. That's how he got the title – sheer outlastedness.'

'I don't like the sound of that.'

'Which is why you'll have to outbox him. And that's something that can be done. He is definitely not a great boxer. He makes all kinds of simple mistakes, the most common one being that he forgets to keep his hands up. He's therefore open to quick shots to the head. Especially high ones. Forget his lower face – he seems to protect it naturally. There isn't much apart from that. His combinations are good to look at but lack power, and he has no counter-punch. As I said, he's not a great boxer.'

'I can beat him on points.'

Reg give me a slap across the face, the way he does during a fight, when he wants me to pay attention.

'Don't you ever let me hear you say that again, alright?'

'Okay, okay, keep yer shirt on.'

'You don't box for points, you box for keeps.'

'I box for keeps.'

'Put him down as often as you can, as early as you can. Fight every round as if it's the last. Don't try to save petrol, don't try to warm up. Les'll tell you the same thing. Don't let him learn your style, because you've got a very distinctive way of holding yourself and moving. If he sees it, he'll figure you out.'

'What's his distinctive style?'

'Classical stance, fairly low gloves, moves a lot.'

'He's hard to hit?'

'Bloody hard. But he always spends a few rounds warming up, as if that's the way you're supposed to box. And his oppos always let him get away with it, thinking that they can do the same thing, and learn his style. But they're mistaken, because there's nothing to learn. D'yer see? There's nothing to learn.'

'Right'

It was just as Reg had said, there was bugger all to learn about Billy that was useful. Though I'd been doing a lot of work with the weights in the gym, trying to get my hip in shape, when I did as Les suggested, and went to see an orthopaedic man, he told me to get used to it. Meanwhile, all the papers had found out that I was going out with Billy's sister, and had made up the story that it was a grudge fight. Ruth pretended that she knew nothing about it, and the family carried on as if there was no fight at all. It was a bloody relief when the fight finally arrived.

I thought Billy looked good as he danced around the ring. Reg was right, he lacked flair, but he looked fit enough. I, on the other hand lacked just about everything, except a record of never being beaten, which was something, at least.

The fight is now history, of course, and it's famous for all kinds of reasons. I said to Billy something like: 'You look good, Billy. Wish it was someone else, though.' He just smiled at me and said: 'I won't keep you long', something like that. When the bell went, I walked up to Billy with no silly idea about making him go the distance, and saw that he did indeed hold his hands a little on the low side, but apart from that his stance was textbook. He threw a whole lot of lefts that missed, and a few rights to the body that I fended off easily. He was, just as Reg said he would be, sparring, and making no attempt to throw a big punch, and for a big fight, this was normal. I lashed out with a right as fast as I could in the middle of all this, and caught him flush on the cheek, which unbalanced him a little, and made him take a little step towards me, bringing the side of his head into view for a split second. I repeated the punch, exactly as I had just delivered it, only this time to the side of his head, just above the ear, and he went down.

As soon as he started to fall, I saw the ref shoot his hand out, and I turned to see where the nearest corner was. In the next second, I saw that the crowd were on their feet and yelling their heads off. A wave of panic roared through me like a bushfire, as I imagined that he had not gone down and was coming after me, and I instinctively raised my hands to my face, and half turned. What I saw was like a picture from a nightmare. Billy was lying on the floor, out cold, the ref was waving his hands, and Billy's corner men were already on the move. I dropped my hands and watched as the doctor was called and a crowd formed around Billy. They carried him away on a stretcher, still out cold, and someone came over, and held up my hand and told the punters I had one the fight by a knock-out in one minute and twenty seconds into the first round and was the new Bantamweight Champion of Australia. It was the worst night of my life.

14 Aftermath

I didn't have the nerve to go around to Ruth's place. I didn't have the nerve to go home. I didn't have the nerve to go to the hospital, but that's where I went. I found out where they had taken Billy, and hung around until I could have a word with the doctor who was treating him.

'Doctor, I'm Archie Taggerty, the bloke who knocked Billy out. He's a friend of mine. How is he?'

'If you're his friend, why don't you go up and join his family?'

'Because I'm ashamed. So how is he?'

'Well, he's still unconscious, though we haven't been able to find anything seriously wrong, no fractures, no evidence of any other kind of brain injury. He might wake any second and tell us he's got a headache. There is one thing you can help me with. Where exactly did the punch land?'

'Well, it was just above the left ear, I think, maybe a bit further back. He was in the wrong position altogether, and I was in the right one. But the punch wasn't hard, doctor, I swear. It wasn't hard enough to knock a bloke out, not even you, I think. You could have knocked me down with a feather when he didn't get up. And he was always fit. He was as fit as a fiddle. The truth is, I wasn't confident of beating him at all. I mean look at me, then look at him.'

I stopped, to let it all sink in, and hoped he got the point. He stood there looking at me hard, and nodded a couple of time, deep in thought.

'Well, we'll get to the bottom of it, one way of another, I'm sure we will.'

But we didn't.

When I saw the family leave, I went up to Billy's room, and looked at him. He was in intensive care, but there was nothing to do, because he wasn't really sick, if you see what I mean, just lying there, like a corpse, but warm, and fairly fit looking. I sat down and just looked at him, and after about an hour or so there was a noise behind me, and a nurse came in and took Billy's pulse and looked at him for a while, and looked at me, sitting there.

'Are you his brother?' she said.

'No, I'm the bloke that knocked him out. He's a friend of mine, too.'

'If he's your friend, why did you fight?'

'We're boxers, that's what we do. It wasn't planned, or anything. It's just that he was defending his championship, and I happened to be first boxer to have a crack at it, and here we are. The funny thing is, by rights, that should be me lying there. I mean, he was the stronger man, I think, and he was the favourite.'

'Then that could've been you,' she said.

'No, somehow, I don't think of myself as being susceptible to a light punch. I think I would have got up again. How long do you think he'll be like this?'

'There's no way of knowing. He could wake up right now, or tomorrow, or not for ages.'

'So will you keep him until he wakes up.'

'No, if there's no change, we'll move him. After all, there's nothing to be done now, but maintain his fluids, you know, nutrients. And wait.'

'Is there anything that might help him wake up, you know, hearing a familiar voice, that sort of thing?'

'I think that helps, but some people don't. Some people say they can hear, but you can't tell. You could try.'

She went back to her spot outside, and left me with Billy, so I moved closer to the bed, and started to talk to him.

'Billy, mate, it's Archie Taggerty. I'm really sorry this happened to you, but I swear it wasn't a hard punch at all, just a little tap – it wouldn't have even put *me* down, and I was half expecting to go down once or twice. But I thought: *Nothing ventured, nothing gained.* Anyway, I just want you to know that I'll stick by you, no matter what. I know I can't do anything, but I want you to know that I'll keep being your mate, no matter what. And if the nurse is right, you know, about you hearing my voice and everything, then maybe it'll help. I know what you're thinking: *Is that that Archie Bloody Taggerty out there, giving me a right royal earbashing? He's got a bloody cheek turning up here, probably came to the hospital to give me another smack while nobody's looking. Little crippled bastard. Just wait till I'm up and about, I'll give him Richmond Bloody Terrier.* You probably will too, worse luck. Anyway, I'll just hang around for a while, if it's alright with you. Besides, I've got nothing better to do. Ruthie's gunna drop me like a hot spud after this.'

There was a gentle hand on my shoulder, and I looked up, and there was Ruth, and she was looking at Billy and crying quietly, and her cheeks were read with tears. I looked at her, I wanted something from her, a sign, I suppose. But she didn't take her eyes off Billy, and just stood there behind me, crumpling up her hanky. She didn't look at me, but she didn't take her hand away, either.

Well, I wasn't welcome in the Magee house, but I found out from Ruth that it was only Billy's mum that put her foot down. Everyone else understood, and it was well known that the punch wasn't a foul, but just bad luck. I spent my days at the hospital, visiting Billy, and the only time I left was when his family came in to see him, and tell him all the news, when the nurse would come and get me.

'Archie, it's the family, they're here. Best you shoot down the corridor and find an empty room and read for a while and I'll come and get you when they've gone.'

I was very grateful for the nurses, because the hospital had visiting hours which the family always observed and which I always ignored, and under the circ's, the nurses seemed to think that this was fair enough. So I'd disappear for a while, or go for a walk, or a get a cuppa downstairs.

The day came when I came in and there no Billy, just an empty room, as if no one had ever been there. I thought he must have died in the night, and I stepped over to the nurses station.

'Sister,' I said, 'could you please tell me what happened to Billy Magee? I'm his friend.'

'Billy has been transferred to an observation ward.'

'Does that mean he's awake.'

'No, it means there's no change, but we can't keep him here all the time.'

'No, I s'pose not.'

I knew how these things worked. In Cairo, they filled the cotton warehouses with the wounded, then, when the flu broke out, they started putting up huge tents like circus tents for them, and then they started commandeering hotel verandahs and so on. They couldn't get enough space.

'Could you tell me where he is, please. I need to visit him.'

The nurse gave me directions, and it turned out he wasn't in the main hospital at all but in some old wooden place stuck out the back, but still big enough to hold a hell of a lot of people. It wasn't an observation ward at all, but a place for old people who were dying, mostly of cancer, I think, or something else pretty horrible. The nurse told me that they only allowed visitors on Saturdays, and if someone died, which happened ever few hours, when they'd send a telegram to the relatives. They let me in because, as usual, they took one look at me and decided that I wasn't worth worrying about. That was the story of my life.

A lot of the patients were unconscious, and a lot of them were just groaning that peculiar kind of deep rumbling groan that comes from opium. I wasn't worried about being in the room, because I knew from Cairo, that they always separate the flu and TB cases and shove them in their own ward, and besides, in Melbourne the TB cases were usually sent down to the leper hospital to die. That's what Billy was there for, I reckoned, to die. The nurse took no notice of him, and it seemed to me that she would only check him when I asked her to. He was still breathing, of that I could be sure, and of nothing else, so I settled in among the smelly, rotten dying, and told him about my day.

It was in the middle of the night some time, when the gas was turned down low, and the coughing and groaning in the huge room seemed to get worse, for some reason, when I felt that familiar touch on my shoulder. I didn't look up, this time – I was too ashamed. And as before, Ruth didn't sit for an hour or so, but just stood there, being sad and, I could tell, rung out, as if it was all her fault. I wanted to tell her that it was all my fault, but her hand told me that that wasn't true either. The long sad fingers told me that this was just a natural outcome, like the sun warming the skin, or the birds chirping. This was the turning of the world. It changed nothing between her and me. She was right about that, I could feel the truth of it, it changed nothing between us, but it reinforced a conversation we'd had before, and would have to have again, an urgent one.

Did I want Ruth to come and stand and look down at me, like that? I'd never thought about how she felt about me in that way, only in the way of a bloke who's on top of the world. But when you're at the bottom of the world, you think about the same things, only differently, and other truths pop up, the ones you couldn't have gotten while you were on the top. Ruth loved me and I had to give up boxing. That was the truth.

Well, Ruth often turned up while I was visiting Billy, as she'd worked out that I was a regular visitor, perhaps by talking to the nurses, I don't know. But we never spoke when we were together there – it was like being in a church; you don't speak to other people because the only possible reason a person could have for going into a church was to talk to God. It was the same with Billy, except that we never spoke to him, either, except in our hearts, at least speaking for myself – no that's not true, speaking for the both of us. But of course whenever Ruth was absent, I'd be talking to Billy about all kinds of things. I'd tell him the news about the pollies and the footy and races, though I had no idea if he was a racing man. But just on the off-chance that he had a fondness for the ponies, as most men of sportsmen did, I told him about all the shenanigans at the Jockeys Club, and which stewards were bent this week, and which horses were carrying a bit of something to snort as well as a lead weight, and which jockeys had been paid to have a bad ride, none of which was a secret, really, except from the ordinary mug punters, who placed their bets without taking the trouble to look into what was what, and believe me, what was always what.

I told Billy about me and Ruth, too, as I thought it was right and proper that he knew how things were, and besides, I thought, what if he does get a bit hot under the collar? Might do him good, you never know. Those bloody doctors had no idea how to help. So I told him the truth. In fact, you might say that that was exactly what I did when I was with Billy; I told him everything about myself, the truth about how I fought, and how I expected to lose, and how bad I felt about how things turned out.

'Billy,' I says. 'Billy, it's Arch again. Yeah, I know, what a pain in the arse it must be for me to turn up every five minutes, bore you half to death and not give you a chance to sleep, which you probably need, and even worse, turn up with your sister to boot. And speaking of Ruthie – yeah, you heard right, there's no need to laugh, I do call her Ruthie – she's probably going to turn up later, so when you're on the mend, I'd appreciate it if you didn't mention these visits of mine – I don't know why I bother, really. I mean, this is just between the two of us, because we're mates. I'm sure Ruthie'd think I was a real no-hoper if she heard the drivel I come out with when I'm talking to you. But what else have we fighters got to talk about, eh? Bugger all, I reckon. Anyway, so I s'pose you want all the news from Richmond town. Well, I'm sorry to say, there ain't none. Nah, just kidding. Actually there's plenty of news, though I'm not sure if you'd know all the people involved.

First of all, let me tell you about the raid on Wing's casino. You know Charlie Wing has a casino above his fish and chip shop, don't you? You don't? Well, I find that very hard to believe, young Billy, because it's been there since the flamin' gold rush, or so I was reliably informed by a boy on a bike. Well, the bloody wowsers – what d'yer mean: *What bloody wowsers?* – the wowsers from the local Callithumpian Bloody Church, I suppose. Well, these wowsers got it into their heads to rid the fair city of Richmond of gambling once and for all, and thought they'd make a start at Wing's casino. So last Saturday, they organised a huge crowd to turn up at the Temperance Hall and gathered until the place was busting at the seams, and then off the went up Church St in a great mob in the night. There were so many of them that they couldn't fit on the footpath, and walked up the middle of the road, holding a big white banner that said *THE WAGES OF SIN*, or some such – I'm pretty sure it was *THE WAGES OF SIN*. So they held up the trams and everything, and as they went they had a tram right behind them ringing his bell like mad, which only created a bigger stir.

Well, Billy Boy, the good Callithumpians of Richmond had but little schooling in the ways of the Chinaman, and certainly were not aware, as is every self-respecting sinner in our fair city, that the only way to get into Wing's casino is through the back door, there being no front door, and that the said back door is in the lane around the back. They were not aware of this important fact, which I think you will agree, should be Lesson One for every Callithumpian, coming ahead of the first rule of Callithumpianism: *Though shalt not thump the Lord's tub after eleven pm, except on the Sabbath when the tub-thumping is banned altogether.*

So they arrive at the doorway between the laundry and fish and chip shop – which is actually the stairway to the cat-house – which is manned by respectable door-keepers who are all for a little bit of fun, and who instantly grab a wowser each and proceed to reduce him to some kind of mash. The other wowsers give a great 'Hurrah!' and pour into the stairway like ants in a treacle tin, and swarm up the stairs. Well, not knowing the area at all, as some of us do, and seeing nothing but what looks might like the upstairs part of a hotel, they open every door, and barge in, wielding axes and whatnot, ready to bust any baccarat tables they happen to see. But do they see these tables, or roulette wheels, or the devil's own cards being dealt amid piles of filthy lucre? No, young Billy, they do not. All they see, before they can avert their eyes, are the bare arses and pretty pussies of Richmond's finest men and hostesses, having it away with gusto.

I am told that the wowsers who happened upon the *Johnny and Joanie* room are still in shock and actually needed to be given a fortifying snifter before they were up to going home and explaining to the little lady wowser waiting there just what went wrong, and why they call it the *Johnnie and Joanie* room, and good luck to them on that score. Laugh, I nearly died. Bloody Callithumpians! The sooner they all join the Union of Catholic Sinners, they better off they'll be. You will excuse me, Billy my son, while I pay a visit to the little boy's room and dream up ... I mean, *recall*, some more news to pass on to you.'

And I get up to take a break from that humid place of loneliness, to get a lungful of fresh air, and look up and see Ruth leaning against the wall, looking at the floor. The only light is a low gas light down at the nurse's station, and it glows behind her head like a halo. She looks up and me and there is tear at the bottom of her face, trying to decide whether to chance the drop to the lino. I put her forehead on my shoulder as gently as she had put her hand on mine the last time I had seen her, and I think it is going to be one of those conversations we have where we don't speak at all, but I hear myself saying to her: 'This is no place for you, love. D'yer see, you're only torturing yourself. I'll do the visiting for both of us, and you drop in every now and then to see how he's going, if you like. Now, come in and say hello to Billy, and I'll take you home.'

She comes in, still without saying a word, and goes over to Billy and kisses him on the forehead, and whispers to him for a while, and strokes his hair. Then she sits and hold his hand and looks down again. As I look at her I realise that she is wasting away, and has not been eating. It lends to her a certain elegance, especially her hands, but it is a dangerous elegance that I've seen before in men who have wasted away from shell shock. I decided that I would never see her looking like that again. I promised myself, and I promised Ruth, as well. All that remained was to tell her.

15 Ruth's Concerns

I didn't have to work. I had money from the USA, lots of it, and I was even thinking of setting up an Australian Company. Les was back, though Shorty was still in America, making money hand over fist.

One Saturday, I took Ruth to the flicks, and as we were walking home, I says to her.

'How'd you feel about me setting up a stunt company, the same as the one over in America, the same as Hard Knocks?'

'What would you have to do?'

'Nothing much, find a bunch of blokes who'd be willing to ride around and take falls, and generally make fools of themselves, and cop a few bruises, find them work, and count money.'

'Is that what you want to do?'

I couldn't tell her the answer to that question, though I wanted to so much it was hurting. I was actually making money from the poems, and Polly Beer had published a few popular books of poems, so I was starting to get worried. Writing was all lies, the thing Ruth hated the most, the one thing, I reckoned, that would turn her against me in a second. I couldn't do what I wanted to do, so I didn't care what I did, and well, Hard Knocks seemed as good as anything.

'Might as well.'

'That's not good enough, Arch.'

'I don't get it, love, I gave up the fight game.'

'You gave it up because of what happened to Billy, not because I asked you to.'

'Well, yeah, I s'pose that's true. But I was going to give it up anyway.'

'So you say, but now we'll never know.'

'Well, it's over, so let's not fight over it.'

'No, of course not. You're right. You still haven't answered my question, about what you want to do.'

'I haven't thought about it.'

'I don't believe you. You've had a lot of opportunities to decide that the thing you were doing was bad for you – being in prison, being in the war, being in the ring. You must have felt how bad those things were for you – you don't have to answer, because I know you, and I know how sensitive you are.'

'Jeez, love, keep it down – someone might hear you.'

'No one will hear us. But I'd like to know what it is that makes you want to get up in the morning and get stuck into it.'

'Into what?'

'Things. Isn't there something special you'd like to do?'

'Well, I dunno.'

'I see... I see, but I don't understand. Arch, this is the first time you haven't been honest with me.'

'You make it hard on a bloke.'

'Rubbish. I'm on your side, and I always have been, didn't you know that?'

'Well, you couldn't have been on my side when I was fighting Billy.'

'I wasn't on anyone's side and you know it. I'm talking about the rest of the time. But now there's something you're not telling *me*.'

There were times when I wished Ruth was as thick as a brick, like a lot of the other girls I'd met, but she was as sharp as vinegar, and never missed a trick. But this was one those women's questions, and you can't do a thing about it.

'I just don't want to talk about all this *what do you want to do* stuff. How would I know? You know me, I just do this and that, whatever comes up.'

'Well, that's not good enough, Arch, as I know you've got it within you to do bigger things that run a stunt company. As far as I'm concerned you'll just be hanging around with the same crowd. And before you try to tell me what a fair dinkum bunch of blokes they are, let me tell you that they only hang around you because you're Archie Taggerty, and you're only Archie Taggerty because you beat a couple of blokes up.'

I couldn't say a bloody thing, of course, because she had me bang to rights, and with not a leg to stand on. She knew my game, and I knew hers, and hers was as straight as a dye, and, given half a chance, I probably would have thrown my lot in with those mugs at the track and casino, and the like. Only Ruth stopped that happening. I was still thinking how hard it is to reason with a woman who's right most of the time, when she piped up again.

'Arch, tell me straight, is Queenie back?'

Well, I was astonished to hear this, for I knew from Les that Queenie was in America, and married to some film producer, and making a fortune looking pretty, which she could do standing on her head, though I'm not sure that's what I meant to say.

'How could you think that? Les tells me that Queenie is married to some movie guy in Hollywood. I don't think she'll ever come back to Australia. Why should she? She's rolling in the stuff.'

'I'll tell why – because she's always been keen on you, that's why. I've known that for years.'

'Ruthie, half the girls in Richmond are keen on me, but the only one I think about is you.'

'Then what's going on? You're keeping something from me, I know it, and I have the feeling it's driving you mad, and then I feel like it's driving *me* mad, as well. What is it Arch, are you in trouble?'

'Nah, I don't need to do shady things to get by, you know me.'

'Then it's about what you want to do, isn't it?'

'Maybe it is, but I don't feel like talking about it just now. I have to think for a while. But you needn't worry, because I won't let anything come between us.'

'I hope so, because I already feel like something's coming between us. So what are you going to do then, start up this stunt company?'

'I don't know. It was just an idea. There's money in it, you know.'

'You said you had lots of money.'

'I just want to think about things for a while, about this work thing. And then I'll tell you what I've got in mind.'

Tell her what I had in mind! Jesus, I was losing my flaming mind, no mistake. My father was a useless man. He drank, he cursed, he worked when he felt like it, which was little, and not so hard that he strained his drinking arm. You might say – those that knew him well enough to watch him knock over a jug said – that he was a fair man with a verse, the poet's gift, the ability, a rare one, to while away the best part of a lifetime spouting verse. Trouble was, you couldn't make head or tail of what his poetic ravings, him being drunk at the time, and so legless, indeed, that he would have to be helped to his feet and supported when the poetic muse grabbed him by the family jewels. He might have been a poet, I don't know. I only know that he was as useful as an udder on a bull, and never produced a memorable line of poetry in his life, leastways, nothing that was ever written down. 'Drunks and poets!' my mother would say, and nothing more, and I understood.

There was a kind of thrill that happened inside me when my father got up to recite some line or stanza that had suddenly came to him, but would never write down. I'm too ashamed to repeat any of that stuff here, as I still remember bits and pieces, of course. But I made a vow, to myself, never to follow in his footsteps. I have never drank to excess, though I'm not a wowser. And I have never struck a woman – well, there was that once. But I have broken that vow, and I have spouted poetry, to my shame. It's true, your worship, that I spouted the said poetry to soothe the torture of a dying mate, I had at the time little choice, for a part of me was dying as well, or maybe it already had, I don't know. Anyway, we were both in that hole together, when that same gun that produced that crater was quite capable of causing another round like the last to fall on that spot and take me to my maker, whatever bastard that was.

I lived with the thrills of the poems, lived with them as I lived with the man, put up with his shameful behaviour in front of his wife and children, and whoever else happened to be there. To me it was a wonderful thing, to hear those cryptic words, or sometimes fairly plain and familiar words, coming out of that silly man in cryptic terms, twisted and meaningful only completely to my father, and to no one else, for poetry is pure self-indulgence, and can rarely be used for any purpose. But the soldier in the hole knew nothing about all this. All he knew was that he was dying, and that he had a mate, and some water, and I had put into his head some images that he might find useful, soothing; I don't know what else, not having died myself.

To become a poet would be the beginning of the end. I inherited my father's misshapen body, and some of his misshapen ideas, about hurting men's bodies for a living, punching men in the nose to show them that I was not a man to be trifled with. I had inherited more than that, I discovered: the power to make poetry, and perhaps more than that, the power to hurt women and children. Would I discover those powers as well? Would I hurt Ruth? I had been content to hate my poetry for what it might do to me alone, but now I found a new reason to be uncomfortable, as if I could be any other way. I tried on the discomfort of the poetry and found that it fitted like a glove, and that it was therefore a kind of discomfort that was made for me, like a horseshoe for a horse, and that I had better wear it. It was just one more form of suffering. Without it I might have fitted in to the world a little more easily, but that was not my destiny.

I knew a bloke in the Light Horse Support Unit, Charles Mansour, he was from Broadmeadows, and he was swept up in the recruitment drive for the war, but as he was a city bloke, they assumed that he couldn't ride, and he was given a job feeding horses, just like every other city kid they rounded up. And that was because nearly all the blokes in the Fourth Light Horse were from the bush, or at least from properties and farms, and had been riding horses since they were kids, and needed no training, though as I discovered, it's one thing to be able to ride, and another to know about horses, and I soon discovered that I had a talent for getting along with horses, which is why, I suppose, I've been so successful at the track.

So this bloke, he was a natural at whatever he did. When he shovelled feed, he made it look as if he'd been doing it all his life, even when he paraded for work, he was spotless and clean, and this is in the middle of a war, mind you. But it was when he hopped on a horse and rode him around for a bit of an exercise, even without a saddle, he looked like he could do no wrong. We weren't supposed to ride the horses, of course, being city louts, but he came from a family of horse people, you see, and knew horses like I knew boxing gloves. For his smart turnout alone he was made a sergeant, and when we got to Cairo, and he was seen riding a horse for the first time, he was given a crash course in officering at the British headquarters, and disappeared into the Regiment as a subaltern. When I last saw Charles, it was at Gaza, and in the middle of a great throng of dirty, tired horses and men, he alone looked like he was posing for a recruiting poster, looking tall in the saddle, and with a moustache a few blokes I know would kill for. I rode up to him, for a chat.

'I knew that smart riding of yours'd get you into trouble, sir,' I said, saluting.

'Archie, what the hell are you doing on a horse? Don't tell me you pinched it.'

'Believe me, it wasn't my idea – things sort of got out of hand. But as it turns out I've got the sweetest mount in the whole Brigade, sir.'

'Well, that's one horse that'll be well taken care of.'

'Thanks sir. Anyway, enjoy your battle.'

'That's the plan, Corporal. Good luck, mate.'

See, now there was a bloke that would fit in no matter where you bunged him. I swear if the Turks had gotten their hands on him, he would have made himself at home, and learned the lingo, and probably ended up convincing them that they would be better off giving up and going home, which someone eventually did – probably him.

It was a terrible thing to leave Ruth in that state, not knowing what was wrong, but being sure that something was up, and worst of all, being suspicious. But I wanted to amount to something, and I couldn't imagine telling even her what was going on inside me. I couldn't ask her to throw in her lot in with a man who'd chucked over everything to write poetry, for that was the desire deep down that was tearing me to bits. If I let this devil out, surely it would turn on me and take what was left of me, the vulnerable part of me that I protected like a new-born baby, and plunge it into drink and violence, like my father, or worse, madness.

Was I not a violent man? Those who knew me thought me a mild kind of man, but only for a boxer. Your ordinary tea-shop crowd would think me a violent man, if they only knew I was a boxer, and nothing else. And they were right. I was my father waiting to happen, all over again. It was bad enough when I had only my self-respect to worry about, but now I had Ruth to think of. I would not subject her to that indignity, of being married to a drunken, woman-bashing or lunatic poet.

But to explain that to her would seem like just so much raving, of the kind for which they lock people in mad-houses. How could she be expected to understand? She couldn't. Even I was having the devil of a time trying to get to the bottom of it. But one thing I knew, this poetry was not the work of God, who is our mate – not that God has ever paid much attention to me, if you don't count Ruth – but of the Devil, who is mischievous and cruel. For poetry in the hands of a strong man may be a gift, and of some use (though I perhaps wouldn't go that far), but in the hands and head of a fool, it's more like the fiery torch of the firebug.

That night I got out the poems and read them. I was hoping to see something in them apart from folly. I couldn't think for the life of me why they were in the world, like people you see who you wonder might be happier dead. I wondered that about my father constantly while he was alive, wondered if he might be better off dead. I know that I would have been better off, and so would Mum and the rest of the family. I was so sure of it that when he did eventually kick the bucket, I thought it was for the best, the way people talk of someone who passes away from consumption.

I enjoyed reading the poetry. It had become my secret vice, so much so that it reminded me of the secret vice of the priests 'which takes hold of a boy when he is alone,' for which reason the priests and brothers exhorted us to be constantly in the company of others – boys, that is. My secret vice had two parts: writing the poetry and revisiting it in the night like a bit of fluff on the side. I would usually wrote the first draft of a poem in a clumsy, furtive hand, using a dirty pencil, on dirty paper. Also, it was my habit to make little hatch marks and chicken scratchings when I wasn't actually writing. It was altogether a dirty business.

Only the poetry I sent off to *The Argus* was written in ink on paper that I bought at the stationers. That poetry was to me just as iniquitous, but I was prepared to pass it off as respectable as long as I thought an editor might fall for it. I wanted it to be baptised, I suppose, because we were taught that even the most despicable person, once he is baptised will, on the day of final judgement, be accepted into God's presence. I was not sure what God would make of this poetry (or, for that matter, anyone else's) but I had a strong faith in the power of baptism. Had I not witnessed the failure of the Turks, who were not lacking in manly characteristics, and had the fastest horses I've ever seen off a race course? This was a failure that was widely attributed to their ungodliness, and the fact that they were not true baptised Christians, as were the rest of us, not counting the Jews (who invented God in the first place) and the Callithumpians, of course.

I read the poems night after night, doing something to my mind in the process, feeding my sinful state, so that it grew fatter. Pretty soon, my anguish became so much a part of my life that I expected it, I looked forward to it. I enjoyed it. In the city, I went to the library and read the *Bulletin*, and the other rags that published poetry. My daimon – I admit it – seemed pleased with me.

I sat there for a while in that churchy place and let the smell of the cedar steady me, as it does, and considered the corner I had boxed myself into. Even If I let the world know that I was Polly Beer – what a peculiar thought to suddenly turn up out of the blue, how silly – I would obtain only the relief that comes from realising that I was a bigger fool than I thought I was, if that is possible. I would be entirely less than I am, and I need all that I am if I am to be any kind of man, and if I am to keep Ruth's respect, which seems at the moment to be in a fragile state.

Also – and this I realised is far worse – I would be seen to be a man who calls himself Polly, and no amount of explaining would change the fact that I did that, and did it as a soldier in the Light Horse Brigade, where if a man happens to get a letter from his dying mum telling him that his name is not in fact Dave but Polly – or any name of that kind – he is expected to slope off to some quiet place and shoot himself, after first shooting his horse, so that his horse wouldn't have to bear the shame.

I had brought that on myself, that Polly thing, as I had wanted the poem – the first poem, which I thought would be the only one – to be not only anonymous, but unquestionably not my work. Let it be the work of some Polly woman. And it was so. I could only shoot my mouth off now if I was prepared to give up everything, including Ruth, and move to a move to a place where men were more understanding, which would be a different country, for one thing.

In fact, the only place I had come across where men were more understanding was Hollywood, which was a kind of lunatic asylum that needed no walls, because no wanted to leave, and in fact, everyone outside was busting a gut to get into it. That was definitely the kind of place where a man might call himself pretty much anything he liked and would not only be accepted but would find himself acting in a movie to boot. Hollywood is a place which knows no shame, because it knows no sin.

But all of this public admission stuff would have meant giving up Ruth, and that was the one thing I would never do. I would have to give up poetry instead.

16 Marriage

Ruth's pregnancy was inevitable, but it changed everything. Her family was understanding, but unsympathetic. My own family was basically stuck in a reaction to the Magees' disapproval of me as a potential husband. I was not good enough for their daughter, sister, you name it. I had been in prison for a serious crime and I was a boxer, and a dirty one at that, and still was, even though I hadn't lifted a glove since the night of the championship fight. Billy was still in hospital, though he'd been moved to Coode Island. After the war the hospital there was kept and used as a kind of hold-all hospital complex for Melbourne's permanent patients: the terminally ill, consumptives, lepers, plague carriers, people who were under quarantine, and the like.

There was also a place, run by the nuns, for people like Billy. It was a huge place, and mostly contained people who had survived factory and car accidents, but who needed to be taken care of permanently. Billy's family visited once a month, as they were told that if there was any change, they would be told. He was expected to die there. I went visiting a couple of times a week, which drove everyone crazy, as Ruth's crowd thought that my mysterious other business was certainly criminal, while Ruth thought I was seeing Queenie, even though I had offered to show her Queenie's letter to Les, in which she discussed her marriage.

The pain of not having that feeling between us was a terrible pain to have, probably for both of us, but for Ruth it was not caused by any kind of rejection by me, but by her suspicion that I was having it away. In the end, matters went too far, and I decided to tell her everything.

'Ruthie, it's time I told you what I've been doing with my nights.'

'No, Arch, you don't have to. You're your own man. If you tell me you've been taking care of business, that's good enough for me.'

'See, that's the problem right there. You say it's alright, but your voice has no softness in it, not trust. It sounds tired and hard.'

'I'm having a bloody baby.'

'That's not how I would have said it.'

'Then how would you have said it?'

'I would have said that we are having a baby, just like that. The way you say it, it's not a good idea.'

'I feel as though nothing that has happened to me in the last few months has been my choice. You're never here –'

'That's not true.'

'That's how it looks to me. Even Les doesn't know where you go.'

'Well that's what I wanted to tell you. And what's this about Les – have you been down the Gym?'

'See, there you go: upset. I suppose you want to know if I've been spying on you.'

'Course not, you've never done that, never would, for that matter. It's just that you hate the gym.'

'Well, I can go down there if I please.'

'Course you can, course. Anyway, how is Les?'

'Never you mind about Les. You were going to tell me where you've been going.'

'Yeah, well I don't want you blowing your top or nothing.'

'I knew it, it's your bloody Queenie again, isn't it? Les told me she was coming back to Australia ages ago, that she'd split up with her rich Yank.'

'I didn't know anything about that – and she's not my bloody Queenie. I wish you wouldn't talk like that. If you must know I've been visiting Billy at Coode Island.'

'None of the nurses mentioned it to me.'

'I asked them not to.'

'Why, for God's sake?'

'Because I've caused enough trouble already. Your family don't want to hear my name again, and they don't want to know that I've been visiting Billy. They don't want me near him.'

'That's not true.'

'Then how come they never visit when we're there? Don't bother answering. They hate me.'

'They can't think of you without thinking about what happened, that's all.'

'And now they can't think of you without thinking about it, because you're hooked up with me.'

'Because I'm having your baby. Arch, I don't think that's ever going to change, not as long as Billy's lying there like that. One day, when he's better again ...'

I let her go to see if she was going to speak again, but she didn't.

'I wonder, sometimes, what it would have been like if it had been some other bloke I'd KO-ed. I wish it had been someone else.'

'Then some other family would be feeling the way our families feel.'

'Yes, but we wouldn't, would we, and our families wouldn't be hating me like this. We always say that that's the risk we take, and so on, but really, this is not about other people, it's about you and me, and me having let you down.'

'I don't see how the pair of you could have avoided fighting. I asked Billy if that was possible, and he said he was bound to defend his title against all qualified contestants, and that's what you were. Besides, he was confident that he would keep the title easily.'

'He said that?'

'No, he didn't have to. I've always been able to tell how confident he was before a fight, you know, by his manner, and he was confident about that fight. And I know you weren't, and that you planned on having a clean fight and probably losing as a result – that's right, isn't it?'

'I s'pose so, but I was going to give those bookies a fright in the bargain.'

'Well, you did that alright. So what do you talk about when you're visiting Billy?'

'Things I think he might like to hear.'

'You tell him the news?'

'No, not exactly, well, I s'pose you could say that. Look, I talk to him, and that's that.'

She laid a hand on my arm, and sat looking at me, and saying nothing, which we'd spent a lot of time doing since we'd been together. When Ruth said nothing like that, but spoke with her touch, I knew that things would work out, and I felt peaceful. When there was a knock at the door, I went to answer it, thinking it might be one of the lads from the gym, as I had had a lot of callers telling me that the fighters were lined up and waiting to have a go at me, and that there was money to be had in the ring, if only I'd reconsider my decision to quit. When I opened the door, there was Queenie.

'Hello, Arch. Long time no see.'

'Queenie.'

'What, not even "hello"?'

'Queenie, this isn't a good time.'

'Replaced me as soon as my back was turned, eh? Well, don't be shy, introduce me.'

'No, Queenie. Maybe another time.'

But it was too late.

'Arch!' came the sharp voice behind me.

I turned around, and saw Ruth standing there, looking pretty pissed off.

'H'lo,' said Queenie. 'Who's been a naughty boy, then?'

Well, there was no conversation after that, not what you'd call conversation, anyway. Ruth was out of there like a St. Kilda tram, and Queenie invited herself in so as not to let the evening go to waste. I tried to catch Ruth, but she was definitely not talking, and told me so in short, harsh words. I have learnt that the best thing to do when a woman is in that state is nothing, because nothing works. I waited until she had caught the first tram that came along, though it was going in the wrong direction, and went home, feeling like everything had gone wrong at once, though really, only one thing had gone wrong, though it was the worst possible thing.

I walked through the open door and found Queenie ensconced in the living room like the Queen of Sheba, wearing not much more than Betty Blythe did, and looking happy with herself.

'So that was the little lady, was it? I know her from somewhere.'

'Doubt it, she's never worked the street.'

'Bit tall for you, isn't she, Arch? Though I s'pose it doesn't matter much if you're lying down, as I see you have been.'

'Ruth is to be my wife, at least she was till you turned up.'

'Lovely. Well, I wish you luck with that one. I'll be off, as soon as I have that drink you were just about to offer me.'

'I'll have to go over and talk to Ruth. We'll have to have that drink some other time. Or maybe never would be better. I'll see you later.'

I walked to the front door, and grabbed my hat on the way out, leaving the door open.

'Ruth Magee,' Queenie shouted, as I left. 'Brother's a fighter.'

I don't know why I went over to the Magees'. I was told that I was not welcome, and Ruth's little nipper even threatened me if I didn't piss off for good. It was as if my face at the door was the plunger that fires the dynamite charges, and they all went off at once. I understood, of course. The family had been eating away at itself like a mad dog since the fight, and said not a word. Bottled it all up, which is the Irish way. Now Queenie had come along and uncorked it, without realising what she was doing, because I knew that, while Queenie wasn't the brightest penny in the till, she had not a bad bone in her body.

I sat on the gutter's edge for a long while, contemplating the way things happen: when you least expect them to, and after a while walked home, which was a long walk. But I wanted to give Queenie time to get bored stiff with her own company, which she eventually would, and go home, wherever that was now. When I got home, Queenie was in our bed, and I had to wake her up, and give her the boot, which was a new thing between me and her, as we had been friends for a long time. But the way she saw it, she might as well stay now that she was here, and anyway, didn't I need the company? It took a while for me to convince her that I wanted to her to go, and that I wanted to patch things up with Ruth, but she finally got the hint. When she left, she was as pissed off as a bull-ant. Whatever I was doing wrong, I was doing it quite nicely.

What do you do with an angry woman? I had no idea, so I decided to wait, and went round to the Magees' place every day and sat on the gutter, until everyone in the street knew who I was and why I was there making a bloody fool of myself. For all I knew, half of bloody Melbourne knew. I was sitting on the gutter. One day Ruth's dad comes out and sits beside me, and rolls a smoke.

'Smoke?'

'No thanks, Mr Magee.'

'She's not coming out. I thought it was time someone came out and told yer.'

'Then I'll wait. She'll come out eventually.'

'No, she won't.'

'Mr Magee, I know you know Ruth pretty well, but I know a few things about her too, and I know she loves me and she knows I love her, and as soon as she remembers, she'll open that door and come out.'

'No, she never will.'

'How can you be so sure?'

''Cos she's in Warragul.'

'Strewth! How long's she been there?'

'A week.'

'You mean I've been sitting out here like a shag on a rock for a bloody week for nothing, and all the galahs in the street knew it?'

'That's about the size of it.'

'Terrific. Well, I'm off to Warragul then.'

'Fair enough. And for what it's worth, I know you've been on the up and up with Ruth, never doubted it. Neither does Ruth, probably. But the whole family's still upset, and will be for a long time. And now there's the baby. Mrs Magee's spittin' chips in there. It's enough to drive a man to drink, 'cept I'm already a drinkin' man, as you know. I reckon things'll change when the baby's born, but don't expect the family to suddenly start treating you like a long-lost son or anything. That could take a hell of a long time. Well, that's all I have to say. Here.'

He passed me a piece of paper, quietly, so that he would not be seen doing so from the house. I unfolded it and read an address in Warragul.

'Thanks, Mr Magee.'

'Yer didn't get that from me, mind.'

I sat there, looking like the bloody fool that I was, and Ruth's father sat beside me smoking his fag and looking like what he was. Finally, he let the butt fall between his feet, and stood up. He was in no hurry to go back inside, where he was going to cop a sharp word or two, no doubt. Before turning away, I shook his hand, and was surprised at how weak and frail his grip was, though I knew the cause.

I was dressed in my good clothes, as I had dressed in the hope of seeing Ruth, and so all I had to do was choof off down to East Richmond station to catch the Warragul train. I found out that that particular train only goes twice a day, and didn't even stop at Richmond, so I spent the best part of the day, doing this and that, and ended up dropping into Ryrie's to see how everyone was going, as it was only a stone's throw from Flinders Street station, where the Gippsland train stopped.

Ryrie's hadn't changed, and it seemed to me that no one was surprised to see me. It was as if I had finally come to my senses, and decided to come back to the ring, and defend my title, which I had not formally renounced, and was therefore still mine for the time being. Everyone gave me the big hello, of course, as everyone wants to know the champ, even if he doesn't know them from Adam. So I'm doing the rounds, shaking the odd hand, and so on, because none of these blokes have seen me since the Magee fight, me having disappeared. I was there for a fair while I suppose, and was settling quite well with Ryrie, and managing to dodge all the questions about my next fight, and I was also keeping one eye on the clock, because I wanted to catch the train without having to hurry, as the trip to Warragul was a longish one, and I wanted to get a good seat.

I finally met someone who was able to tell me where Les was, and it was just across the road at Y & J's, and so I went over to pay my respects, and sure enough, found Les sitting in a back bar having a quiet smoke. Naturally, he's pleased to see me, though I can see by the look on his face that he is surprised as well.

'Arch, mate. I didn't think I'd see you in this part of the world again. How are you?'

'I'm fit as a fiddle, Les. I just thought I'd drop in and say hello to the fellers, before I catch a train.'

'Fair enough.'

'You could've told me Queenie was back,' I says, sitting down.

'Just found out meself. And speak of the devil,' says he, standing suddenly.

'G'day, Arch.'

'G'day, love. You would have to turn up when you did. Dropped me right in it.'

'Arch, since when did you need my help to get into trouble? And speaking of which, when's the big day?'

'Soon, that's all I can say.'

'Les was just filling me in on Billy Magee. I didn't really know him, but I gather he was a straight shooter.'

'He was, and now he's crook, real crook. I went to see him in the hospital –'

I stopped, not sure if this was relevant. They waited.

'He's still unconscious.'

'Strewth, what'd yer hit him with, a glove full of nuts and bolts?'

'That's not funny – I barely touched him. It was a fluke, that's all. I feel as sick as a dog, but what can I do?'

'I hear you've jacked it in.'

'That's right. I'm thinking of starting an Aussie version of Hard Knocks. That should make a few quid.'

'And what does the little woman think of that?'

'She's not keen. Not keen on anything at the moment. Look, I've gotta go. Queenie, do me a favour and give me a bit of room, will you. Ruth thinks I've been lying to her. She thinks ... God knows what she thinks.'

'Alright, Arch, you know me. Anyway, they tell me Les's got a few quid. I might latch on to him.' She grabbed Les's arm. 'Les, let's talk about the Hard Knocks thing some time.'

I was across the road and on the train in a few minutes, and found myself a nice comfortable seat. The train was pretty full, as it was carrying a lot of suburban passengers to Caulfield, where they could change trains. After Caulfield, it would a quite trip. I sat in the plush black leather seat, and thought about what I would say to Ruth when I got to Warragul, a couple of hours away. I must have dozed off, because when I woke up, the compartment was empty, and the train was well out of the suburbs and heading for the bush. All that could be seen through the rushing smoke of the engine was the flashing past of the occasional line of houses beside the railway line.

Eventually, the train stopped, and the last of the city passengers alighted, and a few country types got on, on their way back to Gippsland. We were at Dandenong. As the train started to pull out of the station, I looked out of the window in the compartment's door to the other side of the station, and saw another train sitting at the station, heading for Melbourne. We were pulling away from it, though still travelling slowly, and I saw in the window, Ruth, looking characteristically sad but determined. I jumped up, and slid the door aside, and ran down the aisle, trying to attract her attention, but she was left behind. I went to the door, but we had left the station, and were picking up speed. I walked the length of the train, looking and finally found a conductor.

'What's the next stop, please?'

'Berwick.'

'How far is that?'

'Oh, not far. Twenty minutes.'

'Thanks, mate.'

I went back to my compartment to wait for Berwick and watched as lesser stations came and went, clothed in drab yellow paint. As the train slowed for Berwick, I slid open the passageway door, and took a step through, but a fist hit me in the stomach so hard it knocked me back through the door into the compartment. My fists were up before I hit the floor, because I knew that street hooligans don't mind hitting a bloke when he's down. However, these two weren't using their fists, but their boots, and it was only a matter of seconds before I was incapable of fighting back, and feeling the sickening sound of bones breaking in my face and a body being wrecked. But the most telling blow I received was a kick to my right hip that had me squirming in agony like a worm, for that kick told a tale: these men knew who I was.

They didn't speak while all this torture was going on, and dragged me down the passage to the end of the car, then one of them flung open the door to the outside, and the both dragged me to the door of the train, until I was balancing on the edge of the train. I could hear the steam engine up front, and could barely breath for the engine's stinking smoke, and below me, where the gravel raced by, there was only a green blur. Then suddenly, they pushed, and I was airborne, sailing away from the train. There was a thud and a splosh, and I was drowning in foul muddy water.

17 Down and Out

I woke up in a room in which the walls had been painted a nasty red on the bottom half and a weak white on the top. I felt wrong straight away. I couldn't move so I looked around. On one side of me I could see nothing at all, my brain seemed to register a dull darkness there, and no pictures. It did register pain, though, pain where my eye was. My other eye did better, and gave me the wall and lights, lights that bounced off surfaces that didn't need light, and underplayed planes that I was curious about. There was movement in the form of shadows, mainly on the red half of the wall, and they seemed to be speaking.

Suddenly I realised that I had not been awake, but dreaming, and that now I was awake, not that I wanted to be, not that I didn't want to be. I didn't want anything, and I didn't really think about it. I saw the same wall, but now it seemed a little warmer. The light seemed a little brighter. My body was being touched, pulled and pushed here and there, I don't know where – it was just an idea, and I lost interest. There was sharp pain, where the pushing and pulling was. And I was crying.

Then it dawned on me that the crying wasn't coming from me at all, but someone who was lying in the same place as me, someone larger than me in some places, and smaller in others, who seemed to be having a hard time. That other person was giving *me* a hard time with all his whinging. I wished he would die.

Time had passed, because the present had a quality of nowness about it that told me that some time had already passed, though I couldn't remember its content, and I didn't care. I only knew that I was awake, and felt sure that feeling that I'd been dreaming. But I hadn't been asleep. I was still staring at a stained ceiling and feeling pain. The pain had been poured into me like water, and found its way into every everything, even my ears, where it was cutting into my mind. It was sound, metallic and clanging, but thin and malevolent. The sounds of doctors and hospitals. I remembered it from Gaza, Port Said and Cairo. It was cutting off, cutting into and cutting out pain, the favourite instrument of the surgeon. They were going to cut off my leg. Or had they already? Or...what? I had to know.

In the next instant I was more awake, though I had some way to go. I was trying to be more awake, but my body wouldn't move. I wanted to do all kinds of things, get up, run, thump someone, yell, but I couldn't do any of those things. And I passed out.

When I awoke, I was sure it was now. There was a nurse doing something to me, taking my pulse, and not looking at me. I tried to ask her how she was going, and give her one of my winning smiles, the kind I used at the track to get a tip that wasn't just a mug's tip.

She looked at me and kept taking my pulse, as if the last thing she wanted to do was give me a tip. She was short, and freckled, and kind of dumpy, and had straight hair sticking out from her nurses cap, which made her look more like she was cut out work in a cake shop. She looked at me as though I were a plate of lamingtons.

While she was sitting there, a doctor crept up behind her. He had the look of an undertaker who'd been hit with a bucket of whitewash. His hair was straight and multicoloured, and stuck out all over the place, as if he hadn't combed it, and his nose was just a leftover. I can't say he inspired confidence. He looked at me and shook his head and rocked back and forward a little on his heels, making the top half of the wall move.

'Awake, are we? Good. You've had a bit of an accident. Do you remember?'

I tried to say no and shake my head, but all that did was make me wish I had tried to answer yes instead.

'Well you have. We think you may have fallen off a train. What do you think of that?'

I had no thoughts on the subject. It was all news to me, and I reckoned I would have to wait for tomorrow's instalment to see how it all turned out.

'We're going to move you to a new room, then we're going to do a small operation on that hip, which must be giving you a bit of trouble. So no food, I'm afraid, though I know you must be hungry, as you've been here for a few days now. I should also have some news on your brother by and by.'

I thought of nodding that I understood, and changed my mind. I was glad to hear there was going to be news of my brother, of course – a man always is, isn't he? But I didn't remember having a brother. Oh, well, these doctors always know best. I must have a brother somewhere. It shows you how badly I had judged myself to be wide awake.

It turned out that a lot of my problems were caused by the fact that I had a splint of some kind on my neck, and couldn't turn my head. While they were me getting ready for my operation, a nurse came in with a mirror, and held it above me at an angle so I could see the bed next to mine. In it was a boy, a teenager about ten years younger than me. He was asleep. He looked nothing like me, having thick black hair, and a round face, but I could tell by the knowing smile the nurse gave me that this was supposed to me my brother. *He's in for a shock*, I thought to myself. Then I realised I had no idea who I was.

This puzzle still had my mind frozen when they wheeled me into the operating theatre, and knocked me out. And when I was fully awake again, it returned to give me a hard time. It was days before I could speak again, and gradually I was able to get some kind of mushy food into me and drink again, but that was about it. Nurses came in and fed me, and occasionally spoke to me, and at one stage a big copper came in with a tiny notebook and pencil, and asked me a lot of useless questions about my train trip, and seemed to be pretty cheesed off that I wasn't able to answer them. Who'd be a copper?

The surgeon came back eventually and asked me to write down my name, as I had come in with no identification, and they put a pencil in my good hand and held a writing pad for me, but I couldn't remember my bloody name, and though I busted a gut trying to remember, nothing happened, to my embarrassment. I wondered if my brother knew, and indicated him with my eyes. The nurse piped up.

'The boy's parents came to fetch him. They said he wasn't your brother. It turns out he was fishing under the railway bridge and you fell on him and knocked him out. Sorry.'

I wrote on the pad: '?'

'I see,' said the doctor. 'Having trouble remembering, are we? Not surprised. Nasty cut on the head. It'll come back.'

Well it did come back, though it took weeks, and in the meantime I was moved from the Dandenong and District Hospital, which it turned out was where I was, to the Melbourne Hospital, in the middle of the city. The injury to my hip was a lot worse than they had originally thought, so they decided to start again, and do the job properly. In the meantime, I had no idea who I was, though everyone prompted me as best they could to remember. It wasn't until I had been there for a month that I woke up one afternoon to find a tall, elegant woman sitting by my bed and holding my hand. She had dark brown eyes, with shadows of worry beneath them, and a pale, long face. Her skin was as smooth, and her mouth was wide, and she was pregnant. I looked into her eyes for a long time, and I could see that she knew me well, and I guessed that she was close to me. But as there was no family resemblance at all I guessed that she might have been my wife, though there was no memory of her, even when she kissed me. As I lay there and looked at her, she started to cry, and her tears fell all over our hands. In the end, I let her do the talking, because for me it was all a confused mess.

'I thought I'd lost you,' she said, kissing me again.

I smiled at her as best I could, not knowing how to reply to that remark, which shed no light on the matter at all.

'First, I heard you were dead, then I heard you'd gone bush, then I heard that you'd left for America. I even got Les to find Queenie, and ask her point blank if you were with her.'

She laughed.

'What?'

'I just realized that you didn't know that Queenie has a child – she came back from America with him.'

I knew I was supposed to say something, but I was tongue-tied.

'Anyway, I could see that she was worried too, we both started to look for you. The places she took me, I had no idea –'

I must have frowned, because she suddenly gasped and looked closely at me.

'What's the matter? Can't you hear me? For God's sake, say something.'

'I can't remember anything.'

'Oh Jesus Christ,' she said, and sat crying freely, but still holding my hand.

She leaned her head on my chest, and stayed like that for a long time. I thought in the end that she was asleep. It wasn't until I realised that I could smell her hair, that it hit me who I was, who she was, what had happened, the whole story, at least from the time I got the train.

'Ruthie?'

She looked at me.

'Now I remember some of it. I remember you ... and me. It's just bits and pieces.'

'Do you remember falling off the train?'

'I didn't fall: I was bashed and thrown off. I was on my way to see you in ... in ...'

'Warragul.'

'Warragul.'

'But I ended up in a creek. I nearly killed some kid who was fishing, landed right on top of him. Bet he'll never fish by the railway line again.'

'God, I was worried. We looked everywhere. We even asked at the hospital, but they said you weren't there. Then they sent us a telegram to say they thought they had you, and I took one look at you and said: *'That's my husband'*, and they let me in. I've been coming in for three days. I was worried sick. I thought you might end up like ... like Billy.'

'Who?'

'Billy, my brother, oh God ...'

'We're married?'

She looked around and lowered her voice.

'No, but Sister said they wouldn't let me in if we weren't, so I said I was your wife. We were planning to get married anyway – don't tell me you don't remember?'

But it was coming back to me in bits and pieces, smells, colours, textures, movements. Within three days, I remembered everything in perfect detail.

And I remembered prison, Gaza, and the shame of Billy. And I told Ruth that it didn't surprise me that someone would try to kill me, because I had upset a lot of punters in my short, lopsided life.

'But that'll all change,' she said. 'I'm marrying you straight away, and I don't give a bugger for the plans. I'm not losing you again.'

And that's what happened.

The wedding was a low-key and fairly serious affair, and took place up at St Ignatius', the same church we were both baptised in and first received all our other sacraments. The parish priest refused to marry us, so the new curate, Van Hoyle, a man who looked like he could make up his own mind about things, did it himself. I think what changed his mind was the appearance of Ruth's brothers, who threatened to burn the church down. They were both men of fiery disposition, and had the hair to prove it, and so, as the curate was an Irishman (which the parish priest was not), there was in the end no ecclesiastical barrier.

Only a few people turned up, most of them being members of the boxing fraternity, and Ruth's friends. My mother did not turn up, and neither did Ruth's, though her brothers and father did. This struck me as strange, considering that at the time I suspected them of having been the crowd who had me bashed and thrown off the train, that is, until after the wedding itself. We had a conversation down at the Corner Pub, which had let us have the big room for the night, and they sat me down in front of the nervous gaze of Ruth, across the other side of the room.

'Now listen,' said a red-headed Patrick, lifting a beer to me as if he was toasting me, and smiling though his voice was serious. 'Me and Milo here have been making enquiries, discreetly, mind, and we've come up with a name. Now this man is a serious punter, and he not only lost a packet on your last fight, not that we all didn't - except for Ruth, who I understand was the only person in Melbourne who backed you, and as a result, cleaned up - but he lost his temper, he being a man who gets off his bike at the slightest provocation. That man is Joe Griffin, a bloke who likes to have his pound of flesh. He apparently bet against you in every fight you've been in. Can you believe it?'

'Hang on a mo', says Milo, 'we always bet against him too.'

'Yes, but with us it isn't business - we hate him.'

'That's true, and he's still not out of the woods,' he said to his brother, as if I wasn't there.

'No, you're not,' says Milo, turning back to me.

Joe Griffin was a well-known lunatic. He was a man who was not interested in sports except for the money he could make. He was the opposite of everyone else involved in the sporting life. He was also very dangerous, and had been locked up more often that the crown jewels. The rumour was that whenever he was released from jail, the prison crime rate died for lack of interest. It was said that the last time he was in, they released him early to prevent him murdering some bloke who'd owed him money. And this was the bloke who'd rather that Archbold Taggerty, the most misunderstood cove in town, had a fatal accident, than carry on sharing the same air as himself. My thoughts, alarmed as they were, were interrupted by the brothers grim.

'We're telling you this, because we don't want our sister to become a widow and our nephew a fatherless bastard. We reckon you should take Ruth and move back to America. At least that way we know she'll be okay.'

'Perhaps if I have a word with Joe Griffin, he'll see that I'm not such a bad sort of a bloke after all, and leave me alone.'

'P'raps the Queen'll give Archbishop Mannix a knighthood.'

'America, you reckon.'

I must have sighed a bit obviously, because Ruth soon drifted over to me and sat down beside me.

'So what were they up to?'

'They reckon we should go to America. They reckon some unhappy punter put me in hospital, and might do it again when he finds out I'm up and about and thinking of taking up hurdling.'

'America. I don't know, Arch. I don't know anything about the place.'

'Don't forget, I own a bit of it, and it's making money. We could do whatever we liked.'

'Are you talking about Hollywood?'

'There's no other place to go.'

'Arch, there's a couple of things I've been meaning to talk to you about.'

Now I don't know about you, but in my experience, when a woman says there's a couple of things she's been meaning to talk to you about, what she really means is that there's *one* thing she's been meaning to talk to you about, and that one thing is another woman. You'd think that having just married a man, a woman would stop asking if he was having if off with another woman, but that's women for you. So I put an indignant look on my face, and cut her short.

'Ruthie, I haven't seen Queenie for ages, and even if I did I'm long finished with her as a friend of the kind you mean. But I want you to know that I'm not the kind of man to dump his friends, and while Queenie might be a bit rough around the edges' – I said this, though I didn't believe it myself, for Queenie had no edges at all, and you'll have to take my word for that – 'underneath it all she's a brick, and that's that. And if you're to be my wife, let's agree on that, and let it go.'

'Oh Arch, I know it's true about Queenie. It was her that helped me find you when you were missing. I know what a kind heart she has, but you're her favourite, and it's only out of regard for you that she helped me at all. For a woman, that's a big thing. In case you're wondering why she didn't come to the wedding, it's because she thought it would be too embarrassing for all concerned. See? We talked about it. No, it's not about her.'

I must have breathed a sigh of relief, for I could see she was pleased to see me relax for a second. It could have been my first time that day.

'What is it then?'

I couldn't think of anything that'd be an issue. My conscience was more or less clear. And I knew that she didn't know anything about the poetry.

'When I came into hospital, before you got over your operation, I heard you reciting poetry –'

'Ruth, I was off my scone with laudanum and God knows what else. Poetry! Strike me handsome!'

'But that letter that came from Editor of *The Argus* while you were missing. I had to open it because we had no idea what had happened to you. He said you're name was Polly Beer.'

'Hell, Ruthie, a bloke's mail.'

'Arch, I was your wife, or as good as.'

'Well, that's true, love. Polly Beer, you say? As if I'd go around Melbourne calling myself Polly Beer, me, the Bantamweight Champion of Australia.'

'Archie, you know how I feel about lies and secrets.'

That's what made it impossible for me to tell her, this idea of hers that lies and secrets were the same thing. This bloody poetry was following me around like a bad smell, and it was time I cut loose from the whole flaming thing. And there was Billy. I couldn't run out on him. I needed to talk it over with him.

18 A Desperate Man

Everything was wrong about the marriage, despite the look of it being perfect. I had bought a two-storey house in Brougham Street, not a bad sort of a street, and got my mum to move in, but I had overlooked the influence my mother would have on the household. I have mentioned that Mum hated Ruth, well, it was all a horrible mixture of guilt for what I had done, and the fact that Ruth's family hated my guts – fair enough, I suppose – for taking away their lovely Ruth, and their son and brother, who still lay in the nursing home on Coode Island. Also, Mum resented Ruth just for being my wife.

Ruth made it clear from the start that she didn't want my mother moving in, but Mum wouldn't be left alone in her house, and insisted on being included in the family, at least until the baby arrived, when she promised she'd go home. Her presence meant that she was everywhere all the time, or so it seemed, and we had no time alone. She wasn't critical – I couldn't say that – yet she was, if you see what I mean. A look, a sniff, a raised eyebrow, was enough to send Ruth to the bedroom close to tears.

'I can't stand this, Arch. I've never said this before, but either she goes or I go, and this time there'll be no coming back. She rules your life, she is both mother and father, and she is your conscience as well. You're incapable of making a decision when she's around, and we have a lot of decisions to make. That's it, Arch. It's not an ultimatum. It's just the way it is. And God knows, I don't want to go home, either. I'll never live it down, of course. It'll be *I told you* so to kingdom come. But anything will be better than staying here watching what she's doing to you, and to us. That's it.'

She folded her arms on her belly and sat on the bed, where I couldn't get my arms around her and sweet talk her, which she knew was her weak spot.

'She only wants to help.'

'No, Arch, she doesn't. And it's about time you opened your eyes and saw it.'

Well, the conversation went on in this way for some time, and finally, she told me that she wanted my mother out that day, or she would leave by evening. I couldn't see any good coming out of this situation, one way of another, for no one wants to lose their own mother, and I saw this happening, as surely as if she was about to die. Slowly I dragged myself downstairs, wondering how I was going to prepare the ground for the conversation we must have. But when I got downstairs she was gone.

Sure enough, my mother had decided that she was never going to speak to me again. I had broken her heart, and so on. I didn't know whether to laugh or to cry at the performance she gave, but I knew one thing, that we hadn't heard the last of it by a long chalk.

At home, Ruth brightened up straight away, and even visited my mother, to show her there were no hard feelings, but she had the door slammed in her face. I was hopping mad, but Ruth made me do nothing and stay at home until my temper had cooled. She had a way of soothing me that was marvellous. On this particular night, she sang *Always* to me, until I joined in. The house change straight away, with Mum gone, and we even had a couple of visits from Ruth's dad, who was impressed by the size of the house, and even more by the stories I told him about how I made the money that paid for it, in Hollywood.

'I must see this place for myself, one day,' he said, 'especially as there are, as you said, so many of us Irish people there. That would be a rare treat.'

Until that conversation I had not known that Mr Magee was a film fan, but it turned out he was a walking catalogue of films, both Hollywood and Australian, which was a miracle in itself, as I had never seen him sober, and wouldn't have been surprised to hear that he didn't know what day it was. But I didn't encourage him to make the trip, because I could imagine nothing worse than being trapped on a ship with a drunken Irishman all the way to America. I therefore told him that they had prohibition in America, at which he came close to tears, and had to fork out his hanky and blow his nose and wipe his eyes. It was a sad thing to see, but it had to be done.

Telling Mr Magee about Hollywood turned out to be a mistake. He became obsessed with the place, and took to collecting whatever he could in way of magazine pictures, advertisements, and news clippings, and keeping them in a shoebox. Whenever he came around, which he did frequently, he would bring the box, and discuss his latest find. Ruth was happy to see him away from her mother, as he was a different man, and though he always leaned on us for grog, he never got any, because we had learned to keep a dry fridge, for drinking was something the both of us could take or leave.

The trouble started when Mrs Magee decided that enough was enough, and came around to get her husband. She hated me to the point where she would not come to the door and knock, but must stand outside on the street and yell at the top of her lungs – she had lungs of an Irish woman whose ancestors had been frightening the English for centuries – for her husband to stop being a fool and come home, where he had a family to take care of, which made us all laugh, sitting inside looking at our clippings. But finally, he would slowly put away his bits and pieces, and tie a string around the box, and shove his hat on his head. He would have left anyway, we all knew, simply because he was beginning to sober up, and that was something we had never seen, and truth be told were a little nervous of. So off he would go until the next big scene.

The other problem, not that it was a problem, but it was, was the couple next door, the Morgans, who were a nice enough couple, but had no children and no plans to have any. They lived with the aged parents of the woman, who owned the house, and both of them seemed to have well-paid office jobs. The problem was that the husband had a roving eye which Ruth found a bit irksome, while Vera, his wife, and me became instant best friends, which drove Ruth around the bend. It was one of those friendly relationships that can start any time with any person, and tells you that the other person is okay, and you don't need to go through all that bullshit to get to know them when you reckon you already do. Vera's husband, Frank understood this, and considered it to be a sensible attitude, as they were both educated people, but I was not, and it took me a while to realise that when there is no wrong being done there is no need to feel bad.

But Ruth didn't see things that way at all, and many's the night we only turned in when the judges had handed their cards in, and the referee had declared it a draw. The whole thing came to a head when the Morgans invited us to come over for a friendly drink, and Ruth refused. I apologised to the Morgans, and explained that, with the baby about to be born at any time Ruth was as nervous as a shell-shocked colt. But we never did go next door for that beer, in spite of the fact that we continued to live side by side, in duplex houses, and Vera and I exchanged winks as we came and went, more as a show that we were still mates anyway, because it certainly felt that way.

The kindest thing I can say about Ruth during this period is that she didn't take to being pregnant, not that she didn't want to have kids, that wasn't it at all, and I've met women that didn't want to, but she was a nervous, shy type and the whole experience seemed to make every nerve in her body overreact, so that she it took nothing at all to set her off. She was the most loving and gentle person I ever met, but those final weeks were like living with a prickly pear.

I suppose the worst thing about it all was that she seemed to forget that other people existed, and became a highly touchy and even selfish individual, the like of which I had only ever seen in, well I hesitate to say it, prison. She was like someone in a cage, who wanted to be free, but of course she was a prisoner of her own body, and she didn't share that either. I hated to see it, but she would never eat when she got emotional and upset, and her normal vibrant energetic self was exchanged for a self that didn't seem to care that she was pregnant at all, and became sickly, and coughed a lot. She finally went to the doctor, and he gave prescribed her something for the cough, but it only had the effect of making her listless, and bringing back her morning sickness, so that I worried even more.

All of these problems had their ramifications: in conversation, in daily life, and in our relationships with other people And towards the end of the pregnancy, it got to the point where Ruth stopped talking to other people altogether whenever snapping would do, and they stopped talking to her, and it was just a cruel waiting game where we all just watched helplessly and prayed that things would be different when the baby was born.

Only one unexpectedly good thing, well, half-good, came of all this, which was that because I wasn't welcome in my own house, because I got on Ruth's nerves, I had lots of time to visit Billy, which I did every second day. But every time I saw him, he looked a little thinner than the time before, and a shade frailer. Towards the end of Ruth's pregnancy, there was a day when I went in and sat down and took his hand, and I believed I could see right through it. There was a new nurse there at the time, and when she saw me staring, spoke to me gently.

'His time is just about up. You can see through his skin, and that means he's giving up the fight. Is he your brother?'

'No, he's a friend. At least he was.' And I was ashamed of myself for what I was thinking, which was that when Billy died, I'd be thought of as even worse than before, if that were possible.

I sighed, and buried my head in Billy's side, and held his hand, and prayed for him to have a peaceful death and a fast trip to Heaven.

'What will happen...in the end? How...?'

'How will he pass away?'

'He will just stop breathing, probably quietly, without anyone noticing straight away. One of us will come around to check on him, change his water, and he'll be gone. He'll not wake up, if that's what you mean. It usually happens on the night shift.'

'He's been here for months.'

'Then he must be very strong. What happened to him?'

'He was injured in a boxing match. It was just one of those things. He was a boxer.'

'And are you a boxer too?'

'I was, until I knocked Billy out. Now I'm nothing much.'

The nurse came around and pulled up a chair beside me and sat down beside me and put her hand on top of mine, covering my wedding ring.

'I don't think that's true at all.'

She sat there silently with me in the dull light, in the ward full of silent people, all of us waiting to die.

We were sitting there like that when Ruth walked in. She stood in the doorway, framed by a background of dull colours, and a said nothing. She seemed to have run out of energy. I smiled at her as best I could, it being hard to raise a smile any more. The nurse, who didn't know Ruth, sat still, and said nothing. Then she remembered that there were certain things she was supposed to say.

'I'm sorry, but visiting hours are over for the day.'

'So this is your idea of being straight, is it? Well I've had enough.'

The nurse pulled her hand away as if she'd burnt it, which only made matters worse.

'I'm sorry, madam. I was just –'

'Shut up.'

It's a funny thing about hospitals. If you listen hard enough, it always seems as though you can hear every sound in the place from one end to the other, only faintly. I heard Ruth's footsteps all the way to the front door. Then there was silence. Then I heard a string of railway cars being shunted somewhere.

I wandered around Melbourne for a while, feeling the pain in my hip more than usual, knowing that there wasn't much point in going home, not if Ruth wasn't going to be there. I went over to Havelock's Billiards Rooms, and watched a game, and over to Dick Clancy's pub though I didn't really feel like a beer, and had a shandy instead. I was in the main bar, so it wasn't long before coves were giving me the big hello, as if they were my old mates, which they weren't, so I finished my drink. I dropped in at Ryrie's, and watched a couple of lightweights spar, and wondered how Shorty Long was getting on, and whether his nonactive partner should pay him a visit. When I left, there was a steamboat about to go up the river, so I hopped on and took a seat in the stern, and stared at the wash until it lost its meaning.

At home, I was surprised to find Ruth.

'Took your time coming home.'

'If you'd told me you were going to Coode Island, I would have gone with you.'

'I didn't know where I was going till I got there. So do you want to tell me about that woman?'

'You're driving me mad; that was a nurse.'

'She wasn't behaving like one.'

'Yes, she was. Only something's happened to you, and it's killing me, or us.'

'Oh, so I'm the problem. You're running around fucking every woman in town, and I'm the problem.'

'I've never looked at another woman since I first met you, let alone sleep with one.'

'More lies. Well you can keep your bloody nurse, and good riddance to you.'

'Couldn't you see what I was doing at the home, who I was visiting? You've been wondering where I was going – is that what it's all about? I've been with Billy, every moment I could get, month after month. And now the nurse tells me he's fading away. So I can't stop seeing him just because you're seeing things.'

'Oh, so now I'm seeing things. Alright.'

'That nurse was so new she didn't even know who I was; you can ask her.'

'And I suppose you'll tell me you've been going to the Island to tell Billy bed-time stories.'

'Yes.'

'What?'

'Yes, that's right. That's what I've been doing, telling Billy...stories – he deserves it, deserves something special from me. I know the rest of you love him, and can't stand even thinking about him being in that place, but I think about him night and day, about the next story, as you say, I'll tell him when I next see him. His friends have paid him no attention since the accident –'

'Accident my fat aunt.'

'Ruth, please don't say that. You know the fight game, you heard about what happened. That punch shouldn't have hurt him at all'

'None of your blarney bullshit. I'm not listening to any more. I'm leaving.'

'Wait. I have something to show you. After that, you can do whatever you like.'

'Go to hell.'

She was already packed, and had only been waiting so that she could have a barney with me.

'If your mind's made up, at least let me carry your bags for you. You can't carry these.'

'I'll do as I please.'

But I could tell it was the anger speaking, and she let me take them from her, having at least the common sense to take care of herself. So I follow her out of the house, thinking to myself that the whole thing was touched by insanity, and wondering if I could take any more. Well, she made me follow her all up the way to Church Street, and wait while she caught the first tram that came along, and made the tram conductor give her hand up while paying me no attention at all, as if I was the hired bloody help. On the tram, she made a point of ignoring me altogether, which made it clear to all and sundry what the hell was going on between us, and didn't I get some looks that would have knocked the stuffing out Jack Dempsey.

I gritted my teeth and told myself that it couldn't get any worse, and that she'd soon be sitting at the kitchen table she was brought up at, telling anyone who cared to hear what a let-down I'd been, and how right they'd been all along, and so on and so forth. Though I don't know what she hoped to achieve by talking like that, as the family, and their whole street in fact, regarded me as no better than a red-back spider.

To make matters worse, we had to change trams, and it soon became apparent that she wasn't going home at all, but somewhere entirely different. And then it dawned on me: she was going to Queenie's place.

I was thoroughly confused, but kept my mouth shut, which is what you do with a woman who won't listen to reason, as a bloke's got nothing *but* reason, and a woman is only interested in other stuff, the kind of stuff I'd been writing about, actually, and the last stuff I was going to come out with right then. Time and a place, horses for courses – something like that.

When we arrived at Queenie's place she was not surprised to see us, and gave Ruth a hug at the door and let her in. For me there was not even: 'Hello, you little prick, what the fuck have you done to this lovely woman?' Instead I got a look that said so many things that I didn't know what to make of it. No, that's not true, I did. She looked concerned. Just that. And there was no judgement in her eyes. But that was Queenie.

Before I left, Queenie raised her voice a little, for no reason, as I was so close to her I was almost touching her, and said: 'You've done enough bloody damage, Archie. I think you better piss off.' She then quickly winked and slammed the door in my face. I have never seen so much information packed into a wink, and I've been to betting rings, casinos, boxing houses, and film studios, where there's so much winking and nodding, you'd swear there was an epidemic of some new plague going around. I believe I owed my life to that wink.

19 This Valley of Tears

I can see why the men of Richmond are so fond of throwing themselves off the Church Street Bridge. There are a lot of men being made miserable by their women in Richmond, but the bridge is low enough that a man won't drown. And the river is so dirty that the barman of the Orange Tree swears that one night while out for a walk, he witnessed a man jump off the bridge and bounce off the mud, then get up shake himself off, and walk to the shore. That's why they have a saying in Richmond that Jesus was a local.

But my thoughts were on the bridge for a little while, until I remembered the story, and, as everyone knows, I am man who likes a fine cut of suit, and will not contemplate ruining such a thing in the Yarra's unholy mud. I therefore went over to Ikey's place and had a flutter on the table, and won a brick, some of which I spent on grog, not that that made feel any better. I then went for a walk up to Charlie Wing's to say hello to the girls, for I was feeling in need of company, at least of a pretty face that didn't think I was worse news than a flu carrier. I had no sooner walked into Charlie's place when I turned around and standing there was Queenie.

'I've been looking for you half the night,' she says.

'I had nowhere to go. Home isn't the same without her. Queenie, I think she's gone mad, fair dinkum. Her imagination's gone wild. Is she okay?'

'She's alright, but as soon as you left, she went into labour. Arch, she's sick, very sick. I called an ambulance, and they took her off to the Queen Vic.'

I was bewildered.

'You've got a telephone?'

'Are you paying attention? You better get over to the hospital. Charlie said he'll drive you.'

'Charlie's got a car?'

'Archie dear, it's nineteen twenty-five.'

'Where's this hospital?'

'Charlie knows.'

Charlie turned out to be the worst driver in Melbourne, and we ran over something that was alive in a lane near Latrobe Street.

'Short cut,' explained Charlie. 'Use it all the time, for deliveries.'

'Deliveries of what?'

'This and that. Mostly that.' He gave a little sniff.

'Jesus, Charlie, they can put you away for that.'

'You got to give the people what they want, Archie, everyone knows that. Bit of something extra in the pipe bowl - not Charlie's place to judge. It's business. Bloody government!' He spat out of the window of the car, which shook as it ran over the stonework of the lane, apparently agreeing.

Charlie let me out at the Queen Vic, and gave me a calling card.

'My phone number. Call when it's time to come home, if there's no trams, and I'll come back and get you.'

'I owe you, Charlie.'

'No you don't. I still feel bad about what happened to you when you cut that copper. Bloody coppers!' He spat again.

Inside, no one wanted to know me, as I had been drinking, but finally, after I simmered down I was shown to the nurses station in the maternity ward, and told to wait. I waited all bloody night, and finally was greeted by a sergeant major dressed up as a sister, who informed me that I was the father of a girl and that mother and daughter were doing as well as could be expected, whatever that meant, and I could see her for five minutes. I was shown into a room with two long rows of beds, but only one occupant. I was also given a mask to wear, and told not to take if off under any circumstances.

Inside, I found Ruth, lying in bed, looking washed out, but with the old colour back in her cheeks. She accepted me to the bedside, and held me close to her, and kissed me on the cheek, as if the past nine months had happened to somebody else.

'I'm sorry, Arch, for everything. We have a little girl. They'll bring her in a tick.'

She was breathing deeply and noisily, and sweating like hell. Her body seemed damned uncomfortable, but her mind seemed to be unaware of it. I'd seen that before, many times.

Well, we did have a little girl, and she seemed to have none of my horrible characteristics, and a lot of her mother's good ones, so it was a splendid result, and I was pleased as punch. But Ruth was so weak she could barely move. After having a hold of the baby, much against the better judgement of the sergeant major, I was ushered to the door by the doctor, who had looked in, apparently to have a word with me.

I shook his hand.

'Thanks for your help, doctor. To tell you the truth, Ruth's not been well lately, and I'm glad the baby is finally here.'

'Yes, well, I'm not surprised there's been a problem. Mr Taggerty, your wife has tuberculosis.' He paused to let it sink in.

'You mean consumption?'

'Yes, consumption.'

'Jesus. What, what...?'

'She has probably had it for a long time. She will have to remain here for a while, to be looked after, and then be transferred to the Greenvale Sanatorium for treatment and convalescence.'

I nodded, and looked at him. I was feeling icy cold. But he had only paused. There was more.

'What is it?'

'Your wife has an opium addiction. She brought a bottle of laudanum with her to the hospital. She tells me she has been more of less living on it for months. She has been getting it without a prescription, did you know that?'

'I knew she was having the odd sip – she's had a terrible cough that's been wearing her down.'

'The tubercular cough.'

'Yeah, I see. I thought the doctor was writing prescriptions.'

'Well, I've sedated her a little, and as soon as you're gone, I'm going to prescribe a strong sedative, which should reduce her discomfort for the next few days. You may continue to visit, of course, but she may not recognise you. She may not even appear to be awake.'

I knew what he was talking about. I'd seen many cases of opium addiction in my time, here in Richmond, away in the army hospitals, and well, socially, mainly at the Chinese dens around town. Taken a puff or two myself, of course, but they tell me it did nothing to improve my outlook. In Cairo, I had to have a swig of laudanum every time I thought of it. It can be painful to shake. The sedative would help.

'I understand. I was in hospital in Cairo. I've seen all this before.'

Now it was his turn to nod. Lot of nodding going on.

I stayed with Ruth for a little while, and she seemed to want to talk, however I soon discovered that her opening line was the only one that would make any sense. Not that I minded, as it was like a sweet tune to my ears, like a cross between *The Daughter of Rosie O'Grady*, which always reminded me of her, and *Always*, which we had sung together on the night my mother left.

At Greenvale she was placed in a ward for a month, and then moved to a hut outside the main building. I was allowed to take Jean home, providing a nurse came with us. My mother came back to take care of Jeannie, but it was torture for her. However, she knew that it was either her or Ruth's mother who would take care of the baby. Slowly, Ruth improved and I was allowed to visit, as long as I joined everyone else in treating her like some kind of leper. That was a hard year for us all, as Ruth and little Jean didn't get to see each other at all. But in the end, they reckoned she could go home, as long as the didn't have any kind of fun. I had been secretly dreading the moment when Ruth walked in and found my mother there, but it was like the changing of the midnight piquet in the desert: almost spectral in its passing but for Ruth saying a sincere 'Thanks, Mum', and getting a nod in reply. For Irish women, this was fair running at the mouth.

She was thin as a promise when she left that place, in spite of being forced to eat all kinds of food, in the hope that she might like some of it. But her appetite, which was normally like that of a Waler at an oasis, was absent, and she had to be begged to eat. It was a crying shame to see her beautiful graceful body looking, well, old at twenty-five. Though we went out as often as we could, and I was always careful to make sure that we ate something wherever we went, I felt that the TB had done her some kind of permanent harm.

I asked the doctor about this the next time we were at the hospital for a check-up, and he agreed, nodding a bit more than usual, which told me that I was on to something, probably something he wasn't going to mention under his own steam. I immediately sensed an undertow of some worse entity, something I hadn't thought of at all, but that he had.

'Doctor, there's something you're not telling me, isn't there? There's more. Come on now, you can speak plainly.'

'I don't want to plant pessimistic prognoses where none are called for, Mr Taggerty.'

'On the other hand –'

'On the other hand, there are indicators of a chronic underlying pulmonary weakness, a natural susceptibility.'

'What are you saying, that she won't get better?'

'She will find it extremely difficult to return to the state of health state you have both described for me, that's right.'

He paused again and watched me without moving. I hate doctors.

'Jesus, she's not going to die, is she?'

'Oh, no nothing like that. Put that thought out of your mind, Mr Taggerty. You must be positive.'

'But people die of TB, don't they? I mean, all the time?'

'Well, it certainly can lead to that outcome, untreated. But your wife has been getting the best of care. And she has a lot to look forward to, hasn't she? I'm sure there's no reason to be concerned.'

I have to tell you that I never saw a man so keen on getting out of a conversation unless it was that conversation I saw Gavin

Daly trying to get out of at Ikey's place the night a pair of dice fell out of his pants while he was in the Gents. I paused just long enough for this doctor to take a long gander at his fob watch, and raise his eyebrows as if he just realised he was running late for his own knighthood, and was now going to have to send the King a telegram telling him he'd been held up by an inconsiderate Irishman with a list.

I'm sure I said I hate doctors, so I won't repeat myself.

On my next visit to Coode Island I could tell straightaway that Billy was just hanging on, as he seemed to be losing interest in breathing. I ran into the same nurse at the nurse's station I had sat with the last time I was here. She seemed happy to see me.

'Hello, Mr Taggerty.'

'You know who I am now.'

'Yes, I found out. I'm sorry about the trouble I caused. Actually, nobody knows about it except you and me – and Mrs Taggerty, of course.'

She paused, and gave me a hopeful, anxious look.

'It's okay. I won't mention it to anyone. As for my wife, well, she has had problems of her own.'

'I'm sorry to hear that. When is the baby due?'

'Just had it, a girl.'

'Is everything alright?'

'My wife...she's not well. It never rains but it pours, eh? How's my mate, Billy?'

'He's not doing too well. I think his time is just about up.'

'Oh well, I suppose that's good, isn't it? It'll be hard on Ruth, though.'

'She knew him too.'

'Billy's her brother.'

The nurse looked at me, and I could see her searching for the appropriate look to give me in the circumstances – I have a gift for reading punters' faces – and then relaxing, and settling for her own soft look.

'I'm sorry to hear that. No wonder ... '

'Yeah. If you know who I am, you probably heard that I am pretty good at messing things up as well.'

'My mother always says the Lord works in mysterious ways His wonders to perform – that's what she always says.'

'Your mum would have had a lot of trouble saying that if she saw the Military Hospital at Port Said; she would have been too busy being sick. I'm sorry. I suppose the Lord's ways are pretty mysterious, but I'm not so sure about the wonders side of things.' I needed to change the subject. 'So how long do you think it'll be – for Billy, I mean?'

'It could be any time. Anybody else would have been gone a long time ago. Come on, I'll take you to him.'

Billy was just as I had left him. It was as if I hadn't been away at all. I sat down beside him, and composed myself, as I always did when I was going to talk to him. The nurse had gone and left us alone. The whole place was hot and oppressive. The air seemed to smell of something extra, but my nose told me it was just hospital smells I was used to. I took Billy's hand, and started talking to him, the way I always did. I told him he was an uncle and that he had a niece called Jean, and that mother and daughter were doing well, as that is what you say to someone who is hanging on by a thread.

Then it was into the news as usual. Whenever I came to see Billy I would carry on like as though I was reading the newspaper, only beginning at the back. So I would give him the sporting news first, then a bit of gossip, and then a bit of news that wasn't all that important, mostly about other countries who were having a bit of a stoush. I would finish up by giving him the front page, or headlines, so that by the time he heard it, he'd be dying of curiosity to find out how Manchuria was doing. As it turned out, I did have some extra news, which was that Windbag had won the Melbourne Cup. That didn't surprise him, of course, but it bloody well surprised me, as a little bird told me he was probably going to come down with the flu on the day. I think that little bird got his horses mixed up.

When I ran out of real news I usually did two things. First, I'd make up a bit of news, and sometimes this part of the conversation would go on for ages, as I kind of got into the swing of things. It didn't really matter to me what the news was, as long as it sounded like a bonza yarn. It wasn't only Billy that needed cheering up.

The second thing I usually did was get out some poetry that I'd written recently and read it to him. Sometimes that's all I'd do, and I'd be there for a few hours, reading poetry. Occasionally, I'd read him a poem or two by Polly Beer, who was pretty well known, and now had a few books selling pretty well. But mostly I'd stick to my own stuff.

Well, I'd just finished telling Billy the last bit of news for the day, which was that South Melbourne had beaten the bejesus out of Collingwood and won the Grand Final, and I was looking down at the floor – I'd made that up, of course, because the that match took place in nineteen-eighteen. Still, it did my heart good to imagine what it must have been like, as I had just missed it.

Well, I was staring down at the lino floor and I gave a great sigh of sadness, for I was losing Ruth, and I could see it, day by day, and she knew it, too. I think that in that moment I had no strength left at all, and I found myself sitting on a chair, but more or less down for the count. I was so weak I couldn't move a muscle, except to breath.

My relationship with God had always been a mess – I blame God for that. I reckoned He couldn't organise a tear in a paper factory. But you can't blame a bloke, then turn around and ask him to you a favour, so I was stuffed. But you can play His own slimy game, and offer a deal. So I thought I'd offer Him something He seemed to like, in exchange for Ruth and Billy. It was one of those take it or leave it deals, no negotiating or buggering around, and no reneging.

Well, it was at this point that I always gave Billy a poem. But on this day, I came without one, so I was going to have to improvise, which as luck would have it, was a talent that ran in my family. But I'd only had enough energy to make that little deal with God. And I was firm on that, no reneging. The only thing I had that seemed to have any value to anyone was the poetry itself. Of course, it mattered not to me that people couldn't get enough of the stuff; it only mattered to me that I got the muck out of my system. Otherwise, I think my own life would have been too much for me to handle. But without Ruth, I couldn't imagine life at all. I would bottle it up for good, no matter what, and mention it to no man, and live with myself, if that be possible.

Well, as soon as I made that decision, I felt a great fear, like the fear you get when you come across a scorpion on your bedroll: sudden, deep, with a metallic taste. *I dare you to match that, God, you bastard*, I thought to myself. There was a long silence except for those frightening hospital noises: a dropped bedpan, a raised voice, a hurrying of feet. Then there was a whispering at my elbow, and I turned my head, to see Billy's eyes, looking sideways at me, as if he had just woken from a sleep, which, in a way, he had. His hand twitched a fraction in mine, and I leaned over, to see if he was trying to speak. It was a scene that resembled others I had witnessed many times during the war, except for the circumstances, which must have been unique, I think.

I felt a terrible emotion flood my body like electricity, the same emotion I had felt when I stood on the wagon in Gaza and realised that I was going to be joining the charge on Beersheba. Billy's eyes followed mine, and his mouth began to work as he kept on trying to whisper. I'd seen men like this, and I knew what he needed. I got a towel and soaked it in water and placed it between his lips, and watched him suck it like a baby. His grip tightened, and the desperate look he had assumed became calmer, and he might have smiled – I don't know. I took the towel away when he had stopped drinking, and he whispered to me. He had to repeat himself over and over, until the words started to form properly, and I placed my face close to his and listened. I got the question mark first, and had to listen extra hard for the question before it. But finally it came, as he looked into my eyes, with the faintest of smiles.

'Who won?'

20 The Deal

The naive make deals with God; the crafty shake the bastard down. I was naive. I'd never paid much attention to religion, so I didn't speak the lingo, and I had a record as a bit of no-hoper. Also, everything I touched ended up being broken in some way. I realised all this in those seconds it took me to get the nurse, and bring her back.

'Nurse, Billy's awake.'

'Mr Taggerty –'

'No, fair dinkum, he opened his eyes and spoke to me.'

I hurried back to Billy, with her clip-clopping and swishing behind me like a cart horse, and when we got to the bed, he was lying there just as I had left him. His eyes and mouth were wide open, and his fingers were half curled, as if he was trying to hang onto something. His face was no longer serene, as it had been for months, but had an enquiring look on it, just as it had when he'd asked his question.

The nurse checked for his pulse, closed his eyes, and looked at me.

'You say he spoke to you?'

'Yes, he asked –'

The nurse was waiting.

'He asked...after his mum.'

I picked up my hat, and allowed the nurse to lead me back to her station.

'Mr Taggerty... Archie, I'm going to get you a cuppa. Just you wait here.' She went into the back room and bustled around, then came out again. 'We'll use Matron's tea, shall we? And we'll have a little chat, until you feel well enough to go home.'

So we sat and I sipped and thought hard about what had happened, and wondered if I had fucked up wholesale. I decided that I had. I hadn't actually stipulated how long this miracle was to last, I hadn't even been praying for Billy himself, well, not directly. But naturally, it would have fitted my requirements perfectly if he had woken up. And he did. And I had given my word, solemnly. I was the biggest mug in town. God had paid up, and wouldn't pay twice; He was as slippery as a rat in a grease trap.

I dragged myself home to Ruth and Jean, and found them having a lie down in bed. Ruth was flushed and looked happy to see me, and I thought I hadn't seen her so happy for a long time. It would be a crying shame to take that away.

I sat on the bed and held their hands for a while, then stretched out and put my head on the pillow and let my muscles relax completely. Normally, on a warm day, in the filtered light, with the summer breeze tickling us, and the pain in my hip abating a shade, I would have felt like a nap. But this was one of those days when there was not going to be any sleep. I hoisted myself up on one elbow and looked at Ruth, who was looking thoughtful, as well she might, given the doctor's closed-mouth attitude.

'I've just come back from the nursing home.'

'Billy's gone, isn't he?'

Ruth always knew how to soothe me, no matter what was happening.

'Yes, he's gone.'

'Were you with him?'

'Yes, I was. I was telling him all the news, as usual.'

'How did he go?' I must have paused for a split second too long. 'The truth, please, dear. It's the truth I need.'

'He woke up and smiled at me and asked me ... ah hell, he asked me who won.'

I smiled at Ruth, and she smiled at me, and between us we put together one sad smile.

'That was all, then he was gone. I wish there was something more I could tell you. Oh, I suppose there is one thing. I was, you know, talking to God, just then - when it happened. Maybe I shouldn't have. I didn't want him to die. That wasn't what I wanted. Please don't ask about it. It's just that you wanted to know everything.' I paused, and listened to our Ruth's breathing, which you could have heard over in Hawthorn. 'I don't know God very well, and I'm bloody sure He's never heard of me, so it was probably a silly thing to do. And I'm sure that I got it wrong.'

'You think this is all your fault, after all this time?'

'Course I flamin' do, love. It's driving me crazy, that and -'

'That and me being crook.'

I had nothing to say. I was no good at this kind of talk. I felt like punching someone.

'It's alright, you know, you praying. I pray for you all the time.'

'Go on!'

'It's true. Do you want to know when the first time I prayed for you was? It was the first time I met you, when you got into the ring with Billy. I prayed that Billy wouldn't hurt you.'

'Jesus, don't tell me you felt sorry for me. Ah, hell.'

'No, I knew you were as tough as old boots. I just didn't want him to hurt you, that's all.'

'Didn't want him to hurt me –'

'Billy had never been on the canvas, and I could tell you'd had a hard time – I was right, wasn't I? Yes, I was. And I've been praying for you ever since, every day, in fact.'

It was on the tip of my tongue to say that, as far as I could tell God had been ignoring her as if He thought she was a protestant.

'What is it?'

'I just remembered something I heard this Turkish bloke say in the hospital in Heliopolis – he had the flu and they bunged him in with me. And one day, out of the blue, he said to me in English: '*Silence is the language of God*'. P'raps that's why we never hear Him. P'raps He's speaking all the time.'

I shouldn't have said that, because it made my head hurt so much I wanted to write some poetry, to get rid of it. And then I remembered my deal with God. I could live without poetry; I could keep my end of the deal. But I was so close to crying that I felt like a bloody kid, and suddenly realised that I was squirming a little as I lay there, in the white light of the afternoon sun, in the silence that would have been but for the sound of a tram banging on the rail cracks as it went down Church Street.

'I think He does speak all the time. I think that Turkish man was right. God told me it was alright to fall for you.'

'How?'

'I don't know. It was a feeling I got. I just knew it was okay.'

'Well, I didn't need anyone's permission to fall for you,' I says. 'That was the easiest thing I ever did.'

'Oh I see, so I'm easy, am I?'

'Easy? You?'

'Arch, what did you get those medals for?'

'Turnin' up on time for all the stoushes, and being kind to me horse.'

'I haven't seen any of the men wearing that red and blue one. I heard it was for gallantry. What did you do?'

'Saved a bunch of horses from drowning.'

'Fair dinkum? They have a medal for saving horses?'

'You had to be there, I reckon.'

'See, Arch, I can never get a straight answer out of you.'

'Come off it, a bloke's bustin' a gut here.'

'Yeah, I know – I know. Arch?'

'Yeah?'

'I know you don't want to talk about this.'

I had a sudden bad feeling in my stomach, like I sometimes got after eating Gyppo tucker.

'No, love, I don't. I'm not saying I won't. But it's been hard for me. I've never been able to come to grips with it, not since I was a kid. That's all I want to say right now. I feel bad enough today.'

'Archbold Taggerty, what the flamin' hell are you talking about?'

'Ah...what're *you* talking about?'

'I'm talking about this bloody TB that everyone's pretending I haven't got.'

'Oh, that's all fixed up, love.'

She gave me one of those looks – no good explaining to you if you're not married.

'It's not fixed up, and we have to talk about it.'

My life is full of people having long talks to me – you could look on it as a series of frights broken up by long talks. Myself, I've only ever had one long talk, and that was with Billy, and I had the same talk over and over, just with different words, and usually, it was alright. Billy knew all about the poetry, of course, and just before I made my final prayer concerning him, it occurred to me that if he woke up, he would be able to tell everyone that Archie Taggerty was a sissy. But I knew he'd never do that, because we had become mates, as sure as if he'd been with me at Gaza, as if it had been him in that crater talking to me by the light of a parachute flare.

So Ruth and I talked and talked and talked. And it seemed to me that, after all the important stuff was out of the way, she kept on talking for ages about everything under the sun, as if she didn't want the conversation to stop. But me being as thick as two short planks, I never took the hint and told her what it was that was bothering me, and had been all my life, and would bother me even more now. I just couldn't. I still needed her to be with me, and I couldn't bear her to lose her respect for me.

It was two weeks after the funeral, the worst bloody funeral I ever went to, that I couldn't stand the voice in my head any more. Not that it was the kind of voice you could hear. It was the kind of voice that stirred me in various ways, so that if I tuned into it, I could hear myself thinking ninety to the dozen in words that I could easily have written down as poetry. I went to visit Jack Galloway at *The Argus* to tell him I'd done with poeting.

'Archie, you can't do that. You have a public following. People love your books. You know, you could make a fortune doing public readings.'

'Jack, I came to tell you that I'm not writing any more of the stuff.'

'But what about Polly?'

'Tell 'em she took to the bottle and lost her touch.'

'Archie, what's wrong?'

'It's a long story; I just can't write anymore.'

'Archie, I'll tell you something. I don't think you need to be Polly Beer any more. I think you can use your own name. That's been the problem hasn't it?'

'Well that's part of it, alright, but the fact is, I take no joy in poetry, none at all. It was always just something that I had to do just to be rid of it, as it was gnawing away at me innards, like hunger. I only ever did it to get a bit of relief' – suddenly I thought of the time I had spent with Billy – 'if you catch my meaning.'

Jack looked up at the clock, and stood up. 'I don't believe you. But we can't discuss such matters here. We better go to my other office.'

So we slope off to the pub across the road, and proceed to get outside a few coldies while we discuss the matter. Or rather, while Jack discusses the matter, because I can't for the life of me think of a way out. I have made a deal, and I have to keep my end of it, I tell myself, lest the alcohol weaken my spirit. Well, I'm all set to argue with Jack about my writing, but he comes up me on a different tack.

'I heard about Billy Magee,' he says. 'I'm sorry for all concerned. But I'm not sorry you stopped fighting. You always had more luck than skill, and a splash of cunning, of course, as is well known. I think you would have ended up at the bottom of the Yarra, if you don't mind me being blunt.'

'No, Jack, I don't, for although I've never lost a legitimate fight, I never had the heart to be a boxer. I'd tell you a secret, except it would be in tomorrow's bloody *Argus.*'

'No, Arch, it wouldn't. How long have I known you now? I know just about everything about you, yet never printed a word. Clyde Morris covers the fights, and for all he knows you're teaching ballroom dancing at the Methodist Ladies College. As for Polly, no one knows a bloody thing about her, though she gets more letters than I do. I've got thousands of the buggers.'

'Pull the other one.'

'Thousands.'

'Jesus, they must think I'm a real bastard, not writing back.'

'Not really. They just want to express their gratitude.'

'You'll have me blubbin' into me grog in a minute.'

'That stuff that you hate, they love. I love it too. Clarrie Dennis loves it, for God's sake.'

'Who's he when he's home?'

Well, I thought he was going to have a fit or something, he coughed so hard, for he'd just taken a puff on his pipe. I slapped him between the shoulder-blades until he was back with the land of the living, and we looked at each other in astonishment, though for different reasons.

'Surely you've heard of C.J. Dennis?'

'Course I have. I'm surprised he's heard of me, though.'

'Well, it's time you two met, I reckon. I'll organise it when I get back. He only works over at *The Herald*. He's asked me once or twice about little Polly Beer.'

'My God, what does he say?'

'He says: 'Jack, I'll find out who that Pollywollydoodle bloke is, if it's the last thing I do.'

'Pollywollydoodle ...'

'That's what he calls you. You brought it on yourself, Archie, my boy. Best you come clean. Think of that feeling you get when you step out of the confessional. Ah, the fresh air, the birds tweeting, the laughter of children all over the place. No more dirty little secrets. And the little woman will be so proud –'

'See, that's where you're wrong. Women like strong men, and Ruth comes from a family of fighters. She'd have a fit, not to mention my mum. And what about me daughter, who's just getting over the shock of being born and discovering she lives in Richmond, and is Archie Taggerty's kid, to boot. Turn it up, Jack. Besides, Ruth's not well. The shock'd kill her. No, mate, no.'

'Archie, I know you a lot better than you think. A lot of blokes come through my door, most of them blabbermouths. A newspaper is a marketplace for gossip. I know most of what goes on in this town, and believe me, I know all about Billy Magee. *The Argus* made enquiries, of course.'

He looked over my glasses at me, as he took a sip of ale, and the penny dropped.

'If Clyde Morris can find out, him who can barely stand up or read unless he's had a skinful, everyone else will soon find out, as well.'

'You mean it's in the paper?'

'Nah, not newsworthy enough. Besides, Billy's family would take offence, and I wouldn't blame them. I don't want someone throwing house-bricks through my front window. People might take your relationship with Billy the wrong way. Not worth my reputation.'

'Just what the fuck are you saying?'

'See what I mean? That's what a lot of people would say. But they don't know you as I do, so I let it go.'

'I see what you mean, yes. Christ, I've been stupid.'

'Archie, listen, you were cut out to be a poet, I'm telling you straight. I've never met anyone who's tried so hard to avoid being what he's best at, unless it's that new full-forward Carlton's recruited – what a no-hoper.'

'I always felt that I was cut out to be a fighter.'

'Why? That's always intrigued me.'

'Because it feels so good to punch blokes.'

'Does it? I've never done it, so I'll have to take your word for it. But surely there's a risk that the other bloke will punch you back?'

'Well, there is that side to it.'

The conversation petered out. I was thinking hard.'

'What is it, Arch?'

'I met a bloke in the States, a writer. He told me all about this thing inside him that drove him to write ... and to fight – though he'd never had a fight. I saw him floored by Jack Dempsey. But I knew what he was talking about, and I can't get it out of my head. He said being knocked out by Dempsey allowed him to write. Sorry, I can't explain it any better.'

'Yes, but if you're waiting to be knocked out, don't hold your breath, mate. It's not going to happen.'

'No, I think you're right. Still, it makes you think.'

'You mean, it's making *you* think.'

'Yeah. It's driving me mad.'

'Arch, it doesn't have to be difficult. Does Ruth like poetry?'

'She loves the stuff.'

'Do you think she's read any of Polly's work?'

I didn't know whether to get up and run, or order another round, or tell him I just saw a bloke outside who owed me a fiver. I'd lost control of the conversation, just like I'd lost control of my whole bloody life.

'See, that's the trouble. From what she tells me, she's read all of it.'

21 The Big Finish

When I came home I could see that Ruth was looking in need of some kind of leg up, if you ask me. She was distinctly down in the dumps. It was as if her whole life had decided to announce to her soul that it was time for a snap inspection, like we used to have in the Training Regiment, though ours usually took place in the middle of the flaming night. I knew that when she got into this state, nothing would cheer her up, and she sort drifted off into some distant place that kept her mind pretty busy.

The best thing to do was what I had doing since Jean was born, and that was to bustle around making myself useful, giving Jean a bath, having a go at getting some dinner organised, and doing a bit of housework here and there. I'd fallen into this way of life when Ruth was in Greenvale, and it was just as well, too, because she had no energy at all when she came home, and she had been barred from doing anything that even faintly resembled fun. As it was, she was content to let me do as I pleased, and I could see that she wanted to say something to me, but didn't want to, which was a lot more like me than Ruth. It was like having an unexploded bomb in the house.

So after I just about went crazy with the tension, and hours had passed without her saying a flaming word, except to tick me off for some small thing I might have done wrong in the housework area, she speaks up, with a frown, as if nothing at all had been wrong all day.

'Queenie's son has gone missing.'

She looked at my face, and I could see that she was examining me extra close for signs of what I thought about that.

'Hell, how long has he been gone?'

'A couple of days. You didn't know?'

'How the hell would I know?'

'Well ...'

'Oh, so that's what all this silence has been about. After all this time.'

'I don't know anything about that boy. John Murphy. Oh really, how many Murphys would there be in Melbourne? She might as well have called him John Smith.'

I felt so sad at hearing all this that I just about sank down on the floor and cried. I had thought that all this jealousy was behind us, but I could see that the child that Queenie had brought back from the States was driving Ruth crazy. I thought it was clear to one and all that this kid was the product of a relationship, a marriage, I was told, between Queenie and some film producer who, in the end, had decided to buy her off.

To top it off, the child wasn't like me at all, having swarthy looks, a round face, and a foul temper, all characteristics that were absent from both me and his mother. Even Blind Freddy could see that I was more like King Bloody Edward than that kid. I'll tell you this, though I'd never say it out loud, that that kid was born to get into trouble, and would never be anything but a problem for Queenie. Christ, he was already a problem for me, and I had hardly set eyes on him.

'If she says his dad is called Murphy, then Murphy he is.' She did not reply. And her silence was like a slap to me. 'Ruthie.'

'Don't Ruthie me! I s'pose you better see if there's anything you can do to help, as the coppers haven't got a clue, and ... I owe Queenie a favour.'

'I'd help Queenie find her kid, favour or no favour, you know that, and it has nothing to do with anything except we've been mates for a long time, and that's that. So if you've got more to say on the subject then say it now, for I'm in the mood to hear it and deal with it before I go out.'

She said nothing to this, which was just as well, as I was terrified that this arguing would make her sick again, and I'd been living in a kind of heaven lately just watching her loveliness returning to her.

So I grabbed my hat and left, after trying to give her a kiss, which she dodged as if I'd thrown a jab. That fair put me in a mood to strangle that kid if I saw him, I swear.

I discovered a Queenie beside herself with worry. Everything and every place had been thought of, and Queenie had pulled in a lot of help from all over Richmond, and from the useless bloody police, to boot.

'Hell, Queenie, I'm sorry I didn't come over. I just found out, then I came straight away.'

'Oh, Arch, I didn't expect you at all. I know why you didn't come over. I've seen the way Ruth avoids Jack. It's a horrible thing for a woman to see. She didn't have to say anything. And you've got nothing to apologise about. But I tell you, no one's got a clue. No one. God, what if he's wandered down to the river. It's the one place we haven't looked ... you know, properly.'

'Don't even think about that, love. Is there any reason why he might go down there?'

'Well, he's fascinated by the river boats, of course.'

'Well, we know he'd never be allowed to board one by himself.'

'You don't think –?'

I looked at her for a while.

'Arch?'

'Tell me about his father. I know I never asked you anything about him before, but how did he feel about you coming back with Jack? Queenie?'

'I took off without saying goodbye ... and took Jack with me.'

'Stone the crows, Queenie. Why the hell didn't you say so?'

'It was years ago.'

'What kind of bloke was he, the kind to forgive and forget the kidnapping of his son?'

'I didn't kidnap him – I'm his mother!'

'But Jack's American, Queenie. I'm not sure that you can do that, mother or no mother.'

'You don't think he's here, do you, in Melbourne?'

'I think that if it was him, he's long gone: he's had two days' start. Well, I better get going.'

'His name's Rollo Brik.'

'Rollo Brik – not Murphy.'

'Not Murphy.'

I walked over to Charlie Wing's and called Jack Galloway. He was able to give me the details of ships bound for America. There was only one, the *Orsova*, and it was about to leave. I went down to Station Pier, and there it was, looking like a postcard of itself. I knew it pretty well, of course, and I knew which deck a Hollywood film producer would be living on, too. So I went down to the shop steward's office along the pier, and dropped in to his office. Well, I have always made a point of making the acquaintanceship of every shoppie in Melbourne belonging to the

242

Wharfies Union, because there's a lot of this and that to be had on the wharves for a young man who's in need of a business opportunity.

'Well if it isn't the Richmond Terrier. To what do I owe this honour, Your Highness?'

'Sorry about that, Sheridan. As everyone in Melbourne must know by now, that KO was a fluke.'

He nods towards a chair and puts his feet up on his desk.

'Make it quick, I've got a ship to get off.'

'A friend of mine has had her kid nicked, and we think he might be on that ship.'

'What'd the copper's say?'

'What coppers?'

'I see. Well, who is this bloke?'

'The kid's old man – he's a Yank. And I might be wrong, too. But I reckoned you'd be the one to know.'

I was right about that. This bloke had the power of life and death at Station Pier. He rolled a cigarette, slowly, and looked out of the window.

'Special friend, is she?'

'Do you know Queenie Brennan?'

He kept looking out the window, and blew smoke at the glass, so that it gently flattened as it got there.

'What's this bloke's name?'

'Rollo Brik.'

'What kind of a name is that?'

I shrug, as it's good question, but doesn't require an answer. He writes it down on the back of something and says to me: 'Come on.' And off we go.

Next door, there is a small room full of blokes having a cuppa, and Sheridan sticks his fizzog in the door and says: 'Little job.' He gives the nod to a bloke who looks like he can handle himself. 'Acker, you'll do.' The three of us enter the ship by the loading gangway and go up a few flights of stairs. 'Wait here,' he says, then shoots through for a few minutes. I look at Acker and he looks at me. He knows, it seems to me, why he was picked to go aboard.

'I know you, don't I?' he says, after a bit of an effort. 'Archie Taggerty.'

'Yeah.'

'What happened to that Magee bloke?'

'He died.'

'What'd you hit 'im with?'

'Nothin' in particular.'

'Come on, you can tell a mate.'

'Tell the truth, it was a lucky punch.'

Just then Sheridan sticks his head around the corner and nods us to follow. We go to a cabin on the posh deck and he opens one of the doors without even knocking, and walks in with us behind him. Brik is surprised to see us.

'What the hell is this?' he says.

'H'lo, Mr Taggerty,' says the kid, piping up in his usual wary way.

'G'day, son. Grab your stuff, if you've got any. We're off home.'

'Fair enough.'

'Now hang on, Johnny, you're not going anywhere.'

One nod from me is enough to let Johnny know what's what, as he has been raised in a place were a lot of the conversations consist of only a few words, but a fair slab of nods, winks, and what have you. It wouldn't surprise me if Queenie could recite *The Wreck of the Hesperus* without saying a word. So the kid grabs a teddy bear that has been used as a lure, and walks to me without as much as a glance at his dad, and I open the door for him. The other two close ranks behind the kid as he passes, to prevent the bloke making a grab for him, and remain that way, like a pair of statues, as we leave. Brik says nothing more after that, because Acker has produced a knife, and has begun to tap on the leg of his pants with it, as if he would like Brik to try something. I stop at the door, and look at Brik's pale dial.

'No hard feelings, Brik. I might see you in Hollywood one day.'

I can't help noticing on the way back that this kid doesn't seem to care where he is, and is more interested in mumbling to his teddy bear. Even when I try to have a conversation with him, me having become a bit of an expert on talking to kids, he just gives me a look that tells me that he has said hello, and that should bloody well be enough. So I content myself with enjoying the trip to Richmond, though I am tempted to throw the little ingrate off the Princes Bridge, not because I don't like him much – I hardly knew the kid, really – but because there was something about him that told me that he was going to turn out bad, and in Richmond, which is a broadminded community, that is a hard thing to say about a kid.

Well, of course, Queenie is overjoyed to see the child again, as a mother is prepared to overlook any failing in her kid that doesn't involve passing rabies on to the family, and tells me that I am the greatest thing since electricity.

'So why didn't you call the kid Jack Brik?' I say, after the kid has settle down to stuffing his face with cake as if it was a circus trick.

'Murphy's me mum's maiden name. Thought I'd keep him in the family.'

'Doesn't say much does he?'

'Arch –'

'It's okay, love. Any time you need me, give me a hoy.'

'No, Arch. I wouldn't have done it this time, either, except ... Arch, how was Rollo?'

'Quiet, after he copped an eyeful of this Acker bloke I had with me.'

'Not Akker Williams –'

'Dunno.'

'Big bloke –'

'Yeah, that's him.'

'Didn't hurt Rollo, did he?'

'Nah. Rollo folded like a squeezebox. So you know Akker, do yer?'

'We've never been formally introduced.'

'Course.'

'Well, best you go home, before I forget –'

'Yeah.'

I didn't want to go home, not for the first time either. But for the first time, I didn't want to be married. I didn't want anything I had. I didn't even want Jeanie. I even caught myself envying Akker Williams, who wasn't fit to walk the same ground as Queenie, let alone ...

I wanted to be a drinking man, but I knew I wasn't. I wanted to be the kind of man who can command the trust and respect of his wife just by looking her in the eye, but I didn't seem to be that man either. I sighed all the way home.

Ruth was sitting on the floor surrounded by bits of paper. She picked up a handful of pages and waved them at me, staring wildly. I knew what they were. She let her arms hand fall to her side.

'Did you find him?'

'Yes, his father had taken him on board a ship, the *Orsova*, of all ships - you remember -'

'Good - that's good.'

'So you found something too -'

'Why has this man Galloway been sending you all these cheques - for years, by the looks of it?'

'That's something I've been meaning to tell you about for a fair while. I suppose I was waiting for the right moment. But I reckon there's never a right moment for something you don't want anyone to know. But I suppose it doesn't matter anymore, as I can see that I've nothing left to lose. I'm not the bloke you think I am. I'm a bloke that nobody really knows - a different bloke.'

I took off my suit-coat and eased myself into the big lounge chair, and undid the top button of my shirt.

'What are you talking about?'

'Just a mo, will you - a bloke's all in.' I took off my shoes. 'That poet bloke, Polly Beer -'

'She's not a bloke.'

'That Polly Beer, you like her stuff, don't you, I mean, a lot?'

'What about these?' She waved a hand.

'I'm coming to that - it's connected. What do you see in this Polly Beer's poetry? That's all I want to know, and then I'll explain all this to you. What is it about Beer's stuff you like - I know you like it, I reckon you must have read all of it.'

Ruth answered without looking at me, but just staring at the papers spread out around her.

'She has an open heart, like a child. She says what I think, or what I reckon I'd think, if I could. She tells the truth as best she can. She's not like –'

She had stopped.

'Like me?'

'No, like us, all of us in living in this place.'

'Actually she is; she *is* like all of us living in this place.'

'How the hell would you know, you who ...?'

'Listen:

I saw a ghost tonight, I swear, in Kendall's barber shop;
he stood in darkness and he stared, his face a greyish mot.
He was the place's prisoner, all trapped beyond the glass
So I knew his tired face would not come closer, closer to my
heart.
He wore no hat, for I'd dropped mine, he'd lost his love, as I;
I turned away, I could not help, and left him there to sigh.'

'What are you saying?'

'I dreamed that I alone had sight, in all of Melbourne town
And had the gift of telling and therefore of handing down
Such truths as God allowed.
And He ordained that I would climb, and watch the sun go
down
And, returning, pass on all I'd seen to all those still blinded
by
The sin of being proud.'

'So? You've been reading my books. So what?'

'No, I've never read a one: I wrote the bastards.'

248

The tirade never came, the guns were silent. There was no scream of shot overhead. There was no *dump, dump*, as the rounds thudded into the bodies. There was no storm. There was no need for an order to be given. There were no frightened horses, nor snorting men. The bleeding, there would be none. There was the turning of the world.

22 For Better or For Worse

'You?'

It was a rhetorical question, a tired one. I waited, because there was nothing else to do. I had nothing left. What little self-respect I'd been kidding myself I had vanished. I'd only had one secret, right from the beginning, well two, if you count not really enjoying fighting, just the punching. So many blokes would have thought that that was just a little boxing joke that I didn't think much about, and didn't think of it as a terrible secret. But the poetry thing, the *poeting* urge, as it was, was not a joke, and couldn't be seen as one. Instead, it made *me* look like a joke.

I had heard of ordinary blokes being poets, of course. They were as thick as thieves in Melbourne, especially old warriors who something to say about the war, or some poison in their minds that they had to be rid of. I wasn't like that. I had begun to write the stuff as a kid. And it didn't come to me as a kind of horrible after-thought involving somebody shooting at me. It just came. Its seemed to sense when I was at one of my weak points, and then it struck, like a demon. There had even been times when I'd thought of talking to one of the priests about it – one of the Irish priests. But what would they know of demons, they who took their pleasure from fantasising about the flesh and getting pissed out of their brains? What I needed was someone who knew all about the problems of the spirit.

As I sat and watched Ruth, I saw her face change as she reviewed our relationship, gathering evidence that would make me right. I saw that she was finding it, too. There were numerous occasions when I had let people hear a scrap of verse here and there – there were times when I was too tired to hide it. Polly, on the other hand, was a regular chatterbox, and never shut up, once she got a pen in her hand, or his hand – stone the crows, *that* had never been an issue; it was always just a name, for God's sake.

'Yes, me, love.'

I answered the question anyway. I had no life left. She could ask me whatever she wished.

She nodded slowly with her chin stuck out, as if she was trying to swallow.

'Why didn't you tell me?'

'I was ashamed.'

'But ... ashamed of what?'

'Haven't you ever been ashamed?'

'What are you talking about?'

'Have you ever been ashamed?'

'I don't know.'

I sat there and sighed. I no longer cared if she asked me questions, or just sat there for the rest of her life. I had lost interest in the conversation right at the start. I had lost interest in everything. Finally, when she couldn't stand the silence any more – silence is torture to a woman – she started the conversation up again, because it had died.

'I suppose I've been ashamed, what of it?'

'You wouldn't say *what of it* if you really had been. Tell me what you were ever ashamed of.'

'Oh I don't know. I can't think of anything off hand.'

'Then you don't know what I'm telling you. When you can remember what you were ashamed of, let me know, and we'll start the conversation again.'

'So is that it – you're not going to tell me why you kept it from me?'

I got up to leave.

'I kept it from everyone, not only you.'

'No, Arch you told the whole bloody world, and left me out.'

'No, I've never told anyone, except Jack Galloway at *The Argus*, and that was so he'd publish the poetry.'

'Alright, so you told Jack Galloway. You still didn't tell me.'

'Jack was a bit of a confessor to me.'

'Don't be silly – he's not a priest.'

'He did what the priest does, he took away the pain.'

'That's not his job, it's my job.'

'No matter how much you've loved me, the pain has always been there. Even when I wrote the poetry down, there was pain, just less of it. It was only when I released it to the world that it seemed to leave me – at least for a while.'

'I'm your wife. You're supposed to tell me everything.'

'That goes both ways, you know.'

'What the hell are you talking about?'

'I'm talking about the TB, and the laudanum you were knocking back like lemonade.'

'You knew I was taking it – everyone takes it.'

'I thought you were sticking to the prescription.'

'Look, I didn't want you to worry.'

'I'm your husband – I'm supposed to worry.'

'I don't remember you ever *being* my husband – I remember when you said you *wanted* to be my husband.'

'I still do.'

'You're just like my father.'

'That was below the belt.'

She threw a handful of letters at me.

'So was all this.'

'Alright, then, I'm a bloody poet.'

'I don't give a bugger about the poetry.'

I felt the truth slipping out.

'I do.'

A man needs a place go when he's had a difference of opinion with the little woman. He needs a mate. I had no mate to go to. I suppose all the blokes I knew were out to get something out of someone before they died of TB, or a bashing – I don't think I'm being too hard. Most of them knocked around in pairs or mobs: 'Jack and his mate', 'the Shamrocks', and so on. But I'd seen the sad look in their eyes remain unchanged when they were with their 'mates'. No, cobber, that wasn't me.

I did have Queenie, the closest thing to a mate I'd ever had, I suppose, but just then I didn't feel like her softness, the inevitability of her closeness and her desire for me and, inevitably, mine for her.

And even if I'd had a mate who was a bloke, I wouldn't have wanted to be close to his hardness, his: *'flamin' women, cobber, flamin' women'*. That was not how I looked on Ruth; that wasn't how I looked at the whole thing. My life wasn't about my relationship with Ruth, even though a part of me wanted it to be. What I needed was neither hardness nor softness, but a balance of something that lay a long way outside those two, heart and mind that knew both, the inners of a person who could dish out large gobs of both, and get large gobs of both in return, without caring one way or another. I walked up the low hill towards

Bridge Road, and stopped at the huge grey church. I was a Mick, of course, though I had never given a shit about it one way or another; most of the people I knew were Micks.

We had been brought up to believe that God lived inside the church, inside the actual building, and it had always felt to me as if that was a possibility. But it was just a feeling. When you took away the interior reverberations, the towering perspectives, the constant feeling that something heavy was about to fall on you and squash you like a blowie, there was just sharp-smelling space and tapping heels. And in the space there were people being solemn for one reason or another (though I knew well the reason: they wanted something from God, a deal, a demand, a ransom, a present – something). And they shuffled and genuflected, and blessed themselves, and looked at the floor as if the dead Jesus was hiding between the pews, waiting to jump out and go: '*Boo! Hah, I got you then, Missus.*' I don't think it occurred to any of those Holy Joes that, say what you will about Jesus, he was definitely shit-hot at pretending he was dead.

So what the hell was I doing in here, given my state of spiritual hopelessness? I was escaping from Richmond. This was something that couldn't be accomplished just by getting on a tram and choofing off to town for the day. Though Richmond was definitely as rotten as a suburb can be without being condemned by the State as a plague zone (though, come to think of it, that had happened too), there was a little bit of Richmond in every patch of Melbourne, even in the posh suburbs, where they reckon their shit doesn't stink, and in the outer areas, where the blokes keep farm animals and wives. So trying to escape the rot was impossible, even in the city, where it was all glitter and noise, and songs and such.

But St Ignatius' was not a part of Richmond: it was part of Ireland, or the fucking Vatican, or something, I don't know what. It was another country. If you were to walk in there and buttonhole some old codger and say to him: '*Now don't you just reckon the Mayor of Richmond ought to get a boot up the arse for what happened last week?*', he'd only look horrified and go: '*Shh"*See what I mean?

I breathed the air in that place deep into my lungs, and smelt the cedar, the frankincense, and the *strength* of the place, and peered through the appearance of mist created by the miles of grey stone and pale, high windows. I heard the echoes not just of the people wandering around in the place, but of the trams outside, and of other sounds – I don't know what they were, but they didn't seem to fit in, and were just, it seemed to me, lost and looking for a way out. I took an aisle seat down the back, and relaxed. I'd never felt comfortable in this place, or in any other church, but because I'd been forced to enter them so many times as a kid, I was used to it, and settled in, aware that I was invisible, and that I had nothing in mind.

I must have sat in that church for an hour, not doing anything, not thinking, just sitting. I had a problem, but I hadn't tried to figure it out. I had a life that had not worked, but I gave it not a thought. Every now and then I'd remember that I was supposed to be praying, and think about it for a few seconds, then lose interest. God would have laughed Himself silly. I got up and walked around the church, and went close to the front.

There were a bunch of people congregated down there, and a platoon of altar boys crawling all over the altar and up behind it like white-tailed spiders bunging candles in candelabras and lighting them, and organising the altar for Benediction. I'd done a stint as an altar boy when I was about ten – though I was soon sacked for fighting – so I knew what these young fellers were up to, and what they were in it for: the sheer bloody thrill of being up there on the altar with the priest in front of everyone, looking so bloody good it hurt. So these self-important little buggers got everything ready and slipped out to the vestry with lots of genuflecting and bowing and so on, leaving everyone to wait for the priest.

A part of me wanted to piss off, of course: I'd seen it all before. But of course, that's just what kept me there. You see, ever since I could remember I thought there was something about Benediction that was a little bit magical. In other words, fallen Mick though I was, I had never given up on the Benediction.

The priest – it was Father Garrity, a little twerp who had once ironed a bloke out a few days after he saw him fail to remove his hat as he rode past on a tram – walked out like Lord Muck, keeping one eye on the altar boys, in case any of them needed a thick ear after proceedings had concluded, and one eye on the crowd, to sort out the desperadoes from the regulars. He spotted me, of course, and held my eyes for a second, wondering, no doubt, what the notorious Terrier was doing in the house of God.

On any other day, I would have cringed. I mean, this was a bloke who would have made a fair fighter. However, on this day, I felt a certain entitlement to be there with the Holy Joes. I was a club member, after all; I needed no invitation. But the look that he gave me was unmistakable. I was not welcome in the House of God. I had taken the life of an Irishman.

The sun surprised me by coming out just as I was leaving, and banged me in the eyes like a dose of smelling salts, drying the drop of holy water on my forehead at the same time. I stood outside the church and turned to walk down Church Street, not sure, really, just what was going to happen next, just where I should go, or what imperative, if any, I should obey.

I raised my heavy head and looked down Church Street towards the Yarra, and saw, no felt, no, *dreamt*, of God. A dream outside of me. He took me by surprise. I hadn't been expecting Him; I'd been expecting a Prahran tram, which is funny, as there was more chance of God turning up.

Just at that moment, the sky over Prahran had a kind of newly washed look, as you'd expect from that lot, and the clouds looked like the white patches on a fox terrier puppy who was having a bit of a laze. However, as I looked at them, they seemed to become aware of my gaze, and moved in response to me, spreading like the coloured blobs on a balloon, letting something appear. It was a light, finer and cooler than the sun. It was moonlight without a moon, a light of silvery relieving softness. It was a living person, just grander than the rest of us. I didn't come down in the last shower: I knew who it was. And I immediately thanked my lucky stars that I'd never stopped believing in him, despite the rotten things I'd seen him do.

I just stopped and gawked, feeling the tingles that come with being caught unawares, and feeling like a real dill. I kept my mouth shut and watched as my dream localised itself to the sky above Prahran and God's face took shape and filled not just my eyes but a part of me for which I hadn't had any use for a long time.

There was no message, in case you're wondering. God didn't command me to go forth and baptise in His name or anything. Nor did He tell me to go home and be a good man, and sin no more, the way the priest did, without meaning it. But He did speak to me. At least, I *felt* the words. And what He said was that everything was okay. I know, you're thinking: *Is that it?* Well, yes.

Instinctively, I reached up and put my hand above my head, aware that I was acting like a little kid looking for his dad's hand, and, instinctively, I felt my hand taken. In that moment, trust settled on me, like a crisp, clean shirt, and I accepted it.

The moment passed, appropriately, it seemed to me, otherwise I would have had to sign myself into Royal Park Looney Bin. But that was all that passed. The experience remained with me, like a lambent gaslight flame inside me, lending to my nerves a kind of permit to do things, where before, there had been nothing but compulsion.

Then my mind evaporated, leaving invisible space. I saw the world around me and nothing about it was different. However I was aware that it was happening within a space that was larger than itself, one that would accommodate more. It was this greater space I was drawn to, wordlessly, knowing that I could act within it, safely.

Safely. I savoured the newness of the realisation, like a child with new sweet. Immediately, I wanted to share it: it radiated from me. I recognised it as a new form of expression.

There was a certain stillness about this space that I recognised, again instinctively: it was the absence of thought. Deliberately, I thought into the space and heard the thought. Then there was stillness again. Thoughts with ends. It was, to my mind, the greatest gift.

Part 3 The Decision

23 Going Bush

The year that followed was like a dream. I saw a lot of things happening all around me, but my participation was entirely superficial, and not all that physical. There was a kind of freshness to everything; sometimes it bordered on the exciting. But they were rare; most of the feelings were strange, and their source inapparent. I tried to ignore them, but gave up; truthfully, I guess I wanted to let them live, you know, give them a fair go. My mind still seemed to be faintly interested in things, and so I just sort of followed along with that.

To my surprise, my conversation to Ruth made no impression on my poetry, which still needed to be written. I thought Ruth would stop being interested in my poetry, but I was wrong: she became a kind of student of the stuff, rereading the old stuff, looking for clues, though she didn't say so.

I wrote it without caring whether it was good or bad, but Galloway assured me that the new, thoughtful yet detached mood of it had not been lost on the readers and critics, and that they were taking it in their stride. The conversation made an impression on my marriage, though, and that side of my life faded into invisibility. If I came home late, Ruth said nothing. If I stayed out all night, she said nothing. One day I didn't go home at all.

A lot of the blokes from the Brigade had gotten jobs around horses, and I had taken to dropping into stables and racecourses, and the like, and looking them up, though most of the country blokes had gone back to their farms. I was doing the traps one day and was at Flemington when I ran into Bulldog Micallef, who used to play for Footscray, and had turned to horse training, and we got to talking. I still had my sharp ear, so I can easily remember that conversation, and how I felt about it.

'So, Archie, how's life treating you? I hear you gave up the ring – bad luck, that.'

'Life is life, brother.'

'I see, like that, is it? And what do you think of this here beast?' he says, running his hand over the neck of one of his racehorses.

I had a look at the horse from all sides and then in the face, and said a few quiet words to it. Then I turned back to Bulldog.

'He'll not run today,' I says.

'He bloody-well will' says Bulldog.

'No, he won't. He's crook, and what's more, you know it, don't you?'

'Take him back,' says Bulldog to the strapper, who gives him a sour look. 'So Arch, what I heard about you's right, I reckon.'

'What's that?'

'That you know a thing or two about horses. D'yer know the vet okayed that animal?'

'Someone should okay that vet.'

'Yeah. Well, anyway, I'm scratching him. Been on the look-out for you for weeks. Bloke I know said you'd be a good horse spotter.'

'What bloke?'

'Colin Wren. He said you'd know him.'

'He's right about that.'

'Said I could trust you.'

'Sure you've got the right Taggerty?'

'He wants you to travel around, you know, to the horse sales. Find us a winner or two.'

'He can buy horses himself, surely.'

'Country races, bush sales. Unknown horses, unknown buyer. Bloke like him turns up, looking like Lord Muck, people talk. Besides, he doesn't know one end of a horse from another.'

'Course he does. We were in Palestine together.'

'I heard you got a medal.'

'That's true – they were handing them out with the water ration that day.'

'That's not what Wren told me. So what d'yer reckon?'

'Why not? I got nowhere else to be.'

So that was how I found myself in the horse buying business. It was the beginning of my wandering days, my days of shooting through, of going bush. It was like I was sleepwalking, and had woken up and realised it, but kept on going through the motions anyway. The worst thing about it was that I felt all right about it, I mean about leaving. I should have said that instead of going on about the flamin' horses. Bugger 'em.

Ruth and Jean had lost all their flavour for me. Is that what happens when a bloke shoots through? No, I don't think so; for I've met all kinds of blokes on the road. Most of them were just trying to find work somewhere, anywhere. They were sincere enough coves, many of them carrying war injuries; a lot of them pushing shit uphill to get by at all, let alone make a quid for the wife and kiddies back in Yarraville or some such place. Some of them had become desperate, and would do whatever evil took them to put half a crown into their pockets. At least I had money, so I was able to arrange for the family to be taken care of in my absence.

In Kilmore, I wandered in circles until I was stopped in my tracks by the sight of a red church. I'd been there before, only when it was grey. It wasn't until I got around the corner and had a closer look that I realised that it was the same grey stone as all the other churches I'd ever seen (bar those in America, which might have been for a different god). The dying sun had set it on fire for me, showing me what was in store for those who took religion lightly, like me, I suppose.

I'd been in Kilmore before, having been sent there by the Army to close down the local horse mustering depot. Now I was back. The place had changed, as the Government had gone crazy with their money and were trying to turn the place into some kind of city. It was never going to happen. Already they'd seen the writing on the wall; we all had. Money was getting scarce. The result was that there were half finished public works all over the place. The state had decided to plumb for the roads, a smart decision, I thought, seeing as how it didn't really have any to speak of, except the roads connecting military depots.

The Church, St Patrick's, had a large presbytery with one of those verandahs that makes you smell dripping and think soothing thoughts. The side door of the presbytery was wide open but the screen door was closed, and behind it there was a perfect gloom that warned of judgement. I was drawn to the darkness, and knocked. There was a shuffling sound, and a housekeeper appeared, looking tired and bored, as if she was expecting me.

She opened the door.

'Yes?'

'Hello, Missus. Is Father O'Shea in?'

'And who might you be?'

'Archie Taggerty. I was given his name by a friend in Melbourne – told to look him up.'

'Then you'd know that he doesn't like to be disturbed.'

She wore a floral dress and had a lopsided look about her, like a horse I'd once seen going over the jumps in Cairo, but doing nicely despite the look.

'He told me to expect to be greeted by the sweetest lady in all Christendom, and that would be yourself, I reckon.'

'Well, now, I'm sure Father never said anything of the kind, but if you'd like to come in you can wait in the sitting room, for he hasn't gone far.'

I allowed myself to be led into the sweet gloom that was Kevin O'Shea's house and took a turn of the sitting room. The walls were covered in the strangest mix of pictures, some sacred paintings, including one of a saint giving a bunch of snakes a hard time, our parish's namesake, I assumed, and a wonderful collection of racing photos, mainly of race finishes, photos that were far too professional to have been taken by any of the local coves. After looking at these pictures fairly closely, while bathed in a silence that swirled around me with many threats of sound that never came, I had a gander at a picture of Mannix, looking as if he was just about to protest about some new injustice against the Irish, or just had done that. I was interrupted by the housekeeper, who was carrying a cup of tea, which she set down on a side table next to my bag. She spoke while looking down at the cup and saucer.

'That's the great man himself, may the Lord preserve him, and give him life an make him blessed upon the earth, and deliver him not unto the will of the English. Amen.'

'Amen, Mrs –'

'Jackson.'

'Mrs Jackson. Thank you, and yes, of course, you're right. And thank you for the tea.'

'If you're a friend of Father's then he would want you to be comfortable while you wait. If you're not, he'll no doubt see you to the door and give you a little something to see you on your way, like a swift kick, and I'll be asking you for tuppence for the tea before you leave.'

I laughed my politest laugh, while Mrs Jackson stood with her arms folded like an auctioneer's clerk and her back bent back like a sergeant at morning parade, and frowned at me.

Halfway through the tea, the back door opened and I heard the sound of boots, and of Mrs Jackman giving O'Shea the bad news. A moment later, he was in the room, and walking towards me as if he had been expecting me, which he wasn't.

'Well, well, Archie Taggerty. How are you?'

He walked toward me without slowing down, and grabbed me by the hand and the shoulder simultaneously. He had aged since I saw him in Cairo, burying people's souls. He had slowed down. I wondered if the problem was alcohol – it does some blokes no good to give up the drink, and doesn't seem to work for some Irishmen at all.

'Hello, Kevin. I'm as right as rain, cobber. I'd say I was fighting fit, 'cept I've given up the ring.'

'So I heard, Arch. I got a big surprise when I heard you were fighting, as I was pretty sure you were dead.'

'What made you think that?'

'I gave you Extreme Unction, that's why. I remember you had the flu, and you'd been blown up by a Turkish mortar at Gaza, to boot. They let me in to give you the last sacrament. I heard your confession, none of which made sense to either of us, and gave you absolution anyway. That was the last I saw of you.'

'Don't remember that at all, Kev', though it was very nice of you. Got over the flu, as you see, and came back and got a few bouts.'

'*A few bouts*, he says. Didn't you win the bantamweight crown?'

'I did that. But I didn't come here to talk boxing. I've got a job here and there – it's about horses. I'm on the lookout for a good racer. Now I know you used to ride around with the Brigade, and I also know you take a keen interest in the nags. So here I am.'

'Arch, being a priest in a place like Kilmore is a full-time job. Tell you what, why don't you stay to dinner and we'll talk about it. And in the meantime, we could visit a few parishioners of mine at the local.'

'Parishioners, you say?'

'The publican and his good wife. Both of them upstanding Catholics.'

So we wandered off to the local and had a few beers, and talked about this and that, and Kevin had, I think, a few more beers than me, which was an easy feat to perform, as I made each of mine a shandy. But though we talked about a lot of things, things that to another would be too trivial to warrant more than a word or two, we didn't even touch on the reason for my appearance in town, it being understood that I would continue the conversation when the time was appropriate. It was an unsteady Kevin O'Shea who walked back to the presbytery with me that night, and found dinner ready to serve, as if Mrs Jackson knew exactly when we'd be home. When dinner was served she disappeared as if she were an actress following a script, and we enjoyed a tasty stew and, later, a pipe together in the living room.

'You'll stay, my son.'

'I wouldn't put you out, Kevin.'

'You'll be putting Mrs Jackson out if you leave, Arch, for she is a woman of uncommon hospitality.' He thought for a moment. 'Uncommon. And neither of us would hear of you shoving your feet under someone else's table.'

'Well –'

'Good. Now then, tell me about these horses you're looking for.'

So we talked into the night, and I told O'Shea what it was I was up to, and he listened and nodded, and finally says to me that there is a claiming race on after the cup, which is only a week away, and I should be able to find a nice little starter. Well we took our tea cups into the kitchen as we talked, and I noticed that the dining room and kitchen had been silently cleaned up while we had been at the other end of the huge house, and now looked as if we had never had dinner in there. O'Shea was not surprised at this at all, and I realised that either his housekeeper lived next door, or on the premises.

Well, he was wrong about the horses, though he came with me to the track to see what we could see, and we even visited a few of the local stables, but found nothing. It was only a few days after the races that I found myself at the stable of one Gabrielle Krauss, who'd had a scratching in the Cup, looking at a couple of horses mounted for a pleasure trip.

'Fancy a ride, Arch?'

'To be honest, mate, I've never fancied a ride in my life.'

'Nonsense, you know more about these things than both of these strappers put together.'

The strappers looked at each other, and back to us, and then to then horses, strappers not being a particularly bright species of human.

'Besides, I heard all about how you charged those heathen Turks at Beersheba, and put the fear of Almighty God into them.'

'Oh yeah, I bloody terrified them alright. I can tell you, Kevin, because you're a priest, and I know you'll never tell a soul, but I was only in that charge through the most horrible bad luck, and only managed to stay on that horse because of a flaming miracle.'

'Oh, come on, Arch. Show us what you're made of.'

So we rode our mounts a few miles down the road to a little farm with a few stables, and I was pleased to find that it was no strain at all for me to stay mounted, though I did begin by having one of my quiet words to the horse – Sheila, she was – before I mounted her.

At the farm we met Whitey Gamboli, a man who's family came to Australia to search for gold, and ended up making their fortune training horses. He took us down his stables, and showed us the prettiest little runner you ever saw.

'She was to have run in the Cup, Father. Very long-winded.'

'Now that horse has a bit of spirit in her, Whitey, even I can see that, and you know how much I know about horses. My friend here, on the other hand –'

'Yes, she's a fair horse alright, and we could have used her if she hadn't been trained to race. But she's lame. Why are we looking at her, if I can't see her run?'

I looked from horse to priest to trainer, and back.

'She's with me because I've been giving her the once over, but the fact is, young, feller, her racing days are over before they've begun. I just wanted you to see her before I tell you that she has a brother who's never been seen, and can give her five lengths.'

'Why hasn't he raced?'

'He belongs to a young lady who won't part with him, his only rider. It's tempting, isn't it?'

I had been looking over the horse during this conversation, and could see that she had a mind of her own, and a strong will, but one of those that might make a good partner, if she chose to pal up.

'What happened to her?'

'Fell through a horse float. I don't think she's in much pain, but she's going to wander to the right when she's mended.'

'Where's her brother?'

'Kyneton.'

'A child you say?'

'No, I said young lady. And if you can get her to part with that horse, you're a better man than me, for we've tried, without making too much of a song and dance about it.'

'Do you know this lady, Kev?'

'No, I don't, but I'm sure she'll see reason if the price is right.'

'Well, now, in my experience the price is always right.'

'Now would that be your experience of women, or horses?'

I must have had a strange look on my face, because both men laughed and shook their heads. You can outsmart a priest, and you can outsmart a trainer, but not both at once.

24 Annie

I had a name and an address, but no transport, so I took the train back to Melbourne and got myself onto a train to Kyneton. Well, it was one of those trips that the Arabs call kismet. In other words, it wasn't meant to be just an everyday train trip. The train being totally chockers with bods heading home from the Royal Melbourne Show, there wasn't enough room in any of the compartments to change your mind. So I ended up shoulder to shoulder with a bunch of young soldiers, who were on their way to some God-forsaken spot in the middle of Victoria, to where they were returning from leave, Australia starting to give a bit of thought to getting a standing army going. Well, these blokes were happy to spend the trip playing cards, leaving me to chat with the only other person in our compartment, a lady not much older than me, who seemed to understand the ways of the soldier, for she didn't pay any attention to the lads, who were doing their level best not to swear in front of her, and finding the going tough. So just to put them at ease, I piped up.

'So fellers, it's the army life for you, is it?'

'It is, sir,' says the cheekiest of them. 'We are joining our new unit at Manangatang, where we are to commence corps training on Monday.'

'And where did you do your basic training?'

'Puckapunyal,' they all chime in like the Vienna Boys Choir, and grin at each other for being so clever.

'And what corps will you be in, boys?'

'We'll be in the Ordnance Corps,' they say, as if that is a good thing, though I know better.

'Well, fellers, I hope you have a very pleasant stay in the army, and keep out of trouble handing out bombs and the like to your mates.' And I wink at the lady, to put her at ease, for say what you will of us Richmond coves, we can make a wink stretch a long way.

'We will indeed, sir, thank you. And would you be a soldier yerself? For you look as though you've been in the wars, if you don't mind me saying so.'

'No, son, I don't mind at all. I was in the 4th Light Horse Brigade in Palestine before some cheeky Turk sent me home with half of the Turkish ordnance buried in my hip. Blow me if I don't squeak every time it rains.'

At this they all had a good laugh and asked me if I'd like to have a nip of brandy.

'Well, now, fellers, I'd like nothing better than to take up your hospitality, but only if you'd invite this lady here to join us in a nip, as I'm not really a drinking man. But as the subject has come up, I'd like to drink to the memory of those who didn't leave that heathen place I was in.'

So the lady, for that is just what she was, gives us a smile that'd melt solder, and speaks up.

'Thank you, I believe I will join you in that nip, for two reasons: my husband was one of those men who did not come home, and he was in the same regiment as yourself, and survived God knows what hell in Gallipoli, only to be shot in the back by a Turk who had surrendered to him in Palestine. I'm sorry to spoil your party, gentlemen, but there it is.'

'And the other reason?' I say, taking the liberty touching her arm gently, as if she was a mate, for I can see that she did not mean to put a damper on the occasion, but was merely getting off her chest something that a lot of people were getting off their chests in those sad times.

'Well, boys, as my late husband used to say in his letters, I'm as dry as a camel driver's armpit, though he didn't say armpit, if you catch my drift.'

'To sleeping mates,' I say, and down my brandy, which gives me a bit of a shock, as I've only touched it once or twice before.

Well, now that the ice is broken I decline to tell any of my war stories, mainly out of deference to the lady, and mainly because I know they'll hear plenty for themselves once they start mixing with the other ranks in their unit. So they politely decide to go and inflict themselves on their mates in some other part of the train, there being more soldiers on board than you can shake a stick at, and leave the lady and myself alone.

The lady waits until they have closed the door, and shoves a paw at me.

'Anne Passmore.'

'Archie Taggerty.'

'So you were in the 4th Light Horse.'

'I was, but not long enough to take the Holy Land off Abdul. I'm sorry to hear about your husband. I saw Turkish prisoners do the dirty like that. They didn't get away with it, of course.'

I stopped talking. It was pointless to talk about it. Nothing that had been said about the war had captured the rottenness of it, the suffering. The heroism was talked about and written about as it suited the Army – and the Government, of course. But as far as I could tell, most of those stories had been made up as well. In the end I decided for myself that I would never hear the truth from anyone who was not there. And one of the reasons for that was that the uniqueness of the whole thing made it impossible to grasp.

The paintings and drawings, for example, showing the flashing colours of the regiments on their lances, and the red cross arm-bands, the red blood and the blue sky, the various colours of the horses – all a lie, when the truth was that the sand was nothing but brown talcum powder that clung to everything and filled the air, so that nothing could be seen bar the few yard in front of your horse, and everything was covered in a coat of the same brown powder. Only the freshly exposed entrails of the horses seemed to display their battle colours, as they galloped over the trenches and had their bellies sliced open by the Turkish bayonets.

I raised my eyes and saw that she was looking at me with a steady gaze, showing not pity, which I'm not sure I would have recognised anyway, but something else, something like friendship. It was the same look I'd seen many a time in Queenie's eyes, which I thought strange, as Queenie and me went back to the Ark, whereas Anne and I had just met. I also realised that I was not stuck for words with this lady, even though I'd had not much more experience conversing with real ladies as I'd had baking cakes.

'Well, now Annie,' said I, shoving the '-ie' on the end of her name the same as I had done when I first met Ruth, but not being aware of it at the time. 'It's bonza to meet the wife of a light horseman. In fact, it's an honour.'

'Me too, Archie. So where are you off to, then – Bendigo?'

Anne has her eyebrows raised while she is asking me this question, as if something is funny, but I cannot see it myself.

'No, Annie, I'm off to Kyneton, to see a man about a horse, or rather to see a young lady about one.'

'Well then we'll be getting off together, because I live there myself – always have. So you still like horses.'

'Well, I don't know about that. I'm going up to look at a horse that I hear might make a good racer. Not for myself, but for another – you know, he used to be in the Brigade himself. But I'm under orders not to mention his name.'

'I understand,' she says, and gives me a wink. 'I know how these things work. So who is this young lady, if you don't mind me asking?'

I reach into my pocket and take out the slip of paper I got from Dick Portland at Kilmore.

'A certain Miss Genevieve Oldmeadow, of Malmsbury, near Kyneton.'

'Well now, I happen to know that family has a lot of horses they use for show-jumping and the like, as that's the Oldmeadow girl's passion, so it'll be one of them, I reckon.'

'They don't race 'em.'

'I don't think they are a racing family, Archie. Oh hell, I may as well tell you the whole story: the family are well-known wowsers. So if you want to impress them, you'd better not mention that you're an ex-soldier, or they'll assume you're a drinking man and probably a mistreater of horseflesh, and bang goes your horse.'

I thought about this for a minute. Where I came from there were very few wowsers, if you didn't count the Callithumpians, who were not so much wowsers as a bunch of bloody ratbags, and of course, the Temperance League, a lot of whom were, according to my old dad, secret dipsos. Anne broke into my thoughts.

'Taggerty. Is that an Irish name?'

'Yes, it is.'

'Best you don't use it too often.'

'Anything else?'

'Well, you know wowsers.'

'Yeah.'

'Apart from that, should be plain sailing...that's if they want to sell.'

'Thanks. D'yer know these Oldmeadows personally?'

'No, but word gets around. My whole family is a horsey lot. I hear all kinds of things.'

'D'yer ride yourself?'

'I certainly do. Got a couple of good horses, too. Where're you staying?'

'Dunno.'

'You can stay at my place.'

'I don't know, Annie. I don't ...'

'Then it's settled.'

Victoria Oldmeadow turned out to be the prettiest girl I had ever seen on a horse, though she rode more like a British subaltern than even a British subaltern, and bobbed up and down as if she wanted to have as little contact with her mount as possible. Her horse, on the other hand, seemed happy to maintain a certain aloofness, such as I'd seen in many a horse that would end up being judged unfit for battle, but not for other, showy purposes. I watched her canter toward me having just watched her go over the jumps, and immediately judged her to be the finest female rider I had ever seen, not that I'd seen many.

She gives the horse to a handler of some kind without so much as a whisper or a pat to the horse, which was inexplicable to me, who had learnt that a man's mount is his best mate, and for his sheer guts and friendship, not to mention sacrifice, deserves all the praise he can get.

'Well, Mr Taggerty,' she says, shaking hands with me. 'What do you think of my jumper?'

'He's a lovely animal alright, though I can see he's not been at it for long. Does he know these are not high jumps?'

'What do you mean *know*? He knows what I tell him to know, Mr Taggerty.'

'Well, that's one way of getting a horse to go over jumps, I suppose.'

'And I suppose you've done a bit of jumping?' she says, looking me up and down the way people have been looking at me since I was knee-high to a grasshopper.

'Just a bit, though nothing as elegant as that. In fact, I don't think I've ever seen riding as good as that in my whole life, and I've seen my share of riding.'

'Oh, and where was that?'

'Oh, here and there,' I say. 'But to change the subject for a mo, I've come to have a look at the colt whose sister I saw at Kilmore the other day.

'Oh yes, and how is Delilah?'

'Well, she's lame at the moment, and will never be more than a riding hack, though she has a proud look about her.'

Well, we were walking to the stables as we talked, and there were enough horses in that places to retake Jerusalem.

'If you're interested in Delilah's brother, you can you can forget it, unless you can pick him out from this lot.'

Well I could tell that there was some kind of trick to this game, so I took a slow walk up the long stable and had a long hard look at the horses, and saw a couple of the same height and colour as Delilah, and one with the same flash on his forehead, but not with the same bearing. Then I came to a horse with that same independent look in his eyes, and the same way of holding his head, though not with the same colouring at all. I put my hand out and said a quiet word to him, and he came over and looked me in the eye as if he'd sensed I'd gotten his number.

'Delilah sends her regards,' I says, stroking him.

'Well now, that's a first,' says young Victoria. And she turns to a cove who had come into the stable, and who was dressed in a very fancy tweed jacket. 'Dad, Mr Taggerty picked Garryowen just like that, and seems to have made a friend of him into the bargain.'

'Well then, Mr Taggerty, I suppose you deserve a ride on him for your efforts.' And he comes over and shakes hands. 'King Oldmeadow.'

Remembering what Anne had told me about these people, I reckoned the last thing I wanted was for them to see me on a horse, for the horse soldier has an easy way of riding that comes from living, and even sleeping in the saddle, and having absolute trust in his mount, not to mention the lazy way we has of riding, despite having been to the best riding school the army could muster. A man like Oldmeadow would put two and two together quick smart.

'I'd like nothing better, sir, but the fact is, I have injured one of my hips so bad, I can neither mount nor stay on a horse. But I would like to see him gallop around a bit.'

So I get my wish, and while I am watching this horse galloping an easy circuit of a long track that would tax a stock horse, the girl's old man shoves a pipe in his mouth and speaks to as follows, through clenched teeth.

'You'll forgive me for saying this, I hope, Mr Taggerty, but I'll be straight with you. I will not sell that horse if he is to be raced. I do not hold with horse racing.'

'Then you can rest easy, sir, as I am acting for a party, whom I cannot name, who needs just such a horse for very simple, you might say, showy work as a mount, a horse who is capable of working continuously for an hour at a stretch, and has the temperament to allow himself to be ridden by a schooled rider without trying it on every five minutes.'

He takes the pipe out of his mouth to speak.

'I can't mention the party's name.'

'Mmm.'

'Also, I know this horse's sister had weak spots, and went lame, and why. That won't affect my decision, but it will affect the price.'

'You haven't heard my price.'

'I have heard that it's your daughter who owns the horse, and it's she who'll name the price.'

'She has too many horses already, and this horse likes to be out for a stretch, or he gets restless, and my daughter's only interested in jumping. I reckon she'll probably sell. Mind you, I think she'll want to know who's buying him.'

Just then the young lady rode up, looking a touch out of breath, while the horse was as fresh as a daisy. My mind was made up. That night I sent a telegram to Wren: '*Have two-miler. Need double money.*'

I had an address on the outskirts of town. Anne's place turned out to be a large old house with a veranda all round, completely hidden by trees of all colours and shades, as though it was sitting in the Royal Botanic Gardens. It was at the end of a long drive at the end of a longer street in which it was the only house. Once I got up close to the house, I could see evidence of horses and what looked like a little farm around the back, and wandering chooks, which always have a friendly look about them.

When I got up to the front porch, there was Anne sitting in a long seat with a high back, looking serene, as a body should when they're sitting on their own front porch at journey's end. She had a tea set on a low table in front of her, but no tea.

I went up the steps and sat down beside her, following her silent nod, feeling as if I had done it a thousand times.

'Feel like a cuppa?'

'Wouldn't say no.'

'I'll get us one. Put your feet up and call the cat a bastard.'

I grinned at this, for I hadn't heard it before, it sounding like the kind of thing a country person might say, or a soldier maybe. A city person would have a cat alright, but wouldn't call it a bastard as long as it was catching vermin, which were as thick as footballs at a factory picnic.

'But not the dog,' she added. 'He's got enough on his plate. Haven't yer, boy?' she added, as a blue heeler appeared from around the corner and cast a yellow eye over me as though I'd come to foreclose on the mortgage. 'Don't worry, he won't bite.'

Introductions complete, I give the dog a scratch on the head and settled in to my cup of tea, and listen to tails of the horsey community in the district, which, as it turned out, was rich and fascinating, complete with such skulduggery as would put a city policeman to shame.

'See yer got her horse, Arch,' she says during a silence created by a drop in the breeze, which had made the big eucalypts shush each other in turns. The dog wakes up suddenly and raises his head with his eyes on me and a question in his eyes so that I know he knows that word well.

'How can yer tell?'

'I can tell when a man's made a good deal, whether it's for a horse, a dog or a shotgun.' She was staring out over the front lawn. 'And I can tell when he's dipped out altogether.'

'How's that, then?'

'Ned here bites him.'

'You're pulling my leg.'

'Yeah, but I had you for a sec, didn't I?'

I liked Anne right off. I had never before met a woman who did not try to use her unfair advantages, of which women had more than their fair share, to catch a bloke off balance, and that included a Queenie who could talk Oscar Wilde into changing his ways, to Ruth, who didn't have to say a word at all to get my full attention. She was not at all like any woman I had met, being dressed slightly differently for one thing.

She had not changed her clothes, as women do after a day out, but was still wearing a pale green dress, that matched the pale paperbark leaves all around the house, and had her red hair tied with a bow. She had kicked off her shoes, though, and was now massaging her feet, one at a time, as we talked, whereas a city girl wouldn't be caught dead doing that unless the other bloke was her brother, or some bloke she wanted to get rid of.

We talked without saying much, and I noticed that she never asked me any questions about my past, and never volunteered much about her own. I reckoned that she could see a man had been in the wars in more ways than one, while I could tell the same about her, not that it showed. It was just a feeling.

Wren wrote and thanked me for the horse, and said he could do with another distance runner, if I could find one. He also sent me some money, not that I needed it. The first thing I did was ask Anne's opinion.

'You'll find all the good horses you want at towns without leaving Victoria,' she says. 'Go north-east and you'll be in brumby country.'

'I thought they bled that place dry.'

'Not likely. They left all the foals and young horses, and lots of mares. The horses are all there, and you don't even need to find them as they've already been found and broken in by the locals. Anyhow, have a wonder around – I'll give you a few names and addresses of rellies of mine around the place – and use this place as your base. You'll be right.'

'And what about you, will you be right?'

'Course. I always have.'

'How'd do get to be out here? I can see this place isn't a working farm.'

'My late husband was the son of a successful farmer. He and his father didn't see eye to eye –'

'What, about farming?'

'About anything at all, but especially about the war. His dad was dead keen on going over there and showing those Turks a thing or two, so he enlisted in the Light Horse.'

'I thought that was your husband.'

'His father went first. He'd been in the Boer War, so he was itching to get back into it, and joined the 13th Light Horse. They sent him to France, and he was killed pretty much straight away. But they told us he was badly wounded, so of course, we weren't surprised when the mail stopped. So after a year of no letters, and the family thinking he was still alive, Dyson joins this new regiment, the 4th Light Horse –'

'That was my crowd.'

'Oh yes. Well, that was the last I saw of him. He went to Gallipoli, then to Palestine. He died at Gaza.'

'Dyson Passmore,' says I, trying to remember.

'He was a lieutenant. Over there, they called him Polly, probably because he was a farmer, and some people think we're all cow-cockies.'

I got a shiver as she said this, for I had been at Gaza myself, and saw many a good man die, and many more Turks, though the Turks, who were not stupid by a long chalk, had a way of deciding when to throw in the towel that would bring tears to your eyes. But mainly it was the nickname Polly that did it, and it took me back to Polly Corbett, the bloke who'd died with me, in the night. He'd mentioned another Polly in his Regiment.

'What is it, Arch?'

'I was at Gaza – hell, every man and his dog was there at some time of another. It was well defended, and after we chased the Turks out of there, they came back and defended it all over again. It was there that I was wounded.'

I felt that I had to say to say something, but nothing seemed to do the trick – it was always the same when you wanted to talk about it.

'The last thing that happened to me was that I met a bloke who knew your husband. He mentioned him to me. *Polly Passmore,* he said. I remember because he had the same nickname.'

I looked over to Anne. I knew how valuable information about lost loved ones was.

'Sorry, that's all I can tell you.'

'Thanks, Arch. And what happened to the other Polly?'

I wanted Anne to hear the truth.

'He died right there in my arms, in the desert ... in the moonlight.'

'Did you know him well?'

'I only knew him for half an hour.'

We listened to the crickets for a while.

'Anyway, the Passmores own a fair slab of this district, mostly working farms, though this particular property is my own house. It's the house I was born in.'

'That's about it really. I'm not close to the Passmores, except Mrs Passmore, who is pretty much my own mother these days. You'll meet her eventually, I s'pose, though not out at her place.'

'And have you got any brothers and sisters?'

'I have a brother, who owns the stock and station agency here in town, and a couple of married sisters in Melbourne – that's where I'd been when you met me on the train. And I can tell you're a city bloke through and through, even though you can ride.'

'I am that, though you'd be best not to ask me any questions, or I might lie to you.'

'Tell you what, why don't you lie to me a bit. Then, when you feel like it, tell me the truth a bit, and see how it feels.'

25 Revelations

Well now, this was such a new idea to me, I had to think about it
for a while, and I'm ashamed to say that I wondered what was in
it for Anne, I mean, having a bloke around who might be telling
her porkies about this and that. I probably mentioned to you that
we Taggertys have never been known to be particularly fast on
the uptake where women are concerned, and rely entirely on
luck to preserve the family line. Of luck we do tend to have more
than our fair share, though only in that one department. Then
again, it could be the fact that I tend to list a little to starboard
when I walk due to my being born with a bung hip and then
following up with a series of accidents involving that same hip, so
as I swear that I should be walking round in circles by now.
Anyway, I have been told that women are drawn to such types,
though I don't think that would have been Queenie's or Ruth's
excuse, as they were women who knew what they liked, though
most of the time they liked completely different things.

'But Annie, I don't want to lie to you.'

'And I don't want you pretending to be what you're not, if
you see.'

A thrill of terror went right through me, as if she had worked
me out like some kind of mind reader. It was an effort to speak,
but I had to say something.

'I reckon I see alright, but I don't reckon I understand.'

'Well that'll have to do for now. Now, how about tea?'

Anne had a pleasant way of finishing off every conversation with a suggestion that we eat, and I found this to be a wonderful way of conducting a friendship, as I had never had truly wonderful food, not even from Ruth, who was taught to cook by an angry Irishwoman with a drunken husband and a food budget that somehow never stretched. Anne, on the other hand was a dab hand in the kitchen, and could cook up just about whatever she felt like in a jiffy. I would have stayed for the cooking alone.

'Annie, I like you more than a bit, you know, but I'd stay here for the cooking alone.'

'I know it,' she says, stirring something. 'You've been hurt, Arch, a lot, and I don't mean recently. It's like you didn't have a childhood or something. Am I right?'

'I was a bit of a rough-nut, got into strife. Spent some time at College.'

'What's that, reform school?'

'No, Pentridge. That's how the army got me: emptied the prison.'

'How old were you?'

'Sixteen. Funny part is, before I went to Pentridge I thought I'd get a slap on the wrist and be home by tea time. Nothing's been the same since. Should've seen it coming.'

'Ah, yes, how often do we say that? I thought I was going to settle down and have kids and be a farmer's wife.'

I didn't want to ask a lot of questions, as that wasn't how our relationship seemed to work. Anne gave me a smile, as if to say: '*Well, now where did all that come from?*' and I looked at her face.

It was a face that smiled a lot, and even had a way of looking like it was going to smile when it was frowning, which was pretty all by itself. Her eyes were of a colour that was hard to place, neither blue nor green, but never exactly in between, sometimes bright, and sometimes almost grey. You only get a few seconds to sum up someone's eyes, but that's all you need. I must have looked harder and longer than was polite, because she raised her eyebrow in a question.

'Just looking at your eyes, they being a colour I don't think I've seen before, though pretty,' I was quick to add.

'Archie, it's no wonder that I took to you the moment I saw you, for you've got a tongue that'll turn a lady's head. I'll bet you've had a swag of girls chase you in your time.'

'They might have chased me, but catching me's another thing. Besides, most of 'em would be disappointed if they caught me.'

'You reckon, do you?'

That was a strange conversation. I told Anne a lot of things about myself that others had had to find out for themselves, usually over years. I didn't mind at all. Anne didn't seem to have any secrets at all, and it's a strange thing, but when you're talking to a person like that, not that I'd met many, you tend to forget all the reasons you had for not speaking of your life, which can be a relief.

'So what do you do to keep yourself busy out here, if you don't mind me asking?'

'I give music lessons to the kids of the district, on this piano.'

I had in fact seen the piano, but took no notice of it, as they were a familiar sight all over the place, at least they were in Melbourne. My own mother had one, and she could play it a little, and did on special occasions, but I had never been drawn to it myself.

'They come over here?'

'They come from far and wide; teachers are like hen's teeth our here. It keeps me busy, and it pays for the odd luxury, and for trips to Melbourne, of course.'

'I see you do a lot of reading, too.'

'I read anything that's not nailed down. You could say I come from a reading family.'

I looked at the titles, and saw that there was a lot of poetry, including some familiar Australian poets.

'I love poetry,' she said, following my eyes.

I stopped and picked up a volume by Polly Beer.

'I bought that one because of her name,' she said. 'You know how it is. Anyway, it turns out I like her poetry. They say she was a nurse in Egypt during the war. I can't believe what a small world it is.'

I held the book in my hands and felt it take on a great weight, as though it was solid lead, and then felt it grow even heavier, so that I felt like I wanted to drop it. I even felt my hand and my arm grow tired, then my bad leg, then the rest of my body.

'What is it?'

I turned and looked at her. I could see she was at the very least puzzled, and probably a little concerned. The words in that book had become such a burden to me that I could barely lift my own little book of verse. It was time to come clean.

'I have a confession to make.'

'You're married, I know.'

'How do you know?'

'Sticks out a mile.'

'Hell.'

'It's not a problem for me. None of my business. So, is that it?'

'No, that wasn't it. I was going to say that I wrote this.' I held the book up.

'You're Polly Beer? Are you sure?'

'Oh I'm sure all right. 'I got the "Polly" from the bloke I told you about, and the "Beer" from Beersheba.'

I realised that she hadn't moved.

'You okay, Annie?'

'Yeah, yeah. I'm just finding it hard to ... are you pulling my leg?'

'Wish I was. I started publishing the stuff while I was in Cairo, and somehow I just couldn't stop. Sometimes it drives me mad.'

I opened the book at the first poem and looked at it. I expected to see a stranger's work, something so changed by age that it was no longer recognisable. Instead, I heard my own voice, surrounded by the noises of 1918 Heliopolis. My voice sounded different, though, and I knew why, instantly, though I doubt whether anyone else would have. It sounded like the voice of an old man. It was the voice of most of the blokes who'd survived casualty evacuation. It had run out of ways to express its weariness and pain, and had become simply the generic patient's voice.

I closed the book and handed to it to her as she sat and stared, and began reciting the first poem, surprised that I could remember it, but not bothering to stick to the printed word, and editing and embellishing as I went, carelessly, like an editor who has been distracted by the news that the pub across the road has just burned down.

Anne had not opened the book, but sat and watched me with keen eyes, like a hawk that has found something to observe without feeling inclined to pounce. I stopped after I had more or less covered the first stanza, and sat down. There was the sound of a gum creaking outside as the wind picked up, and there was the sound of an answering creak somewhere in the house itself, as if the two had suddenly decided they'd had enough of me and my poetry, and wanted to swap a yarn themselves.

Anne produced a little hanky with flowers embroidered in the corners, and wiped the forming tears from her eyes.

'Sorry, love, didn't mean –'

'No, Arch, it's alright. I wasn't thinking of my husband just then, but of you. Arch, what has happened to you? You've had a hard time, haven't you? You wrote all of this?'

'There's a lot more, you know. They reckon people like it; they're always asking for more. But I hate it.'

'You can't be serious, you can't. How can you say that when you wrote it? How can you hate something that so many people love?'

'I don't know, Annie. The fact is, I haven't told anyone that I did write it – just one, in fact.'

'You told your wife.'

'She loves the stuff. She couldn't get enough of it. In the end, I had nothing to give her except my secret – it was a secret, you see.'

'She must have been proud of you.'

'You'd think so, wouldn't you?'

'If she loved the poetry, she would have been proud, you can take it from me.'

'It wasn't enough.'

'You said you hated it, the poetry.'

'I've hated it all my life, since I was a kid.'

'You've been writing all your life?'

'Where I came from, that wouldn't have gone down too well.'

'I can't believe what I'm hearing. The sheer bloody effort of keeping this to yourself. You're not a weak man, Arch, I can see that. My God ... my God.'

'Take it easy, love. It's just history, you know, a bloke's story, that's all.'

'No, Arch, it's not. This poetry is not a bloke's story. It's something special for everyone like me, who lost something – someone.'

'There are lots of war poets – I've read a few.'

'I'm not talking about those lost to the war. I'm talking about the sad parts of life, and the exciting bits, too, like the poems about horses.'

I laughed my head off at that, and after a few seconds, so did Anne.

'You know, everyone thinks Polly is a country girl of some kind, the way she writes about horses.'

'I should have known.' She slapped the arm of the chair. 'Ha! I should have known. A horse soldier – of course! You'll have to tell 'em.'

'They'd hate me.'

'What do you care? You said you hated being a poet.'

'It's just that –'

'What?'

'People in the city know me. They'd have a fit.'

'I thought you'd put all that behind you.'

'What gave you that idea?'

'Arch, when you're guard's down, I can read you like a flamin' book.'

That boxing term put me on suddenly on the defence, like the word itself.

'Touched a sore spot, I see. Sorry Arch, not prying or anything. People say I'm not backwards in coming forwards.'

'It's not you, love. I told you, a bloke's got a bit of a past, that's all.'

'I've never met a bloke that didn't have a bit of a past. But usually that's all there is to it: a flamin' bit.'

We let it rest. Anne was a bit embarrassed at the thought that she'd pried, and I was embarrassed at being alive – I think that just about sums it up.

Well, of course, my past had a way of catching up with me, overtaking my present and turning into my future, if you see what I mean, which is uncanny, if that's the word I want. And it did just that the following day, when Anne and me had taken a break from whatever it was she did and what I was supposed to be doing and turned up in my face. I should have known it would.

Anne and me had gone over to the Frangipani Cafe in town to get ourselves a proper lunch, to celebrate nothing in particular, when who should I bump into in the street driving a carriage and two horses but "Swingin" Sam Burns, an old mate from the Regiment who'd been recruited with me from the Coburg University.

'Well, I'll be blowed if it isn't Trooper Burns,' says I. 'Annie, this here scallywag is Sam Burns, late of His Majesty's Light Horse, and not a man to be trusted with a horse that hasn't got a rider on him.'

'Well, well, well. Archie Taggerty, the Richmond Terrier, as I live and breathe. I heard you'd shot through back to America after, well, you know, after ...'

'Sam, this is Mrs Passmore.'

'Anne,' says Anne, giving Sam a smile I'm not sure he deserves. 'What's all this about the Richmond Terrier?'

I make a face, but the cat is out of the bag and half way to the next town. Burnsie can see it too, and says nothing, just gives an embarrassed laugh, which turns into a wheezy cough.

'I used to do a bit of fighting...it's in the past.'

'Arch was the Australian Bantamweight champ. Retired unbeaten after ...'

'That's enough, Sam. You'll bore everyone in town to death with your tall tales.'

'Well, now, Sam, we were just about to have lunch in the Cafe. Would you care to join us? Archie's shout, eh Arch? I'd like to hear all about the Richmond Terrier.'

Now this was a situation that I couldn't say no to, as times were extra tough all over the place, and one look at Burnsie was enough to tell me that he was just getting by, and this cart was not his at all, the horses wearing gear that was in pretty good nick. So I was not going to put my foot down and deprive young him of a square meal, especially when I could afford it.

So here we were, all tight and cosy, sitting in the cafe having lunch, and me reluctant as hell to talk about the past for the simple reason that dragging it up had never once in my whole bloody life come to any good, and often had caused me a lot of grief.

My mind drifted back to 1916 and the Melbourne County Court, where some beak or other – all I remember is that he was a cold-hearted swine who deserved the number one field punishment, that is, being propped up on the firing line to be shot by anyone who happened to be at war with Australia that day. The judge had got my number all wrong and had not allowed half of my witnesses to appear on the grounds that they were known criminals and prostitutes and couldn't be trusted. The result was that not only did he get a very one-sided picture of the young man in the dock but also found it pretty difficult to warm to him, and decided that the rest of society would probably not warm to him either. I was therefore sent to the only place that would do me and the rest of the said society any good at all: *HM Pentridge Gaol*, Coburg.

What I didn't know, and the judge probably did, was that I would eventually be sent to the slaughter in France or Gallipoli. The judge said I was the most vicious little animal it had been his displeasure to try, and his pleasure to punish. I have to admit I smarted at the word little. I was more than a shade shorter than the rotten cop I bounced, and the unevenness of the fight should have been taken into account, but was not.

But young Burnsie was off and running, so I had to step in before he painted a wholly unfair picture of myself, any picture being probably unfair.

'That's a bit steep, Sam,' I said. 'I mean, it is well known that the fighters in the lighter classes have to employ a bit of subterfuge occasionally to get by – besides which, the punters love it and are prepared to throw coins for it.' I realised as soon as the words were out of my mouth that I hadn't put up a good defence. 'What I mean is – oh, I don't know.'

'They didn't call him the Richmond Terrier for nothing. What about Billy Magee?' he says, getting worked up, but suddenly realising he's said too much, clams up.

'What about him?' says Anne, looking amused.

'Nothing,' says Burnsie, catching my eye again, and seeing that I'm in no mood for him to take one step further. Of course, Anne's no fool, and she can see that the rest of the story would have made juicy listening, but she is nothing if not polite to a fault, and stirs her tea as if we'd been talking about the weather. However, Burnsie is now hell-bent on trying to paint me in a good light.

'They gave him a medal, you know. Bet he didn't tell you that?'

'I'll thump you in a minute.'

'Now what've I done? You're a flamin' hero. He is, you know.'

'Everyone got a medal, for God's sake, except them that talked too much.'

At this Burnsie laughed like mad and slapped his thigh. That took me back, that image, because it was just the way a bloke would laugh if he was in the saddle and something tickled him, like his mate nodding off and sliding out of the saddle, which happened quite bit in the Sinai. I had to join him in laughing, and pretty soon we were laughing and trying to push each other off our mounts, which is to say, our chairs, because that's all we had.

'Well, now Anne, your friends seem to be enjoying my tea-cake more that anyone I've ever seen,' says a buxom lady behind the counter.

'You'll have to forgive my friends, Maude; this one's' – she nodded at me – 'shell-shocked; and this one, well, I don't know about him.'

'He's a trouble-maker,' I said, 'and should be shown the door.'

But we were allowed to carry on, thanks to Anne being with us.

Still, we judged it best to leave, and headed out into the street where Burnsie had left the pair tied up. We left Sam heading for the pub and took off in the opposite direction.

'You might as well tell me, Archie, as I'll only get Sam drunk and get the truth out of him, you know.'

'Ah, hell, well now, let's see. Ah, hell.'

I didn't know if I was coming or going. I never talked about Billy, not with anyone. I didn't want to start now. Especially not now. But I felt safe with Anne, safer than I had felt with anyone I could think of, including Queenie, including Ruth – what was I saying, *especially* Ruth.

'It's just that I had a bad fight when I was in the boxing game, my last fight in fact. I hurt a bloke. Later, he died. I knew him. He was a mate. After that, I gave up the fight game. Ruth ...'

But I'd said about twenty times more than I'd meant to, and I pulled myself up. Both Queenie and Ruth often said they could read me like a book, so I reckoned I'd said enough. If I was that easy work out, I suppose Anne could do the rest herself.

'Arch,' said Anne, looking at me and stopping in the street, 'I was only asking about the medal.'

Talk about a mug. 'Jeez, I must be slippin'.'

26 Return of The Terrier

It's funny how life seems to keep an eye on you, just in case you develop a weak spot, one that it can take unfair advantage of, like when you're not looking, or when you're having a hard time. Life had had its evil eye on my for some time, I see that now: it's clear as day. Life was ready to spring, had followed me to the bush, saw me making friends, doing a job for an old mate, patching up his rotten maggot-eaten life, as it was, I guess. Life sort of follows you around, hiding in the shadows behind you, so that look around you as you might, you will never see him shoving his hand over his mouth to stop himself from laughing out loud at your naivety, your stupidity, I would even go so far as to say.

Life can take the form of an enemy shooting at you, like it did in Palestine, so that you can see it a mile off and take the appropriate steps. Or it can take the form of some lovely thing that fools you into thinking that everything has come up roses. It took the latter form when it got sick of following me around and sprung out of the shadows at me in Kyneton.

It was Sam Burns who was the messenger of the fate that was the rest of my life. I had stopped writing poetry, having figured out that a man who's more or less at one with the world has no need for that sort of relief. The poetry did not pressure me to get back into it. Instead, it cleverly sent Sam Burns around to Anne's place only the following weekend with a piece of news for me.

'I thought you'd like to know,' says Burnsie, 'that there's a boxing troupe in town.'

'I don't fight any more. Whose outfit is it?'

'Cal Kennedy's.'

'The trainer?'

'Things have changed, Arch. You've been out of touch. Kennedy's been banned.'

'I see.'

And I did. The fight game had been cleaned up since I quit, and the writing had been on the wall even then. There was a lot of talk about my last fight, and the purists – and the wowsers – had used it as an excuse to get rid of the larrikin element, the colourful side of the sport, you might say. Had I stayed I probably would have ended up being on the receiving end of all that hard feeling, though I personally felt that that would have been most unfair in the circs, my last fight being squeaky clean, despite the sad and spectacular outcome.

Kennedy had told his kid to do something dodgy, take a dive, something like that, and that had upset a few punters who'd lost a few quid as a result, important punters, like members if the Sportsmen's Syndicate.

So the Kennedys of the world were doing whatever was necessary to get by. And the world economy didn't exactly look kindly on the struggling sportsman.

'So what's the drum?'

'The usual, a few dollars for standing up to their champ, range of champs, take your pick.'

'You wouldn't get a fight, Sam. You're a pro. Kennedy'd spot you. Anyway, he might have seen you fight.'

'I know that, Arch. I thought I might be joining the troupe, you know, be a plant. I could fight unorthodox, look a bit silly, draw the mugs.'

'Fair enough. Have you talked to Kennedy?'

'Yeah, it's practically settled. It turns out he's short a lightweight.'

I looked at Sam. He was, properly speaking, a featherweight, but was carrying a bit of lard from all the drinking he'd been doing.

'Yeah, I know, I'm a shade heavy. No one'll know the diff.' And he suddenly launches into a few quick boxing moves at me to show that he's still got what it takes. But I can see he hasn't. 'So what d'yer say?'

'What, me? You must be mad. Ruth –'

'Who?'

'Nothing.'

'The little woman made you swear off the ring, did she?'

'Not exactly.'

Sam looks up at the house, and back at me, without saying anything.

'She's just letting me stay here while I buy a few horses.'

'I didn't say anything.'

'Well, see that you don't.'

'Touchy subject. Sorry, just talking to meself.'

'And you can stop that, too. I said I'm out of the game.'

'There's a few quid in it.'

'I'm a pro. I might hurt someone.'

'Nah, you're past it; no chance of that. I reckon Mrs Burns could do yer.'

'What, your missus?'

'Me mum.'

I didn't rise to the bait. I wasn't fighting.

'You might enjoy it.'

'Are you on a finder's fee?'

'I won't lie: there's a fiver in it for me.'

'Well, you're straight, I'll say that. But tell Cal I'm finished.'

But Sam had said something that gave me a tiny thrill in some place way down the back of my mind, where I'd stowed it a long time ago. He was right: I *might* enjoy it.

I went down to the Cal's show that night. He had his own tent on the outskirts of town in someone's back yard, not that you could tell one person's back yard from another's, under a circus tent of sorts with painted boxers all over it, even Jack Dempsey, which I thought a liberty. Cal himself was out the front spruiking for all he was worth, and filled the tent, to my astonishment, given that it was hard times and the game was definitely illegal. But I swear everyone in town turned up, even the parish priest and his off-sider, a pale young man with sandy hair and big hands who looked as if he could take on the crowd himself.

'Well, well, well. Look what the cat dragged in,' said Cal, and I remembered the first time I ever heard that voice, down at Ryrie's place.

'H'lo young Cal. See you're making a go of it, my boy,' I said, playing the larrikin.

'I heard you were up here,' he says.

'Sam'd be the guilty party,' I says.

'Ah yes, a willing fighter is Sam. He should pull in a few punters. You game?'

'Nah. Someone'd spot me; nNo one'd get in the ring with me. You'd wind up looking like even more of a mug than you do now, if that's possible.'

302

I said the words, but I was secretly hating myself for it, for I realised in the moment, smelling the canvas and hearing the punters murmur, that I sorely wanted to give someone a slap, even if it was just to get rid of the growing feeling I'd had since meeting Anne that I needed to clock someone. Not that I'd said as much to any man – or woman – nor would I. But I knew the feeling, for I'd been born with it, I reckoned. But Kennedy was a trainer, and trainers can read minds like mothers, and sergeant majors, and like a lot of the girls I knew at Charlie Wing's place.

'Tell you what: keep it a secret who you are; get you in the ring with one of my bantamweights; see how you like it. If you win, double the prize.'

'What if I lose?'

'*What if I lose?* he says. Well? Make up your mind; you're holding up the queue.'

'I'll make up my mind when I've seen a few bouts.'

'Fair enough.'

Well, of course Cal played the punters like a flaming church organ, but there was little need to, as it looked like every able-bodied sporting man in town wanted to have a go, and there was no shortage of coves who just wanted to thump someone for their present predicament, and there were a lot of them in one of those round about then. But it looked like a reasonably well-run affair, if a little rough on the punters at times. You pays your money and you takes your chances. But the fighters were under orders not to wipe the floor with anyone, so most blokes could go home with a little bit of self-respect, which was important, as women were allowed in.

At one point in the proceedings, Cal jumps into the ring and starts shouting and waving his arms about as if the Queen has just given birth in the dressing room, so the crowd shuts up and pays attention.

'Now for our next bout, young John B. Kanga, formerly of the Republic of Queensland, and a runner-up to the one-and-only King Rex, bantamweight champion of New Zealand, will take on all comers for a bout of three rounds.'

At those words, a young man who seems to me to be a kiwi of some kind ups and hops into the ring and dances around as if he's a kid who's all alone in his bedroom and imagining the day when he'll be a real boxer. I like his style, but I can tell that he's no has-been, and can probably box pretty well. So I'm wondering what he's doing working for Cal Kennedy, when Kennedy tips me the wink and I can see that this is the cove he wants me to spar with.

'What about you, young man? Three rounds with the champ, who, by the way, has promised his mum that he'll be home by ten, and so can't stay for more than that.'

The crowd all think this is very funny, of course, and look at me as if I'd be a drongo to say no to this dare.

So I say okay and the crowd claps politely, if a little nervously, for they can see I'm a little worse for wear, and take me for a returned soldier who's been run over by a tank or a blown up by a German mine, which is half right.

'Don't be silly, mate! Can't you see he's a digger?' rings out a voice in the crowd, sounding a lot like young Sam Burns, who's not finished earning his fiver.

'Yeah!' yell the crowd. 'Why don't you pick on someone else.' And some of them boo Cal, which makes him put on a very serious face indeed.

'I'm dreadful sorry, young man,' says he in his performer's voice. 'But I'll not be responsible for harming a brave lad such as yourself. You have no reason to prove yourself to me.'

In reply I say to the crowd, getting the hang of the occasion, 'Hang on a mo. I need a few quid; it's for me mum.'

And would you believe someone jumps up, and shoves his hand into his pocket and yells, 'If that's all you need, cobber, you can have some of mine – I'll only drink it.'

And I can see that if I don't do something the punters are going to finance my dear old mum and me, which would be downright dishonest, not to mention flamin' dangerous. So I wave a wing and shush them dramatically.

'Thank you, brother, no. I'll fight any man who tries to fling as much as a farthing at me. Let me earn me money fair and square.'

So the audience goes crazy of course, and I head for the back of the ring, where I strip and let myself be dressed in some boxing kit. While the crowd claps slowly, and Cal, a man of many talents, leads them in a chorus of *It's a Long Way to Tipperary*. Then I climb into the ring and do a bit of a slow shadow-boxing, slow because my hip has seized up a fraction from all the horse riding I've been doing, and I find that I have probably made the right decision after all. While all this is going on, John B Kanga, goes over to Cal and has an earnest conversation with him with his eyes fixed on me, and I can tell I've been spotted like a camel in a horse race. But I can see Cal frowning and shaking his head, as if he's not sure if Kanga knows what he's talking about.

So finally Cal calls us into centre ring and recites the standard cautions as if he is the ringmaster at a circus, and winking wickedly at the crowd as he says 'no rabbit punches', and 'no kidney punches', and the like, which makes the crowd shout in a great long wail of delight with each fresh caution, as it is a well-known fact that in the matter of travelling boxing shows, there are really no rules, as long as the punter doesn't actually get killed, as that could land the whole troupe in jail for a long time.

So the bloke whose job it is to ring the bell holds it up for all to see, but before he can dong it, up jumps Sam again, pointing at me, and says in a voice I swear he has copied from Cal Kennedy, 'I knew I'd seen that bloke before – that's Archie Taggerty, the Bantamweight champ.'

You could just about hear the bones in the punters' necks crack as they whipped their heads around to Sam, and then back again to me. There wasn't a closed mouth in the house. There was no movement. Sam stood frozen, seconds away from looking like either a complete drongo or a man of remarkable perspicacity, waiting for it all to sink in, remembering, if you will, that half of those present had had a glass or two before turning up.

There was a murmur, then a few shouts from here and there to the effect that I should be allowed to fight, and one or two – probably a few who'd bet against me in the old days – who thought I should finish off what I started. You could see that my image as a war hero had now dissolved like baccy smoke in a willy-willy, now that the crowd had something much more interesting to look forward to: the champ versus the bloke from the Republic of Queensland, wherever that was. And thanks to a few angry voices in the peanut gallery I could tell that the crowd were now hoping to see me get ironed out.

It was just like the old days in the Collingwood Town Hall, with me the bad bastard facing the straight bloke, never mind that he might have just finished two months for emptying a pub. There I was, lopsided and shifty-looking – that's what the papers said – facing this John bloke, who looked like he might still be loved by someone, and wanting to put one over him and everyone else in the place, and show him that the Richmond Terrier could be a nasty little bastard if he wanted to be, and in the ring, at least, he did.

'This changes things, ladies and gentlemen, I think you'll agree. I mean, John here's got a family to feed. I can't having him get beaten up by a man who killed his last opponent, can I now?'

At hearing this, a great crowd-shaped gasp rises up into the smoky air and the audience falls into a state of dark and hungry contemplation. Plainly, they are torn.

'Let him fight me, and I'll show him who's a killer,' pipes up Kanga.

And it's on.

The bell-ringer rings the bell and the Cal gets all formal, and says, 'touch gloves' and steps back to the ropes.

It was a three-rounder, and I for one am glad of that, for it was only my mind that was in shape to fight, for my body had gotten soft and sore, and rusty in the joints.

As we touched gloves, I put my face right up against John B. Kanga's and said to him, softly, because I could, 'What he said is right: I killed Billy Magee, and tonight, I'm going to kill again.' And because I was shorter than my man, and needed him to be at a disadvantage of some kind, I spat in his face, and danced back a step, knowing that if he was a fool he would wipe his face straightaway, which he did.

Up went his left, to wipe his face, and up went my right at the same level as his glove, in the hardest place to see, and I smacked his fist into his face with a neat hook. To my amazement, John didn't fall, but stood with his feet glued to the canvas, and shook his head like a dog with a bee-sting on his nose. I'd underestimated the man, and took a step back to see what he would do next. He walked up to me as bold as brass and snarled from somewhere down in his boots, not, I think, to think to put a scare into me, but because it was in his nature to snarl.

The audience were as happy as Larry at the way the fight started and one and all were heartily in hatred of me, and hoping I would get my comeuppance for that dirty trick. Well, of course, that was the sort of reaction that I had fed on for all my years in the ring, and seemed to move me to get things done in the way I knew best, which had little or nothing to do with the Marquess of Queensbury and his mob.

I now faced Kanga in my southpaw stance, which for me was completely arse-about and calculated to give him the idea that I was left-handed. He took the bait, and even though the bloke in his corner yelled, 'No, ya drongo, no!' it was too late, and Kanga lead way too long with his left in his confusion. I stepped in fast and hit him a few times over the top of his arm, and made him pay attention to his corner. I was feeling better than I thought I would at this point and was beginning to feel the old confidence when bang! I was sitting on the canvas looking up at John and not really thinking about anything in particular, not even why I was down there.

When I realised I was being counted I was up like a rabbit, but the trip back up made my hip hurt as if it was broken and with a yell of pain, I crumbled and went back to the canvas. The pain was about as bad as it had ever been, and I felt it hurting my soul, which was worse, as that was my weak spot. Cal was uncertain about what to do next, and by rights should have declared me unfit to box, except we were not at West Melbourne stadium but in a circus tent in a paddock in Kyneton, and there was already a lot of cash floating around the place.

I grabbed hold of Cal and dragged myself back to my feet, then did as John had done and roared like a freshly gelded colt, and shook my head wildly; not to show my anger, but to handle the pain, which was killing me.

Once I had found my footing I gave Cal a shove to get him out of the way, and took a step up to Kanga, as if I was going to fight, and Kanga, thinking it was all too easy, came in and ignored my extended right hand, his corner man having told him I would switch my stance, so of course, I didn't, as I couldn't put any weight on my right side, which was all heat, pain and pins and needles just then.

Kanga said to me at that point something about my mother, I think it was, but he was mistaken, as my mother had never made a living on her back, so I let his mistake go by me. Instead, I let him walk right up to me and punched him sharply one-two in the nose, his most prominent feature, which he was not defending all that well, then went on the back-peddle and found I was on the ropes with no way to go and no dodging power. I was only left with one punch, a short right to the bottom of the sternum and I gave it my best from about one foot away. It seemed to hurt Kanga, as he fell onto me, just as the bell rang, and I sat down where I was, with Kanga leaning on me as if I owed him a tenner.

Cal came over and pulled him up straight and he said he was okay, but went back to his corner breathing pretty hard, and I knew I'd found a weak spot.

Round two saw Kanga holding his gloves close to his face, and his elbows in tight, like a man who doesn't want anyone to know who he is or that he's got wallet in his inside pocket. I switched to the unorthodox stance for the first time, letting him see that I was a man of many parts, and wasn't going to give him a look at my best just yet.

We boxed on like that for the best part of the round, getting our faces slapped and getting tied up, but Kanga wouldn't let me get a look at those ribs again, not matter what I did, so I let him get me onto the ropes again, and slipped my left glove through his left elbow, as if we were going to doh-see-doh at a square dance, and pulled him square to me. Kanga didn't resist this, as he was breathing hard and noisily and was looking forward to a few seconds rest; but as he turned I gave him a mighty thump in the ribs exactly on the other side to his heart, and that upset him like nobody's business.

Of course, Kanga complained to Cal, and, of course, Cal told him to box on, and the rest of those in the tent were none too happy about all this, as they wanted to see as fair a fight as possible without me actually winning. I then commenced to landing as many blows on the back of Kanga's head as I could before Cal stepped in. But before he could separate Kanga I gave the kid a hard blow to the left buttock, wondering what effect it would have.

Well it gave him a fine limp which kind of mirrored my own; but he still hadn't worked out that the way to get the best of the Richmond Terrier is to box, not brawl, for I knew bugger-all about how to box. And now he was about as elegant as a drunken dogcatcher. And his corner was yelling at him to put me down, while my own was trying to catch the eye of some filly in the crowd who were all, by the way, hoping I would get up after all – it's always the way when they see a little man copping it left, right and centre from the organisation.

He did eventually limber up enough to box the way he was trained to in the first place, and had finally got it into his head that he was in a boxing match and a not a street fight, though for me they were all street fights.

I had no trump cards. My best bet was that he hadn't fought a decent opponent for a long time, and his best bet was I was just another mug. I didn't give the young feller chance to find out. I switched to my natural stance for the first time, and tucked my head in, which was my style, and put my hands in front of my face, which made me look a lot more defensive than I really was. As he walked up to me, a bit crookedly, I thought, I planted my feet and gave him a right cross that would have made Les cry. Kanga's head snapped back, and he fell straight down on his back and didn't move. I thought: *Christ, I've killed him*, but then I saw that various bit of him were twitching and quivering, and it was all over bar the shouting.

Well, to cut a long story short, there was practically a riot in the boxing tent, as there was a lot of pent up anxiety in society generally in those days, and it all came out like a bomb going off. The crowd threw a lot of money into the ring, and I just indicated to young Kanga that he could have it, and went over and told him I was sorry if I bent the rules a bit, but I could see if I didn't he'd probably have me for breakfast, which seemed to cheer him up a bit. Then I got down and slipped out of my boxing togs and into my street gear and made an exit, though not before stopping to collect my earnings from Cal.

'Archie,' he says, 'you are a crafty bastard, and no mistake. Seeing you fight fair took me back, it did. I'll be in touch.'

I don't know how I got out of that place. It seemed that everyone wanted to shake my hand – God knows why – the winners and the losers, those that like me and those that hated me – everyone. A few of them said they'd seen me before and when I heard that I didn't know whether to run like hell or shake hands. When I got to the exit, who should be standing there but

Anne, looking at me as if she's never seen me before, so that I knew straight away she'd seen the fight.

'So that's what you used to do?'

'Pretty much.'

'And did you ever lose?'

'Nah. Got a few aches and pains for me trouble, though, like tonight.'

'And how's that bloke you flattened...Kanga?'

'He'll live.'

I regretted saying it straight away, but there it was. I kept my mouth shut. We walked away from the yelling and clapping and the raucous voice of Cal making an announcement, and into the dark street that led to town, and Anne slipped her arm through mine.

27 Goodbye to Kyneton

The next day being Sunday, Anne and me walked down to Our Lady of the Rosary church for Mass, even though I hadn't been for years. It just seemed natural. The church was packed, as a lot of people had taken to praying for better times, and hoping, I suppose, that it was true that the squeaky wheel gets the grease. A few people recognised me from the previous night, I thought, and there was a whisper or two. I was used to that, as it happened all the time when I was a Richmond lad, though for all the wrong reasons. The priest, Father Meaghan, found my eye during the sermon and fair twinkled at seeing me in his church, so I guessed he'd been at the fight, as it is well known that no Irishman can resist the sight and sound of a stoush, priest or not. After Mass, he ran around the front and collared me while Anne caught up with an old neighbour she hadn't seen for a while.

'Archie Taggerty! What a fight, what a fight! Would you be all right, my boy?'

He was ringing my hand as if he was pumping bore-water.

'Yes, Father, I don't think young Kanga laid a glove on me. Must be the luck of the Irish.'

'Surely, not my son. It's just that God can spot one of His own when He sees him – just as He can spot a heathen,' he added cheerfully. 'Now tell me, what's the story with you and Mrs Passmore – not one of liberal and sinful living, I hope?'

'No, indeed, Father, and you would be surprised to hear that I've had very little of that in my short and often regrettable life.'

At this he gave me a friendly clip on the ear that nearly knocked me over.

'Oh, for a man who can fight like the devil you are an easy man to kid. I know all about your hunt for horses, and I know your friendship with the good lady is above board. Oh, yes, I know everything that goes on in this sinful town, the good and the bad. Now, as that was the last Mass for the day, I would be honoured if the both of you would come over to the presbytery and join me in a cup of tea and some of Mrs O'Loughlin's scones. I can't eat 'em by meself; sure a man's not made of cast iron.'

Anne caught my eye and walked over and off we went to the presbytery, with Father Meaghan hurrying on ahead to warn his housekeeper that we were coming. When we arrived we were shown into a cool, subdued sitting room, one of which seemed to exist in every presbytery in Victoria, and Father Meaghan announced, with an exaggerated look at the mantle clock: 'Well now, look at that. No wonder I'm feeling as dry as a protestant's icebox. I think I'll forgo the pleasure of Mrs O'Loughlin's scones and have an ale – it was the preferred drink of Our Lord Himself, you know. Will you join me? Anne?'

'B'lieve I will, thanks, Pat.'

'Arch? And please call me Pat – me sainted mammy does.'

'Thanks, Father.'

'Pat.'

'Pat.'

He disappeared and reappeared a few minutes later with the beer, and a hungry look on his face.

'Anne has been telling me about your adventures, and also how the word has got around the district that someone is buying horses. In other words, young man, the jig is up.'

He laughed heartily at the look on my face, and didn't stop until he had rolled himself a cigarette and taken a drag.

'Ah, that's better. Don't ever take up the cloth, young man: the vices that go with it cost too much. Now, as I said, you'll find the diggings are worked out around here. With one exception, that is.' He winked at Anne and took a mouthful of the cold beer. 'The bishop himself has a modest stable, you know.'

'Yes, but Pat, I'm looking for horses that haven't already been snaffled.'

'Ah yes, well, His Grace is a crafty devil after me own heart, and does not train any but his claimers in Melbourne. He trains his specials out here, and as luck would have it, he has a distance runner fresh in from the Upper Murray. Never raced. Low price. What His Grace doesn't know, and so on.'

'But Father – Pat, too many people would know.'

'Not if the horse had to be put down. His Grace has never seen him.'

He took another gulp of beer. *No sips for this man*, I thought.

'Okay, Pat, what's in it for you?'

'Let's just say l will get to clear a debt and get the best of an old adversary at the same time and leave it at that.'

'Sounds okay.'

'Anne, my dear, will you get bit of fresh hay from that brother of yours? I'll see that the horse is delivered in the next day or two.'

Anne, who hadn't said a word while all this was going on, now allowed her glass to be clinked by Meaghan, and promptly began a conversation in such a suspiciously Sunday way that I knew she had been in on it all along. She was, it was turning out, a woman of parts.

Of course, the horse turned up, and Anne went for a ride on him and declared him at least a contented enough animal, but in need of testing, and I looked the horse over, and saw that he would made a good whaler, having the right mix of muscle and sturdiness, but with a will to work and a spring in his step. Such a horse cannot be talked out of or into anything, except by a mate.

The next day we took the horse down to the local racecourse and a jockey of few words turned up and jumped on the horse and took him for a gallop the long way around. He was a lovely runner, ready to pace hard, but ready to come home hard too. I could see him at Beersheba, running the plain, a three mile run into the cannon and machine guns, half dead from thirst and with the scent of Abraham's Well in his nostrils. *Good boy*, I said to myself as he came home. *Good on yer, mate.*

'Annie, I'm jackin' in this horse lark.'

It was a week after the horse had been taken to Melbourne, and the two of us were sitting on the front verandah having a cuppa and some scones and jam that Anne whipped up.

'Thought you would. You know your horses alright, but you're much better at beating the daylights out of other blokes, Blind Freddy can see that.'

'Truth is, I'm restless. Being here with you, it's getting to a man. I don't know whether I'm coming or going.'

'Was it that letter you got?'

'That letter was from my business partner in America. The studios are going out of business. No one's working. Tax problem. That was my income. And Ruth and Jean's.'

Anne didn't say anything for a while.

'Work's impossible to get out there, I hear. You're welcome to stay here with me as long as you like - you know what I mean.'

'I know, Annie, and don't think I haven't thought about it. But I need to earn money.'

'You're going to fight, aren't you?'

'It's what I do.'

'What about the poetry?'

'It wouldn't be enough. There's bloke's out there willing to pay good money to see a prize fight, and throw away what's left on the book. I was only stripped of my title for failing to defend it. The syndicate never got around to banning me.'

Anne took a bite out of her scone and looked away. She was pretending to be more interested in an old gum she'd only seen every day of her life. When she turned back, she was as close to tears as I've seen her.

'You're not going to hook up with those drongos, are you, love?' She nodded toward the town. 'It'd only be a matter of time before someone from Melbourne found out and came up and flattened you, then where would you be?'

'Nah, not them, love. You're right about them being bloody drongos. I wasn't born yesterday. But while I've still got a few bob to me name, I best shake a leg.'

'I s'pose you'll be going back to Ruth and Jean.'

'I haven't thought that far.'

'Well, p'raps you should. I have a feeling it would be the first time.'

Anne took me to the station in the sulky the next morning. To my surprise, I was also seen off by Pat Meaghan, the rogue priest. I hadn't thought we'd become close, but there he was, and seemed to be completely without judgement as to my coming and

317

going. We stood on the station for a long time while a small crowd made their way onto the train, then waited until the last minute before seeming to feel it was time for me to go. There was little to say, and that's what I said. Anne, on the other hand had quite few words to say, and said her piece, while the priest went for a stroll over to the stationmaster and bent his ear about something.

'Now listen to me, Arch. It seems to me that you don't know what's bad for you or what's good for you, so I'm going to step in right now and give you a piece of my mind, not that I mean any harm by it, but in the hope that you'll listen, if you care anything for me.'

'Now, you know I care.'

'I don't want to hear your blarney, Arch, 'cos I'm guessing you know how to use it when a woman's affection are at stake.'

'That's not fair, Annie.'

'No! That's enough. Just let me speak. Now, sometimes coincidences happen, out of the blue, lucky circumstances, you could say, out of nowhere, that need to be grabbed and acted on, if you get my meaning.'

'No, I don't. I don't know what you're talking about.'

'All I'm saying is, if you suddenly feel the hand of coincidence on your shoulder, think twice, then think again, about what's possible, why God might have chucked you a few crumbs.'

I'd never heard her speak like that, eloquently, poetically. I wondered for a moment if that was something all women possessed, and if that was the reason people liked Polly Beer's poems so much. But the train had begun to move, and I had to be on it. I kissed her on the cheek, then she kissed me back, and

I quickly got myself on board, and watched as she and Pat waved. None of us was smiling.

I sat for a long time watching the countryside go past, and not even capable of thinking about the future, but dreading seeing Ruth and Jean again – I had been away too long. I had been away so long that to my surprise, all I was capable of feeling was guilt and pain. I knew the feelings well; I believe they were inherited by every Irishman in Australia. No, I *knew* it. I wasn't sure if I had the strength to face them, or the will, or the guts. I had found it impossible to live with Ruth; she wore me out. As for Jean, I had no power left to love her. I had been her mother and her father when Ruth was in hospital, and I had hoped and prayed that I would grow to be a loving person through the experience, and that Jean would somehow pick up on that and forgive me in some way.

But love doesn't work that way. It works the way Queenie loved, and Anne love, with a sense of the moment having arrived and being important because it was already packing up to leave. They loved not for a reason, but with a sense. And I think it was that sense that Ruth lacked. She had a more desperate way of looking at the world. Irish again!

I gave up and pulled my focus back for a moment, aware that the window was mirroring a man's face in the compartment window. I looked up and saw a bespectacled face, serious and happy at the same time, smiling, I realised, with one side of his face, and hinting at some weight with the other. And yet appearing peaceful.

He slid the door aside and shoved his head in just a little. 'Mind if I come in?'

'No, not at all.'

He sat across from me and smiled a sociable smile as if he was going to speak. He was, I knew, sizing me up. I'd seem many a bloke do it, in prison, the Army, in the ring, at the track - I'd done it myself. But this bloke and me were, it seemed to me, no adversaries.

'Mind if I smoke?' he asked.

'No, go ahead. I'd have one myself, 'cept I don't smoke,' I said with a look of resignation.

'Spoken like a poet.'

'Was that an odd choice of words, or do you know something I don't.'

'I know who you are, if that's what you mean,' says he, having a bit of fun.

'And who might I be?'

'Pollywollydoodle, that's who.'

That rang a bell, though I couldn't place it. But I knew he had the right bloke, all right.

'I am Polly, all right. You have me, friend. But how did you spot me? I mean, I didn't know anyone knew Polly was a bloke.'

'Think hard now. One man knows; one man has always known.' I frowned. 'Right from that first poem, sent from Cairo.' He raised his eyebrows.

'Ah yes, Jack Galloway told you. So you know Jack. But I haven't seen him for a while. How'd you know I'd be on this train, er, sorry, I don't -'

'Clarrie -'

'Clarrie.'

'Shall we call it coincidence?'

There was that word again. What had Anne said about coincidence? I should pay attention? I should, that's what she's said. I looked at Clarrie, puffing his pipe and looking out the window. I couldn't believe it was a coincidence, but I couldn't help thinking this would be a good time to let go and trust. Anne had never steered me wrong. She had become my best mate. It was true, I realised. She *had*.

'I don't think I believe in that, never have, really. Most of the things that happened to me, well, I could see why they happened, further on. Most of the time it was just plain due to me. And that's that.'

'What about your poetry? Do you think there's a cause for that? I always think it just appears in a man spontaneously, regardless of the circumstances.'

'So you know about that, do you?' Then it hit me. 'Ah, Clarrie Dennis! of course. Pollywollydoodle! That's what Jack said you called me. And that would make you the *Triantiwontigongolope* man, I reckon.'

'I s'pose it would.'

We laughed and shook hands. I'd been set up, but I didn't mind, as it had been done by friends.

'So, are you in a hurry to get back to Melbourne?'

'Why do you ask?'

'I was going to ask you if you you'd like to come out to my place for a day or two. A man can write poetry out there. It's a special place...you'll see what I mean.'

I went inside for a moment, thought of Ruth and Jean. I needed to see them. Suddenly I needed to see if it was a lost cause, or whether there was any point in carrying on.

'That's very kind of you, Mr Dennis.'

'Clarrie –'

'Clarrie. And I might take you up on it. But first I have to take care of a few things. Are you going home?'

'Catching a train from Melbourne up the Albury line. Anyway, think about it.'

I thought about it all the way to Melbourne, of course. It was one more thing to think about. And none of the things that had happened to me in my life had become old memories. They still had noise, sensations, and smells. They still had the feeling of excitement. I couldn't put them away. And the strongest memories were of Ruth, and the way she had spoken to me the last time I saw her.

28 Toolangi

Melbourne had changed. It had become a mess of frantic behaviour and taut looks. Galloway admitted to organising my meeting with Dennis without his usual sly smile.

'We journos can find out all kinds of things about people: where they are, and with whom they are, even, at a pinch, which Melbourne train they plan on taking. Besides, I know everyone in Kyneton: I started out there. So where to next?'

I sighed.

'I see. Here's Clarrie's address. He telephoned me you were coming. I haven't given you any serious advice before. But here's some now, take it or leave it. Go home and see your family. Then, when the time's right, go and visit Clarrie up at Toolangi. You'll be doing yourself a favour. Sooner or later you have to face up to the fact that you're a writer, and a good one. Den'll put you straight on that score. It never does a young bloke any harm to have a bit of mentoring. Mind you, I've sent blokes to the bush before, and permanently cured of them of their city ways. You might like it.' He looked at the clock on the wall. 'Looks like it's about that time.'

I had blokes to see in the city, and a bit of business to take care of. But once I was satisfied that I was not in the poorhouse, I caught a tram to Flinders Street, and walked down the steps to River Walk.

Ryrie was where he always is, out in the middle keeping an eye on proceedings while the young bucks impressed. He winked at me as I entered, and I walked up to him and shook his hand.

'Heard you been training horses, or something.'

I laughed. 'You don't miss much. Who told you that?'

'Little bird. He also told me you beat the bejazus out of John Kanga the Maori in Cal Cameron's travelling circus.'

'I see. Cal.'

'Nah. Cal's no friend of mine. It was a certain priest I grew up with right here in Melbourne.'

'Blimey, am I the only cove in Melbourne who hasn't got a mate in Kyneton? A man can't get any peace.'

'He tells me you looked as if you were in form.'

'He'd probably had a skinful.'

'Yeah. Look, all I'm saying, you should have a word with Les –'

'You know it's a mug's game, Dave. And I'm not a mug, no matter what the papers say. I quit because I had to. It's no secret.'

'You had an obligation to defend.'

'Don't give me that.'

'Not to the syndicate. Fuck 'em. To yourself, for your self-respect. When you take it all the way, you know something about yerself.'

'I know a lot about meself. I know I've fucked up everything I've ever touched.'

'Your too hard on yourself. You never thought you could box. You always fancied yourself as a street fighter. But you know as well as I do the punters don't turn up to see a couple of Gentleman Jims; they turn up to see a couple of Archie Taggertys, and they're happy as Larry if they only get one of 'em.'

324

I was silent. I was thinking of Ruth, and how suddenly I wanted to see her, to be with her again, like it used to be. And Billy. If I wanted to see Ruth, I had to get out of this place and go home. Ryrie mistook my introspection for interest.

'You can make a lot of money, and believe me, there aren't many blokes doing that the moment. As I said, talk to Les.'

'Ruth'd never have me back.' It was a silly thing to say, as I realised as soon as I'd said it that Ryrie would probably know by now that it was me who shot through, not Ruth who threw me out.

This time it was his turn to clam up. What could he say?

'I'll think it over. First things first, though.'

Going back to Richmond was hard to do, because I was afraid of the tongue-lashing I'd get. And I felt terrible guilty about the whole thing, though, strange as it might seem, I didn't know what I had done to feel guilty about. Ruth had made life unbearable for me. Our marriage had turned into one long argument about non-existent girl-friends, and opium-induced horrors, from somewhere deep inside Ruth, somewhere I didn't understand, but something that had to do, I knew, with her family. As for the family, they were Irish battlers, like the rest of us. Like my own family, they'd had a fighter, though they now regretted that. And like my family, they'd supplied one of their members for a marriage, which I know they regretted like hell. Our mothers were both hard cases, and our fathers either lost or as good as. And that was the story of Richmond.

I had hoped to lift Ruth out of that, take us both to a higher level, where we could at least breathe the Richmond air without being fouled by the rottenness of those who'd breathed it out. As if I could talk. Ruth was pure, despite being in pain, and angry, deep down.

She was home when I turned up. The fact is, she didn't have the strength to do any kind of work, and even the house work was too much for her, so she kept it to a minimum, so my mother wouldn't turn up every five minutes with her clucking tongue and critical eye. We'd had to make the marriage work alone, and then we'd found that there weren't two of us in the relationship. At least that was how I saw things.

Ruth opened the door herself, and immediately put her light arms around and cried big sobs onto my neck, while I stood in the doorway with my hat in my hand and wondered how the world worked when really I would settle for a just a hint about how women ticked.

'Archie,' she sobbed, over and over. She pulled me in gently and close the door, and looked into my eyes with a pained smile on her face, and tried to smile at me. But all that happened was that her face turned into a grimace and she began to wheeze badly. I took her into the living room and we sat down together. Jean was playing on the floor and immediately went over to Ruth and grabbed her. I felt so bad about seeing this kid who didn't even recognise me that I felt like I didn't deserve to be there, even thought it was my own house and home.

'Hello, Jeanie. I'm your daddy. Hello Ruthie love.'

Jeanie could only hang onto Ruth more tightly, while Ruth in turn clung to me more tightly too, but the lack of strength in her hand and arm almost made me cry.

'I didn't think you wanted to see me anymore,' I said.

'How could you think that? This is your home.'

'All we ever did was argue.'

'I was sick. I hated myself.'

'Ruthie, how can you say that. You are the only woman I have ever loved, or ever will love. I only wanted to be with you. I tried to understand when you were expecting, but I couldn't. I didn't know how to talk to you.'

'I'm sorry, Arch. I went mad, I really did. I'm as sorry as hell. And I'm sorry I drove you away.' She turned her face to mine and there were tears all over her cheeks. Some parts of her long face were deathly white and others a weakly spotted in red. Her eyes were sunken and large, yet still had that gentle shine I saw the first time I ever saw her. 'How long are you going to be here?'

That was a bloody good question. I had come home expecting to cop an earful about my supposed girlfriend, Queenie, who I hadn't even see in a month of Sundays, see how they were surviving without me, because I'd had no mail, then scoot over to Mum's for a quick visit. I hadn't expected to be welcomed, much less apologised to. It was all a bit overwhelming, and I found tears coming into my eyes. Ruth kissed me as tenderly as she ever had, and clung to me, though I she seemed to have the strength of a sick child. I was so worried about the state she was in I thought she might pass away right there in front of me and Jeanie.

'How long have you been like this, love?'

'Not long,' she said, with a faint smile.

'I see.' Ruth couldn't lie to me. I knew this was bad.

'Love, when was the last time you saw the doctor?'

'You know him, Arch. He wants to send me back to Greenvale. But if I went back there, there'd be no one to take care of Jeanie.'

I felt as rotten as hell when I heard that, because we both knew that if I'd been there, I could have taken care of Jeanie, and that the last thing either of us wanted was for our mothers to get their hands on her, and make her life as sour as theirs were. Ruth was thinking the same thing.

'Arch, where've you been? I mean, I don't blame you for shooting through, but I got no word, not even a letter.'

'But I wrote you lots of letters. I wrote from every place I went to. But when you didn't write back, I just assumed you'd had it with me.'

'I didn't get any of them.'

We stood their staring at each other, uncomprehending.

'But you came home. Why, anyway?'

'I had to, to see how you and Jeanie were. I mean, I love you, don't I?'

'Oh, hell. What a mess. I didn't get those letters, not one.' She started crying again, and I noticed that she seemed to cry with an ease she hadn't shown before, as if the crying was normal for her, and not just occasional, the way it was for the rest of us. I don't think I'd ever seen Queenie cry in the whole time I'd known her.

'Where'd you go?'

'I went up the bush, buying racehorses. I've been all over the place.'

She turned my face and looked at my cheekbone. 'You've been in a fight. Oh, Arch, not again.'

'Nah, just a travelling boxing troupe I came across. It's just a bruise. You should see the other bloke.'

She looked at me long and hard. For the first time, she didn't criticise what I'd said, just kissed me on the cheek, and then kissed me again, over and over, till Jeanie came along and wanted to get a few kisses herself.

'How's Mum, and your mum?'

'They're doing okay. Your mum comes over every five minutes and tries to run the place...Oh, hell, the mail! So that's where it went. God, I wish you'd been here –'

'No, love, you didn't want me here at all. That's why I left.'

'I was mad. It was a mixture of things: the laudanum, the pain...other things.'

'I'm here to stay, if you'll have me. I'll take care of Jeanie, and you can relax and just enjoy life. I'll go around to Mum's tomorrow and read the Riot Act and get those letters back. I'll make sure she leaves you in peace. You know, hard times are coming.'

'They're here already.'

'Nah, this is nothin'. Times are going to get worse. The company's got problems in America. The money might dry up altogether.'

'There's the poetry ...' She cut herself off, and studied my face for a reaction.

'That's won't pay the bills, love. Sorry, but it never did make me rich. No, there's only one thing –'

'No, no. There must be some other way. Desperate times means desperate men will turn up for a fight, men who'll do rotten things. I don't want to lose you too.'

Ruth was as beautiful as ever. Suddenly, she was as passionate as she was when we met, her Irish blood getting up. I held her close to me for a moment.

'I need to think about all these things. And I need to visit a bloke. How'd you and Jeanie like to come visiting with me up to Toolangi, in the bush. We've been invited up there by Clarrie Dennis – you know, the poet, the one who writes for *The Herald* –'

'C.J. Dennis?'

'Yep, bumped into him on the train down to Melbourne. Nice bloke. I'll send him a letter and see what he says. We could stay at the local for a few days. What d'yer say?'

'Sounds good. We could to with a little holiday. But I have to tell you the truth, now that you're home. I don't see how I can avoid Greenvale. I can feel my energy getting lower by the day. Darl' – she looked at Jeanie – 'I don't know how long I can hold on.'

'Then it's Greenvale for you, my love, if the doctor still says so.'

As it turned out, the doctor thought the country air wouldn't do Ruth any harm at all, so after I got the go-ahead from Clarrie, we were off on the first train to Healesville, a lovely little town at the bottom of the mountains. From there it was a ride by trap through the Kinglake forest, full of bellbirds, whipbirds, and cockatoos. Clarrie had obtained a little house at Toolangi, which was a sort of village, and built an extension onto it so that he could work. His poetry and column for *The Herald* took up most of his time, and had to he sent by horse messenger to Healesville every morning so that it could make the next edition.

As for Clarrie, or Den as we came to call him, he avoided the city like the plague. He reckoned he'd had enough of it. The house was called *Arden*, and his wife had been hard at work putting in the prettiest garden we'd ever seen. It was the kind of place you could spend all day in just getting to know the place, and not caring what was happening to the time. In fact, just forgetting you'd had a life somewhere else.

We moved into the Dennises' house after a few days, and stayed for a few weeks. Den and me took long walks and talked about poets and poetry, and I was surprised to discover that I had accumulated enough knowledge of my art to converse about it with a kind of depth that made Den shuffle his feet and frown at the ground. It also turned out that he'd read most of my poetry, which was, I realised, quite a bit. He encouraged me to write, and I often took myself out to his gazebo and worked while the bush thrived around me, and teased me from time to time. Ruth barely wheezed at all while we were there, and Jean remembered her habit of calling me Daddy. So all in all, it was an idyllic time. But then, it was that kind of place.

'What are your plans, Arch?' Den asked me on the last night of our visit. Do you think the poetry will be enough to see you through this rotten slump?'

'No, Den, I'm not kidding myself. I've been supporting myself with the profits from a stunt company I own in California; but they've fallen on hard times themselves.'

'Stunt company. You mean, blokes falling off horses?'

'That's exactly what I mean. I used to do some of the horse stunts myself until they started to get a bit dangerous. I mean, I know my way around a horse, but I'm not fit enough to take a beating every day. So we hired blokes who were. Anyway, that's going under, I reckon. So I might have to think of something else.'

'Do you ever think of fighting again? I mean, it hasn't been that long since you stopped boxing, has it?'

'You don't know what happened, do you?'

'Actually we do. It must be bloody hard to come to grips with. I've heard, though, that they want you to make a comeback.'

'It's not that simple, Den. The boy who died in that fight was Ruth's brother, Billie. In fact, it's been tearing us to bits, hasn't it, love?'

'It's been hard, as hard as hell.'

'I'm sorry, Ruth, I didn't know', said Den.

'That's all right. It's messed up both of our families as well as our own. But even if that hadn't happened, well, we still don't see eye to eye about fighting.'

'Ruth can feel as righteous as she likes, you know, but she never has. All that's gone by the board, and been replaced by sheer bloody sadness, hasn't it love? And to make matters worse, I never stopped loving the game. I've hated myself, that's true, but never the fight game itself. I suppose you could say it's in me, and always has been.'

While I was making this little speech I was looking at Ruth, who was looking at me the way she used to, in the old days, in my boxing days, with quite acceptance, the way you tolerate a kid who's been giving you a hard time, but whom you still love. When she spoke, she said something I wasn't expecting at all. She laid her gentle hand on mine first, so I knew she was using her powers of persuasion.

'Arch, I want you to do what's best for yourself. I don't have to ask you to do your best for Jeanie and me – I don't have any worries on that score. But the best for *you*, that's what I want.' She turned to the Dennises. 'That's really what he's worst at.'

'Well, my boy, you've done yourself a favour with this poetry of yours. It's sweet as apple pie, this stuff. No wonder people love it. My advice, for what it's worth, is: keep it up.'

'If you knew how I felt about it you wouldn't say that, Den. That poetry and me have never got along, never been mates. I've tried to stop writing it, you know, many times.' I looked at Ruth, because this was for her, too, as she didn't know any of this. 'Many times. When I was only a kid, I discovered that the same thing that makes me want to hit blokes makes me write poetry. It's a kind of demon. I hate it. Well, the poetry was better out than in, I reckoned, so I wrote it. I've only seen it in print a few times. Pretty bloody stupid, eh?'

'Would you like to see it in print now – I've got your books right here?' said Den, nodding towards the bookshelf.

'Nah, Den. Me and it, we would only stare at each other like a couple of drongos. I've always reckoned it would go away when it was good and ready.'

'Go away! You mean you want it to stop?'

'Yes, I always have. It doesn't suit me to be a poet. I'm not even much when it comes to being an ordinary cove, as you can see – all lopsided and out of line with the world. I've never had a day in my life when I've been free of pain, you know.'

'Arch, I never knew that – you should have said something,' said Ruth.

'I'm not complaining, mind. Just trying to tell you a bit about myself. My damn hip never worked properly since the day I was born. I'd fall over and it'd take me half an hour to get up again. When the kids at school worked that out, I used to get pushed over every five minutes. Then I learned how to stick up for myself – flattened a couple of bullies, and the rest is history. It was the only thing I could do right, and I kept on doing it.'

'But Arch, the poetry. You can do that right. It's wonderful.'

'Yeah, but I do it to get rid of it; I do it for a bit of peace and quiet. I don't even remember most of it, and I don't want to.'

'But others do, don't you see? People all over Melbourne.'

'All over Australia,' said his missus.

'Yeah, everywhere, they love the stuff. That's your legacy, not a championship you won in terrible circumstances.'

There was silence. Den pushed on.

'Have you ever thought of writing out of the sheer enjoyment of the act?'

'You know, I don't think I have,' I said, aware that I was staring at them like an idiot.

'Well then, perhaps it's time you did.'

29 The Prodigal Son

That last evening at Toolangi was one of the happiest of my life. I don't think I'd ever met anyone who'd made an effort to understand me, and in some ways succeeded. Den had not been in prison, had not smelled the sting another man's blood, and wanted to draw more, had not left his family – though he had gone bush. Ruth, bless her, made an effort – I could see her struggling at it – but I don't think she knew what it was she was supposed to get.

I'd never asked another to fathom me – I'd never asked myself to, or so I thought. But it dawned on me, as I walked in the bush, and as I talked about nothing and everything with Den, that the poetry itself was capable of asking questions. God knows, there were enough questions in the poems themselves. People had noticed it, I knew that. 'The Quizzical Poet' was what the newspapers, then the bookshops, and then just about half of the readers, were calling me. It's funny, but in all the years I'd been writing I'd never one thought of answering those questions. I suppose I'd assumed the poetry would do that for me. Maybe it did – I don't know. But I knew I'd have to keep thinking about it.

These were some of the many thoughts that woke me in the middle of the best kind of sleep a man can have, the lover's sleep. It was not dark when I woke: a very low flame burnt in the hurricane lamp on the table, to comfort Jeanie. Outside, the mountain ash forest was gently moving, rubbing against itself, groaning like a ship at anchor in a swell. The house seemed to creak a little - Den had told us that parts of the new section were still trying to find their feet - and whisper to me that it was aware of everything that was taking place inside it. But in my mind there was a confusion of images, some more or less clear and colourful, some still spectral. It was fanciful, in the main.

Could I imagine me a poet, strutting up and down the Royal Arcade like a toff, hoping to be noticed - *The Great Polly Beer* finally exposed as *The Great Archbold Taggerty?* No, I couldn't really see it. But I could easily see me strutting around the ring, sweaty and bloody with one hand raised, giving a wink to Queenie - why had I said that? I immediately thought of Ruth, beside me, and hoped she couldn't read my mind in her sleep. She'd have a fit.

That what exactly what I was thinking when it happened. Ruth stirred suddenly, as if she'd been frightened by a snake, and I half sat up. I turned and saw by the lamplight her eyes flash open, and stare at me in - what? I still don't know - panic, I supposed. Then she coughed a whole chestful of blood all over the place.

There was no doctor at Toolangi, so we took her down to Healesville in the trap, with Jeanie staying at Den's place. The doctor could do little, and would not have her moved again, so she stayed in his back room, and I dossed beside her on the floor. I was able to send a note to Jeanie explaining what was happening and give it to Den's courier. There was nothing for it now but to return to Melbourne, and we took the train as soon as soon as Ruth was able and Jeanie had joined us. I had hopes for Ruth. She was in a bad way now, but people had passed through this same illness and lived to be, well, lived.

'Ruthie,' I told her on the train. 'You'll come through this.'

'Don't make me laugh, love: that'd be the end of me.'

'Sorry. Look, don't say anything, don't even whisper. Just don't move a muscle. Just relax and breathe. And let me take care of everything.'

'Arch, I don't think I'm going to make it to Melbourne, much less to Greenvale. I can feel the life leaving me.'

'No, Ruthie. I've seen a lot of blokes die, from all kinds of things, especially flu and TB, and you're nowhere near it.'

'It's happening,' she said, and kissed Jeanie, who was having a snooze beside her.

I looked at her, and wondered if I'd ever fathom this person, who was, at times, like her own mother, who'd given me a hard time since the moment I'd met her, and at times like her old man, who had a heart, but no sense at all. But Ruth was the sensible member of the family. It was to her that I had turned time and time again for common sense, when my own constantly short supply ran out.

But as I heard her say that – and I couldn't argue all that hard, because I'd seen many brave men accurately predict their own deaths – I saw in her the quiet power that I'd seen every time I'd looked at Billy. He had a self-confidence – it was the self-confidence of the Irish, of course, all blarney and a mile wide – but it was there, in the blood. I looked at Ruth, and saw it, not in her eyes, but in the restless set of her face, and her mouth, not beautiful and soft, as it usually was, but taut and pushed forward, like a fighter daring his opponent to have a go.

'No, it's not, darling. Go to sleep.'

Greenvale was not my favourite place. It reminded me of Coode Island during the war, only without the stench. The dying there was quiet because of the power of opium, which flowed like water. In fact, I believe the nurses and doctors used it even more freely than the army had, because it had been in short supply in Cairo, whereas it was grown by the ton in the farms around Melbourne.

The improved building had been completed, and the outer huts for those who, it was judged, would live, had greatly increased in number. The morgue, I noted, now spread out to accommodate a whole yard, which had once been occupied by stables. The bus that took us the final leg of the journey from the station at Fawkner passed several other buses going the other way. They contained only a few returning visitors. At the hospital, we were met by a nurse, who grabbed one of the dozens of wheelchairs at the reception area, and put Ruth in it.

'I'm sorry, Mr Taggerty,' said the nurse, not sorry at all, 'but you can't go any further.'

Ruth grabbed my hand and held it as tightly as she could. She looked at the nurse with a look that was meant to kill. The nurse's face softened and she looked at us both in a new light.

'The contagion is too high inside,' she said. 'I'm thinking of the child.'

We gave Ruth a hug and a kiss, and looked at her crying eyes. Jeanie was aware only that it was goodbye time. But I was busy storing memories for a long haul, maybe a lifelong haul, for all I knew. There was nothing to say.

'I'll take care of little Jeanie, love,' I said. 'You won't have to worry. And I'll stay put, so you needn't worry on that score, either.'

'I know, love,' she whispered, and pressed my hand, to affirm it.

'We'll come to visit every weekend, and eventually, we'll take you home.'

Ruth didn't know how to let go of us, at least that's my story. So there we were, the three of us, looking a pathetic excuse for a family, and the nurse just getting so fidgety I thought she was going to jump in like a ref and tear us apart with a sharp warning. At least there would have been a kind of comic honesty in that. Instead, she grabbed the handles of the wheelchair, which was at least her property to do with as she pleased. She was so close to us that she was touching all of us simultaneously, and for half a minute became a part of the family.

'Nurse, wait just a minute.'

She relaxed her grip, but did let go.

'You'll be back next Saturday,' she said to me and Jeanie. It was a prediction.

'Yes, love, we'll be back on Saturday.'

The ride back to town was a mystery to me. There was air, and it was warm, and blossoms were beginning to appear in the trees. That's the sum of my memories of it. I might as well have been a sleepwalker, or mad. I stared about me, and clutched Jeanie, who didn't appear to be all that worried about what had happened. But the fact is, I felt very little and observed nothing else of consequence.

I found myself on the bus. Found myself prattling on to Jeanie about this and that. Found myself waiting for a train. Platform. Train. A river. Another river. East Richmond station. I remember when they build it. It became dirty overnight. *DO NOT SPIT*, the sign said. There was so much TB that if a copper caught you spitting, he'd cuff you over the ear so hard, you'd genuinely feel repentant, which was the general idea.

The concrete ramp. Church Street. My heavy, sore feet on the footpath. My sore body. My numbness. Jeanie's sweaty hand. The cool dimness of the hall. The tapering sound of Jeanie's running as she penetrated the house. My awareness, after a long while, that I had ceased to move.

Next morning I was off to Charlie Wing's place with Jeanie in tow.

'No kids, Arch.'

'I have to use your telephone, Charlie.'

'Who do you want to call?'

'I had to put Ruth in Greenvale.'

That word was not synonymous with hope, return or health.

'Solly, Arch. Okay. Come on.'

We went into a back room, where a large, bull-necked man sat drinking tea, like a tame rhinoceros.

'G'day, Arch.'

'Donny.'

'Heard you made a comeback.'

'No, Donny, just a few rounds in a tent. Wouldn't call it a comeback. Anyway, how'd you hear about it?'

'Bloke in the pub.'

'Fair dinkum, I don't know why they invented the bloody wireless.'

'Here's the phone, Arch. Who do you want?'

'Greenvale.'

'What's the number?'

'What d'yer mean: *What's the number?* – how the hell would I know?'

I watched while he got in touch with someone at the other end of the telephone line and asked to be put through to

Greenvale. He wrote down the number he was given and handed the phone to me.

It turned out Ruth was doing okay and was sleeping. They didn't seem to think there was anything to be concerned about. No, I couldn't talk to her. I felt as though I was back in the bloody Army, taking orders. I had to be happy with that, because the nurse had no intention of giving me any more intelligence.

I took Jeanie home and got her some ice-cream on the way. While Jeanie talked to her dolls, I sat on the front porch and looked at the sunny day, a day that seemed to be unaware of the human suffering all over the place. It took me back to the day at Gaza when I went into the sea after the horses. It wasn't a case of battling the seas: the sea really couldn't have cared less. It was just splashing around, pummelling the hell out of the beach because it could, because it loved it. *It loved it.* I thought about that, and it took me, in its turn, to what Den had been saying to me, about doing poetry for no particular reason, like breathing.

I saw that I could be like the day, carrying on, despite the suffering all around and inside me, simply because it was just happening, and, if realised, *I* was just happening. It was my turn to happen, and for no more reason than that. I didn't have to hit people to make myself feel good: I could just fight – just like that. And I didn't have to write poetry just to relieve myself, to obey the call of nature, because that's what I'd been doing all my life. I could write out of respect for myself and no other reason. That's what Den did; I watched him do it day in, day out. Writing was his daily life, like pissing and breathing and sleeping. None of those things had a greater or lesser place for him. They were all his way. And his life still had its ups and downs. And so would mine.

I saw all this in the day. I looked up and saw the cloud mass drift in the form of the lamp post outside the house sweeping across the sky. It was all relative. The world of illusion was right there, dead handy for those who preferred it. I just had never realised it. I had been living the illusion of life all those years. The thought struck me dumb with embarrassment, and I was glad I was alone at the time. I overcame the embarrassment with a set of my eyes. I would never do again. I asked God to let me live my life from this moment on not in a state of self-delusion but in a state of realisation, no matter how ridiculous I realised I had become. I resolved to experience what I wanted to experience without the prop of bullshit I'd been leaning on all my life.

When I turned up at Ryrie's, he barely looked at me.

'Took yer time, Taggerty.'

'Never mind that. I'd like to spar with that bloke over there,' I said pointing.

'He's shaping up for a bout this Saturday. I don't think he'll be interested. You'll have to talk to Mick Mulligan. He nodded. Mick was ready for me.

'It's okay,' he called. 'We'll have a few minutes.'

I got into my togs and shaped up to the corner.

'This is not a street fight, Taggerty – you're not in Pentridge now. I don't want my boy hurt.'

'As if I'd hurt your boy. Heaven forbid!'

'He's got a fight coming up, so all we want's a little workout.'

I faced this feller and touched gloves and for the first time I had nothing to gain by being in the ring. I wasn't trying to impress anyone, or work out a new dirty trick, or strengthen my leg, which now quivered mercilessly as I adopted my old fighting stance. I was just being the person I reckoned I had become, a bloke who loved to fight, but who loved to win as well, the two essential ingredients of a boxer.

It was a good sparring match. The other boy was five years younger than me, and would have been easy pickings had I been in form, as he fought as if he'd never been fouled in his life. When we were well and truly sweaty, his trainer called a stop, but his boy wanted to keep going, and so did I, for I was getting into the swing of things again. Warmed up as we were, we could have turned the spar into a nice little dust-up if we'd wanted to, except for one thing: we weren't getting paid.

His trainer came over to me as I was resting my leg, and sat down beside me.

'Haven't seen you for a while. I see it's true what they say: that you've jacked it in.'

'Yeah. What's it to you?'

'Saw your last fight. I don't know how you did it. No one does. No one liked it, either, except me. Had a few bob on you. Did well out of that. How's that other boy, Billy Whatshisname?'

I sighed. 'He died.'

'Sorry, mate. He was a good fighter too.'

'He was a good boxer. Let's leave it at that. Which reminds me.'

'What?'

'That kid of yours. You know he's a pushover, don't you?'

'Don't you believe it. The game's a lot cleaner these days. He'll go the distance, and that's what counts. More fights go the distance than not these days. You'd find it hard to get a fight with your record.'

'Care to put your money where your mouth is?'

'Okay, find a trainer and get permission to fight again, and we'll see. We've got our own plans.'

He left me deep in thought.

'Dave, where can I find Les?'

'Parker? Over at Sanky's – got a few new boys.'

'Thanks. I'll be seeing you.'

'You'll never get a fight, you know. The syndicate blokes have long memories.'

'I'll think of something. Maybe I'll go over and see their boss.'

'Ted Beauchamp? You'd never get past his front gate.'

'You throw in the towel too easily, Dave.'

He had no answer to that, for it was true, though no one ever said it to his face in the old days. And he didn't have to remind me about Beauchamp's front gate, as I had heard that he had turned himself into a gentleman and had practically been adopted by the Prime Minister. But I knew someone who would get past more than his front gate.

After a few enquiries I found myself at George Di Gianopoulous's casino, a place that had both happy and unhappy memories for me. George Di G had not seen Queenie Brennan for donkey's.

'Sorry, mate. The likes of us are not good enough for Queenie. She decided to look for a man at the Monte Carlo club and caught a tram across the river.'

'I know all about Ted Beauchamp. They've been an item for years.' He relaxed. 'You know, Beauchamp's driver lives just across the road - bloke called Pauly Poulos.'

He nodded in the direction of the street. 'Arch, you didn't hear any of this from me. I'm not going up for accessory to murder.'

'Jesus, George, I only want to ask Queenie for a favour. I don't care if she's giving it to the King of bloody England.'

'Pauly –'

'Poulos.'

'Family?'

He shrugged. I headed for the door, and he spoke as I reached for it.

'Arch, they reckon he keeps a gun in the car.'

'Well, does he or doesn't he?'

He shrugged again. Why, I wondered, do Greeks do that?

30 A Flaming Miracle

Pauly turned out to be as shifty as shit-house rat, and twice as Greek. He opened the door as if I was trying to repossess it.

'Yeah?'

'I'm a friend of Queenie Brennan's. They say you know where she lives.'

'And did they say I'd tell you to fuck off, you Irish bastard?'

'No, Pauly, they forgot that bit. But me and Queenie are old mates from years back. In fact, we met just up the street from here. I've been up the bush, and lost touch with her, and now I need to say hello to her. It's important. You can even stay while I talk to her. I know who's paying the bills. I don't want to rock the boat or anything.'

He whipped out an ugly looking knife. 'You've got a bloody nerve. I oughta cut you right now and teach you a lesson.'

Well, I could see I wasn't going to get anywhere with this bloke, who was probably someone's cousin, and could probably get his family to make life difficult for me if I lost my temper, which I would have if I hadn't had once spent the night lying in my own blood and filth in a hole in a desert with a dead mate listing to the taunts of the Turks, who made this bloke's threats sound like a child's.

I drove a right up under his ribs, and knocked the air out of him so hard I felt it punch me in the face as it shot out of him. He dropped the knife and fell to the ground clawing and writhing like a snake, trying for all he was worth to get his diaphragm to work. I bent over and slowly crushed his balls in my fist until he managed to get enough breath to cry out.

'I think that makes us quits, doesn't it Pauly?'

I left him on the floor and went round the back to his garage and let myself in. Pauly had been dressed up his best clothes, so I guessed he was going to take the car over to Toorak. I opened the boot, hopped in and closed it gently. Sure enough, it wasn't long before he came out, still making a song and dance of his pain, and hopped in and drove off. I knew where we were until we got across the bridge, then I opened the boot a little and had a look at the road behind us.

We went to a pretty good address in Toorak, and he stopped and hopped out and went to a door. I closed the boot and pretty soon we were off again with his employer in the back. Not far away I saw out of the back that we had come to a South Yarra address. I waited until Beauchamp had gone in, and let myself out of the boot. Pauly stayed in the front. Throughout the trip Pauly had kept quiet and didn't mention our little difference of opinion. As I guessed, he would not have seen any advantage in talking about it. I slipped behind the car behind and made myself scarce a little way down the street. When the boyfriend left, I went to Queenie's place.

It was a small block of four flats with name-tags on the doors. Getting in required a key, but I found it easy enough with my own front door skeleton key. I knocked and I heard Queenie's voice on the other side.

'Just a sec.' Her voice was toneless, neither happy nor surprised. She opened the door and saw me and blinked a few times, them quickly looked behind me, then grabbed me and hauled me in I like a fish. 'Archie!' This time her voice was excited.

'Hi, Queenie, love. Don't worry, he's gone.'

She gave me the big hello. 'It's lucky for a lot of people you didn't decide to join the Force, that's all I can say. How'd you find me – not that I'm not pleased you did?'

'Pauly gave me a lift.'

'Yeah and pigs can fly.'

'In his boot.'

'Jesus, Arch. You should watch out for that bloke: he's a bad bastard.'

'Funny, the last time we spoke I left him incapable of hurting a fly.'

'He'll cut your bloody throat.'

'Ah, fuck 'im. So how're you and little Johnnie Brik getting along – pretty bloody well, by the looks of it?'

'We are, Arch. We have everything we want. And Ted doesn't hurt me; he's a gentleman.'

'Does his wife know?'

'I think so, but she hasn't turned up on the doorstep, if that's what you mean. Jesus, it's good to see you. Where've you been? I heard you were in the States.'

'Nah, I've been wandering around the bush buying racehorses for your posh neighbours.'

'Have you seen Ruth?'

'Yeah. She's not doing too well. I've had to bung her into Greenvale again. She's changed, Queen', she's not the Ruth she used to be. But I think we'll be all right – that is, if she makes it.'

I let my breath out, becoming aware that my chest had been tense and puffed up.

'Sit down, Arch. Feel like a cuppa?'

'Yeah, thanks. I've grown rather fond of the odd cuppa.' I suddenly thought of Anne, and wondered how she was going.

'So, wandering around the bush, eh? I know you, Arch, and you're not the kind of bloke who wanders around the bush.'

'Been busier than a one legged tap-dancer though – don't ask.'

'I don't have to ask. I know what effect you have on women better than you ever will. See you've been fighting.'

'It was a travelling troupe. A bloke roped me in. Bloody silly, really.'

'King Bloody Kanga.'

'My God! Now how'd you know that?'

'Ted told me. He's big in the Sportsmen's. No one dongs anyone this side of Albury without him finding out. He pays for information, you know.' She put down her cuppa. 'Oh, so that's it. You want to know about Ted – silly bloody me. And here's me thinking it was me you wanted. When will you ever flamin' learn, my girl?'

'No, Queenie, I did come to see you. But I want to get back into the game for a while.'

'You don't need to fight.'

'I do. The company's doing badly.'

'Can you still fight, though? You know dirty fighters are on the way out, don't you? Sorry, love, but we are calling a spade a spade, aren't we.'

'I can win without gettin' up to my old tricks. I can train.'

'I see. So you've made your mind up. Oh, well. What d'yer want me to do?'

'Just whisper a word in Beauchamp's shell-like, that's all – bit of pillow talk.'

'He won't go for it.'

'You'll find a way. All I want's a fair go.'

'Even if he agreed ...'

'Now you're talkin'. He will. I know you: you've always got a few secret tricks saved up for a rainy day.'

'It's only because it's you, Arch. I mean it.'

'I know you do, love.'

I had warned Les that he was going to get a call from Beauchamp, and that he might set conditions. When I caught up with him, he was not optimistic, but he was able to tell me that I would have my licence renewed.

'So what's the catch?' I said.

'The catch is you can't fight in Victoria.'

'Then what's the point?'

'They'll give you a licence issued in Victoria, and that'll let you fight anywhere in Australia.'

'That leaves Sydney. Jesus, I don't want to spend the rest of my life in that place. What about Ruth and Jean? I have to be here, mate, in Melbourne.'

'That's the deal. If you get a shot at a national title, he'll let the conditions drop for good. Sound's fair to me, though I'd forget about a title fight. Those days are over, my son. It's all as clean as a whistle these days. I don't think Archbishop Mannix'd himself'd get a fight.'

'I bet Queenie could get him one.'

'So that's how you got to Beauchamp. You've got a gift there, you know. If you bottled it you'd make a bloody fortune.'

'Look, I'll train here and go up to Sydney for the fights. We can do that, can't we?'

'We'll have to. When can you start?'

'Now. Let's go over to Ryrie's.'

Ryrie only shook his head when he saw us coming.

'They're going to let him fight,' said Les.

'Says who?'

'Ted Beauchamp.'

'Fair enough. Off you go, then.' Not like Dave to run at the mouth.

I trained hard, most of time at home, while Jeanie watched and threw punches across the room while she was playing. It wasn't long before she was punching her dolls. I could see she was going to be a feisty woman one day. She had the blood of the Irish, Scots and the Welsh in her, and they were all born with the desire to dong somebody. When she started to knock the stuffing out of her dolls, I brought her the biggest teddy bear I could find. Actually, I ran into an old mate from the jam factory, and it turned out he knew a bloke, and so on. He did me the favour because he'd followed me in my boxing days and made a quid or two, and now he had a job and things were looking up. We kept up our visits to Greenvale, though neither of us were allowed to touch Ruth, which just about broke our hearts.

The ward where Ruth was kept was almost exposed to the elements, there being a roof, and large windows that were apparently never closed. It was raining like hell the day Ruth found out I was fighting again. I had told Jean never to fight in front of Mum, but it was like trying to stop the tide. As soon as she got restless and I tried to quieten her down she started to box me in a way that left no doubt what had been going on at home.

'What did you teach her that for?'

'I didn't.'

'I suppose she learnt it all by herself.'

'You know how kids are.'

'Arch, no!'

The truth had dawned.

'I have to make a quid, Ruthie. Things are crook. I'll be okay.'

'You'll be okay. And how long have you been saying that? Anyway, you can't fight. You lost your license.'

'I'll get it back. Everyone likes to see a comeback.'

She lowered her voice and whispered through spitting teeth. 'And what about our marriage, Arch. Are you going to make a comeback for that, too, or what.'

It was always the same: Ruth would do her block, then rake up the past and throw it at me. She'd never be happy as long as I was in the game. But I had to be in it.

Just then a nurse came at me like a mad fox terrier and shushed so loud, I thought she was going to go for my ankle next.

'What are you doing to this lady?' she asked as if I had Ruth in a headlock. 'She is not to be excited or upset in any way. Is that clear?'

'You know where I stand,' said Ruth. 'When I get out of here, I want to find you at home and in one piece, with a good job.'

'Good jobs are as scarce a hens' teeth, these days, love.'

'You'll get one or you'll never see me again.'

The Magee blood. I don't know whether I loved it or hated it. But I reckon that it was Ruth doing her block that saved her life. To cut a long story short, Jeanie and me were given the bum's rush and Ruth was left coughing and spluttering as if she was drowning. The nurse who threw me out told me I ought to be ashamed, and that if I ever saw Ruth again it'd be a miracle. And I could tell by the look on her face that she wasn't pulling my leg. When I got to Flinders Street, I went looking for Les.

'Les, I don't know if I can go through with this boxing thing. Ruth's put her foot down. This time she's fair dinkum.'

'Well she can relax, I s'pose, because it's all off. Beauchamp's been overruled by the Syndicate. If you've got another plan, now's the time to wheel it out.'

When I got back to Richmond, I took Jeanie up to St Ignatius', on the Hill, to ask God for a favour. I knew He didn't listen to blokes like me, but I reckoned that if I softened Him up by letting Him go a few rounds with Jeanie, He'd be useless.

'Where are we?' asked Jeanie, as soon as we stepped into the cool gloom of the entry.

'We're in a church. It's the church you were baptised in, and the church your mum and me were married in.'

I thought Jeanie's eyes were going to bug our when she looked up to the ceiling, which was so high I could swear there was a mistiness about it.

'It used to be the tallest building in Australia,' said an Irish voice behind me. I turned and there was a priest wearing a day suit. He had the face of a man who had gone a few rounds in his day and still had a lot of fight in him. 'I don't believe I've seen you in here before, though I feel as if I know you.'

'I haven't seen eye to eye with God since I got a look at His handiwork in Palestine,' said I, for I could see I was talking to a man who liked to stand firm, and that's how I wanted to face him.

To my surprise he blessed himself and closed his eyes for a moment. I half expected him to burst into tears. 'It's the trouble; it's everywhere: in my homeland, in the Holy Land, and right here, in this little bit of Ireland, Richmond itself. It's alright, my son. But you must never speak of the Lord like that again, d'yer hear? You came into His house, don't forget. You came into *His* house. And why, may I ask, did you do that?'

'I wanted to ask Him to soften my wife's heart. For she won't let me fight, when fighting's all I want to do.'

'And why in God's name do you want to fight?'

'To get back my bantamweight crown, Father.'

He looked startled, and I wondered if I'd said the wrong thing, but there it is: better out than in.

'Well, now, bless me! It's the Richmond Terrier himself, back from ... just where did you go? Never mind. So what's stopping you?'

'The Sportsmen's Syndicate. They banned me for not defending me title, Father.'

'I know the story,' said the priest. 'And I know the reason you wouldn't defend it, and it's a credit to you, my son. But a woman's heart must always give way to her husband's will, that's God's Holy Law. So I want you to leave it to me. I know a few people. And it seems to me that what you're asking's a small thing in itself. And now: *Benedicat vos omnipotens Deus, Pater et Filius et Spiritus Sanctus.*' He made the sign of the cross over us, and winked.

After he had whisked away, walking more like a horse colonel than a priest, I took Jeanie down the front of the church, so she could see the sights, and prayed out loud for the both of us, that God would spare Ruth and somehow make the family whole again.

Two days later I received a visit from Les, who had news.

'You'll never believe what happened.'

'Don't tell me we're at war again,' I said, for I had heard that Europe was in a crisis, and I'd heard that kind of talk before.

'No, the Syndicate has changed its mind. They're letting you fight, and you can fight wherever you like.'

'I don't get it. What happened?'

'I heard from a little bird that the Archbishop had a word to the Chairman. You didn't tell me you knew Mannix.'

'Wouldn't know him from a bar of soap.'

'Then why have you got his picture on the mantlepiece?'

I looked around, and he was right. It turned out Mannix and me were mates.

It was a terrible choice that faced me now. Ruth had made herself clear: no fighting or no marriage. But she didn't know what it was like, to be able to do something special, and to be denied the freedom do it. She didn't know that a man's got to do certain things, whether others can see it or not. There were men in Gaza, on both sides, who fought like that. They didn't care about the right and wrong – you couldn't follow that anyway.

I mean, the Turks had been in that place for hundreds of years, they reckon. They just did their best. And there were men like that in Pentridge. They battled on, whether they deserved to be there or not, and most did not. Their crime was their Irishness. Queenie would have understood. She never whinged and whined about the lot of women, and she had a few things to complain about. She just made the best of her life, even if that meant sometimes making the worst of it, if you see what I mean.

'Listen to me, Les. Meeting Mannix like that in the church the other day was a flamin' miracle.'

'A flamin' miracle,' said Jeanie, looking up at Les.

'She's turning into a regular little parrot, isn't she. I can hardly wait to see Ruth's face.'

'Les, it *was* a miracle. I have to use that miracle to do what I can, win or lose.'

'Ruth won't see it that way. She'll eat you alive.'

'She'll be all right on the day. Women like winners. And I've never been beaten.'

'In Australia.'

'In Australia, though America doesn't count, as those bastards couldn't punch their way out of a wet paper bag.'

Les looked deep in thought at Jeanie, who looked back at him the same way.

'Wet paper bag,' she said, seriously.

31 Back On The Horse

After my meeting with Mannix, things moved quickly, which didn't bother me, as I needed a few quid. My return bout was at the Collingwood Town Hall, against an old soldier like myself, a bloke who'd been swinging a pick down at the new dry dock. Les told me he could box, that he had muscles like a bodybuilder, and the crowd loved him.

The good news was that he was the same weight as me, and had been building his muscles in all the wrong places for a fighter. And because he was muscle-heavy he was shorter than me, which was a rare thing. His mates called him Tich, and that was in fact the name he fought under: Tich Fegan. He was a busy little bloke, sniffing as he shadow-boxed while I was introduced. The ref wasn't allowed to refer to me as the former bantamweight champ, but he was allowed to say that in my last match I was victorious under very controversial conditions, which was a polite way of saying that I'd killed the other bloke. This was something that Tich reminded me he knew.

As we came into the centre of the ring to receive the referee's instructions, Tich began a conversation of his own, with a sniff between every second word.

'So, Pegleg (sniff), gunna kill me too, are ya (sniff)? Are ya?'

'No, mate, I promised me mum I wouldn't kill any kids.'

'I've killed Germans, I 'ave (sniff).'

'What'd you do, sniff 'em to death?'

'Fuck you, ya murderer.'

'I'd love you to; you do look kinda cute.'

So this was all pretty much the normal banter that goes on in the centre ring. We paid no attention to the ref and he paid none to us.

It turned out Tich had been told to expect dirty tricks, and tried to defend all the wrong places at the same time, which gave me lots of scoring shots to his head. As the fight wore on, he gradually began to take notice of his corner, and box, but by then I had boxed myself into a handy position. My hip was giving me such a hard time that in the end, I had to stop moving and stay in the centre, pretty much flat-footed.

I could tell that Tich thought I was propping for a big right-hander, because he began to work extra hard to get to me to move off the spot. But his problem was that he didn't have the reach to hurt me. He had to take a chance and come in close, as he was being told. By the time he made the decision to fight close, he was tired, and I managed to get in a very handy body blow that made him lean on me and hold on. That was how round seven ended.

At the beginning of round eight, he came out walking, and still in pain from the body punch. I drew him once more, and let him have identical left to the midsection, and this time he couldn't stand up straight and backed away. His corner was yelling at him to do the same thing to me, but this time I chased him into the corner and let him have it with both fists the diaphragm as many times as I could. The only way he was going to get out of this mess was by flooring me. When the ref broke us up, I stepped back a few steps to box on, but Tich was fading fast, and fell to his knees. I went back to my corner and watched as he tried to get his breath, and failed, then finally passed out altogether. I felt better than I ever had. For the first time, I felt completely happy about fighting.

The audience, fickle lot that they are, were happy as Larry about the outcome, and remembered me well enough. I think they were just as surprised as I myself was to see the Richmond Terrier win a fight without cheating.

'I never saw you use those combinations before,' said Les.

'I couldn't dance; I had to think of something, so I decided to try something I picked up from watching a few of the blokes at Ryrie's.'

'Yeah? What was that?'

'Box.'

On Monday the paper said that Tich had been so '*badly mauled*' by the Richmond Tiger that he'd had to have emergency surgery and that his spleen had been removed. He'd never fight again.

When I saw Les during the week, I told him about it.

'It's a risky business, of course. But he would have known that.'

'I want you to give him my share of the purse, Les.'

'He'd never take it. Besides, he's not the only one with a family to support.'

'What's next, then?'

'Strengthening your legs, that's what. If Fegan had had the reach, he would have wiped the floor with you.'

'No, I mean, who's next? Come on, Les, I know you've got someone in mind.'

'No, I haven't, for once. Give me few days; we'll see what turns up.'

What turned up was an article about me in the *Sporting Globe* under the headline:

'Taggerty backs down from fight,' it said. *'Up and coming bantamweight, Milo Magee, has challenged Archie Taggerty to a fight, only to be turned down. Magee's brother, Billy Magee, never recovered consciousness after his last fight, in which he lost the Australian Bantamweight crown to Taggerty. Taggerty, the Richmond Terrier, was stripped of his title shortly afterwards for refusing to defend it. Milo Magee said:* Taggerty was the dirtiest fighter in Australia until he retired, and never fought a clean fight in his life, including the one that killed my brother. All I want is a chance to avenge my brother's death. I can't ask fairer than that. But Taggerty wants to stick to fighting broken down wharfies *".*

Taggerty's last fight was last Saturday night at Collingwood Town Hall, where he defeated Michael "Tich" Fegan, who was seriously injured and, shortly afterwards, announced his retirement. Taggerty was unavailable for comment. However, his manager, Les Parker, said, "Archie doesn't want to fight the boy, out of respect for the family. That's the kind of bloke he is. Besides, he doesn't want to hurt young Milo, who is like a brother to him. *"*

'Les, what the fuck is going on?' was the first thing I said to him when I caught up with him. 'Since when do I back out of fights, Milo or no Milo?'

'You'll back out of this one, or Ruth'll have your balls. She'd never talk to you again. I don't want to be part of that. I've known you two for too long.'

'But he'll drive the punters mad. You know how much they love this stuff. I didn't know Milo was a fighter. Is he any good?'

'I've seen him fight a few times, mostly prelims. He wins 'em, but he lacks Billy's style. He's not in your class. And with a bit of luck he won't be.'

'Jesus Christ, this is crazy. What if he improves? What if he gets a shot at me? What am I supposed to bloody do, run home to Mummy? No, this is no good. Put him in the ring with me. Let me give him a hiding and to hell with the consequences. I'll take him the distance and win on points so Ruth can see I'm trying to satisfy all parties. Or maybe she won't find out. You know, they don't have wirelesses or newspapers in that place. What do yer reckon?'

'I reckon when you show up the day after a fight she'll take one look at your dial and read you the Riot Act.'

'Yeah. I'm buggered coming and going.'

'Well, you wanted to make a comeback. What if Billy's got other mates out there who're still in the game? Look, Arch, you've got one of those images, the kind that says: *I'm as slippery as they come. I dare you to catch me.* It works because yer a terrific fighter. But it attracts a certain undesirable element.'

'I always thought the punters liked me.'

'Nah. It's the way you fight they like; they *hate you.* But that idea of yours is probably the best of a bad lot. Fight him early. Beat him without killing him. Then get on with earning some money.'

'I wonder if I should tell Ruth about the plan.'

'Let me worry about Ruth. But not before the fight, okay? Now, I'll go and have a word with that reporter bloke. Tell him you'll let the kid take a poke at you. That should get a mention in the sports pages.'

'Just tell 'em I'm going to sue them for libel. That'll wipe the smile off their faces.'

It turned out the kid's handlers were just as furious as I was, and had no intention of letting him fight me. They'd seen what I'd done to Tich Fegan, and didn't want their boy to end up the same. I also heard from a little bird that his parents were completely torn about the whole idea. On the one hand, Mrs Magee wanted him to wipe the floor with me, and preferably put me in the morgue where I belonged, while Mr Magee, who I knew to be a halfway decent bloke, wanted to put an end to the violence, and at the end of the day wanted Ruth to be happy. But they were a boxing family. Irish fury. Dong someone and it'll all be better – I understood. There would be a fight. And as far as I was concerned, the sooner the better.

The Fegan fight was to be my last fight at a small venue. The powers that be reckoned there was no point in hiding the talent and experience at small rooms, and let Les know that I could fight at the Stadium from now on. That was both good and bad. Good because of the money.

There were no small fights at the 'Shed'. But there was ten times the publicity, and big fights were hard to keep secret. The papers kept referring to me as the ex-champ. It was: '*Ex-champ gets comeback fight at Stadium*', '*Ex-champ calls Magee coward*', and '*Ex-champ says he's ready for Dempsey*'.

My hip had not healed, but I was now as strong as ever, thanks to some clever body work by a physiotherapist Les had found. That bloke knew exactly what the problem was, and how to fix it, and was the first person who knew what was going on. This bloke, Vincent Parnell, had a way to take away every pain in a blokes muscles and bones just by twisting bits here and pressing bits there, and so on. He was like a piano player on the human body. It was Vince who turned my career around, or rather, rebuilt it, beginning with the sinews and muscles.

Vince was one of those blokes who like to keep to himself, if you know what I mean, and often move from town to town, doing whatever they can to get by, I'd met a bloke like him once before, I mean to talk to – I was thinking of that bloke called Daryl, the painter, back in my Pentridge days. There were many of them around, of course, but they had to keep their noses clean and their lives quiet, in case the worst possible thing should happen to them: prison. But a bloke can't choose how he's going to be born, and I'm as good a case as any I can think of.

The first time I laid eyes on Vince, I had to ask myself how a bloke like him can make it from birth to whatever age he was, about my age – I reckoned – without getting himself killed, or at least, getting his face rearranged every ten minutes. I say that not because he was the kind of bloke who rubs you the wrong way – not at all – but because he was tall and had blond curly hair and smooth skin. But there was something else about him that marked him as a man that you couldn't help noticing: he was a man with a smile in his eyes, not just for his friends, or for the ladies – hell, we were all casting our best smiles at *them*, weren't we? – but for all the coves he met as well. I mean, a bloke can be too friendly.

So all in all I reckoned, and so did Les, who liked him well enough, that he was safe as eggs with us, and we'd keep him on as a kind of physical trainer, for a slice of the purse.

'Les, that won't be necessary,' says Vince. I know you fellers are finding it hard to make ends meet and I don't want to make thing worse for you.'

We were having this conversation while sitting in the *Marvellous*, which was a large cafe in the middle of Melbourne that had seen better days, and eating some soup with the winnings we had made from the Fegan fight. Les had found Vince somewhere – I really didn't know where – and brought him home the way the cat does. Apart from a lot of blokes wearing suits – I later discovered we were close to *The Argus* newspaper offices – the place was chockers with women who were hell-bent on talking the place to the ground. Vince seemed to be right at home in that place, and paid a lot of attention to the ladies, and vice versa, though I think they were wasting their time.

'What d'yer mean?' says Les.

'I have some money of my own, enough to pay the rent, anyway. I just want to be a trainer for a while, help you out. We'll talk about money again when you've got some.'

I had been looking at Vince while he spoke and I was thinking that I'd seen many blokes like him in the States, especially in California, where everyone was trying everything, and in the cellars of New York, where there are no rules. But Melbourne could be a dangerous place, and Vince looked out of place. In the States a bloke like him would be snapped up by a movie producer in nothing flat and put in front of a camera. He looked as though he had been cast in gold.

'Vince, I don't mind taking you into the team,' I say, 'Don't mind at all. But this money of yours – I have to know – no, Les, I have to ask him straight – did you make it on the street.'

'Fair crack of the whip, cobber!' says Les.

'No, Les,' says Vincent, laying a gentle hand on Les's forearm. 'He's right to ask, he's right to ask. No, Arch – is it all right if I call you Arch? – not a penny. I'm not anyone's. I've got a rich mummy in St Kilda.'

'Well why didn't you say so?' I said, as if he'd suddenly remembered a secret password. 'But why the hell are you hanging around with us, then?'

'I like the view.'

'Oh.'

'See?' said Les, 'He likes the view.'

'Yeah, all right, keep your shirt on. A bloke can ask, can't he?'

So that was how we acquired what turned out to be the best physical trainer this side of the Black Stump, and I ended up springing around like a Mexican bloody jumping bean. We kept Vince under wraps, and not only because he was a great body-worker. A bloke like him wasn't safe around the traps, and could end up in jail with a chest full of broken ribs any tick of the clock. He had a habit that was close to suicidal in the circles I moved in: he liked to smile at everyone.

When we were ready we sent a note around to Iggy Coghlan, the promoter at the Stadium, asking him to organise a bout with Milo Magee.

32 The Magee Stoush

On the night, I found out that the big money was on me to floor
Magee, and a lot of the money was coming from the same bloke
who'd had me thrown off the Gippsland train and on to some
poor kid's head.

'It's definitely a funny old world,' I said to Les when he told
me this, when we were sitting in our corner.

'I heard that he reckons you must be a tough bastard after all,
and he'd like to see you earn him a bit of money for a change.
Mind you, if you don't give it your best, you'll find that instead of
throwing you off a train, he'll probably throw you *under* one.'

'Thanks, cobber.'

'You're welcome. Just remember, don't hurt the kid, and
don't let him lose face. And don't –'

'Give it a flamin' rest, mate. I'm not his bloody mother.'

'Speaking of which,' says Les, nodding to one side.

I follow his eyes to the middle of the third row and spot
Ruth's – and Milo's – parents, staring at me grimly. At least, Mrs
Magee is. Mr Magee is looking around as if he's never been to a
boxing match before, which, it occurs to me, is just possible. But
his wife looks right at home there, placed as she is to get a good
view of the action, unobstructed by the corners. I nodded politely
to her, but she looked at me as if she didn't know me, except as
the man who took her son away from her, when the truth was
that that was God's doing. I had not arrived at that conclusion

easily, but arrive at it I did. Otherwise I don't think I could have sat there and contemplated what was coming up.

'What's the betting,' I asked Les.

'It's well in your favour.'

'That'll be good for the kid's confidence, keep him going.'

'Yeah, that's what we reckon.'

The bell went and the referee, who was the same ref I'd had against Tich Fegan, came over to inspect our gloves while we were being announced. I was a bit worried that the announcer might say something dodgy about one of us, especially me, but he seemed a polite enough bloke. He called Milo 'Mighty Milo Magee' and me by my usual moniker, and the crowd cheered me and gave Milo not even the most piddling clap. I jumped up and waved to the crowd and, as I was returning to my corner, spotted sitting not far behind Les and Co, Queenie, looking serious and thoughtful. She burst into a big smile when she saw me wink at her and gave me an encouraging nod. I saw that the seat beside her was vacant so I guessed she had chosen the spot and that her boyfriend had gone off somewhere to place a quiet bet.

Seeing Queenie perked me up like mad, because I always felt quite alone at a fight, which I did not ever do for the love of it, but for reasons that no one knew about, and also, on this occasion, because I needed a quid.

The ref called us into the centre ring, and put his hands on our shoulders as if we were two tarts he was trying to choose between, and stuck his head down in a confidential way, which was necessary as he was a head taller than both of us. While he gave us the standard instructions, Milo stared at me with a vicious, angry look on his face, as if that what was expected of him, and I looked at him standing there, almost touching me with his forehead, and tried not to think of Billy, which was bloody impossible. I could see he'd been planning this moment for a long time, and was prepared to let him have his way, as that is the easiest way to fight a fool.

When the ref told us to shake hands, Milo spat in my face, which was taking a serious risk, but which the ref paid no attention to. His only reaction was to turn to me and look at me deadpan for a split second. That look told me a lot: it told me that I had one foul in the bank, in other words, that my first wouldn't count. I heard Milo's manager groan and slap the canvas with frustration when all of this happened, as he knew his boy had done a stupid thing. The punters, on the other hand, lapped it up, and booed the kid like mad, though, truth be told, it was nothing in itself.

I knew that this whole incident was going to go down badly with the Syndicate, which every second person in the game had told me was now so clean it'd bring tears to your eyes and make you wonder if you were in the right state, let alone the right country. I had to remind myself that under no circumstances was I to get up to my old tricks, and that Milo would prove to be his own worst enemy if he kept up these shenanigans.

When I got back to the corner, saw out of the corner of my eye Mrs Magee shouting encouragement to Milo, whose action she heartily approved of. The female of the species, I have heard, can be a spiteful piece of work, and that McGee woman was living proof.

Back in the corner, Les shoved my mouthpiece in, while looking at Mrs Magee, who was shouting like a fishwife that she hoped I'd get my comeuppance.

'Jesus, Les, that woman's the grandmother of me daughter,' I said.

'Look on the bright side,' said Les, as serious as I've ever seen him. 'She might have a heart attack and drop dead.'

I felt that I should have ticked him off for that, but the feeling soon passed.

When the bell went for round one, Milo came out ready to box. He was under orders not to do his block, not because I might outfight him but because, I reckoned, his manager wanted to get a look at me. Everyone in Melbourne had seen me fight dirty, but only those who were at the Fegan fight knew I was capable of putting that behind me. I let round one pass with a few cautious but well-placed shots that I knew would score points, and as many body shots as I could get in at a fairly strong work rate. At the end of the round the kid needed a bit of a breather, while I was as fresh as a daisy, thanks to Vince putting in a lot of good work on my legs and hips. The kid's corner were not all that happy about the fact that I had easily outscored their boy, and I could tell by their faces that they were telling him to keep up the work rate, and that I would tire. I had spent years watching other corners giving that advice. It had yet to work.

'Their plan is to wear me down,' I said to Les.

'Good. That means they won't do anything silly that might put their boy on the canvas.'

'Queenie's here.'

'I saw her. She's still by herself, too. Okay, let's go.'

Round two was a bit rough for young Milo, as his brothers and his mum were calling on him to stop prancing around and murder me, which, as far as they were concerned, was the point of the evening. I could tell that this was mighty hard on the young feller and told him so when we got a chance to chat.

'See yer brought yer mum. Why don't you give *her* the gloves, ya flamin' fairy.'

'I'll kill you –'

He would no doubt have elaborated, but I had distracted him enough to get a left rip into his liver, and made him groan our loud and pull in his elbow. My next punch was identical, and caught him on the forearm. There was a snap, and a look of surprise came over the kid's face. After that he spent the whole round poking at me with his left as hard as he could, while I watched carefully from behind my gloves to see if what he was doing what I thought he was doing.

'Les, I think his right arm's busted.'

'Nah, he's just resting.'

'I heard the bugger snap. That's why he's not using it.'

'We both looked over at his corner. His trainer was looking at the arm carefully and looking for sore spots.'

'See?'

'Shit, now you'll have to floor him.'

'No, I'll keep boxing him.'

'The ref'll DQ you if he thinks you don't want to fight.'

'We'll see.'

The third round saw the lad working hard with his left and holding his right in reserve like a fighter who's only got one punch. This time his corner were fairly restrained in their coaching, and everyone could see he was fighting according to instructions. With a broken arm, he was going to have to avoid being floored and lose points for not boxing hard enough, that or get knocked out. The alternative was forfeit, and that was unthinkable, in view of all the name calling he'd been doing all over the Melbourne.

To make matters worse, regardless of the outcome, he was going to have to stop fighting while his arm healed, and that'd be a problem all by itself, and one the Magees would blame me for.

In the end, the kid's fight got weaker and weaker and I thought I could see a lump on his arm. The only thing I could do was give him a bit of a fair go by not fighting all that hard. By round six, the whole house was pissed off like mad, and the ref went over to the Magee corner, to find out was wrong. He was giving them a chance to throw in the towel. He knew something was wrong but not what it was. I could see they were waving him away. So then he came over to my corner and leaned in over me and put his head beside Les's.

'Listen, I don't know what's going on between you two, but if you don't box to your best ability, I'm going to disqualify you, do I make myself clear?'

We nodded, and he went to have a word with the judges, probably to tell them what he'd said to us. One of the judges gave him a note, which he read, and folded up and put in his pocket. Then he signalled, and the bell was rung, late. The crowd had developed a low murmur, because they were expecting him to announce that I'd won on a TKO, but they were to be disappointed.

'You'll have to KO him, I reckon,' said Les, in his workmanlike way.

'Leave it to me, Les. I've got an idea.'

When the bell went for the sixth, the kid came out with a spring in his step and threw a couple of quick punches to my head which I dodged and returned, only to see him do the same. I could see that he was just letting the crowd know that he had lots of fight in him, and their bets weren't safe yet.

After sparring for a while like this, I could see the ref giving me the evil eye, so I sighed, and spoke to the kid out loud, so the ref could hear.

'It's time for your nap, son. See ya.'

And the next thing I did was cover up and walk in close, copping a few stinging lefts for my trouble, then letting two hard lefts go to his abdomen while pushing him backwards onto the ropes. He was covering his midsection with his injured right at that moment, so I hit him hard on his fractured spot as hard as I could. There was a lot of give in the arm where there should have been none, and I felt the end of the protruding bone right through my glove. I thought I even heard more bone breaking.

The kid was furious, sick with pain and mad as hell, and lashed out as hard as he could with his left, trying to sting me into backing off, which I did, making him follow me away from the ropes. Then, as he tried to give me a straight left designed to send me off to the fairies, I feinted and poked hard at his face with my left, once, twice three times, until, finally, reluctantly, he put his right glove in up beside his temple, where I found it. I gave him my best hook and drove it deep into his forearm with no intention of making it past his guard. He was already a bit grey around the gills, and when I did that, he went as white as a sheet and his legs buckled a little. Then he looked at me without seeing me for a moment, and fainted right into my arms like a sleeping child.

I looked at the ref and he looked at me, and I waited there like a flaming idiot while the kid's cornermen came in and took him back to the corner to bring him around. The ref, meanwhile, grabbed me by the wrist and drove my fist up towards the rafters. It's a rare thing to see a fighter pass out like that without having been concussed, and the crowd was in an uproar. I looked at Les, and he shrugged. He looked back at me and tilted his head philosophically. I hadn't knocked the kid out, though the win would be recorded as a TKO. I had done my best to carry him to the end, but in the end my old mate God had intervened as only He can. Life is rum, and that's the truth.

In the dressing room I met Queenie, who hugged me as if I was her long-lost son.

'Nice to see you, love,' I said, and I meant it, too.

'Had to come and see what you'd do. Jesus, I thought you were going to put him away – you could've, you know.'

'Yeah, well I wanted to go the distance; you know, try to upset as few people as possible.'

'Yeah, now that's the story of your life, isn't it, not upsetting people? And what does Ruth think of all this? Or doesn't she know?'

'She's back in Greenvale sanatorium. She's pretty crook. She's been talking about dying, but I think it's just the laudanum talking.'

She placed a hand on my arm, while Les unbandaged my hand.

'I'm sorry to hear that, Arch. I suppose I'd better visit her.'

'No visitors allowed except me and Jeanie, and her mum once a month. Her mum'll be over there tomorrow, to tell her what I did to her brother, and that'll be that, I reckon. I don't think that would be a fair thing to do to Ruth under the circs, but she'll do it anyway.

'Well, you wiped the grin off her face tonight anyway. You should've seen her.'

'Hey, what happened to your boyfriend? I didn't see him?'

'He left before your fight – business. I told him I'd get Pauly to take me home.'

'And where's Pauly? Still holding his gut? He should be after the punch I gave him.'

'He's waiting with the car. He knows that if anything happened to that car his life wouldn't be worth living. Geez, I've never seen a fighter pass out before.'

'Shock,' said Les. 'That was your plan, wasn't it?'

'Yeah. I knew if I mashed his arm up a bit more, he'd cave in.'

'Hell, Arch, is that legal?'

'Funnily enough, it is.'

'Milo won't be laughing when he finds out he'll be out of the ring for three months,' said Les.

'Well, that wasn't what I wanted. I better go in and tell him no hard feelings.'

'You can tell him at the rematch,' said Les without even looking up, and I realised he was right. This feud of theirs wasn't going to go away.

33 Trouble At Home

Next day I went over to Greenvale with Jeanie. It took all
morning to get there, and it was a rotten trip because Jeanie was
crook and didn't even want to see her mum. Trouble was, Ruth
was going downhill, and despite the brave face I was putting on
for the world to see, I was worried. When we got to the hospital,
we ran into her parents going the other way. I doffed my hat to
Mrs Magee, but all she could do was spit at me, which, under the
circs was fair. When we got into the ward we were refused
admission.

'I'm sorry, Mr Taggerty,' said the nurse, but Mrs Taggert is
not well enough to have visitors. You'll have to try again next
week.'

'Did she say anything?'

'I really don't know.'

'Did her parents see her.'

'They may have. I'm not at liberty to say.'

'So that's it, the bastards! Well we're her family now, and we
have a right to see her – her daughter has a right.'

The matron pulled up beside us like a timber truck when she
heard this and put her threepence worth in.

'I decide who has rights in this place, and your wife does not
want to see you. So please leave. Or do I have to show you out
myself?'

We left quietly, as I didn't want Jeanie see her dad outclassed by a woman, though she was about six weight grades above me.

This was one of those rare occasions when I felt like a drink, but I took Jeanie home instead and we had a little tea party, which made her feel pretty good for about five minutes. Then she threw up on me. It turned out she had the measles. So she was as sick as a dog for a while, while I was kept busy being the doctor, nurse, and mother all rolled into one.

There were long stretches with Jeannie when I had nothing to do, so I found myself sitting in the front room, which was the room with the best light, writing poetry. I realised as soon as I started that I was not being urged to do it by some inner demon, or *daimon*, as Gallico had called it. The daimon seemed to have gone for the time being, and I felt something I'd never felt before, a kind of freedom to be what I wanted to be, and do as I pleased. I felt it in my bone and muscles as well, as I was relaxing for the first time.

I wondered if indeed that was what it was. Straightaway I was worried that the poetry would pay me back by not working, and would be rejected as rubbish. But that thought had never occurred to me before, and so for the first time I felt vulnerable as a writer. And I began to wonder if that meant that I would be vulnerable as a fighter as well.

I was filled with fear, not the fear of losing something, though it crossed my mind that I might, but the fear that I might change in some way. I didn't know what that meant, as I'd never had it before. I'd changed over the years, of course, but it had always crept up on me and washed over me the way a dream does when you're asleep, without doing you any harm. I came to see that I needed something that I hadn't experienced in a long time, maybe ever. I needed to be accepted just as I was, without any strings attached, just once in my life, before I could move on. I realised there would be a price, because there always is. But I'd had a good run. I hadn't shirked paying my way, and I had, as a result paid in all kinds of areas. And now it looked as though I was going to lose Ruth.

Still I kept writing, and still the poetry came out easily. Was it as good as it usually was? I couldn't tell. I began to read the poems aloud, the way Galloway had told me others did. It sounded okay, though I couldn't hear my own voice in it. It was just a voice of a poet coming from somewhere. Was this the way Ruth heard it when read it? No, I was sure it could not have been, because everyone thought Polly Beer was a woman, including her.

There were even stories about Polly. It was rumoured that during the war she was a nurse in Cairo. That would have been Galloway. He told me once that the public were hungry for information about her, so he had begun to invent it, much to Den's disapproval. The fact that so many of the poems were of the war made it easy for him, and I never objected.

I realised as I sat and worked, with Jeannie coughing away in the next room, that the poetry was never really my creation at all, no more that my own breath is. It just appeared in its way, in its time, more or less carrying the message to the world that its source was – is – alive. I felt as though I'd had this thought before, and ignored it. But it seemed now that it contained a holy point within it, a sanctity of sorts, that was worth respecting. I had always been guilty of a sin, if that were true: the sin of disrespecting my own soul. I thought I might stop doing that.

But that discovery led to another, the possibility that my fighting fell into the same category. After all, they'd been born at the same time, on the same day, possibly from the same impulse that gave birth to twins. The fighting made me feel good when I struck, hurt, punched, and so did the poetry, though its relief lasted only a short time. I could go months without donging someone, but only days without writing, and even when I was writing I'd think to myself sometimes: *Arch, that was an interesting thought; I think it would look good on paper.* Then there was an even chance that I'd forget it. Not that it mattered. Those thoughts never went over the horizon.

Suddenly, one night as I lay in bed, I realised that my body had lost its pain for the first time in its existence. I felt not just physical relief, but mental pain – guilt for not noticing the exact moment when it happened. Something had changed. A cold thrill went through my heart, as I wondered if it meant that I had lost someone dear to me. I went into the bedroom, noticing my footsteps had a lightness, that my hip, though it rolled a little, had no pain, and looked in on Jeannie. She was breathing normally for the first time in weeks. She was no longer sick. I looked out of the window towards the west, and wondered if the daughter was mirroring the mother. I went back to bed and dreamt of camels.

I was offered a fight, a real fight. This was to be the return bout I had wanted. I was to matched with a man who had never fought me, but by all accounts had always wanted to: Leonard Jenkins. He was a famous fighter, even in my early fighting days, and you could say he followed me up the ladder. But my sudden departure from the ring had robbed him of the chance to fight me for the crown. In the end he had fought his way to a championship bout with Stephen Stanley, the "Stanley Steamer", but had lost on a TKO. He had dropped a few positions in the rankings, then got a return bout and lost on a KO, though many said the ref counted as if he just remembered that he had to be somewhere. Then Boardman, the champ, was beaten by Jack Morris, whose name was not Jack but something like Joshua, but who had taken Dempsey's name, and it was from him that Jenkins took the Crown. After defending the title against Morris, the first thing Jenkins did, so they say, was say my name.

What everyone from Brunswick to Bullamakanka knew was that this Jenkins bloke was famous for two things: winning the championship, and keeping his licence to fight when the clean-up of Melbourne boxing took place. How a man with so many foul points against him had managed to discipline himself like that was a marvel of modern sports, and one that I think I might have, in my way, rivalled. He had, it was said, a constitution of steel, and though his many detractors gave him a hard time during his fights, and in the paper, hinting that the man had shown himself to be a bit of let-down.

However, his camp let it known to our lot that it was going to be on for young and old, and that Jenkins didn't care if he won by hook or by crook, as long as I was on the receiving end. This was the kind of fight the Sportsmen's Syndicate had taken pains to prevent, having guaranteed all and sundry that boxing was as clean as a whistle, and contained no nasty elements of old, they having been retired, had the stuffing knocked out of them, or learned to toe the line in the interest of feeding the little woman and the kiddies.

But as the sports writers pointed out, I was none of the foregoing, and had only given up the game when I did after beating my opponent to death. Since then, it was said, I had only been playing the good boy in the hope that I might get a crack at Jenkins, which wasn't true, of course. They stopped short of calling Jenkins my nemesis, as that would have only had the punters scratching their heads.

Though I trained well, and prepared for the fight better than I ever did, Les and Co were nervous and quiet.

'You're not talking to me, Arch. What's going on?'

'Something happened to me, Les.'

'I can see *that*. You okay?'

'There's nothing wrong. In fact I feel better than I've ever felt in my life. You know, my hip isn't hurting much at all, though it's settled into a new sort of stiffness.'

'I can see that, too. What're you on?'

'Now, Les. You know me better than that. No, this is something different, something I can't explain.'

'Are you going to be okay, against Jenkins?'

'Yeah. Les, I have a bit of feeling about this one; I think the best man will win.'

'Where'd yer get that stupid bloody idea? This isn't a bloody cricket match - this is fucking war. I want that bastard dead, and so should you.'

'I'll be happy to beat him.'

'There's something wrong with you, all right. Look, if ever there was a man to kill, it's this bloke. I'm not kidding. You'll not give him a fair go, like Magee.'

I had no answer for that.

'You'll kill this bastard. That's what I want.'

'Les, I never heard you say that before.'

'If you don't, he'll do it to you - that's what he wants. Jenkins is a bad bastard. He shouldn't even be in the game. He's put one over everyone in the hope of getting a bout with you. They say winning the title didn't impress him at all, because he didn't take it off you.'

'Well, I know how he feels on that score.'

We said nothing more about Jenkins. As usual we dug up a bit of dirt on the champ, but there wasn't much to go on. He had been a dirty fighter because he had a mean streak in him, and not because he knew he couldn't go the distance, like me. And like me, he seemed to enjoy hitting people. You might think that all boxers have that in common, but you'd be wrong. Most of them just liked the glamour and the purse at the end of the night. For most of them, there wasn't anything else they were good at.

I trained well right up to the fight, and the team was happy enough, but Les, in his gruff way, was worried I'd gone soft. He didn't say anything; I just knew.

There was one thing Jenkins could do that I don't think I could: go the distance. He didn't seem to have anything wrong with his body, and was reasonably fit. What he wanted was to push me as hard as I needed to be pushed, and that meant being ready to go the distance. And that was something I'd never done. The punters all knew this, of course, and went by form. Jenkins was priced to win. On my side of the ledger, I'd never been beaten, and a lot of people knew me to be crafty bugger.

On the night, we boxed as best we could, with me switching from southpaw to orthodox and back again every now and then, until everyone in the place was thoroughly confused. I even fought unorthodox for a few rounds, which made Jenkins strop boxing and throw his hands up at the crowd as though he'd had enough. As far as points went, we traded rounds. We had the same reach and weight, but completely different styles. I preferred to fight in a head-protected stance, and Jenkins in a wide stance with his arms wide and his fists set to reach out for a hook on either side. His hook was quite smart but not quick, and most of the time I fended off. His wide stance made it hard for him to dance, but to the annoyance of his corner, he had no intention of doing that, and made me come to him.

One reason he stayed pretty flatfooted was my quick straights and uppercuts, which he hated. When I finally cut his face, I was relieved, as I knew his corner would tell him to dominate the fight, and that was something I had expected. In the eighth round I made the ref stop the fight and take a look at his face, and while that was going on went to my corner and looked down and saw Queenie. She was dressed to kill, and had her hand on Les's shoulder. Oddly, I thought, he didn't seem to mind – as I said, he was no ladies' man. She was giving me the signal that she was alone, or at least not with Beauchamp. But he must have been here, because this was the fight of the night, a fifteen-rounder for an Australian title.

Jenkins finally got sick of the ref fiddling around like an old woman and shoved him aside impatiently. The ref called for the fight to resume, and I wondered what Jenkins would do to compensate for being vulnerable. I soon found out. We resumed our battle the centre ring, neither of us willing to risk backing onto the ropes, and a lot of ineffectual leather being thrown as a result, when Jenkins deliberately hit me low. There was no pretence at all, no attempt to fake an accidental blow. He had simply given up a point, just like that. The ref told him off, then went to the judges and told them to penalise him.

Meanwhile, I was on the canvas, but I was not resting. I was totally paralysed, and couldn't fight, but there was no count on me, and the ref simply waited for me to recover. As the bell went, I was helped to my corner, and sat there, gulping air and hoping I would be able to come out. The doctor was brought over to rule on whether I was fit to fight. If I was not, Jenkins would be disqualified, but the title could not pass to me that way, so for me, at least, and for Jenkins too, I would have to fight on if he was to get his wish.

Round nine saw Jenkins copping non-stop boos from the crowd, who had come to see a fight, not a dirty trick their mothers could have pulled. The booing had an unsettling effect on Jenkins, who even pulled up for a moment to tell the punters to fuck off, which didn't improve the judges' opinion of him. He then attempted to box, no doubt to prove that he could. With only seconds to spare I tore into him with a combination we'd practised for this stage in the fight, when Jenkins was not at his best. The focus was the diaphragm, and the sides of the abdomen, where the viscera were less protected by muscles. Three times I used the combination, and three times, he weakened. When I went for it for the fourth time, he finally had had enough and bought his crablike gloves in to defend his body.

At that moment, when he seemed distracted, time seemed to go away. If I'd been looking at a clock I swear I would have seen it as stopped. I could hear individual voices in the crowd – I know every fighter can *remember* individual voices, but this is not the same thing – I heard them as if they were the only ones in the stadium. I smelled Jenkins' sweat. It was almost overpowering in its potency, and I wondered why I hadn't noticed how strong and virile it was at any other time in the fight. I heard Queenie's voice break through. She wasn't shouting, like the rest. She was encouraging me in a loud voice, though for many that would he shouting, but for me it was just Queenie getting excited about something.

That was the moment that time seemed to be waiting for, to catch up, so to speak. My feet were reasonably square, so I reached out with a right hand, and gave Jenkins my two year punch. It was the most measured punch I'd ever delivered, and in the fight game it isn't often you get a chance to throw one of those.

I believe Jenkins was unconscious before he hit the canvas. He did not move, and I did not care.

34 The Last Stand

Queenie and I had dinner at the Marvellous that night. Everyone and his dog wanted to be my friend, and dinner was on the house. Queenie chatted away as if we were the best of friends and had just returned from a movie or a day at Luna Park. Every now and then she would hold my hand, the hold of familiar friends, not of lovers, not of wives and husbands, not of aunts. I realised, as Queenie looked at me with her frankly flirtatious eyes, that she would never change, would always be there for me, would always be just as she was in this moment.

'What's up, am I boring you?' she asked with a mock-serious look.

'No, love, no. I was just thinking: you know, just before Jenkins went down –'

'I've never seen a right cross like it.'

'Yeah, so you've said – well, just at that moment, I found myself in a strange place where there was no time, none. It was as if I was a character in a fairy tale, you know, *Alice in Wonderland*, or something. You don't get it, do you?'

'Actually, I do, Arch, I had a similar experience when I gave birth to John. There was a moment, just before the very end, when he was just about to finally appear, when I realised that my life as an individual was about to end, and I felt a sudden quiet, and believe me, I was not *being* quiet at the time, if you see what I mean; I was screaming my head off. And you know how I can do that, don't you darling.' She squeezed my arm like a little girl. 'In that moment I thought of you, Arch.'

'Why don't you pull the other one: it plays *The Road to Gundagai*.'

'No, really, Arch. I thought of what might have been, if things had turned out different.'

'You mean if you hadn't pissed off with a movie producer with a name like a building material and left me like a shag on a bloody rock.'

'I thought I was in love.' She laughed. 'Anyway, that's what happened.'

'And what might have been?'

'You know as well as I do, Arch.'

'No, Queenie, I don't. You're the most infuriating woman I've ever met.'

'I thought that was Ruth's job.'

'Nah. Ruth's had good reason to be pissed off at me.'

'You're in love with Ruth. It's alright, Arch. I'm in love with you and you're in love with Ruth. I've got John, you've got Jean.'

'You've also got whoever wants to pay the rent and keep you in grog.'

'That's not fair, Arch. I would have been happy with you for good.'

We'd been down this track before and it led to silence. I didn't want that, and neither did Queenie.

'So tell us about your moment when the clock stopped. Was I in it?'

'Yeah, I could hear your voice.'

'What was I saying?'

'Give a man a chance, girl'

'Sorry, Arch.'

'You were telling me to hit him, Jenkins, as if I wasn't – going to hit him, I mean. But the thing is, I could hear you as if you were right beside me, even though you weren't screaming your head off.'

'I *could* scream my head off if you want me to, you know.' She cuddled up to me as she said this, spoke into my ear, though I think if you'd been sitting at the next table, you'd have got the message.

'Shh!'

'So that's when you hit Jenkins?'

'Yeah, well I was planning on hitting him anyway. It's just that at that moment there seemed to be was no time passing. It felt as if the punch took no skill at all; it was all in a day's work.'

'They'll be talking about that punch till the cows come home.'

I laughed my head off.

'What's wrong with you,' she said, punching my arm.

'Cows. You wouldn't know a cow if you tripped over one.'

'I'll have you know I was a farmer in New Zealand for a couple of years.'

'Couple of months, more like. And if I know you – and I do – it was Arty Curran who did all the cowboy stuff.'

'He was a cowboy, alright.'

'What d'yer mean?'

'Got his head turned by a station hand, didn't he?'

I kept my silence; Queenie had been as unlucky in love as I'd been lucky in the ring, and didn't need to have it rubbed in.

'I'm sorry, Queenie. It's just that I know Arty from way back. I could have given you the tip.'

'What'd be the point of that? You were never available.'

That stung me like a lacing to the ear, as it wasn't true. Queenie and I had a couple of good years together, broken only by her shooting thorough with that Brik drongo. If only she didn't drink like a fish, things might've turned out different. But she did.

'Anyway, that's when I hit Jenkins. And down he went.'

'Was he okay?'

'Yeah. I spoke to him in the dressing room. You know, he couldn't remember the punch at all. In fact, he couldn't even remember round ten. But he was okay about it. He even said he was sorry about the low blow.'

'Jesus.'

'It was all bull. I should have been more careful.'

That night I went over to Queenie's place, as Jeannie was being looked after by Mum at my place. Next morning, we turned on the wireless while we made breakfast. The announcer said that Jenkins had had a stroke, and was finished as a boxer. He called me the Richmond Terror, and likened me to a murderer.

I had nowhere to go after that. I had my home, of course, but in my heart there was nowhere to go, just cold wasteland. The papers bunged me on the front page. Billy's name was bandied about by the press sluts. I had become a monster, not fit to be alive. I was a consumer of other people's lives, no better than a leech or a vampire bat. I was Killer Taggerty.

Mum had heard the whole thing on the wireless. She could be hard, and it seems she was that day. She had prevented Jean hearing the news, though she wouldn't have had a clue what it all meant.

'I suppose you'll be giving up the game now.'

'Yes, Mum, I'm supposed to defend the title, but the truth is, it's over for me.'

'Never. You'll go on for as long you want to. They're already saying you're one of the greatest boxers who ever lived.'
However, she was saying it to herself, not to me.

'No, Mum, what they're saying is that I'm one of the most vicious bastards who ever stepped into the ring; that's what they're saying. They're saying I'm a bloody animal.'

'I think it's time you owned up to being the great fighter that you are. So some rotten swine gets himself half-killed. They say he hit you low – did he?'

'Yeah, nearly KO'd me, which would have mucked up everything for him, of course. What a game!'

I told Jeannie I was sorry that my face was hurt and that I was going to spend the whole week with her, and then at the end of it, when I wasn't so ugly, I'd take her to see her mum. That brought a smile to her face and like me, she hadn't had too many of those over the course of her little life.

I wrote poetry every day, and it felt very freeing, and made set no conditions for its presence.

I remembered the days when Ruth smiled all the time, even when she was registering disapproval, in the days when it took something pretty bloody serious to make her really downhearted, despite her hard upbringing. In those days I'd be smiling every time I saw her, thought about her, touched her. That was something that happened inside my heart and sort of found its way to my face. I knew how to restore that time. I'd spent all night thinking about it. There was something about me she loved, and it was still there, whatever it was. As for the things about me I knew had been poison, I'd start chipping away at those as soon as Jeannie and me were dressed for the day.

Acknowledgements

Many thanks to the following for their help during the writing of this novel.

My fabulous sister, Kate Twohig, for illustrating and designing the cover.
Ann Parry for her reading of the book and editorial comments.
My agent, Lyn Tranter at Australian Literary Management, and Kirsten Tranter for their comments and suggestions.

Also by Peter Twohig

THE
CARTOGRAPHER

'If...you enjoyed Safran Foer's *Extremely Loud and Incredibly Close*, you are going to want to read this book.'
Bookseller + Publisher

Melbourne, 1959. An eleven-year old boy watches as a murder is committed in a strange house. Just one year before, he had looked on helplessly as his identical twin, Tom, suffered a violent death. God, who he no longer counts as a friend, has a pretty sick sense of humour.

Having been seen by the murderer, he is now a kid on the run, and takes refuge in the dark drains and dangerous drains tunnels beneath the city, recreating himself as a series of superheroes and creating a remarkable map to help him avoid the bad bastard he has locked eyes with. His only protectors are his very shady grandfather, a professional standover man, and an incongruous neighbourhood couple who intervene in a very unexpected way.

A captivating novel bristling with outrageous wit about a tragic figure in a rotten place who refuses to give in, and the crowd of shifty, dodgy and downright malicious bastards he has to match wits with on his extraordinary journey. *The Cartographer* is a fresh, poignant and deeply touching novel that you will never forget.

The second book in the Richmond triology

THE
TORCH

'Not since *The Curious Incident of the Dog in the Night-time* has there been such a compelling child narrator'

Herald-Sun

Melbourne, 1960. Mrs Blayney and her twelve year old son, aka 'the kid', live in Richmond. At least, they did, until their house burnt down. The prime suspect – one Keith Aloysius Gonzaga Kavanagh, also aged 12 – has mysteriously disappeared. Our narrator, the kid, sets off on a covert mission to find young Keith, who he privately dubs 'Flame Boy', to save him from the small army of irate locals – not to mention Mrs Blayney – who want to see him put away.

Flame Boy has not only made himself scarce, but he's disappeared with a very important brief case of secrets, which the kid is keen to get hold of for his grandfather, a shady character, who's got some secrets of his own. But the kid has got a lot going on: he's also organising a new gang of kids; coping with the ups and downs of having a girlfriend (who likes to kiss – a lot); trying to avoid Keith's dangerous prison-escapee father, Fergus Kavanagh, also an arsonist, who is suspected of selling secrets to the Russians; and all the while dreaming of the most covetable item in the world: the Melbourne Olympic Torch.

A madcap, slightly shambolic and irresistibly fun novel about loss, discovery and living life to the full, The Torch is a little ripper of a ride.

The third book in the Richmond trilogy

THE

MAZEMASTER

Melbourne, 1960. One Saturday morning, in the middle of busy Richmond, the Blayney kid's brand new brother is kidnapped right out of his pram, setting off a train of events that couldn't possibly have been anticipated. First, the Blayney family, who are a very mysterious crowd with dubious connections all over town, decide to take matters into their own hands. Then, the kid himself decides to conduct his own enquiries, knowing that this is probably a very bad idea, and that he might be next.

In the guise of The Mazemaster (one of his many superhero alter egos), he mobilises his friends, some of whom come from the dodgiest of families, and swings into action, collecting evidence all over the place, getting involved in a shooting, another kidnapping, an unwelcome hospitalisation, the theft of a train, being chased down into the maze of drains and tunnels beneath Richmond – territory he regards as his own – in spite of dire warnings from his grandfather (a very scary bloke in his own right), and a man from ASIO, finally getting into the stickiest mess you could possibly imagine.

A brilliantly daring, touching and downright funny novel about loss, discovery and the kid in all of us. *The Mazemaster* is a crazy ride.